Searching for Julia

A Novel by

Martin F. Sorensen

Searching for Julia
© 2017 by Martin F. Sorensen

Published by Sand Hill Review Press, LLC
All rights reserved
www.sandhillreviewpress.com,
P.O. Box 1275, San Mateo, CA 94401
(415) 297-3571

ISBN: 978-1-937818-57-9 paperback
ISBN: 978-1-937818-58-6 case laminate
ISBN: 978-1-937818-70-8 ebook
Library of Congress Control Number: 2017940093

Cover art by Shutterstock
Graphics by Backspace Ink
Art Direction by Tory Hartmann

SHRP
Sand Hill Review Press

For Charleyne

Chapter 1

Carolyn, Elizabeth, 1980

CAROLYN STUART LIES AWAKE, excited and restless. An intense thrill pulses in her chest as she imagines Marc Silver's brown eyes and smile when he welcomes her into the UC Berkeley Art Institute.

The heat that radiates from Damian next to her on the bed interrupts her happy morning daydream. She raises herself up on her elbows, and in one slow fluid movement she lifts the covers up and swings her legs over the side of the bed. The floor chills her feet. Muscles pull on her back as she yawns and stretches high, smiles to herself and then stands and tiptoes to the window. Separating the blinds, she studies the view down the Berkeley hill to the lights of the Bay Bridge and San Francisco across the water. One of the lights beyond downtown has to be her mother's upstairs window in Sea Cliff, even if Carolyn can't pick it out from so far away. Is her mother Elizabeth awake yet?

Her stomach hurts, but excitement keeps her from going to the kitchen. Damian shifts in the bed and she wonders whether this self-taught abstract artist will be proud of her. She doesn't know the answer to the question and shakes her head of blond hair, uneasy as she walks to the bathroom.

A photo of her mother and herself stares at her on the wall, from last spring when she graduated from Mills College. Sorrow comes over her as she thinks of the argument they had later at dinner, over her decision to study art at Berkeley instead of business at Stanford.

That would have meant copying her mother's career path, and Carolyn hates math. There was enough of it in high school and college. By now, she knows who she is.

Warm water cascades down her body as Carolyn pictures the opening of her show at the Whitman Gallery on Hayes Street. In her reverie, she walks around, her green and brown pastels on one wall, stark black charcoal drawings opposite. Large oil paintings with bright reds and blues are lit from above. Her mother leads wealthy bejeweled friends around the gallery, sparkling amber wine in hand, and when she spies Carolyn, smiles with warmth. "I'm so happy for you, Darling. Maybe I didn't believe in you before, but no question I do now. A new show for you, that's what I want to do." Carolyn sees an appreciation in her mother's pale blue eyes she has never seen. Then the stark falseness of the image stops her daydream.

Steam keeps the room warm and damp, so she opens the window and shivers as the cool early morning air pours past her body. The chill makes her fresh and ready to take on the day. Cold air, invigorating, arousing, is the clear sign of great things to happen.

Carolyn slips on her Chanel panties and bra and studies herself in the mirror to make sure her nipples aren't showing. She brushes her blonde hair into neat wavy lines. A black sweater and new Jordache designer jeans appeal to her. The outfit is neat, clean, studious, but contemporary and expensive. Expressive highlights and shadows complete her makeup. Her large hazel eyes with rays of green dominate her face as she applies extra, unneeded mascara. She wonders whether she's overdoing it, if Marc Silver, the director of the institute, will think she's flirting with him, but takes the chance he'll like it.

She knows that Marc likes his men and women as he likes his art, beautiful and well-dressed. Marc's office displays his eclectic tastes, so she believes he'll appreciate her eclectic projects.

For her interview, Carolyn has prepared a wide-ranging sample of her work to show off. In her portfolio, she has placed an impressionistic watercolor landscape of the Berkeley pier and an abstract oil with predominant earth tones. She added a tempura in beige and blues of expressionist sympathies, and to top the selection off, a Brazilian-looking tropical gouache.

Her portfolio leans against the door waiting for her, a concession to her nervousness. She carries it to the coffee table and studies each work, then leaves the watercolor. That medium works for hobbyists, not for serious artists. The three, the oil, tempura and gouache, will show him her talent well enough.

She hesitates again and wonders if they suffice. Maybe she needs another oil, something more representational. She pulls canvases back from the wall, studies each one, and recognizes one of her favorite works, a portrait of her mother Elizabeth. Her mother refused to sit for it, so instead, Carolyn modeled the painting on her favorite picture from a few years ago at Christmas. Elizabeth Stuart is radiant in a dark red dress and pearl earrings. I should have seen that earlier, she thinks. That will be the perfect complement—it will show a great range of talent. She picks it up with care, she doesn't want to scrape it, and brings it over and adds it to her portfolio with a satisfied sigh.

When she opens the door, the morning cold air rushing up from the Bay hits her face. She remembers she hasn't said goodbye so she goes back in to Damian. Asleep on his back, dark morning stubble on his chin, he's oblivious. She kisses him on the forehead and touches his shoulder with the tips of her hands.

He mumbles and turns, opens his brown eyes into a slit, sees her and smiles. "Hm. Why don't you come back to bed and let's get it on, baby."

Carolyn pulls back a step. It would be great to jump back in bed with him, but not now. "Damian, you know I can't, I have to go for my interview."

He lifts himself on his elbows and speaks, groggy. "It's not even light out there. You've got time. Come on."

The warmth from his body fills the air as he moves over in the bed and pulls the sheet off his chest.

"No, Damian, I can't."

With a lazy stretching of his arm he tries to pull her down on to him, but she pushes away and stands up straight. "I've got to go. After the interview, I'm having lunch with Andrea. I'll come back after that. You need your sleep." She leans back down and taps his shoulder. He tries to pull the sheet down to expose himself, but she stops him, even as she smiles. "We'll have champagne and celebrate. The whole afternoon in bed, you and me." She resists the strong urge to lay her palm on his chest.

Damian falls back on his pillow, and turns and pulls the covers up to his waist. Carolyn pulls them over his shoulders, gives him a little pat, lets out a sigh, and leaves the room.

In the living room, she takes her portfolio, opens it and checks the items one more time, nodding with satisfaction, and closes it. She surveys the room as if she were missing something, checks her watch, and opens the front door. The phone rings in the bedroom, but she shakes her head and shuts the door behind her. Even if it's Andrea wanting to change something, she's got to go.

Cold air blows past her face once more as she steps out the short dark hallway to Rose Street, but stops as a young kid with wild hair flies past her on a skateboard. The portfolio just fits in the back seat of her red Jaguar convertible, and Carolyn gets in the front. She sits for a moment and breathes several times, then pulls out into the street on her way to San Francisco.

Carolyn drives downhill on the empty street in the dark to Interstate 80 and heads south to the bridge. The mist rises from the Bay, and the City sparkles around her while she takes the Van Ness exit and drives up to Bush Street. The traffic is the normal early-morning delivery vehicles blocking lanes on the street as the first long shadows settle over the city. On Bush, she turns right and heads downhill until she parks across the street from the brown brick of Notre Dame des Victoires. A truck passes, then she hurries up the steps to the church entrance and pulls the door open with both hands, careful to not make any noise.

An older woman in a faded gray coat, who smells of mothballs, sits motionless in the last pew, as if she hoped to be a statue herself. Carolyn passes the woman and walks to the alcove with the statue of Our Lady of Victories dressed in white and blue, crowned in gold. Blue votive candles put flickering highlights and shadows on the statue from below. She takes a long taper, lights it on one of the burning candles and holds it in her hand for a moment. Without praying, she lights a new candle and blows the taper out. In the still air the small flame wavers for about half a minute and then glows steady along with the others. Silence hovers about her for a long time, then she steps back and puts a dollar into the small rectangle on the top of a wooden box.

Carolyn peers up at the Virgin to let her know she is here, pauses for a time and thinks about her art goals and long it's taken to come to this point. As the dark gray light turns yellow from the East Bay sunrise, she leaves the church, crosses Bush Street, and makes her way back to the bridge. For the second time, only now traveling in the opposite direction, Carolyn crosses the Bay, merges onto 80 and follows University up to campus.

CAROLYN PULLS INTO Bancroft Parking next to a beat-up gray VW bug. She takes her portfolio out of the back seat, then sees Andrea Frohman getting out of her car.

"Andrea, hi."

Andrea, dressed in her signature bib overalls to hide her weight, turns to Carolyn with a smile. "All ready to go. It's exciting, isn't it? I can't believe we're here today. You're seeing Marc Silver, right? Today?"

Carolyn stares at Andrea with a dismissive frown. "You're not going like that, are you?"

Andrea looks down at herself, at her grandma shoes, but keeps on smiling anyway. "Hey, it's not a cheerleader audition. It's what's in the portfolio that counts."

Carolyn smiles back at her, knowing that Andrea will never change. "Well, every man for himself."

Andrea rolls her eyes. "I guess. But I sense Lady Luck's on my side. Why don't we splurge and have lunch at Chez Panisse?"

"Okay, how about two hours from now?"

"You got it."

They walk together in the bright morning sun to the Art Deco building of the Art Institute. Andrea waves goodbye and disappears inside as the distant Campanile chimes three-quarters of an hour.

Marc has remodeled the lobby of the Art into sparse, cold, and modern. A large vertical abstract bas-relief combining rays of black, white and grays dominates the wall facing the chrome and black visitor chair. The exterior of the building has an old architectural air to it, but the entrance door with "Marc Silver" in bold lettering beckons with new mahogany and brass. Carolyn sits in the chair and puts her portfolio beside her. A quick check of her watch reassures her that she has arrived with time to spare.

The office door opens and a tall, thin blond man with angular features appears. It's him, his grey mock-turtle sweater, black jacket and jeans. His smile shows perfect white teeth underneath vivid pewter-gray eyes. He holds out his hand and says in a formal, crisp voice, "How do you do. I'm Marc Silver. Please come in." He holds the door open for Carolyn.

His office functions as an art gallery, she remembers. Modern, renaissance, Greek, eclectic.

He offers his hand as he says, "May I peruse your portfolio?"

Carolyn hands it to him.

He lays it on a large black table, and opens it. "Let's go through it together, shall we?"

Carolyn nods.

Marc spreads the work out on the table. As he picks up each one, he moves it, perhaps to discern the effects of lighting. He is oblivious of Carolyn's presence. With a shrug and a long sigh, he puts the final piece of art back on the table and closes the portfolio. He turns and hands it to her, and focuses on her eyes. "You have three different paintings. Some are chromatically intense, others appear washed out. You are experimenting with your style. That is clear. I'm afraid it won't work for us."

Carolyn's heart sinks and her head spins. "I'm sorry?"

"We don't teach technique here. We guide artists who are self-aware. You are not. You wouldn't fit." His hand behind her back nudges her toward the door.

She stops, resisting his pressure. Her voice carries her indignation. "I have a letter from Robert Henry. He recommended me."

"Yes," he said. "I know Robert. I read his letter. In my view it wasn't strong enough. And it doesn't make up for your work."

Carolyn can't accept his decision. Something more has to be said in her defense. "I won awards at Mills."

Marc raises his voice. "This is not Mills, Miss Stuart. You should consider art history, perhaps, or commercial art. Now, if you will excuse me, I have other appointments." He pushes the door wide open for her and stands in rigid sentinel for her exit. Somehow, Carolyn moves through the door and hears it shut behind her. And the world shuts with it.

On the steps in front of the institute, her portfolio falls down to the cobblestones below, lying there for anyone to walk on, Carolyn sits in despair. Her hands cover her head to shut out people walking by. She shivers in the cold shadow, and the shivering is proper punishment. She searches left and right for a pay phone to call Andrea and cancel lunch and commiserate with her, but finds nothing. Instead, she picks up the portfolio and drives down Shattuck to the restaurant.

Andrea waits in the upstairs café, half hidden by a giant dark green fern. She smiles with excitement when Carolyn arrives at the table, already set with a bottle of white wine. "Carolyn, can you believe it? Kroeber Hall! The Art Institute! We've got it made in the shade." Her friend stands, jigs two steps of a victory dance and opens her arms.

Carolyn pushes her back. "What? You got in? And I didn't? Shit. I don't believe this. Dressed like that?" She folds her arms across her chest and scowls.

Andrea appears close to tears. "Oh, I'm so sorry. I can't believe you didn't get in."

"Yeah, well neither can I." Carolyn sweeps her hand across the table and sends water and wine flying, glass breaking on the tile. "I wonder what you had to do. On your knees, I bet. You can go to hell!"

Carolyn stomps back to Bancroft parking. Once in the car, she bangs hard on the steering wheel. Andrea, she thought, goddamn Andrea? And not me? In a fury she hits the sides of her head with her fists and grunts all the air out of her lungs.

In a fog bordering on depression, Carolyn drives to the apartment. She needs Damian's love.

CAROLYN OPENS THE door to the apartment and hopes for Damian's sympathetic brown eyes on the sofa or at the kitchen table. Not there. Damn him!

A strong musky odor permeates the air. The bastard is still asleep and hasn't opened any windows. She bites her lip as she shakes her head and walks down the hallway to the bedroom. Damian is making a muffled noise inside.

Determined to wake him without caring how he reacts, she pushes the door open and looks over to the bed and pain spikes down her chest. A naked red-haired woman moves up and down on Damian. They do not see Carolyn, but continue grunting and thrashing. Carolyn tenses her whole body and screams. The woman falls off and Damian grabs a sheet to cover himself. His dark eyes glare angry and defiant as he comes up on one elbow, breathing hard.

Carolyn backs out of the room, slams the door shut and kicks it. As she turns to leave, the portrait of her mother looks down on her from the wall. Before, it was the radiant red dress, the glamorous pearls. Now it's the stern, analytical eyes accusing her.

She goes out to her car, sits sideways, her feet on the ground. Her head is light, she's ready to vomit. She waits. The nausea passes and she moves inside the car. She glances at the San Francisco skyline in the distance.

Her mother. Despite all the tension-filled history between them, Carolyn has a mother. Elizabeth. She wipes her eyes and starts the car.

CAROLYN STANDS INSIDE the elevator on the 47th floor of the Bank of America building in San Francisco. The tears she has held back well up in the warm air, but she brushes them away. As she enters the hushed offices of Elizabeth Stuart Financial, LLP, the quiet elegance of wealth surrounds her. On the right, glass windows display rows of young men and women in professional business suits, typing away before banks of computer screens or on the phone, while older men prowl among them. On the left, a giant door, made from a single board of European walnut, as she knows, with a gleaming brass handle. Nothing but the best for her mother. Except not today, Carolyn realizes.

A handsome young man with curly blond hair, white shirt tight and neat, appears in front of her. "May I help you?"

Carolyn smiles in an attempt to be polite and keep her emotions to herself. "No thank you. If you please, I'm here to see my mother." Without waiting for the man, she turns left and heads for the door. She opens and closes it without looking behind her.

In front of her, Marian Brooks, white hair, severe, at her gilt-edged Louis XIV desk, smiles at her, leans forward, and holds out her hand. "Carolyn, how nice to see you. It's been a while since you've been here." Still smiling.

Carolyn nods. "Yes, that's true. But I'm here to see my mother."

Marian frowns and speaks in a warm voice. "Oh, I'm sorry. Your timing isn't good. She's in a meeting. Does she know you're here?"

Carolyn responds with her own best imitation of a warm voice. "She's always in a meeting, isn't she? That's all right. I'll go in myself." Determined and confident, she walks to the end of Marian's desk and turns toward the door.

Marian, her lips a thin line, stands and blocks her way. "I beg your pardon, Miss, but she is in an important meeting."

Carolyn's eyes widen and her voice rises enough to convey her resolve. "She is going to be in a meeting with me. Please get out of my way."

Marian sighs and returns to her desk.

Carolyn opens the door. Elizabeth Stuart sits at the end of a long green marble conference table, Alcatraz shining white in the distance behind her, her auburn hair tied back, accentuating her strong jaw line, large pale blue eyes with flecks of gold, red lips, and the diamond pendant earrings. Everyone in the room stops talking and watches Carolyn, who stares at her mother.

Elizabeth stands. "Excuse me, please." She smiles with a formal business face at the four gentlemen at the table. A Valentino black stretch wool dress shows off her figure and her height. She moves forward to Carolyn, taking her by the arm and leading her out of the room. Before closing the door, she leans back in and says "Gentlemen, she's my daughter. This won't take long." The men all nod politely and twist left or right to face each other in conversation.

Elizabeth leads Carolyn two doors to the right and pushes her into a plush office with a view of the Bay Bridge. Two steps in, she stops and faces her daughter, arms folded across her chest. "What is this all about, Carolyn? I'm in there with Goldman Sachs."

Carolyn hesitates, confused about where to begin. "Mother, I..."

"Yes? Tell me. I don't have time for a chat."

Carolyn focuses on her mother's eyes, so blue, thinking she had always wanted them to be the same hazel-green as hers, hoping for recognition. "Berkeley didn't accept me." She wants her mother to hold her so that she can let the tears flow.

Elizabeth throws her arms up in the air. "You came here to tell me this?" Without saying a word of welcome or greeting to Carolyn, she walks to the window and then spins around to show her irritation. "I don't have time for a career discussion, Carolyn. You should have come to work here. You could be the one talking to Goldman Sachs."

Carolyn gives up on receiving any comfort from Elizabeth and abandons any idea of telling her about Damian. Instead, now standing in her mother's office, she makes up an excuse. "I need a key to the house, Mother."

"Where is your key? Oh," Elizabeth glances at her diamond Rolex. "This won't do." She picks her Coach purse up off a chair and removes a key chain, taking a key off it and handing it out toward Carolyn. "Here." But she puts it back, shaking her head. "I don't need a distraction right now. And you don't need a key. Alice will still be there. Just go."

"Mother, please, I…"

Elizabeth opens the door and stands ready to go out into the hallway. "Carolyn!" Her eyes blaze with frustration. Turning from her daughter, Elizabeth shuts the door.

Carolyn stands, silent, stiff, cold, her head down, shoulders stooped, heart empty, amid the splendor of crystal chandelier, designer carpet, burled French wood, Renoir, and leather chair. "Goldman Sachs. God, Mother!"

Chapter 2

CAROLYN PARKS HER car half an hour later on Camino del Mar, walks to the side gate of her home and follows the brick path to the back yard. In the distance, through the span of the Golden Gate Bridge, are the dark Berkeley hills, far away. Distant from this morning. The memory this morning takes hold of her, when she had searched out the window, wishing she could see the lights of this house.

The low brick wall at the end of the yard overlooks the restless sea below, waves crashing against the rocks. Carolyn leans over, moves her head down and becomes dizzy, mesmerized by the whitecaps moving in and out, and the swaying water pulls her downward. She turns away from the view, closes her eyes for several seconds, and then stares at the home she grew up in. On the third story on the right is the window of her room.

In the past, she had been so anxious to leave that room, the departure that symbolized her adulthood. Now she needs to be in it, to see the world as a child again, to know she could start all over. Without rejection, without betrayal. Escape from her rejection by Marc and the betrayal by Damian.

But there is no escape from her mother's stinging criticism. There is no way she can leave that behind. Goldman Sachs. As if that's the be-all and end-all of life.

Carolyn walks back to the house. The door stands open to the rec room. Inside she climbs the stairs to the first floor. From the kitchen comes the sound of pots and pans. Alice. Carolyn steps into the kitchen, and when she sees Alice, who has raised her, standing there, a chocolate cake on the counter ready for frosting, she bursts into tears. Alice has always been there for Carolyn, taking the place of both grandmothers and grandfathers. And Carolyn's father as well.

"What's the matter?" Alice, in a staid blue dress with an apron, her sympathetic brown eyes widening, opens her arms and pulls Carolyn in and holds her for a long time, patting her on the back. A white paper napkin appears from nowhere to dry Carolyn's tears.

Carolyn takes one step back from Alice, holds her hands for a moment, and sits at the kitchen table. "Mm. Can I have a piece of that delicious cake?" The comfort of Alice is mostly the comfort of food.

Alice smiles and her eyes light up from being asked for a piece of cake. "Of course you can, Darling. Let me cut a piece and put some frosting on it for you."

Carolyn slouches down in the chair and watches Alice move in quick easy steps around the kitchen, getting a plate, cutting the cake, putting frosting on the piece. She, Carolyn, is where she belongs, at home. Until now she has not realized that she's missed home, missed being home with the comfort of Alice.

The creamy chocolate density of the cake and frosting anchor her. She sighs and relaxes, and eats the rest of the cake, concentrating, following every bite on the fork from the plate to her mouth.

Alice stands with her hand resting on Carolyn's shoulder. "There, now. Why don't you go up and take a nice long bath. That's what you need. You need to relax." Alice is like a talisman to Carolyn, irresistible.

Carolyn licks her lips and smiles. She stands, gives Alice a hug, and goes upstairs to her room.

The art on the walls of her bedroom stuns Carolyn. The whole effect is what Marc Silver had pointed out. Something of everything. Every style, every hue, every nuance of brush stroke, medium, line and atmosphere. Nothing that tells you who Carolyn Stuart wants to be. An excess of eclectic, whether of her own or of great painters. She has plastered every inch of space on the white walls with art. It isn't inspiration, its dizzying distraction.

Without waiting she gets to work taking it all down. The framed paintings come off first, and Carolyn yanks the nails hard out of the wall, not caring where they fall. Next she pulls the taped pieces of art paper off and throws them on the floor. She gathers them all up and hides them behind the sofa. As a final act she retrieves Spackle and a spatula from the garage and patches every hole in the wall. The blank wall tells her that this is the state of her life. There is nothing to look forward to.

Her clothes fall in a heap on the floor when she undresses. In the bathroom the water gushes into the bathtub and she sits down in the middle, her legs outstretched, and waits for the warm water to come up to her neck. Surrounded by silence, covered by oblivion, she rests there. The sense of the nothingness of her existence lulls her into a dreamless sleep.

When she wakes up, the water has cooled, and the orange glow of sunset filters in through the window. Carolyn gets out of the tub, dries herself, and goes out into her bedroom. Her clothes lie in the same undisturbed pile, which she picks up and puts into the hamper knowing Alice will take care of them. On the table she notices a sandwich and diet soda. She smiles to herself. What a wonderful thing for Alice to do.

Carolyn puts on Ralph Lauren: dark blue wool pants and fall colors wool knit cardigan. To show her mother she is not going to give in. Cold water on her face brightens her mood and she straightens her hair out, puts on light lipstick and goes downstairs. She has no idea what to say to her mother. But one thing for sure, it doesn't involve going to work anywhere near Goldman Sachs. And not for Elizabeth Stuart Financial, sitting in front of a screen while millions of meaningless numbers march by.

Carolyn steps into the living room. She expects to see her mother there, but she has not come home yet. Logs burn in the fireplace. She stands before the fireplace, turning to let the warmth surround her. In the kitchen, she finds Alice at the vegetable-strewn counter, who smiles and insists on another long hug.

"Are you feeling better now, dear?"

Carolyn nods. "Rested, and clean, Alice. Thank you for the sandwich." The long lawn stretches out beyond the kitchen window. "Do you know where Mother is?"

"Your mother, she just came in. I'm sure she's in her room, changing. She knows you're here. Why don't you just go wait in the living room?"

Carolyn takes a Diet Coke out of the refrigerator, goes to the living room and sits on the sofa, then picks up a coffee-table book and flips through it. A soft noise prompts her to raise her head and see Elizabeth standing in the hallway at the entrance to the room.

Elizabeth wears her white terry cloth bathrobe, her hair dry but messy and hanging down. No makeup, no jewelry, and bare feet. A smile graces her face. In her hands, she holds two short Waterford cocktail glasses with bronze liquid. "Carolyn, will you have a cocktail with me? It's dry Oloroso and a drip of Johnny Walker Blue. Not a strong drink. We could have a drink together, you and me. I would like that." She gestures to the can of pop on the coffee table and smiles again with some condescension. "Something more grown-up, maybe?"

It's obvious Elizabeth thinks that's clever, but Carolyn doesn't take it that way. It's not the way to start a grown-up kind of conversation, if that's what her mother wants. Not today. Enough happened to her today.

"Mother," she says, her voice full of sarcasm, "if you don't think I'm grown up, you shouldn't be offering me liquor."

Elizabeth is disappointed, hurt even. "No, Carolyn, I didn't...." She sits next to Carolyn on the sofa. "I'm sorry, maybe I did talk that way, but I didn't mean to. I just wanted us to have the same drink, and it came out the wrong way." She leans back and lets the drinks rest on her thighs. "I wanted you and I to be two women having a cocktail before dinner." She holds a glass out to Carolyn. "I know you had a bad day. Please share it with me."

Carolyn accepts the drink without paying attention to her mother. Elizabeth holds her glass out toward Carolyn and waits for something from her daughter, cheers or a gentle clinking.

Carolyn stares at the floor, and then raises the glass to her lips and lets the sweetly burning liquid just meet them. She focuses on her mother, who is taking a drink from the glass while peering over the top at Carolyn.

"I appreciate that you're making an effort, Mother. It would have been helpful to me if you would have made an effort this morning."

Elizabeth stands and speaks down at Carolyn from an imperial height. "You can't get it through your head, can you, that the world does not revolve around you."

Carolyn puts her drink down on the coffee table. With an athletic movement she pulls her legs back underneath her and folds her arms across her chest. As she speaks, she keeps her eyes on the floor. "No, Mother, I don't think the world revolves around me." Still facing the floor, she brings the glass to her lips, then raises her head and empties the glass. She stands and says, "Sorry, I think one of your two grown-up women in the room needs another drink." At the bar cart, Carolyn fills the glass half-full with the sherry and then pours another inch of scotch into it. After sitting down, she holds the glass in her hand and stares into her mother's eyes, waiting.

Elizabeth sits and shakes her head before answering her daughter, as though her eyes were trying to penetrate Carolyn's mind. "Getting drunk will not solve any of your problems. And this stuff will just make you sick at the rate you're pouring it down. Suppose we slow down on the drinking and then talk."

Carolyn tries to determine the attitude in her mother's voice. Is she criticizing her daughter's behavior and at the same time trying to sound empathetic? But Carolyn can't bring the two into agreement. She hears the criticism, not the empathy. Feelings had never been important for her mother. For Elizabeth only success matters, as Carolyn witnessed this morning. So now, it is obvious that her mother is trying a pop psychology trick to get her to calm down. Carolyn drinks the whole glass of liquor in response. But then she becomes queasy and the room starts to spin around her. She rolls off the sofa on to the floor, gets up and walks to the bathroom, holding on to the sofa, the table, the chair, the wall, and the bathroom door. Then she throws up in the toilet.

Carolyn sits on the bathroom floor, hoping to hear her mother's voice above her sounding comforting and worried. She hears nothing. She pushes herself up and washes her face and cleans her mouth, then walks back to the living room. Elizabeth is on the sofa, drink in hand. Her mouth is a straight line. One leg is over another, the foot moving up and down in slow rhythm.

Carolyn stands near the fireplace, sick to her stomach and sick at heart. She studies her mother's aging face, her beauty fading, but still vibrant, and wonders if her mother will ever accept her as she is.

A small black-and-white photograph in a silver frame is on the mantelpiece. It's a picture of Elizabeth as a young child in Central Park holding the hands of her mother and father. Carolyn takes the picture down from the mantelpiece and holds it in front of her mother. Elizabeth studies the picture with eyes that show how much the picture means to her. For just one second, her mother seems helpless, as if Carolyn controlled in her hand everything that is dear and precious to her.

"You know, Mother, this is your whole problem, isn't it?" Carolyn steps back as if making sure that Elizabeth can't reach out and take the photograph back from her. "Except for this miniature photo, there is no picture of my dad in this house, is there?" She holds the picture out in front of her so that Elizabeth could see it. "You have no mother, your father disowned you, and my father ran away from you. So you take it all out on me. You want me to be rigid, and controlling, and hateful, just like you!" Carolyn throws the picture at the fireplace. It hits the brick and falls to the floor, the glass broken in jagged triangles.

Elizabeth stands, her eyes blazing, her lips quavering, her hands shaking as she points at Carolyn. "You...you...you are the reason I have no husband!"

Carolyn glares at her in in shocked disbelief. Before her out the window, lies the long lawn, the brick wall, and the sea beyond that. She runs to the hallway and out the back, slamming the door. When she reaches the wall, she climbs and stands in the wet breeze. The wind whipping her hair in her face, she extends both arms out and is mesmerized by the waves crashing into the rocks. And waits, confident that her mother will see her and come.

Strong arms circle her leg. "Carolyn! Please, I beg you."

Carolyn opens her eyes. "I don't know who I am" she shouts to the wind. Elizabeth holds her tight, then lifts her hand up to her daughter, her eyes full of tears. Carolyn takes her mother's hand and steps down from the wall. They walk close together back to the house. Inside, Elizabeth leads Carolyn back to the sofa in front of the fireplace. They sit, quiet, in each other's arms. Then Elizabeth, shaking now, holds Carolyn.

"Carolyn, I love you. Do you understand me? I want to help you, not work against you. I have an idea. Will you listen to me?"

Carolyn nods, watching her mother's eyes, moving from one to the other to perceive her mother's feelings. Not yet convinced. *Listen to her mother, that's what she is supposed to do, when the real problem is that her mother doesn't listen.* Her mother holds her tight against the pull from beyond the walls, from the brick wall and the sea, the rocks below it. Carolyn sighs, slumps down in the sofa, and says, "Yes, I will."

Elizabeth tightens her grip on Carolyn's hands, then lays her hand on her daughter's shoulder and shakes it with a gentle movement. She waits, and Carolyn opens her eyes.

"What I want…."

Carolyn sits up. "Wait—I will listen to you, Mother." Her voice is begging. *"If you will listen to me."*

Elizabeth lets Carolyn's hands go. "All I want is for you to listen to my idea. I have no control over you. There never was a time when I did. At least, not for a long time. I paid for you to study art at Mills College. I paid for you to go to Paris in the summer to study Picasso, Florence in the summer to study Michelangelo, and then Louvain in another summer for medieval jewelry. Don't say I have failed to listen to you." Carolyn starts to speak, but Elizabeth holds up her hand. "Hear me out, will you?"

Carolyn falls back into the sofa again, nodding to herself. "Ok," she says cautiously. "Tell me what your idea is." Carolyn watched her mother's face carefully. There might have been a faint smile.

"What if you went to New York?"

Carolyn sits up in a hurry, her eyes widened. "What do you mean?" She wants to be interested, but she wants the conditions to be right. Trust in her mother is still something unnatural to her. Her voice betrays her skepticism. "You're going to put conditions on it."

"Let me finish. We can worry about conditions later on. But let me tell you upfront I am worried about one thing. It's Damian."

Carolyn rolls her eyes.

Elizabeth throws her hands up. "There you go."

"Mother, you don't have to worry about Damian. I'm through with him."

"Well thank God for that."

There is a moment of silence and Carolyn knows that her mother expects her to explain why she doesn't have to worry about him, but she can't tell her about another failure, especially when Elizabeth didn't even say she was sorry for her.

"All right, here's what I propose. You know your Grand Aunt Beatrice lives in New York."

"Aunt Beatrice? I have never even met her."

"I know that, honey. But she is my father's sister, and she lives in my father's house on the Upper East Side."

Carolyn is interested in New York, but she doesn't let herself believe that her mother's interest coincides with her own. That would be too much to expect. Her memories of her mother's support for her interest in art aren't positive. "You have a house in New York?"

"No, I don't. Beatrice does. My father left it to her."

"Why did he leave it to her?"

"I don't know, Carolyn. When he cut me off, he cut me off. His sister was married and living in Canada at the time."

"Maybe you were in his will. Well, of course...." Carolyn knows the answer before she finishes the sentence. She has known it for a long time.

"No. My lawyer saw his will, and there was nothing in it for me."

"You didn't see the will yourself?"

"No."

"Why didn't you contest it?"

"My father already told me, to my face, a long time ago, that he was leaving me a trust fund. Fortunately, he also left me something more valuable."

"What was that?"

"His list of friends and contacts. That's what I used to start my own business."

"Mother?"

"Yes?"

"How well do you know Aunt Beatrice?"

"Not well, I admit."

"Don't you see her when you go to New York?"

"Carolyn, I tell you, except for business meetings, the place I go to in New York is the New York City Marble Cemetery where my mother is buried. I leave flowers there every time I'm in the city. And that brings up my idea."

Carolyn waits without moving.

"I propose that you go to New York and stay with Aunt Beatrice."

Carolyn's eyes light up. "And?"

"You stay there while you...now please don't get upset with me. Hear me out." Elizabeth exhales. "I think you should explore the schools there." For her, this seems to be a revelation that would solve the problem.

"School. What kind of school?"

"Okay, I want you to consider business school. Columbia, or NYU, or even Wharton."

Carolyn's eyes widen. A trap. New York. But not my New York. My mother's New York.

"I can see your reaction," Elizabeth said. "Please hear me out...."

Carolyn doesn't wait. "Mother, I'm not prepared for business school. They won't even let me in."

Elizabeth laughs. "Oh, my Dear, I'll make sure they let you in if I have to buy the whole damn campus."

Carolyn resists. Her mother always buys what she wants. "I'm not going to do it, Mother. You can't force me. I'll just go live with Andrea until I get a job." But she doesn't tell her mother that she has burned her bridges with Andrea.

Elizabeth shakes her head, her voice raised and taking on a hard edge. "A job? Doing what? For how much money?"

"You don't get it, do you, Mother? I'm not going to business school. I'm not you. I'm not a math person like you."

"Things will work out. They have an international program. You go to London, to Paris, not just New York. You concentrate in art philanthropy, or in the financing of art collections. Whatever you want."

"Oh, great, just like Marc said. Work for a museum."

"Good god, Carolyn. Art collecting is what you'll do. Your home becomes a museum. New York art galleries will be waiting for you. That's what I'm offering you. And nothing's stopping you from taking art courses on the side. I'm offering you the world. Don't you see?"

This confuses Carolyn. She doesn't want to do what her mother's proposing. A flurry of ideas fly around her head. She does want to go to New York. But she knows in her heart she isn't an MBA student. It would be marvelous to work with art galleries in SOHO and Chelsea. And London and Paris. The real question is whether she can accept her mother's help and not go to business school. "So I would have to stay with Aunt Beatrice, is that it? So she could watch over me?"

Elizabeth puts her lips together and thinks for a moment, then says, the frustration still in her voice, "Beatrice has no children. She would enjoy having you stay there. It's not control, Carolyn. You will be too busy."

"How do you know all this? Have you already talked to her about it?"

"Yes, I have."

Carolyn's voice rises. "When? This afternoon?" She can't believe she's hearing this.

"No. Not at all. Earlier in the summer."

"Mother, you mean to tell me you worked this whole scenario out with your aunt and you didn't say a word to me?"

"I think you should calm down. I didn't work out anything. We talked, and she mentioned that she lived in a large house on the Upper East Side, and she would like for me to stay there when I go to New York, and she mentioned you as well. It was her initiative, not mine."

"Are you going to stay there?"

"I don't know. I don't have any plans to go to New York at the moment, so I haven't given it any thought."

It's true, Carolyn thinks, this Aunt Beatrice can't control me. I can do as I want. "All right, Mother. I agree. I will go to New York. But I can't promise you that I'm going to become a banker."

Elizabeth smiles for the first time, her eyes and her voice softened. "All I ask, Carolyn, is that you try."

CAROLYN FASTENS HER seat belt and sits fascinated with the view out the window as the American Airlines 747 jet accelerates on the SFO runway, lifts into the air and banks over Golden Gate Bridge on its way to Idlewild Airport. Out the window she sees the bridge she might never have to cross again. As the plane climbs into the sky, into the clouds, the whole Berkeley episode disappears. The blue sky appears above and the clouds below, New York lies ahead and San Francisco vanishes beneath her.

Chapter 3

Elizabeth, New York, 1960

ELIZABETH GEORGIA STUART focused on Rockaway Beach through the dark circle of turning propellers as the Eastern Airlines Douglas DC-6 floated down to a perfect smooth touchdown at Idlewild airport in clear skies with a slight breeze from the West. She took her black alpaca car coat from the overhead rack and walked straight down the airplane stairway and out through the terminal to the waiting line of taxis. "Park Avenue and 85th Street."

Forty minutes later the taxi swerved sharply to the curb. She stepped out and stared with apprehension at the imposing four-story red stone house. The cold Atlantic air made Elizabeth pull her coat tight around her and button it up. The chandelier shone in the window of her father's office, as he no doubt scrutinized his return on investment. He waited up there, his anger radiating out the window, as if he already condemned what she had to confess.

She faced the street and raised her arm for another cab. "60th and Madison, Please. Between Madison and Park."

TWENTY MINUTES LATER, Elizabeth entered Midtown Internal Medicine and made a forced smile at the receptionist wearing a starched white nurse's uniform and cap. "I would like to see Dr. Rivlin, please."

"Hello, Elizabeth." The young woman, with dark brown hair and no makeup beneath her olive eyes, put her finger on the open pages of a large thick appointment book and searched for a moment. A smile. "Did you call to schedule an appointment? I don't often miss them."

"No, I didn't. I just flew in from California."

The young woman frowned. "I'm sorry, he is booked for this week. If this is an emergency, perhaps you..."

The door opened behind the reception desk and an elderly woman in a wrinkled nurse's uniform came out. She had white hair and round horn-rimmed glasses and she spoke with genuine warmth, also visible in her light brown eyes. "Elizabeth, how unexpected. I didn't think you had an appointment today."

"I don't, Colleen, but I just arrived from California, and I need to talk to Dr. Rivlin. Can you fit me in?"

"Let me come around." Colleen disappeared behind the door, and reappeared from a side door in the reception room. Shaking Elizabeth's hand, she said, "It's nice to see you again. Let me talk to him. I'll be right back." One minute later she came through the door again. "He can spend time with you, but not right away. Can you come back in an hour? Will that be all right? He's...."

"Of course, that will be all right. I appreciate this, Colleen. I'll be back in an hour. Thank you so much."

Elizabeth stepped out on to the street to catch her third cab, then changed her mind and walked back to 59th and Lexington and caught the #6 subway headed downtown. Getting off at Bleecker, she bought a small bouquet of yellow roses, then walked across Bowery, to 64 East Second Street, the address of the New York City Marble Cemetery.

Her heart beat faster as she entered the rustic black wrought-iron gate and walked across the perfectly-mowed dark green lawn to the old sycamore tree with the gnarled trunk, covered with vines. She pulled her skirt up above her knees and knelt, placed the roses on top of the small cement square that read Vault 238, Julia Marie Stuart, and touched her mother's name. "Hi, Mama. It's me." With one hand, she sighed and wiped tears from her cheeks, but kept the other on the plain dark gray slab for half a minute. "Pray for me." She walked toward the cemetery gate, but halfway there she turned her head back and watched the small concrete square diminish in the distance as she walked out the gate and retraced her route back to the doctor's office.

DR. RIVLIN, tall and broad-shouldered, energetic for his sixty years, welcomed her into his office. His silver hair offset black-rimmed glasses and a red bow tie. "Welcome, Elizabeth. It's nice you came in, though I must admit I'm intrigued. I understood you were still way out there at Stanford. Your father is in good health I trust. At least I haven't seen him in a while."

"I haven't seen my father in several months, either. Two weeks ago I talked to him and he was fine."

"Why, then, Elizabeth, have you come all the way to New York? Some problem?" He adjusted his glasses, sat back in his chair and interlaced his fingers on his chest.

Elizabeth inspected the floor, then looked up at him. "I need to ask you to do something that is important for me."

"Well, you have piqued my curiosity."

"I must leave school for several months. I am asking you to write a letter to the school explaining my absence. Letting them know that I have mononucleosis, and that I need total bed rest."

He pursed his mouth and frowned, sitting without any motion, studying her. Then he sat up. "Elizabeth, I can see from where I sit, you don't have it. Your movements are energetic...." He studied her. "Your neck is fine. You don't seem to have a fever. In any case, I would have to examine you. What you are talking about is an infectious disease. I would call the school today, and you would have to give me the names of people you had close contact with." He stood up. "This is a surprise. Let's go to an examining room."

She shook her head and shrugged her shoulders. "I'm sorry, Dr. Rivlin." She noticed his Columbia diploma on the wall, then back to him. "The problem is something else."

He nodded, saying, "I think you have to tell me what the something else is. I have been giving you physicals for your whole life, Elizabeth. You can confide in me."

She did not know this would be so hard. "Doctor, I'm pregnant. I can't be expelled from Stanford. I need your help."

"Does your father know this?"

"No, he doesn't. I'll tell him when it's time."

"And the father of the child? Is it a student...or a professor?"

Elizabeth reddened at the insinuation, at the sudden accusatory change in his attitude.

Dr. Rivlin continued, noticing her reaction. "You should have come here with the father, Elizabeth. In any case, I'm not a gynecologist, as you know. I could give you the names of several good people in the building. Perhaps a woman…"

This childhood doctor now became a cold, objective clinical threat. Elizabeth put her arms across her chest. "Thank you, Doctor Rivlin. I'm not quite ready for that yet. Excuse me for taking up your time. I must see my father now." She stood to leave.

He held out his hand, but when she didn't take it, he shrugged with seeming sadness, followed her out to the reception room and opened the door for her. "Elizabeth, please come see me whenever you want," he said, nodding. "I am still your doctor."

She thanked him and went down to the street. A cab stopped to let an elderly woman in a red coat get out, and Elizabeth took a step toward the cab but stopped and walked the long way up to 85th and down to Park Avenue.

Her father's house, the home she grew up in, loomed high above her. The light was out in her father's office window. She had not brought a key with her, so she rang the bell and waited, nervous and unsure of how to tell him.

The door opened and Mrs. Willow, still gaunt, with her long white hair streaked with black, brushed back from her face, brings her hand to her chest in surprise. "Miss Elizabeth, how unexpected." Then she took a step back, concerned. "No one told us you were coming. I would have prepared your room. I…"

Elizabeth waved her off. "It's a bit cold. I'd like to come in."

Flustered, the woman opened the door wide and backed away.

Elizabeth entered the hallway and called up the marble staircase. "Is my father at home?"

"Yes he is, Miss. Excuse me, doesn't he know you're here?"

"No, I didn't tell him. Where is he?"

"He's in the library. He was on the phone a few minutes ago."

"Thank you, I'll just go up there."

Mrs. Willow took Elizabeth's coat. "Will you be staying long? Would you like something to eat?"

"I don't know how long I'll be staying. And I'm not hungry right now. I'll just go upstairs."

"Will you be staying for dinner?"

28

Elizabeth touched Mrs. Willow's arm and smiled in sympathy for the woman's worry. "I don't know. We'll see. Thank you."

Elizabeth walked up the long staircase, pausing to observe the grand master paintings on the wall. At the top, she stopped to listen, but the house was quiet. She put her hand up to knock on the library door, held it, then brought it down. She adjusted her skirt, then opened the door without making a sound. At the far end of the room across the dark Oriental rug the fire burned brightly in the fireplace. The graying auburn hair of her father peeked out above the red leather wing-back chair. She paused to see if he was awake, or reading, or just thinking, but she could not tell. He did not move.

She closed the door. At the sound of the click, Hugh Stuart swiveled around in the chair and inspected her, a snifter of liquor in his hand. His mouth sneered, and his pale blue eyes observed her with contempt. Elizabeth froze.

"Why did you come here?"

"Dad..." she had no idea how to begin.

Hugh moved back to face the fire, taking a sip of his drink.

Elizabeth walked toward him until she was in front of him. "Dad, why are you so angry?"

He stood and walked away to the center of the room. "Angry? Why should I be angry?" He waved his drink back and forth as if trying to find the words in the air. "I get a call from Dr. Rivlin, and what does he tell me?" He glared at her. "'That my daughter, my own daughter,'" his voice rose with each phrase, and he then faced her, pointing with the glass as if offering her a toast, "Elizabeth Georgia Stuart, upon whom I have lavished my time, my fortune, my influence," and he was straining his voice now, "I could say my love and my life, that this daughter is pregnant and she is leaving the university. Tell me, Elizabeth, is our family doctor lying to me?"

She sat in a chair, silent, surprised and stunned at this total lack of sympathy. And at the betrayal by Dr. Rivlin. No, more than that, this hostility from her father. She said meekly, "No."

Hugh continued, pacing back and forth, his voice now changing to a lower but more sinister tone, "And then he tells me you tried to get him to lie about it to the university?" He put his drink on the library table. "Is that also true, Elizabeth?" He did not wait for her answer, but lifted his eyes up to the ceiling, expressing his frustration at the event threatening his composure. "But, of course, it's true. You lied to me about being pregnant." He took a deep breath and shook his head back and forth as if he were shuddering. "You want to lie to the university. What other lies are you keeping from me?"

Elizabeth sat in the chair, hunched up and closed in, helpless. "Dad," she said, pleading. "I…"

He resumed his loud accusatory tone. "Don't, Elizabeth. You have nothing to say. After all I have done for you. Raising you with love and generosity on my own. All the people I have told that you would be following in my footsteps. The charitable donations I made in your name…," another deep breath, "…all the associations I have prepared for you…to one day…take over this firm." Hugh stopped, out of breath. Out of accusations.

He waved his finger at Elizabeth when she opened her mouth to speak. He spoke as if the voice of the devil spoke for him. "You are just like your mother." He got up, once more, and stepped to the center of the room, searching for an answer to why this plague visited him.

"Dad, please, I was just at mom's grave."

Hugh's face reddened and blood vessels stood out on his temple. "Grave?" He asked the question as he searched in the air for its meaning. "It's not a grave, Elizabeth, it's a vault. She is dead to me, is that clear, young woman? Dead! She was a vicious slut, just like you."

"Daddy…."

"Oh, yes, yes, that's it. Dad, Daddy." He pursed his lips. "Elizabeth where is your husband? Why are you here alone?" He stomped his foot and slapped his thigh, then stood ramrod straight. "Where is the baby's father?"

"I don't know."

"You don't know." His eyes widened in disbelief, his fists tightened. "What do you mean you don't know? Was it a student at Stanford?" Then he stood silent for one moment of possible shock. "Was it a professor?" The word sounded like an explosion coming out of his mouth. He forced himself to stare at her face as he waited for the answer.

Elizabeth had enough. She stood, back straight. "No, not a professor. He was a student."

"Was?"

"He left school."

30

"So, he left school, and he left you and I'm supposed to just pick up the pieces after your slatternly behavior."

"I'm asking for your help, Dad. You don't have to be so hateful toward me."

"Hateful? I don't think so, Elizabeth. It's you who have behaved as if you hate me, after everything I have done for you. I'll tell you how it's going to be. I'm going to go to the University Club and will be back on the weekend." He leaned and pointed to her. "You had better be gone by then or I will have you thrown out."

"Dad!"

"No! No! It's over. You are the same as your mother." His lips tightened into a straight line, his eyes moved back and forth as he thought. "I will leave you a trust fund, and a trust fund for the child. Go to JP Morgan on Monday and it's yours. But I will see no more of you."

He pounded in heavy steps out the door. Elizabeth stood. No tears. A pain ran down her back. The door slam shut downstairs.

Sunday morning, she left the house with one small suitcase. Besides her clothing, there was the picture of her as a child with her mother and father. And a copy of every item in Hugh Stuart's Rolodex file.

A few hours later, she sat in the first row of an American Airlines four-engine DC-7 airliner bound for Chicago, the first leg of her trip back to San Francisco. Her hand rested on her purse on her lap. The picture was in the purse.

Chapter 4

Elizabeth, Julia, New York, 1940

THE BROADWAY LIMITED streamlined steel car pulled into track 17 in Pennsylvania Station. Porter Malcolm West in his neat beige uniform pulled down the pieces of luggage and backed out the door of the drawing room. When he had left, Hugh Stuart moved out to the passageway, followed by his wife, Julia, and Elizabeth, their two-year-old daughter. Down on the platform, Hugh gave Malcolm a tip. "Our automobile will be waiting out on 8th Avenue, as usual."

The porter thanked him, smiled politely, and moved the luggage cart out to the station.

Julia Stuart held her daughter tight as they walked through the sprawling Beaux Arts concourse. Elizabeth strained her neck to see the gray light from the glass-and-wrought-iron ceiling.

A man's voice droned on in tired monotony out over the concourse. "The Pathfinder, bound for Pittsburgh, Chicago, and St. Louis, leaving at two o'clock...."

Elizabeth, puzzled, searched for the source of the voice. "Our train, Mommy?"

"No, Darling, it's a different train."

"Where's our train?"

Julia smiled at her little girl, her hazel eyes smiling in enjoyment. "Our train waits on the track for more people tomorrow, sweetheart."

"Oh. Look there. Can I have candy?"

"Lizzie, you had dinner a little while ago."

"Oh, all right."

She let her mother's hand go and ran over to Hugh. "Daddy, I want a candy bar."

He glanced sideways at Julia with a smug grin, then smiled down at Elizabeth. "Hm. Sure, why not?"

She pulled her dad over to the newsstand, jumping up and down while he paid for the candy.

"But you can't eat it till we're home, okay?"

"Okay." Elizabeth smiled at her mother, but held on to her father's hand while they went up the grand staircase to the 8th Avenue exit.

Hugh opened the door to the street for his wife and daughter to pass through then took Elizabeth's hand again and pointed her to the long black Cadillac Fleetwood limousine at the curb where the porter had closed the trunk and was walking back inside.

Grace Stuart, Hugh's mother, white-haired, square-jawed and severe, appeared in the rear passenger window her dark green-blue eyes took in the scene. She waved at them. "Come, Elizabeth, come sit next to me."

Elizabeth smiled up at her father, who nodded. She ran over to the car, where Timothy Gibbons in his dark brown chauffeur uniform tipped his hat and opened the door for her. She scampered in.

Hugh watched Julia, who had moved back to the station door. She was talking to a middle-aged Mediterranean type of man carrying a battered suitcase with several large tourist stickers on it. He smiled at Julia and patted her on the arm before disappearing behind the doors. Hugh's face became rigid.

Julia continued gazing inside for a moment, then walked toward the car, her eyes down in some private thought. When she approached Hugh, she smiled, took his arm and said in a normal, pleasant voice, "Let's go home."

As Gibbons held the door open for them, Julia saw Grace's eyes locked on Hugh, the straight line of her lips and the coldness of her eyes a mark of hauteur and disapproval.

Elizabeth sat between Grace and Hugh, while Julia sat on the jump chair that folded out from the back of the front seat.

Grace chided Elizabeth. "My dear, be careful with your hands, they are dirty from the train and you do not wish to soil your nice dress."

Elizabeth surveyed her father and mother before responding. "I'm sorry, Grandmother."

"You needn't be sorry, but you must be careful." Grace gave the child a smile of approval and then faced the window in a distracted manner although she couldn't see much through the curtains.

WHEN THEY ARRIVED at their townhouse on Park Avenue, and Gibbons opened the door, Elizabeth stepped out to the street.

"Oh no, be careful." Grace reached out to the little girl.

Gibbons ran over, put his arm on Elizabeth's shoulder, and waited for the others to get out.

Hugh opened the front door to the house for them all while Gibbons went back to the car. As soon as they were inside, Mrs. Willow, in a black dress with white lace, came scurrying out of the side door to take coats and hats with a little curtsy.

Mary, the household maid, stood at the top of the staircase, her hand held out. Elizabeth ran up the marble staircase and took Mary's hand and the two of them stepped right, facing the hallway toward her room.

Julia took a quick step up. "I'll be right there, Darling. Wait for me."

Elizabeth stopped and informed the adults walking up the stairs, "I want to play music."

"Lizzie, you're not old enough to do that."

"Mary will help me." She disappeared with the maid.

"Try to be quiet!" Julia called after her.

"That child has too much energy." Grace patted her hair. "She needs to be controlled or she will run wild on you both. I know she will end up destroying that beautiful record player. It shouldn't be in her room."

"I think it's wonderful that she has so much energy," said Julia, and after a quick glance at her husband continued, "and Hugh bought her the machine, remember?" She knew that when it came to her granddaughter Grace accepted whatever Hugh said or did.

The three of them went on in silence up the marble staircase. At the top, Grace walked to her room. Hugh and Julia went into the library.

Julia sat on the green brocade sofa, her hands folded on her lap, her eyes fixed on Hugh. He walked to the library table, picked up the Wall Street Journal and opened it wide. She cleared her throat. He paid no attention. She cleared her throat again, louder. He folded the paper, irritated, and raised his eyebrows.

"Hugh, who do you think is Lizzie's mother, Grace or me?"

"I think that's a silly question. Don't you?" He studied her with a frown and his chin lowered.

"Silly? No I don't think it's silly. I think it's important."

"Julia, you're making too much of this. What's got into you anyway?" He spread out the newspaper again.

Julia stood, walked to Hugh, and pulled the newspaper out of his hand. She threw it on the carpet.

He angrily demanded, "What's got into you?"

She folded her arms across her chest. "You're not listening to me. It's not about me, it's about your mother."

"Keep her out of this."

Julia put her hands behind her and focused on his eyes. "Hugh, I am Lizzie's mother. Today in the train station when I said she couldn't have any candy, she went right to you to get what she wanted. And then all the way home her grandmother acted like she was in charge of our daughter."

Hugh put both hands down on the table and leaned on it, turning to Julia. "What am I supposed to do? If you controlled Elizabeth yourself, then my mother wouldn't be getting in the middle." He stepped back, put his hands in his pockets, and leaned in close to her. "Have you thought of that?"

Julia raised her arms up, let them fall down at her sides, and gave a sigh of helplessness. "If your mother would stay out of the way I could control my daughter."

Hugh sighed and walked over to the fireplace. He rested his elbow on the mantle and tapped his toe. Then he faced Julia. "All my mother did was try to keep Elizabeth clean and safe. That's hardly controlling her."

Julia's voice rose in exasperation. She flipped her head back and said, "You think that's it?" then walked out of the room.

Hugh picked up the intercom phone. "Have Gibbons bring the car out front. I'm going to my office." He left the library and walked to his mother's room. He knocked gently on the door and heard her voice inviting him in.

She was sitting in the chaise longue, dressed in her green satin robe, her head back on the pillow, her fingers holding a small book open on her lap. "Hugh, Darling, I heard you and Julia in the library. I don't know what you were saying, but I'm afraid it had something to do with me."

"No, Mother. Nothing about you." He smiled at her.

She raised her eyebrows. "Don't patronize me, Hugh. You chose her as your wife against my wishes, indeed against the wishes of all the family, including your sister Beatrice. You both got married too soon."

Hugh sat down at her dressing table and moved her mother-of-pearl hairbrush out of the way to make room for his hand. "You can leave Beatrice out of this. You weren't happy with her husband either."

"Well you can't blame me. This man takes her off to Canada and they go traipsing around the Yukon. Who knows what kind of danger they'll be in? I might never see her again."

He covered her hand with his and waited a moment before speaking. "Mother, they settled in Montreal. Give Beatrice a little room to get on with her life."

"But she's in another country, for God's sake. And don't they speak French there?"

"You've been up there yourself on the Montreal Limited. It's a day's ride with a great Pullman lounge. Everybody speaks English so stop worrying." Hugh stood up and gave his mother a kiss on the forehead. "I have to go."

He left the room hearing his mother's long sigh and walked around the banister to his office. Inside, he held at the stock market ticker tape, which had curled up in a long paper snake on the floor, a day's ticking. He picked up the section of tape closest to the now-silent machine and began reading. He pursed his lips as he drew the paper through his fingers. The paper swished to the floor when he let it drop. He moved to the gold ticker and held up its short tape, then tore both tapes out in disgust, dropping them in the mahogany bin in the corner. He picked up the intercom phone and cancelled the car. Then he called his office on Wall Street.

"Stuart Financial. How may I direct your call?"

"Hanna, put me through to Luther Bollinger."

After a few seconds, a high-pitched man's voice came on the phone. "Yes, Hugh. I hope you had a pleasant holiday."

"Luther, did you see the gold ticker today?"

"Yes, it went down a couple of pennies."

"Well, buy some more."

"But...Hugh...is that wise?"

"Wise? What do you think? You're so...cautious. You're too cautious, Luther."

"Sir, I am neither cautious nor foolhardy. I buy and sell on instruction."

"I instruct you to buy five million dollars of gold. Today. Now."

In a voice that was shivering, Luther answered, "Sir, if that is your instruction I will carry it out. Will you be available to sign a check today?"

"Of course, I will. When we're finished, I will call Accounting and make sure they do their part."

"I remind you again, Mr. Stuart, that the price of gold is declining."

"It is indeed, Luther. For now. There's going to be a war. England has transferred millions of pounds of gold to Canada. Gold will be the most precious commodity on this earth and I plan on owning as much of it as I can. I'm just getting started."

"Sir, a war would be calamitous."

"Luther, I am not discussing world politics with you. You are valued for your ability to make trades. That is all I require of you."

"I'm sorry, sir. You brought up the subject of war."

Hugh hesitated. "Hmm. So I did. Now, make the trade and get me a check to pay for it."

"Yes. Right away, sir. I did not mean to offend you."

"You did not offend me, Luther. You irritated me with your caution. Now, transfer me back to Hanna."

"One more thing, sir, if you please."

"All right. What is it, Luther?"

"It's too late to make the trades today, Mr. Stuart. I'll have to make them first thing in the morning."

Hugh held the handset tight in his grip and let out a frustrated breath. "Of course, that's right. But first thing in the morning. As soon as you've made the trades, you call me, you hear?"

"Yes, sir. First thing."

"Now get me back to Hanna."

The phone went blank and Hanna was back on the line. "Yes, Mr. Stuart."

"Hanna, put me through to Kurt Walther."

After a click, another voice. "Mr. Stuart, this is Kurt."

"Kurt, first thing tomorrow morning, Luther will be coming down to see you with a request for a check for five million dollars. Do you understand me, five million?"

Silence on the line, then, "May I ask for whom, sir?"

"Dammit, I don't know, Kurt. I'm buying gold. Perhaps he will require checks to several different traders. And it might not be exact. That's beside the point. When he brings the request to you, I want you to get me those checks to sign as quickly as you can. Understand?"

"Yes, I do, Mr. Stuart. I will bring the checks up to you myself."

"I'll be waiting for them." Hugh put the handset down. He swiveled around to face the window, leaned back with his hand behind his head, smiling to himself and watching the trees sway back and forth down 85th Street.

His phone rang. He picked it up ready to do battle, sure that someone downtown had failed to do his job. "Yes?"

"Mr. Stuart, this is Elmer Griesbeck in the real estate office. Do you have a moment?"

"I do. But it's late in the day, Elmer. As they keep telling me."

"Then let me fill you in, and you can decide how you want to proceed. It's about the apartment building on the Lower East Side. I think you ought to go see it."

"Elmer. What do I pay you for?"

"You pay me for management, sir. And I do it. But I think this building could end up causing you a lot of problems. A fire... people hurt...."

Hugh snorted at the handset. "I have important trades tomorrow morning. Before I do anything else. By then you'll be able to do your job. Is that understood?"

"Thank you, sir. I understand, sir. I will inform you tomorrow of how the situation develops."

"No. Do not inform me tomorrow. You take care of this."

Hugh hung up the phone and slammed his palms down on the desk. He stood and put his hands in his pockets and stared out the window again, at the traffic moving and stopping along Park Avenue. His mother, his wife, his daughter, his staff, and now his damn tenants pressing down on him. This day trip had been damn unproductive.

He went back to the library and found Julia lying down on the sofa, reading *The American Weekly*. He gestured at the cover. "Look at that rot. She's naked. Why are you reading that?"

Julia closed the magazine and noted the cover. "Why, I didn't pay any attention to the cover. It's Henry Clive. It was here, and I felt like something relaxing. I think we both need something relaxing."

He ran his fingers through his hair and pulled his tie off. Then he took the carnation off his lapel and threw it in the wastebasket. "I hope you don't plan on painting lurid images like that. It's hard to know what you're doing with your art."

She put the magazine down and walked to him. With her palms resting on his chest, Julia gazed into his eyes.

He backed away.

She put her arms out, making a point of still staring into his eyes. "Hugh, Darling, anytime you want to know what I am doing with my art I would love to tell you, but you never have time so I'm all on my own, I'm afraid."

"What do you mean, alone? You have Elizabeth. And you have Mother, too. A household to run. You have no time to yourself. Didn't you enjoy today?"

She sighed and backed away. "Enjoy? A trip to North Philadelphia to see your cousin? The highlight of my day was getting a facial massage in the salon car coming back."

"Elizabeth had a good time."

"The trip bored Lizzie, Hugh. She's too young for a day trip like that."

"I see. Then why didn't you tell me about this sooner?"

"Why? It seems to me I didn't have any choice in the matter. Your mother arranged the whole trip without any advance word to me."

Hugh sucked his lips in and rocked back and forth. "Mother. Oh, yes, Mother. She took time to make arrangements, Julia, and you should be appreciative instead of complaining. And we had a wonderful meal in the dining car before arriving. They have quite excellent cuisine."

"Yes, I know. Cuisine for you, cousins for your mother. What about time for us? "

He sat in his dark red wing-back chair and put one leg over the other. "Perhaps we would have more time together, if you would spend less time at that art league of yours." He put both legs on the floor. "Who was that man at the train station? He seemed to be awfully familiar with you."

"That? That was Carlo De Luca, my professor. He's a painter, and a rather famous one at that. He has a painting in the Metropolitan museum. Which your mother contributes to. Which you would know if you took your nose out of finances long enough to pay attention to art."

Hugh stood. "Fine. So he's a famous painter. What's that got to do with you, Julia?"

She went to him again and took his arm and spoke in a soothing voice. "Nothing, Darling. Nothing at all personal. He was at the Art Student League last week and did a master class."

"Oh, a master class. I suppose there was a nude at the center of it all?"

Julia laughed, cupping her hands over her face. "No, I'm sorry, Darling, nothing as lurid as that." She smiled and still laughed. "There were twenty people there. He critiqued one of my portraits, and was rather complimentary if I do say so myself."

"And that gives him the right to put his hands all over you?"

Julia recognized she was having no success with him. The humor left her face. "Not everyone is as reserved as you."

He stood straight and bent back. "Yes, well, I may be reserved, but I would never touch another woman, Julia." He stared at her with piercing eyes. "Does that make any sense to you?"

"It does. You're reserved, he's not. That's not what he was doing, not the way you make it sound." She put her arms across her chest. "Why don't you come to the Art League and see for yourself?"

He pointed to paintings on the walls. "Observe, Julia. What Mother and Father have collected. Beautiful, all of them. Impressionists, Post-Impressionists, Renaissance, Old Masters. Cross's *La Terrasse Fleurie*. Isn't it beautiful, those flowers? I mean stunning, don't you think? There, a genuine Signac. It's the Grand Canal in Venice, for God's sake. See," he said, pointing, "there's San Giorgio. Now what's wrong with that?"

Julia noted Hugh, then the painting, confused. "Why should there be something wrong with that?"

"Don't you think...it's not...modern...is it? It's impressionist, Julia, it's modern...yes, in the timeline, but you can make out what it is. That's what art is, not that awful contemporary chicken scratching."

"Oh, Hugh. You think that's what art is? Is that why you won't come, because you think all we are doing is awful chicken scratching? Have you seen my chicken scratching?"

He toddled his head back and forth trying to decide how to continue. "Chicken scratching? You? My God, I should hope not. Your portraits are nice. Yes, they are. I've seen your portrait of Elizabeth, and one of Grace. And then there's...well...okay...that's what I've seen. And I like them. They are fine there on the wall in Elizabeth's room."

"Oh, there you go, "she said, turning around, her hands out in front of her, "on the wall in Elizabeth's room. That's where you think they belong, don't you?"

He thought for a moment, then smiled at her in an attempt to keep the emotions within control. "I thought we agreed, Darling. They are there for a reason. They are something for Elizabeth to be proud of."

"Right. But not something for us...for you...or your mother...to be proud of."

Hugh turned around the room again, with a sweeping gesture. "I know you didn't think it would be appropriate to put your student work up on the wall with these...." he pointed at each as he spoke, "with... Ostade...and a drawing by...Gainsborough." He rested his chin on his hand, waiting for her.

Julia stood still, stunned. "It doesn't matter what I think, does it?" She felt hot. She spoke to the floor. "Since you insist on the truth, no, I don't think I'm up there with Rembrandt and Michelangelo. But I did think I was up there with you!"

"Oh, Julia. I didn't think you were this petty. Up here with me? What's that supposed to mean? I'll tell you, if you want to know. It sounds like you married me for money and now you're expecting me to make sure my money guarantees you a career. That's what this is all about."

Julia shook her head in disbelief. "You've been talking to your mother, haven't you?"

"Leave my mother out of this."

"Your mother is in this, Hugh. You and her money. You and she and our daughter."

"This makes my point."

"What makes your point?"

"My point that you are indifferent to my mother, who wants to help you in every way. And, also, in some ways, you are indifferent to me."

Julia's face crumbled, her muscles pulled tight. "Indifferent? To you? Now you are becoming bizarre."

"Perhaps. So it would seem to you. Bizarre, I mean. You object to my mother, in whose house we live. In the house of my birth. As a matter of fact, that's more than indifference, Julia, it's...it's...well, let's leave it at indifference. But you object to my mother who tries to help you. And you object to me because I don't show you sufficient cultural deference."

"Hugh...I love you." Her voice was pleading.

"Love, yes, you say you love me. I hear you."

"Am I not good enough for you in bed, Darling?"

"Ah. Yes. I knew you would bring that up. Love and sex. An artist talking. Love and sex. Tell me something, Julia."

She felt hot and thirsty.

"Elizabeth is two years old. Why haven't we had another child?"

Her eyes opened wide. "Why? How am I supposed to know?"

"I think maybe you do know."

"Hugh, you're scaring me. Do you know something I don't? Has Dr. Rivlin told you something?"

"You tell me."

She folded her arms across her chest. "Me tell you? What's there to tell?"

Hugh hesitated, bit his lips, seemed to be thinking, then raised his voice and blurted, "Why can't you get pregnant, Julia?"

"I don't know."

"Have you talked with the good doctor about it?"

"No, I haven't."

"Why not?"

"Why not? Good God. Lizzie's two years old. It wasn't that long ago I was still breastfeeding. Why should I get pregnant?"

"Don't you want to get pregnant?"

"Hugh, what's going on here?" She shook her head in disbelief. "I'll get pregnant when I get pregnant. I'm not doing anything to keep from getting pregnant. Yes, I want another child. Yes, I hope it's a boy. There, is that what you want to hear?"

Julia waited to hear a sigh of relief from Hugh.

He remained silent for several seconds, as he took the time to ingest what she said. He stared at her, smiling, but he forced the smile. "Ah, you see, indifference. That's it. You say you want a boy. Have you asked the doctor why you're not getting pregnant?"

She laughed, her voice full of cynicism. "Oh, I know. Pregnant, that's what you want. That's all that matters to you and your mother. Children. Heirs."

Now Hugh laughed. "Wouldn't you like more children laughing in the house? It would make Mother so happy."

Julia sensed his laughter was as full of cynicism as hers. "There you go. Your mother's house. You can't stay away from the topic, can you? It's always there in between you and me. I wish we lived in our own house, Hugh. You and me and Lizzie and little Hugh as well."

"Little Hugh? Are you making fun of me? Because I'm not making fun. I've been to see Dr. Rivlin and I know there is no reason for you to not be pregnant. At least when you haven't even been examined. You haven't even tried to find out if there's a medical reason."

She walked to the door. "At times you are preposterous, Hugh."

Chapter 5

JULIA GOT OUT of the yellow cab at 215 West 57th, entered the Art Student League building, and walked to the second floor. She entered a busy classroom with walls full of practice canvases where she studied basic oil painting. The students moved around the room putting away their paints and brushes. Carlo de Luca stood in the corner of the room, hands in pockets, watching the chaos. He ran his hand through his black wavy hair.

Julia walked up to Ann Bayle, a tall girl with long, straight dark brown hair and outsized round glasses. "Ann, what's going on? Am I late for class?" Julia raised her wrist to see her watch and quickly glanced over at Carlo.

"No, not at all. We're going to Harlem."

"Harlem? Whatever for?"

Ann moved her eyes to the corner. "Carlo is taking us over there to study the murals in the Harlem Hospital."

"That's a long way. Why didn't he tell us before?"

"I don't know. Who cares? I think it'll be fun, and he thinks it's important."

Julia thanked Ann and walked to where Carlo stood. "Professor, I'm sorry I missed your remarks this morning. Can you tell me why we are going to Harlem? I thought we were going to continue discussing brush techniques."

Carlo smiled with a row of perfect white teeth. His cinnamon-brown eyes surveyed Julia's eyes. "Of course, Julia. It's simple. The murals at the Harlem Hospital are modern painting at its best. This is a class in fundamentals. It's not all about getting the paint on the canvas. It's about the meaning of art. And this work is about the social justice in art."

"Social justice?"

"Julia, where have you been? You don't learn brushstrokes and then figure out what to paint. It's all part of the same process." He put his hand out and with care laid a finger on her upper arm, the same as he had done at the train station.

She withdrew a step.

"Julia," he said in a warm, personal voice as he took a small step toward her, "if you think pure abstract art is what you want, perhaps you should be in another class. People in other rooms are throwing paint on the walls. Is that what you want?"

His accusation stung. "I signed up for this class, sir." She grew nervous, pressing her lips together.

"Please, call me Carlo. And forgive my behavior, I didn't mean to cause you any discomfort. But I believe in my mission. Will you come with us?" He defended himself with his smile. "You like to do portraits, I know, but perhaps you will see something helpful."

Julia ran her tongue along the inside of her lip. "Thank you... Carlo." She glanced left and right to see if anyone was close enough to hear them. "I'll meet you up there."

"Thank you. Listen, everyone's going on the subway together. I'm glad you're going to join us. You're going to be delighted and enlightened."

JULIA FOLLOWED DE LUCA and the group into the subway and up into the Harlem Hospital and walked with them down the hospital corridors with the WPA paintings along the walls. He pulled Julia to walk along with him. The first mural showed Charles Alston's *Magic in Medicine*, and on the opposite wall, his *Modern Medicine*. De Luca stopped the group halfway down the hallway, in the middle of the two murals.

"This is what I'm talking about. You know these murals caused a great controversy several years ago? Too much Negro subject matter. Can you believe that? But observe these two murals? Do you see the difference? Do you see the social justice in these murals? Walk around and absorb this art." He stopped and made a sweeping gesture with his hand. "Go on. I'll wait."

The group moved in a slow, chaotic dance walking up and down the hallway, stopping to talk and point.

De Luca waited until they had all observed enough of both murals. "See, that's modern medicine, but there are more than Negroes in it? " His eyes brightened. "Look, that man in the center, that's Louis Pasteur. And that woman, holding the baby, that's Dr. Logan, the painter's wife." He stopped speaking and surveyed the group, making sure they were paying close attention. "Do you get my point? This is the power of art. This is what brushstrokes and mixing oil are about," he said, hesitating, waving his hand at the murals again before continuing. "And perspective." He stopped, his hands folded in front of him, waiting for it to sink in. "It's not only about medicine, or social justice. It's the Cotton Club, too!"

Julia held back as the group of artists wandered down the long hallway. Carlo leaned close to talk to Ann Bayle, and Julia let them all go on ahead, until she had the hallway to herself. Carlo did not notice her absence from the group, which gave her relief. She made a mental note to keep her distance from him in the future. The thought of him close to her body chilled her. She ran her fingers through her hair and walked back to the lobby and out to the street.

Chapter 6

JULIA ARRIVED HOME hot and sweaty from the long excursion. As she reached for the knob, the door opened and Mrs. Willow stood impassive as a sentinel to the side, with a slight but rigid bow, and Julia entered the house, passing the woman in her black and white uniform, her hair pulled back in a tight bun. The servant's eyes showed deep brown as if the iris and pupil were one large disk. She was a perfect complement to Grace. Julia knew that Mrs. Willow was focused on Julia's appearance no matter how much she wanted to seem inattentive. How long would it take for Grace to hear of Julia's unkempt state?

Before changing, she went to Lizzie's room. She opened the door to find Lizzie sitting on the bed, dressed in a beautiful pink pinafore dress. Grace stood in the middle of the room with a stern face. The little girl contemplated her mother, then Grace, then down at the floor. Mary stood quiet in the corner, smoothing the little white apron on her uniform.

Grace dominated the scene, standing straight with her hands folded across her abdomen on the dark blue Valentina dress. She studied Julia's eyes as her daughter-in-law surveyed the voluminous folds of the skirt.

Julia broke the tense silence with a smile. "What's going on?" She glanced at Lizzie, then Grace, then Lizzie again, and waited.

Lizzie said nothing. She wasn't near tears, but she strained her neck to see her grandmother.

Grace gave out a close-lipped smile of triumph as she swiveled in place back and forth to survey the room from on high. "Elizabeth was going to play with her watercolors. She was going to get the room dirty. The set you gave her, I believe, Julia. And she was wearing atrocious clothes. Mary was having a difficult time, so I stepped in to set matters right." She set her gaze on the maid.

Mary folded into herself and kept her dark eyes pinned on the floor.

Julia sat on the bed next to Lizzie. She put her arms around the little girl but focused her attention on her mother-in-law. "Thank you, Grace. I know you stepped in to help and I appreciate it." Julia's smile was as cold as the marble floors in the house. "I'm home now, and I can take care of her." She pulled Lizzie more tightly to her and bent down and kissed her head. Then she returned her gaze to Grace, still forcing a smile.

Grace stood rigid and silent, eyes locked on Lizzie, maybe feeling disgusted with the little girl's lack of discipline, or disappointed at the loss of her own triumph over Julia. "Come, Mary." Grace moved out of the room with her quiet determination.

Lizzie shuddered and sighed in relief. Julia held her still for a moment, then stood up and said, "Let's get you out of these ridiculous clothes." She opened the closet and saw Lizzie's play clothes on the floor. "What's this?"

Lizzie smiled. "I changed." Julia noted that Lizzie did not say that Grace had made her change. That was clever.

"Why?" But then Julia realized something threatening to her and her daughter. More threatening than had appeared at first. Lizzie was protecting herself from her grandmother. Julia nodded with understanding. "I came home in time." Raising her eyebrows, she said, "Let's do drawing, okay?"

Lizzie nodded, but she was still unsure of herself. She changed into her bib apron and red pants, standing as close to Julia as possible. When she had them on she rubbed her hands over them, making sure they were clean. Then she sought her mother's approval.

"Honey, you're terrific. I am so proud of you." Julia adjusted the bib. "Now, let's have some fun!"

Lizzie was not ready yet to adopt her mother's happy demeanor. She pointed at the bed.

"What is it, honey? Show me."

Lizzie walked to the bed, then climbed on it and scuffled over to the pillows where she picked up a book. She brought it back and showed it to her mother.

"I see," Julia said as she flipped through the book. "A coloring book." She opened the book to the first page and saw the scribbles in various colors. She noted, in particular, that Lizzie had concentrated all the colors in the center of large spaces. Lizzie had made sure she didn't go near the black borders. Don't go near them and you won't go outside them. She knew what it meant. More of Grace's control. "Okay, you know what, I bet grandmother got you this book, didn't she?"

Lizzie stared at her mother, after all this still not clear exactly whom to trust.

"Darling, I know grandmother is trying to help you be neat. But it is hard, isn't it?"

Lizzie nodded again with the same insecurity.

"Do you want to do the coloring book?"

Lizzie shook her head.

Julia smiled and put an arm around her daughter. "I think coloring books are good and your grandmother was nice, but they are for older kids. For now, let's you and me do our own drawing. You have some blank paper in the closet, don't you?"

Lizzie was smiling now and stepped toward the closet.

"All right then, bring the paper and the watercolors over here to the floor and let's have some fun."

Lizzie picked up the box of watercolor paints, but hesitated.

"It's okay, Darling. You're wearing your play clothes, it's fine."

Julia knew she had her work cut out for her to keep Lizzie free to grow up. But she worried about how she was going to do it unless she stayed home all day or somehow was able to teach Mary how to take care of Lizzie. She sat back and ran her fingers through her child's red hair, then leaned over to view the paper Lizzie diligently worked on. "Oh my," she said, "that's lovely. Something beautiful. That one goes on the wall. Next to mommy's." She smiled at the yellow sun and blue-green-purple sky and dirty-brown something else. Deep inside, she spoke to her daughter. That's right, Lizzie, you keep on painting from your gut, from your heart.

Lizzie giggled and beamed. Julia beamed. Julia pulled her little girl over to her and hugged her as tight as she could without hurting her. The little girl pulled away and went back to her paper and paints. Julia put her hands up to her face and wondered what Lizzie was feeling right now. Lizzie dipped her brush in red and drew a sun and then dipped the brush in blue.

Julia patted Lizzie on the head and kissed her forehead. Then she stood and said "I've got to change clothes, too. Will you play alone for a while?"

Lizzie didn't answer. She stopped the blue brush in the middle of a line and waited.

"I tell you what, I'll ask Mary to come in for a while. Will that be okay?"

Lizzie waited for her mother.

"I think it will be fine. And Mary will be happy, too."

Lizzie continued with her blue line. Julia called downstairs and Mary soon opened the door. She came in, but a small frown appeared on her forehead, and she moved her eyes around the room to see who was present.

"Mary, will you watch Lizzie for a little while. I need to freshen up. It won't take long."

Mary curtsied. Julia laughed. "Mary, that's kind of old-fashioned."

Mary smiled, but hid the smile behind her hand. "Yes, I know, I get used to doing it because Mrs. Stuart likes it. I usually do it when I'm alone with her."

Interesting, Julia thought, Mary didn't hesitate to share this information. She's sympathetic. I can take advantage of that. "Well, you can do it or not with me and Lizzie. We don't care."

"I wish I could work for you."

Julia remained silent for a moment before speaking. "Thank you, Mary...I'm thinking out loud. But, if Hugh and I were to set up our own house...somewhere near...would you come with us? I know Mrs. Stuart hired you, but...."

Mary's eyes sparkled, her hand came up to her mouth. "Yes, Ma'am, I would."

Julia frowned and spoke with warm sympathy in her voice. "That's nice, Mary. It makes me feel good. Let's keep this between us. I'm not even sure it will happen."

Mary nodded and knelt down beside Lizzie.

Julia stood and walked down the hallway. As she opened the door to her bedroom, Grace's cold voice came from behind her.

"Julia, may I have a moment with you?"

Julia wiped her forehead. "Do you mind, Grace. I'm hot in these clothes. Give me a moment to change. Will that be all right? And I'll be right there. In your room? Or in the library?"

"In my room, if you please. It will be more private."

Julia showered fast and changed into black slacks and a scarlet cardigan and walked down the hallway to Grace's room. She knocked once with a quiet little tap and waited.

"Please come in, Julia."

Grace sat at her Chippendale desk, wearing a white satin robe, poised with a silver pen in her hand, as if writing a note in a book. She pulled one side of the robe over to cover her legs, and beheld Julia with her stern green-blue eyes. "Do sit down, Julia," she said in a warm voice that didn't have honesty behind it. She pointed to the French antique chair upholstered in cream brocade.

Julia knew that the emotion in Grace's eyes meant more than the honey in her voice. "If you don't mind, Grace, I prefer to stand."

Grace nodded and the warmth left her voice. "As you wish, my dear. I'll come right to the point."

"Please do," Julia said, folding her hands in front of her to imitate the schoolgirl demeanor that she thought the treatment warranted.

Grace put one leg over the other, adjusted the robe, put her hands one on top of the other on her knee, and sighed. "It has come to my attention...."

Julia frowned and moved one step closer to Grace, who raised her head to stare down her nose. "Your attention that what, Grace?"

Grace held her gaze on Julia's eyes, head not moving. "My attention, if I may continue, that you are engaging in behavior that will bring disgrace upon this house."

Julia wanted to laugh but could see that Grace would take it as insulting.

Grace stood. "Tell me I'm wrong, Julia. Tell me where you were this morning."

Julia couldn't speak for a moment. Then she understood that Grace had some agenda. "Where I was? Where I was this morning is no business of yours."

"Oh, but it is, my Dear," Grace replied, her voice rising. "Where you go is important to your husband and to your family."

Julia scrunched up her face, almost in mockery. "Grace, not every detail of every day is important."

"Don't try and change the subject. Tell me where you went."

Julia decided to play along. "I was in art class."

Grace scoffed. "Art class. Indeed. I expect you to be honest with me."

"Honest? I'm afraid I don't understand, Grace. You have me at a disadvantage. I don't know what you're talking about."

Grace sighed. "All right, if you force me." She shook her head at Julia. "You were in Harlem today. And with some Italian man. And we know that Italian man would be the same one who met you at the train station."

Julia put her hands over her face and laughed. "What? You have got to be kidding. I go to art class and study art in New York, and you turn it into something...sinister?"

"I'm not turning anything, young lady. One of my best friends called me today. Your reputation is already something of gossip, it appears. She called me out of friendship." Grace put her hands together. "Who knows how many other people she has called."

"Grace....."

Grace stood up. "Oh, no, don't act so righteous." She took three steps. "Don't act so indignant. You owe me a proper explanation." She stood straight, arms down at her side. "You owe your husband an explanation."

Julia put her hands behind her back, lowered her head, and realized that Grace was not going to give up. She lifted her head, stared into Grace's eyes, and waited several seconds before speaking. "I don't owe you an explanation, but you seem to think you need one. I already told you I was in art class. The class went to Harlem to view paintings in the corridors of the Harlem Hospital. I wasn't there with the professor, I was there with many other students. Does that satisfy you?"

"Well, it's up to your husband to decide."

"Good God, Grace, will you ever get out of my marriage?"

Grace's eyes widened. She walked to her desk, sat down, and leaned on her elbows, facing away from Julia. She lowered her voice. "You don't know what you are doing, Julia." She remained quiet.

Julia waited, then walked out of the room, her heart pounding.

Chapter 7

JULIA OPENED THE door to Lizzie's room and shielded her eyes from the sunlight streaming in the window. Lizzie sat on the red Persian rug, her dolls arranged in a row, and before the dolls, a small car. A tiny baby doll rode naked on top of the car.

Julia smiled with delight. "What's going on, darling?" she said as she knelt by her daughter. "Ooh, doesn't she have any clothes?"

Lizzie laughed and moved her head back and forth. She leaned over and picked up a pile of small pieces of paper. "She had a bath. Now ticker tape."

"Oh, that's wonderful. Who's the parade for, Lizzie?"

"The king."

"The king? Oh, my," Julia said, covering her cheeks with her hands in great feigned excitement. "Can I help you?"

Lizzie nodded, but her puzzled eyes showed she was uncertain about how her mother could help.

"What shall I do?" Julia said.

"Watch, Mommy."

"Who's going to move the king's car?"

Lizzie quietly studied the little car and at the scraps of paper in her hand. "You." She held her hands cupped to hold the paper ready and waited.

Julia knelt and pushed the car an inch along the rug. Lizzie let the paper scraps fall and jumped up and down with joy as the pieces covered the baby and car. Julia sat back and gave Lizzie one-person thunderous applause and yelled "Yaayyy!"

Lizzie laughed and joined her mother in the small chorus of joy.

Hugh's loud and angry voice came from down the hall. "Where the hell's my ticker tape?"

Lizzie's frightened eyes fixed on her mother and pulled her lips in between her teeth. Her eyes welled up.

Julia felt her little girl's fear inside her own breast. She slumped. Her face showed concern but she tried to make it seem not so serious. "Darling, is that your father's tape?"

Lizzie stared for along moment at her mother, then nodded. She dropped to her knees and began picking up all the little pieces.

"Did you take it from the wastebasket, sweetheart?" Julia spoke in a warm, comforting tone, hoping to shield her daughter from her father's anger.

Lizzie didn't respond. She remained frozen, her hazel eyes wet.

Julia smiled. "You got it off the machine, didn't you, honey?"

Lizzie hesitated, then nodded once and her chin lowered to her chest.

Julia patted her on the head, then pulled her up and wrapped her arms around her. Lizzie's warmth and smell of warm soap made Julia want to hold her forever. Julia held her daughter out from her, lifted her chin with a hand, and spoke in a warm whisper. "It's all right." Then she pulled her back in again and whispered in her ear. "Don't worry, I'll talk to Daddy." She let the little girl down.

Lizzie backed away from her mother and held out her hands with the scraps she had been able to pick up.

Julia put her hands out and let her dump the paper in them. She picked Lizzie up, wiped her eyes, and then put her on the bed. "If you wait just one minute everything will be okay." She kissed her daughter on the cheek. "I'll be right back."

Julia stood, blew a kiss and smiled, then went out, closing the door behind her. No more yelling was coming out of Hugh's office, where the door was open.

When Julia entered the room, Hugh was sitting behind the grand oak desk, papers strewn across the top, with his finger on the phone, ready to turn the dial. He pinched his lips together, put the receiver down and leaned back in his chair. The room smelled of cigars, even though Hugh had never smoked in his office in the past.

Julia sucked her cheeks in and folded her arms across her chest as she stood, legs wide apart, eyes staring, voice hard. "Hugh, you scared Lizzie, yelling like that."

He sat up and pointed to the two ticker tape machines on his right, his eyebrows lifted.

Julia put her hands behind her, cocked her head and softened her voice. "She is a little girl."

Hugh stood so that he viewed Julia from up high. "Yes, well let me tell you something. Now I had to ask the office about the market." His voice grew louder and more insistent, almost threatening. He spit out the word 'office'. His eyes widened, and he threw one arm up. "I seemed like an idiot. I never want to ask them what's on the tape when I'm home. Never." He came around the desk and put his index finger on the gold ticker tape. "It's like they know more than I do."

Julia bowed her head a little and moved it from side to side. "You're kidding. They work for you. You could've said the machines didn't work."

Now he reared his head back. "My business is my business, Julia. I don't want Elizabeth interfering with it. Is that clear?" He tightened his lips in disbelief at this conversation she forced him to have. "Can't you control your daughter?"

"Yes, sir." Her hand out over the desk, she let the pieces of tape fall like a little parade on his papers. "There." She walked toward the door, then stopped and hesitated, thinking for a moment, then pivoted on one foot and faced him, breathing at a slow pace. Her voice was quiet. "Your little girl's terrified, you know. Won't you come and tell her it's all right?"

Hugh was already sitting in his chair, an unlit cigar in his mouth and his finger in the rotary dial, the skin white from pressure, the phone to his ear. He froze for an instant, his eyes on her, questioning. "Maybe later," he said. Then he put his head down and continued his dialing.

Julia left the room, walking with deliberate movements back to Lizzie's room at the end of the hallway. Before going in, she stopped to turn a vase of light yellow orchids, using the time to listen for Hugh's footsteps, wanting him to think of her and Elizabeth. She heard nothing, so she continued on into Lizzie's room.

Lizzie sat motionless on the pink bedspread, surrounded by dolls and teddy bears. They were all sitting, waiting for judgment.

Julia knelt in front of Lizzie, smiling. She spoke with a soft voice. "Honey, your father says it was all right to take the paper this one time."

Lizzie burst into tears and leaned forward to her mother. Julia pulled her down and sat on the floor with her, cradling and rocking her. "Lizzie, sweetie, it's all over now. There's nothing to be upset about. Your father loves you."

But Lizzie let herself snuggle into her mother and continued rocking back and forth. She jumped up and took a teddy bear and sat back down, holding the fuzzy brown bear tight with one hand, and her mother's sleeve with the other, until she finally fell asleep. Julia put her to bed and gave her a gentle kiss on the forehead.

Chapter 8

HUGH HEARD A STAMPEDE of little feet and then a yellow blur ran past the door to his office. He slapped his knee and leaned back in his chair. "Elizabeth?"

The footsteps stopped.

"Elizabeth, come in and see me."

The footsteps started at a more measured pace and then a small hand held onto the door frame. A redheaded girl, a green ribbon in her hair, peeked around the corner and peeked in with a serious face. She waited at that awkward angle.

"Sweetheart, sit on my lap. I'm not mad at you." Hugh swiveled his chair away from the desk and put out his arms.

Elizabeth came running into the room and climbed up on his lap and laid her head on his chest. Hugh rocked her back and forth for a few moments and patted her on the head. She sighed and relaxed. Then she sat up and smiled as he ran his fingers through her hair, and put her hands out on the desk on the papers.

"What's this, daddy?"

Hugh laughed. "Oh, it's some papers I'm working on, you know, Daddy's work, so we can pay the bills."

Elizabeth sat back again and put her finger in her mouth and moved her eyes around the room, tired and bored again.

He picked up her little hand and held it. "You know what? You know I don't care if you play with the ticker tape as long as you take it from the wastebasket. Will you do that for me?"

She nodded, her fingers still in her mouth.

He held her and made her sit up and twisted her to face him. "I have something for you. Of course, I don't have it yet, but I do have something for you. Would you like to know what it is?"

Elizabeth clapped her hands together and smiled.

He smiled back at her. "I love you, you are my wonderful little girl. You know we live two blocks from Central Park, the best park in the whole world. And I have something there for you."

She took a deep breath and waited.

"Okay, I can see you are impatient. I'll tell you what it is. It's a pony."

She screamed and jumped up and down and wriggled on his lap and put her hands over her face and said "Oh no, where will we put it? Can I ride it now?"

Hugh laughed and rubbed the top of her head. "It's in Central Park, honey, we couldn't bring it here, it's too big." He gave her a hug, pulled her head down to his chest and began rocking again. "A pony can't live in a house. It needs a stable with lots of hay to eat. And oats."

Elizabeth pulled herself away, a puzzle on her face. "What are oats, Daddy?"

"Oatmeal, Elizabeth, but uncooked. Horses love them, apples, too."

Elizabeth stared off in the distance, dreaming. "Let's take apples to the pony."

Hugh began to recognize a child's infinite line of questioning. He picked her up and put her on the floor and held her hands and said, "Hold on a minute, my little cowgirl, we don't even have the pony yet." He also realized he didn't have a good handle on children's reaction times. "All in good time."

"When, Daddy?"

"I have to talk to the people in the Park, but I promise you next week."

Elizabeth frowned. "When?"

Hugh frowned back at her, knowing he had put himself in an untenable position. "All right, Elizabeth, I will call tomorrow. You can ask me then. Now run along and play."

Elizabeth smiled at him and ran off trotting like her little pony.

Before she reached the door he called out, "Daddy's little girl?"

She kept on prancing out the door.

Hugh leaned back in his chair, drummed his fingers on the desk and thought, "Hmmm. Yes. My little girl."

The phone rang, demanding attention. Hugh walked at a deliberate pace back to his desk. No rush for a phone call. He sat at his desk and studied the picture of himself, Julia, and Elizabeth in Central Park. His arm possessed his wife's waist and she gave herself to him in admiration. In between them Elizabeth stood in a rigid pose, her body facing the camera, but her head, following her mother, focused on her father. He stared into the camera, mouth firm and straight. That's the way he viewed his family. Adoring him.

Hugh picked up the phone ready for a fight, as if the pleasant interlude with his daughter hadn't even happened. He lifted an unlit cigar up off the ashtray and let the caller wait while he lit it and puffed a large volume of smoke. "Yes, what is it?" He said it loud to make sure they understood he had no patience for wasting time.

"Mister Stuart, this is Elmer Griesbeck."

Hugh rolled his eyes and took the cigar out of his mouth and put both elbows on his desk. "This better be good news Elmer. I hope you have taken care of everything."

A short silence. "Well, sir, I did what I could but things have gotten out of hand."

Hugh's voice rose. "Out of hand? What the hell do you mean? You said you could handle this." *Shit*, he said to himself, not caring whether Elmer heard him. "Shit," he said again out loud into the telephone. "Tell me what it is, Elmer, that you cannot do."

"You see, sir, a little boy died in the apartment on Orchard Street. From his burns." Elmer's voice began to shake.

"I see. I'm sorry. What started the fire?" Hugh could hear Elmer breathing into the phone. "Elmer, tell me how it happened, dammit."

"We don't know, sir, there was a fire and the little boy was killed and a couple of other people were burned."

"What am I supposed to do?" Damn. Passing the buck. Smoke swirled around his head as he inhaled and let it out in a long breath.

"I'm sorry, sir.…"

Hugh slammed his fist on the desk. The picture jumped up and fell flat. "Elmer, you're not competent at this. I'll find somebody who is.…"

Elmer didn't let him finish his sentence. "The fire marshal is here, sir." There was satisfaction in Elmer's voice as he announced with relief that the pressure was off him and now on Hugh. "I'll put him on the line…." His voice faded away in mid-sentence.

Hugh let out a sigh. Damn, he didn't even know where the building was. He had never been there, he inherited it and never mixed with tenants. He had people for that.

A new voice came on the phone. "Mister Stuart?"

Hugh let his cigar drop into the ashtray and his hand fell on his thigh. "Yes, this is Hugh Stuart. With whom am I speaking?" He shook his head. He stood, as if to gain leverage over the voice.

The voice was much more assured and self-confident than Elmer's pusillanimous squawking. "Mister Stuart my name is Theobald Matthew. I am the fire marshal for lower Manhattan. I understand you are the owner of the building at 108 Orchard Street, is that true?"

Hugh didn't know the building at all, he'd only seen totals for rent receipts. "Yes, I suppose I am," he said, his voice showing his irritation.

The marshal responded with a voice that had a hard edge. "You suppose you are. Now either you are the owner or you are not, Mister Stuart. Which is it?"

Hugh sat and leaned over his desk. He knew that he was not going to be able to intimidate the fire marshal the way he was able to intimidate his own employees. There were lawyers for that. "What I meant was that I do not manage these properties myself. The gentleman there with you now manages the property. He is the one who knows the exact house numbers."

The line went silent, and you could hear the fire marshal talking to Elmer away from the phone. Then the fire marshal came back online. "You are the responsible party, Mister Stuart. I'm calling to inform you that one of your tenants has died in a fire and several others suffered burns as well. We are in the middle of an investigation as to the cause of the fire, and I am informing you now that you are a principal participant in this investigation. And by principal participant I mean you, Mister Stuart, not your manager and not your secretary. Is that clear?"

The man's tone shocked Hugh. He forced the man to wait several seconds. Then he said, in as pleasant a voice as he could project under the circumstances, "Mister Matthew, I understand my rights and my responsibilities as a property owner in the City of New York. You can have complete confidence that myself and my company will support your investigation to the fullest. We will help you find out how these tenants started this fire," and here Hugh stopped to feel for the right word for these lazy, uneducated... "and they will be assisted to learn the proper fire safety for the places where they live."

"Ah, I see," said the fire marshal, "you appear to have made your own investigation and determined that the people who live there are responsible for the fire. Well, Mister Stuart, we don't act so fast. Our investigators study the scene thoroughly and only then do they prepare a report. Only then will we determine whether those poor burned people did it all by themselves, or," and he paused for effect, "whether there were any building code violations that contributed to this unfortunate loss of life."

Hugh fumed. He gnashed his teeth. He fixated on the cigar in the ashtray, at its ashes. Then he took a deep breath and let it out in a long sigh and composed himself and smiled as he spoke into the telephone. "Mister Matthew, you will have our full and unimpeded assistance. We will help you in whatever way we can. Now, if you would be so kind as to put my manager back on the phone, I will say the same thing to him."

"Thank you, Mister Stuart, your cooperation is appreciated by the Fire Department of the City of New York, always striving to protect." Hugh heard the smile in the fire marshal's voice.

Elmer Griesbeck came on the phone. He had not gained any more self-assurance. "Yes, Mister Stuart...."

"Elmer, you are to give the fire marshal your complete and undivided attention to resolve this matter, is that understood?"

"Yes, I understand, sir."

"Elmer, keep me informed."

"Yes, sir."

Hugh slammed the phone back on the receiver. He picked up his cigar and lit it, sucked on it, then blew out smoke toward the ceiling. He picked up the phone and dialed his lawyer.

"Good morning," came the pleasant voice, "law firm of Krause and Stone. How may I direct your call?"

"This is Hugh Stuart. Put me through to Leonard Krause."

"I'm sorry...."

"Don't be sorry, young lady, get me Leonard. Now."

"Yes, sir," she said in a shaky voice, "I will try."

"You tell him I want to speak to him now, got that?"

"Yes, sir."

"Now go tell him. Tell him Hugh Stuart wants to talk to him and it's important. Tell him somebody died and they want to blame me. You understand?"

"Yes, sir." Then the line went silent.

Hugh puffed on his cigar until a cloud hovered over his head. He swiveled his chair around to the gray buildings across the street.

"Hugh?"

"Leonard."

"What can I do for you? You will have to excuse me, I am with somebody in my office right now."

"Leonard, I have a problem and you had better fix it. When can you get over here?"

"Not this afternoon. It's a day of emergencies. In the evening. I could have one of my associates handle this if you like."

Oh, there you go, shoving your subordinates off on me. "Hell, no. You're my lawyer."

"That's fine, I'll be there. Do me one favor, Hugh, I'm going to put someone else on the phone who can do some preliminary research on this and then I'll bring that with me."

Hugh sighed, defeated for the moment. "All right, put him on."

The line went silent for several moments and then a young woman's voice came on the phone. "Yes, Mister Stuart, can you please hold on for one minute?"

Hugh shook his head in frustration. "Who the hell are you? I need a lawyer, not a secretary."

"I understand that, but Mister Krause asked me to hold the phone, sir."

Hugh fumed, but waited until a man's voice came on the phone.

"Yes, sir, Mr. Stuart, this is Albert Williams. I'm taking notes on what you say, sir."

"The fire marshal is investigating a fire in one of my buildings. I need to know my liability. You got that?"

"Yes sir, I do. Thank you, sir."

"Okay." Hugh put out his cigar, turned away from the phone and mumbled, "I hope I don't have to do everything myself."

Out in the hallway, he straightened his vest, and listened. Elizabeth could be heard at the end of the hallway in her room singing to herself. Hugh went into the library. Nobody. No answer when he knocked on his mother's door. His and Julia's bedroom. Empty. Damn!

Back in the library, he pushed the button to ring the kitchen, then poured himself a finger of Johnny Walker Black and sat in his red leather, wingback chair. In the quiet, he sipped on the scotch and moved his toe up and down. When the door opened, he jumped up and twisted around to face Willow.

She stood quiet and mute and rigid with one foot inside the door.

He swept his arm in a grand arc and said, "Where the hell is everybody? "

Willow answered in a mousy little voice, "I don't know, sir."

"Is Elizabeth in there by herself?" He frowned and took another sip of his drink.

Willow's eyes were studying the floor. "Oh no, sir, Mary is in with her."

"Where's my wife?"

Willow moved her head up, her eyes opened wide. "I'm afraid I don't know, sir."

"Where's my mother?"

"I don't know that either, sir. They didn't say anything to me."

Hugh put his arm out on the chair and tapped his toe on the floor. "I see. Well then, I will tell you, Willow. We're having a guest for dinner tonight. Make sure that a place is set for six-thirty. What are we having?"

"I'm afraid it's leftovers, sir. From last night. Mrs. Stuart said that was alright. She said I should...."

Hugh shook his head in frustration. "Well, I'll tell you what, Willow, you get something nice for dinner tonight from the delicatessen. Can you do that?"

"Yes, of course I can, what should I get, sir?"

He raised his hands up, spilling a large drop of Scotch on the floor. "Shit!" He frowned at her. "How the hell do I know? How long have you been doing this? Go do it."

Willow went out the door, closing it without making a sound.

Hugh sat back in his chair. So, here I am, he thought. He grimaced. Now I have to do the cooking. Gold's going through the roof. I have the opportunity of a lifetime. And I have to spend my time putting out fires. His pun, unintended or not, made him laugh. His drink finished, he left the library, but before he opened the door he did what he always did, glanced at his father's portrait over the fireplace. Stern, solemn, strong, demanding, George Randolph Stuart. But Hugh wasn't aware that he did it every time he entered or left the room. Or that he wanted his dead father's approval.

"Why the hell do I have to do everything myself?"

Chapter 9

LEONARD KRAUSE, DRESSED in a black pinstripe suit, with a dark red tie set off by his starched white shirt, stood before the painting of Hugh's father above the mantelpiece. He swirled his single-barrel Jack Daniels around the glass, sipped, let out a breath, then pointed at the painting. "Your father was a great man, Hugh."

Hugh nodded, shaken by the hard eyes that glared at him. "Yes, he was." In imitation of Leonard, he swirled his whiskey in his glass.

Grace's voice came from behind them. "A great man," she said with admiration on her face.

The two men faced her. Leonard raised his glass to her, and smiling, said "You're beautiful as always, Grace."

Hugh, trying to catch up with his lawyer on civility, raised his glass.

Grace smiled and raised her glass of white wine but faced Leonard. "Why thank you, sir. It's Christian Dior." She smoothed the long line of the black silk skirt.

"Oh?" Leonard said. He smiled at Hugh in feigned embarrassment, "I'm afraid I don't know him." Then he swiveled back to Grace. "If it's a him. But then I don't know dress designers except the ones that my wife wears and she thinks I should know."

"Oh, yes, he's a new designer for Robert Piquet. I thought I would try him out for tonight."

"Well, I will recommend him to Marianne. I'm sure she will be calling you." He viewed her over his glasses. "Probably soon after I get home."

"Who's getting home?"

Julia walked in with a smile and wore a bright orange floral dress with large ruffles across the top. Her blonde hair fell in long curls to her shoulders. She carried a martini glass.

Leonard gave her a grin. "I will be, Julia. You're lovely tonight." Then he swiveled to face each of the women in turn. "You and Grace both."

Julia curtsied, careful to keep her cocktail glass from spilling. "Thank you, Leonard. I hope Marianne is well."

Leonard nodded. "Thank you, yes, I'll tell her you asked after her."

Grace's smile stayed on her face, but it lost its luster.

The room fell silent. They sipped.

Grace's eyes betrayed her concern at the lawyer's presence in her house, but she didn't ask why. She said to Leonard, "Dinner will be ready in a while. I have to thank my son for ordering it. We were all busy doing other things today."

Leonard laughed. "Yes, he has the burden, since he invited me to dinner tonight, with not much advance notice, I can tell you." He laughed again, leaning toward Hugh in companionable sympathy.

"Is there something special, Leonard?" Grace's voice carried a note of concern.

Leonard pushed his drink toward Hugh.

Hugh shuffled his feet. "You see, Mother, it's about the property on Orchard Street."

Grace straightened. Her fears had been justified. "Oh, I do hope it's nothing serious. I remember when your father purchased that property. I must tell you, I thought it was...what shall we say? Below par. I won't go there, but Papa said it'd pay off in the long run. Now I sense something is wrong with that property. Is that right?"

Hugh waited for Leonard, who remained silent, his face expressionless, so he spoke to Grace. "There's been a fire there. One of the tenants died. The fire marshal wants to talk to us. But I'm sure we have no responsibility for the fire." He pointed his glass at the lawyer. "Leonard is going to tell me the details. The timing couldn't be worse. I've got a meeting tomorrow, to increase our holdings in gold, and now this has to happen." Hugh motioned to Leonard to continue.

Grace and Julia, both quiet, heads rigid, eyes open wide but moving around the room, waited for Leonard's response. Grace's eyes shone with fear. She had twitched with news of the death of a tenant and now watched Hugh and Leonard with restrained disapproval. Why had she not been told?

Leonard shuffled his feet and gave a quick glance at Hugh before speaking, unsure how much he should reveal. "Well, as you know, he left this property in equal parts to you, Grace," he said, lifting a finger from his glass and pointing at her, "and to Hugh. So it's not merely a financial matter, it's a family responsibility. And I understand completely Hugh's situation."

"I see," Grace said. "The three of us ought to discuss this alone. This doesn't concern you, Julia."

Julia, surprised, said, "This concerns me if it concerns my husband. Especially if a tenant has died. What do we know?"

Hugh raised his eyebrows and cocked his head toward Leonard. "That's why he's here. I wanted him to come earlier, but we're not his sole client."

Leonard finished his drink and searched for a place to put it. Grace held out her hand and took it from him.

"We should sit," he said.

When they found seats, he spoke. "We know these people aren't careful… if you know what I mean." His eyes surveyed the room, lingered on the painting above the mantel. "Someone there—we don't know who—started a fire in the apartment. The marshal hasn't completed his investigation, so we are not sure of the details yet. These buildings…."

Julia interrupted him. "Buildings? You mean more than one?"

Leonard smiled, but he kept his lips closed as he did it. "No, Julia. The one apartment. Several buildings were constructed in the late 1890s. This is one of those buildings. And that's important to our case."

Grace sat up, bewildered and afraid. "Our case? Oh my god, what does that mean?" She swiveled her gaze between Leonard and Hugh.

Leonard smiled again and held up his hand. "No, no, Grace. I'm sorry. That's the lawyer talking. There is no case. Not in the legal sense. I should have said 'in this instance.'"

Grace relaxed and smiled at Hugh before turning to Leonard. "You were saying, about the buildings?"

Leonard continued. "The building, as I said, was built in the late 1890s. That means they have been grandfathered."

Grace interrupted again. "Grandfathered?"

Hugh said, "Mother, it's a technical term. You haven't been involved for years. Father did it for you, and now I'm doing it. I don't want Leonard to have to explain every legal term you're not familiar with."

Grace was clearly ashamed, but she didn't let her worry go as she glared at her son, her voice quavering. "Don't insult me, Hugh. First you tell me the fire marshal is coming after me, and now you want to keep me in the dark." She sat back in her chair, satisfied that she had made her point.

Hugh nodded in deference. "Yes, Mother, of course, you're right. Leonard, will you please explain the term for us?" He made a quick glance over to Julia and back to Leonard.

Leonard continued. "Let me explain the issue first. The fire started with the wainscoting. You know, wood paneling three feet up the wall. It has varnish on it, and varnish is flammable. Now, Grace, this has been superseded by modern building codes. But back in early 1890 building codes permitted it."

Julia shrugged her shoulders. "So why didn't we change the wainscoting when the new codes came out?"

Hugh frowned at her but moved his eyes sideways to Leonard. "This happened before us. So it doesn't apply to our assets."

Leonard nodded. "That's right. You see, Julia, property owners can't change everything they own every time the code changes. That's ridiculously expensive…."

Hugh interrupted. "So, then, when new buildings are constructed, they fall under the new codes. Wainscoting with varnish is proper on our old property. It was, after all, constructed in the last century."

Julia spoke with anger in her voice. "Yes, property, I understand." She stood. "Varnish I understand. But this was a human life, Hugh. We can't treat a human life like property."

Leonard put his hand out and stopped Hugh from speaking. "You're right, Julia. I applaud your concern. But I'm here as your attorney. I'm here to discuss your legal situation."

"Legal? No." She put her hand up to her forehead, then addressed them with a loud voice. "This is a moral problem," she said, with an emphasis on 'moral.' She hoped for support from Grace, but as soon as she saw her eyes, she knew there was none. She understood that Hugh was leaving the defending to Leonard.

Leonard sighed. "It may not be polite, but I must correct you. My position is as your lawyer, not your pastor. No bill for that. And you must understand this, Julia. I have talked to the fire marshal for Lower Manhattan. That's what I came to see you about. I know him, he's a fine man, but he tries to go beyond his authority. He thinks he's a one-man crusade to convince people to upgrade their property according to his modern standards. He's Irish, you know, the tenants are Irish, too, well, I can tell you, he has no authority. He now knows that we won't fall for this tactic."

Grace let out an audible sigh. She moved in her chair, smiled and laughed at the same time. "Thank God for that, Leonard. Can't thank you enough. Oh, my goodness. What a relief. I'm up for a refill on my wine." She stood and walked over to the wall and pulled open a cabinet and picked up a long, fluted bottle of white wine in a silver cooler. Still smiling, she filled her glass and took a drink. "Now that's refreshing. Can I get anyone else a drink?"

Julia took a sip out of her glass and shook her head, her lips straight. Leonard said no with a gesture. Hugh sat back in his chair, raising his eyebrows at his mother's unusual behavior.

"It's not over yet," Leonard said, cocking his head and observing them over his spectacles.

Grace put her wine glass on the green marble counter and turned to face the room. She sucked her lips in, switching her gaze between Hugh and Leonard.

"I don't mean to alarm you, Grace. And it's why I don't give people information outside of the office. I should have spoken to Hugh alone. Here we are in your magnificent library discussing this...trage—er... this mess."

Grace came back to her chair and sat straight, her hands on her knees.

Leonard continued. "The fire marshal's investigation will show that the tenants were at fault. But it's your property, and your property management people must pay careful attention. This property will now be on the marshal's list, his watch list. I merely want to advise you to take this opportunity to make sure that the property is up to code in all respects."

Hugh responded in a strong voice. "Leonard, I will talk to Elmer in the morning. I can't thank you enough."

"Oh, yes, we are grateful, Leonard," Grace said. "Now I'll take my wine in and get ready for dinner. If you wait here a couple of minutes, I'll call you. Hugh should do this more often. I didn't know he was a wonderful cook." She laughed as she left the room, stepping in awkward jerks, and drank more wine as she walked. Quite out of character for Grace.

When she had disappeared, Leonard turned to Hugh. "I'm glad I made at least one person happy."

Hugh's smile was tepid. "I'll make sure that Elmer invites the fire marshal to see the apartment when the work is complete," Hugh said. "And, I appreciate your visit, Leonard. As you have seen, Mother has been relieved of stress. As have we all."

Julia's face darkened. She cleared her throat and the two men turned to face her, both waiting for her to say something.

Hugh did not wait for her, but said, "My Dear, Mother has dinner waiting. Why don't we eat. You and I can talk later?"

She straightened her spine. "No. I want to clarify this. My so-called moral situation."

"Which is?" Hugh said in an irritated voice, first to Leonard then to his wife.

Julia knew this was the first time she had gotten involved in his business affairs. At the moment, she wished she had done it earlier. She had naively assumed that the business Hugh was the same as the Hugh she loved. And now this shock. "Which is, that you have now settled the question of the assets, but what about the people?"

Hugh moved his head back in disbelief. "The people? What do you mean by that? I will have Elmer get right on top of this."

She opened her eyes wide. "No, Hugh. Not your staff. The person who died. The people who now have nowhere to live."

Hugh waited several moments before he responded. He turned halfway toward Leonard, then came back. "Julia those people are not mine."

"But they have nowhere to live."

"Then they should have thought about that before they lit matches."

"Oh, Hugh, please. That place is a firetrap and you know it."

"Well, so is Yankee Stadium if you start fires."

"This isn't Yankee Stadium, it's your building."

"Dinner's ready, everybody." Grace's happy voice came from the dining room.

Julia folded her hands across her chest. Hugh, hands in his pocket, studied the floor.

Leonard pursed his lips, then said in a quiet voice, "Why don't we go in to the dining room. Grace is waiting on us." His eyes moved between Hugh and Julia.

Julia unfolded her hands and started to walk. "Yes, you're right. Let's have dinner."

THAT EVENING, as Julia and Hugh prepared to go to sleep, she sat on one side of the bed in her black satin night slip, her arms hanging between her legs, her shoulders hunched over, head bowed. Hugh sat on the other side in his blue striped pajamas and took his slippers off, pulled the covers back, slipped into the bed and turned the light off, without saying a word. Julia turned her light off and lay on her back, facing the ceiling, listening to Hugh breathe in and out. She was relieved that he didn't come over to her side.

Chapter 10

WHEN JULIA OPENED her eyes in the morning, Hugh's side of the bed was empty. She listened, but his bathroom door stood open and no sound came from it. She didn't check the time, she took a shower and got dressed in beige slacks and a cream blouse. Without makeup or jewelry, she went out to the dining room. Lizzie sat alone eating oatmeal. She glanced up when she saw her mother, spoon still in mouth, but didn't react. Julia went to her and put a long kiss on her forehead and hugged her tight.

"How's my baby today? Are you doing all right?"

Lizzie nodded without missing a spoonful.

Julia turned around the room and saw toast and coffee on the sideboard. She took a piece and began to eat it dry.

Lizzie dropped her spoon and said, "Mommy, today my pony."

Julia frowned but then raised her eyebrows. She spoke in a cartoon-serious voice. "A pony? Hmm. When did this happen?"

"Yesterday."

"Yesterday when?"

"Yesterday Daddy told me."

"Oh, he must not have been busy."

"I don't know." Lizzie twisted her body in an awkward contortion. "He said."

"And he said he would get it today?"

"Uh-huh."

"You know, honey, he forgot to tell me. But I haven't seen him yet. He got up before me. I was a lazybones today."

73

Lizzie laughed. "Lazybones," she repeated. Then she volunteered, "The Park."

"Oh, I see, you're going to ride the ponies in Central Park."

"No, my pony. In the park."

"Okay, if Daddy said that."

"Where is Daddy?"

"I don't know. He must be at work. I'll go see if I can find him. You'll wait here for Mary, okay?"

Lizzie nodded and dipped her spoon in the oatmeal.

Julia walked along the hall to Hugh's office. She heard his voice behind the closed door. She started to knock, and then held her hand back. A sound of footsteps disturbed her. Then she knocked. No answer. She knocked again. Still no answer. She knew that inside Hugh talked to someone on the phone, and that he waited for his checks. Maybe he talked to the fire marshal, or...she realized she had made up excuses for herself. Why did she hesitate? Was it unpleasant? Or was it that she couldn't stand him?

"Mommy!" Lizzie ran to her mother and opened the door to Hugh's office. She stood with the door open, watching her father.

Hugh sat at his desk, listening to his phone. He waved Lizzie to stop. Then he motioned her to leave the room.

"My pony," she said, loudly.

He shook his head and tightened his lips, pointing to the phone, but smiling.

Lizzie stood still.

Hugh noticed Julia standing in the doorway. He became serious as he moved his eyes to his desk.

Lizzie studied her mother. Julia pulled her out of the room, closing the door. She knelt and ran her hand over Lizzie's hair. "Darling, you can see that Daddy's busy. Now is not the time to talk to him about the pony."

"He promised."

"Of course, he did, Lizzie. But can't you see Daddy's got things on his mind?"

Lizzie watched the door, restraining herself from running back into Hugh's office. More footsteps came from the hallway.

Lizzie turned as Grace came around the corner. She ran to her grandmother and grabbed her hand. "My pony. I want my pony."

Grace smiled at the child with a face of bewilderment. "Oh my, a pony. Is it in your room?"

"No, it's in the park."

Grace frowned at Julia. "Do you know what this is about?"

Lizzie turned back to watch and listen to her mother, her eyes opened wide in anticipation.

Julia sighed. "Elizabeth said that Hugh promised her a pony today."

Grace leaned to speak to Elizabeth. "Sweetheart, your father meant a stuffed pony. I'm sure. Why don't you go down to your room and see if that's what he meant?"

Lizzie ran back to her mother. "No. A real pony. He said a real pony."

Grace turned around and walked swiftly to the library. Julia led Lizzie to her bedroom and tried to interest her in a book.

Chapter 11

HUGH LIFTED HIS head up from his paper-strewn desk when he heard the knock on the door. "Yes?"

Mrs. Willow appeared, her head peeking inside the door, the bravest position she could muster. She said, her voice quiet and respectful, "Mr. Kurt Walther is here to see you, Mr. Stuart. He said you expected him."

Hugh nodded. "Yes, I'm waiting for him. Bring him up here. He won't be staying long. Leave the front door open and show him up here."

In a few moments, Kurt Walther walked in the door and strode like a soldier up to Hugh's desk. His dark brown hair was combed straight back from his face, and the large wrinkles on either side of his mouth made him appear to have a permanent scowl. He held up his black leather briefcase, took out a check, and handed it across the desk to Hugh.

Hugh studied the check, turned his head up to Kurt and nodded, then put the check on his desk. Kurt stood still.

Hugh said, "Nothing more," as he put his finger on a piece of paper on his desk.

Kurt Walther pivoted and left the room.

Hugh picked up the phone and dialed. He waited. Then, "Yes, this is Hugh Stuart. Inform Hans Seifert that I will be there in half an hour? He is expecting me."

"Of course, Mr. Stuart," said the accented voice. "We know you are coming. Thank you for your information."

Hugh frowned and hung up the phone without waiting for a reply, and then called Gibbons to bring the car around. He put the check in his inside coat pocket and walked out to the street. "Nassau and Wall, Timothy."

WHEN THEY ARRIVED at Wall Street, Hugh got out of the car and told Timothy to wait in the underground parking until a messenger came for him. With that, Hugh walked into the ornate building, with complex wrought-iron railings on the balcony in front of every window. He went up the marble steps to the second floor offices of Zurich International Bank, where he announced his appointment to the young receptionist with short curly blond hair, who showed him into a large conference room and pulled out a black leather chair for him. The long rosewood table drew the eye to the far wall with its huge color photograph of the Matterhorn. The other walls displayed photographs of skiers, picturesque towns, and trains chugging up the Alps.

"Coffee, sir?" she said, her voice cool and courteous. "We have excellent Black Forest cake today. May I offer you a piece?"

Hugh put his briefcase on the table and shook his head.

The woman adopted Hugh's perfunctory demeanor. "Very well, sir. Herr Seifert will be with you in one moment." She walked with brisk steps out of the room.

Hugh removed his check from the briefcase and put it on the table and aligned it square before him. He heard the door open behind him, and turned to see a tall man wearing a black double-breasted suit, with white shirt and black tie.

The man peered out from black glasses, his blond hair a perfect crew cut. He smiled and offered his hand. "Hello, Mr. Stuart, I'm Hans Seifert."

Behind Hans Seifert came two other men, each carrying large folders of papers.

"May I introduce Hermann Eisner and Rudolph Felber?"

The two men bowed to Hugh, and then the three sat opposite him.

"We understand you are prepared to buy gold on the open market. That is what we learned from Mr. Bollinger. For five million dollars." He waited for Hugh's answer.

"I am." Hugh moved the check an inch.

Seifert turned briefly to his colleagues before replying. "Let me first say, Mr. Stuart, that we at Zurich International Bank are pleased that you have sought our bank to help you with this transaction. We believe we will be able to meet your requirements."

For an instant this formal vocabulary puzzled Hugh, but then he understood these were Swiss bankers. "My requirements, as you put it, are to buy gold. I can give you my check today. So, gentlemen, I believe the question is as to how we can proceed."

Seifert nodded. "The first question we must resolve is how you wished to take ownership of the gold."

Hugh frowned. "Ownership? I don't understand."

"You have two choices. You may purchase gold bullion, that is, a number of actual bricks of gold, which will remain in the vault as your property."

"But I...."

Hans raised his index finger and continued. "Or you can make a bulk purchase of gold. You receive a certificate of ownership of gold in the value of five million dollars. But you do not have title to any specific gold bullion."

Hugh thought for a moment. "Bullion is not certificates, of course. But what the difference means to me, I don't see."

"It's this, Mr. Stuart. If you purchase gold bullion, you pay the money and you receive the number of bricks of gold according to the price. If the price of gold goes up, the value of your gold goes up with it. And vice versa. I assume you are purchasing the gold on your own behalf?"

"Yes, I am."

"It is, certainly, not our position to question what you intend to do with the gold, but you understand that there are many documents which must be completed for an international transaction."

"Of course," Hugh said, with impatience. "But you have not told me about the gold certificates."

"Yes, yes, how careless of me. The gold certificate is for a fixed sum. At the time of purchase, you are entitled to a defined but variable weight of gold bullion. And the value of your gold always remains the same. It does not vary. If the value of gold on the market increases, then you are entitled to a lesser weight of bullion. And, once again, and vice versa. Certificates are for those who wish to hedge their risk. Gold bullion is for those who are willing to accept more risk in order to make a profit."

"I don't want to buy certificates, I want to buy real gold bullion."

"Thank you for that clarification, Mr. Stuart. That makes our procedure straightforward." He laughed to himself, then stiffened in embarrassment. "Excuse me, an international transaction in these times is never simple, but now we know the direction our efforts will take."

"And that is…."

"Well, you must complete import-export documents. I believe you have not done this before, is that correct?"

"No I have not. I am doing this for the first time."

"Understood. We will not need your check today. We must complete our transfer and other international documents with Zurich first. When we have identified where the bullion is located, that is, the vault where it lies, et cetera, then we will communicate with you as to the next steps."

"How long will this take?"

"I shouldn't think it would be more than a week."

"And then, after that, how long before I receive the gold?"

"Mr. Stuart, you cannot take possession of the gold here. It must remain in the vault in Switzerland."

Hugh cocked his head.

Seifert stared at Hugh several moments, and then continued. "I am sorry to disappoint you. I see it's another sign that you do not have experience in these transactions. We cannot transport the gold here. It is out of the question. And I will tell you that you cannot find another Swiss banker to do it. Or any other banker, for that matter. Go to Rothschild even, or whichever, they will not do it."

"I don't understand."

"Mr. Stuart, have you heard of U-boats?"

"U-boats? You mean German submarines? Of course I have heard of them."

"Then you understand the reason why we cannot ship gold across the Atlantic. We could not even get insurance for a ship with a gold cargo. Not when U-boats have sunk one hundred merchant ships. If that is your requirement, you will be severely disappointed."

"But the British have shipped tons of gold bullion to Canada for safekeeping."

"Unsubstantiated rumors." Seifert leaned across the table. "And even if true, large elements of the British and Canadian navies guarded the gold. I don't think you have a destroyer at your disposal, do you? And correct me if I am wrong, but I doubt you can persuade the United States Navy to do it for you."

Hugh sighed and folded his hands on the table. "I do understand, believe me. I see my position. But, then, why do you believe my gold will be safe in Switzerland?"

Seifert laughed. "Mr. Stuart, the Swiss Federation has stood independent for a thousand years. Even Napoleon Bonaparte did not try to conquer our great confederations in the Swiss Alps. And now this little corporal and his beer hall Nazi party are not going to threaten Switzerland. When war breaks out, they will need us."

"Germany will need you?"

"Of course. They will be at war with France, Poland, and England, who knows. And as they did in World War I, they will need Switzerland to make transactions with the outside world, including their enemies." Once again that sidelong glance at his partners. "We have gold now for the reason that others, across Europe, above all in Poland and France, are selling their gold to us. Still others are buying gold. Swiss gold is now the center of the market. And you know this too, Mr. Stuart. That's why you want gold bullion, because you hope that the value of gold will go up when war breaks out. Do you think you are unique? Did you think we were ringing cowbells in the alpine pasture until you came along?"

Hugh recognized the defensiveness. "Mr. Seifert, please believe me, I do not wish to argue history with you. I merely hope you understand my concerns."

"Oh, yes, we do. There is no question of that. But now you must make a decision. We will go ahead and make the necessary inquiries in Zurich so that we can have your documentation available to you. If you choose to withdraw from the transaction, it does not matter to us. Perhaps you will even feel better if you go to another bank, and see what answer you receive."

Hugh stood and held out his hand. "No, I do not wish to go to another bank. Luther Bollinger has complete confidence in you, and so do I. I will await further word from you. But, make no mistake, I wish to make an order." Then Hugh thought for a moment and smiled. "Perhaps I could open an account with this five million dollars?"

Seifert nodded and smiled. "Of course. Leave the check with me and I shall arrange it. If you will just wait another minute, I shall expedite the matter."

After shaking hands, Hugh waited another five minutes to sign, then left the building, sought out Gibbons, and went home.

THE NEXT MORNING, Hugh fidgeted in his office until the phone rang.

"Mister Stuart, it's Hans Seifert from Zurich International Bank. I have received a communication from the bank headquarters. We are able to fulfill your order for five million dollars in gold bullion. The documents are ready and I suggest that I bring them to you today. This presumes of course that you wish to proceed with the transaction."

Hugh took no time thinking. "Hans, if I may call you that, now that we are business partners, you suggest the time and I shall be waiting for you in my office here at the corner of 85th and Park Avenue. It's my home, so you won't have any problem getting in the building. In fact, I should be here all afternoon and you may choose your time."

"Mister Stuart, oh yes, excuse me, of course, Hugh, I shall be there at two p.m. precisely. Good day to you, until we see each other again. For now, goodbye."

Hugh hung up the phone and leaned back in his chair. Then he went in search of Grace and Julia. He found Grace in her room, at her Victorian mahogany writing table. "Mother, we have an important person coming this afternoon. I would like you to meet him, and perhaps join us in the library for sherry or something."

Grace raised her eyebrows." Oh my, I hope this isn't going to be like the last person you brought in without warning."

Hugh laughed. "No that was a semi-emergency, Mother. This is an important business transaction."

She stood and put her pen on the table. "Well, I am pleased to hear that. Who is it this time?"

"Hans Seifert, from Zurich International Bank. I am buying some gold from them and he's bringing the paperwork over here."

"How convenient."

"I don't think it's a matter of convenience. It's a matter of treating your customer right. I'll review the paperwork and then we'll go to the library. I will ask Julia to join us."

Grace frowned. "Is that necessary? She went off this morning, ran out the door saying she was going to the art league, or wherever she goes these days. Quite frankly, Hugh, I don't like it at all and I think you should talk to her about it."

Hugh sighed. "Mother...keep to the topic at hand. I don't think we need to discuss this any further. Tell Willow to expect him around two and have her show him up to my office as soon as he's here. I don't want him to wait any time at all."

"Of course, Darling, I think it's exciting."

Hugh went in search of Julia. He found Mary with Elizabeth and Mary said that Julia was at an art class. Hugh thought about that, then gave Elizabeth a little kiss on the top of her head and started to leave."

"Daddy, where's my pony?"

Hugh turned back and smiled at his daughter. "I'm sorry, sweetheart. Yes, your pony. I have not forgotten that. No I haven't. Here's what's going to happen. I went over there, to Central Park, to the stables. And they didn't have anything available now."

Elizabeth lowered her head and began to cry. Hugh knelt next to her, and put his hand under her chin. He took out a handkerchief and wiped her eyes. "Now, my little Elizabeth, don't you worry. I have worked it out. You know what I did?"

She rubbed her eyes and shook her head, waiting for good news.

"I have ordered a pony from Kentucky. You know, that's where they have the thoroughbred horses, for the races. It's on a truck. It'll be here in a few days. Okay?"

Elizabeth nodded, her eyes brimming, then pulled the picture book up close as though she concentrated on it. Hugh stood, patted her on the head, and left.

As he followed the hallway to his office, the front door opened and Julia came through the door. Her blond hair was a mess, her face hot. Hugh waited at the banister while she walked up the stairs.

"Julia, you are really atrocious. Why are you so sweaty?"

"Why? I don't know. I guess because it's warm outside."

"Where were you?"

"Where I most always am when I'm out. At the Art League. Studying. Haven't we had this conversation before?"

"My god, why don't you ever tell me where you're going?"

She stared amazement, halfway up the stairs, her hand on the banister. "Oh. Maybe I will, when you start telling me."

He pulled away from the banister and half-twisted, and then turned back. "You are not presentable. A gentleman from the Zurich bank will be here in an hour, and you are not fit to be introduced to him."

Her eyes opened wide. "Oh, Zurich bank. And you want to introduce me? Why?" She finished climbing the stairs and leaned against the wall, then thought better of it. She pulled her hair away from her face.

"This is important for our future, Julia. For the family. It's a valuable business connection. He's coming here, that shows that the bank considers us to be important partners. Now would you please go and get ready."

"Sure."

"And from now on, take the car. Gibbons is here for that purpose."

"The car? A limousine with a chauffeur? I don't think so, Hugh. That's ridiculous. The subway's an easy walk from here." She turned and went into their room.

Hugh pounded his hand on the banister and walked to his office.

Chapter 12

IN HIS OFFICE, Hugh sat up when he heard the doorbell ring. Instead of waiting for Mrs. Willow he went to the entrance foyer, waving her off when he saw her coming in from the kitchen. He opened the door, greeted Hans Seifert and took him up the stairs to his office.

"Please, have a seat." Hugh pointed to the red leather chair in front of his desk.

Seifert put his briefcase on the floor and spoke as he opened it and searched for documents. "Hugh, as we discussed on the phone, your transaction has been approved. Our Zurich headquarters expedited your order...important under the circumstances of events in Europe. We have deposited your check with our New York bank, J.P. Morgan and Company, you see...."

Hugh was surprised as he interrupted Seifert. "J.P. Morgan? That's another bank."

Seifert nodded and smiled. "Mr. Stuart, we are an international business bank, not a retail bank. By design. Is this your first international transaction?"

Hugh, humbled, responded. "No, but it's my first one for five million dollars during a time when we are headed for war."

"I see." Seifert thought for a moment. "Any questions? You did diligently study Zurich International Bank before you came to us, did you not?"

"Oh, yes, of course. Luther did that for us. No problem there."

"First time jitters. Or caution. I understand perfectly. Why don't we proceed with signing the necessary documents?"

Hugh nodded.

Seifert brought the stack of documents to Hugh's side of the desk and put them before him. "I'll go through them one by one, and we'll both sign each one at the same time. Is that satisfactory for you?"

"Yes, it is."

When they had finished signing the documents, Seifert gathered one set and handed it to Hugh, then walked back to his chair and put the other set in his briefcase.

Hugh put the papers in a drawer in his desk. "Can I offer you coffee, or a cigarette, or a cigar, for that matter?"

"Thank you, Mr. Stuart, but I don't smoke."

"How about we go to the library then, and have, say a glass of sherry or something?"

"That's fine. I am interested in your library. You have a fine home, that much is evident."

"Wait one minute, Hans, while I make arrangements for my wife and mother to meet us there."

"I'll wait."

Hugh found both of them in the library, each reading. Julia had changed to a black silk pleated dress, and her hair fell in lovely curls around her shoulder. Grace wore a Navy blue day dress with small flowers. They both smiled. "I'll be right back," he said.

Hugh ushered Hans into the library and introduced him. The women stood. Hans offered his hand with a formal Germanic bow to Grace, and kissed her hand as he wordlessly praised her eyes, which she accepted with a wide smile. She glanced over to Hugh in obvious approval. Hans turned and did the same to Julia, who smiled, but the smile was formal and reserved.

Hugh spoke. "We have completed the transaction for the gold bullion. I hope we will be able to complete more transactions in the future."

Hans nodded. "Yes, It's my hope as well. We do have war preparations in Europe. As you know, the Spanish civil war ended last April, but now the German armed forces are poised on the border with Poland, and so, matters will become complicated." He moved his gaze back and forth between Grace and Julia. "Mr. Stuart was wise to complete these transactions before war breaks out again."

Grace sat up and folded her hands on her chest, her eyes dark. "War? Surely there will not be war?"

Hans sought a hint of how to continue. Hugh turned to his mother.

"Mother, you do read the papers. You know that war is likely in Europe. War is always likely in Europe. But we shall stay out of it. We learned our lesson the last time."

Hans smiled, then said, "And, as you know, Switzerland has been a neutral country for over a thousand years. Your investment is safe with us."

Grace sat back, relieved.

Hans's eyes moved around the room, and then he made a sweeping gesture with a hand. "I see you have lovely paintings in this room. May I view them up close?" He said this to Grace, who left it up to Hugh.

Hugh motioned for Hans to follow him to a wall. Together they stood before the Signac.

Hans nodded in appreciation. "Of course, I am not an art expert, but as an amateur of painting, I see you have something wonderful here." He made a movement to get closer to the painting. "May I?" After Hugh gestured, Hans took out a pair of glasses, leaned in, and studied the painting. Then he turned to Grace. "I'm not familiar with Signac, but it's exquisite. I admire your taste." Then, as if he recognized an error, he turned to Julia. "Everything in this room is superb. We do have a painting by Paul Signac in the Kunsthaus Zurich, but I don't remember its title. So, we have something in common, then. The next time I return home I shall be certain to visit the museum."

"Are you from Zurich, Mr. Seifert?" said Grace.

"I am from a small town near there. Schubelbach. It's on the road to Liechtenstein. I live in Zurich now. And...." He made a bow and smile of pretend embarrassment. "Albert Einstein did his famous work in Zurich." He waited for their reaction.

Grace and Hugh smiled.

Julia said, "You must have many famous paintings in the Zurich museum, Mr. Seifert."

Hans nodded. "Yes, the Kunsthaus is a major European museum. But, you know, you have your own museum here in your home."

Hugh said, "The pieces here in the library my mother and father collected over the years. In my office, you may have noticed, the walls are bare. I have not yet started collecting art." He took a step toward Julia. "My wife is an art student, and perhaps one day we shall also collect something."

Hans turned to Julia. "Do you have a favorite painting, Mrs. Stuart?"

"I'm with you, Mr. Seifert. My favorite's the Signac. But I also like Cross's *La Terrasse Fleurie.*"

Hans bowed slightly. "Yes, I can see that. And may I say you have a perfect French accent. Have you studied in Paris?"

Julia laughed. "Thank you. No, I haven't been that fortunate. But my mother was French, and she taught me as a child. I'm afraid I don't speak it much, but I do remember my mother's wonderful accent."

Hans gained their attention by hesitating and observing them both in a deferential manner. "May I make a suggestion? Hugh, you stated that you want more art for your office. Did I understand you correctly?"

Hugh, puzzled, nodded and said "Yes, I would like that."

"Well, then, I can be of service to you. I have a friend from Zurich, who could show you paintings that might interest you. His name is Karl Eppl. He doesn't have a gallery per se, but he has a home here in Manhattan where he has what you might call an informal gallery. You see, he has but recently established himself here in the United States. I myself was satisfied to be able to help him find suitable lodging. If you would allow me to introduce you to Karl, I would be happy."

Hugh deferred to Julia. "My Dear, what do you think?"

"Of course," she said. "We haven't as yet made any plans for acquiring art for Hugh's office. I think your friend Mr. Eppl is an excellent place to start." Hmm. Without warning, she had become valuable to Hugh, she whose art hung in a child's bedroom.

"You are correct," Hans said. "But you see, I note that you have fine taste, it's important for Karl, Mr. Eppl, to have you as patrons." He bowed in feigned deference. "Too strong a word. Customers, shall we say? There's no obligation. I am happy if I have brought people together. I can arrange it for next week if you like?"

Julia said, "Where is his...his...informal gallery...Mr. Seifert?" The term 'informal' aroused her suspicion, and she hesitated because saying it made her sense that they were complicit in something illegal, or worse.

"He has a brownstone on the Upper West Side...on 95th. It's his home, actually."

"We're interested. Don't you agree, Hugh?"

Hugh's smile was one of immense satisfaction.

KARL EPPL STOOD in the hallway of the house, holding the door open, as he gestured for the three of them to enter. He was tall and thin, with round black glasses, his impeccable black double-breasted suit offset by a European-style charcoal cravat showing around his neck. "Guten Tag, Hans," he said, then, aware he had spoken German, smiled to himself. "Please introduce our guests."

"Karl, may I introduce Hugh and Julia Stuart. Grace Stuart, Hugh's mother, you remember, I mentioned she might come, but it's not the case."

"Please, come in," Karl said. He held out his hand to Julia, and when she took it, he made a short bow and feigned kissing her hand. Then he stood straight and offered his hand to Hugh. "I am delighted to make your acquaintance. Hans informs me that you are connoisseurs of art."

"That's nice of him," Julia said, arching her eyebrows at Hans. "That implies more experience than we have." She turned to Hugh to let him continue.

"I think," he said, "it's more accurate to say we appreciate art, and we understand you have some paintings available for purchase." He in turn faced Hans. "That's what we understand."

"Yes, yes, you are right. That's why Hans has brought you to my small gallery. It has been open for several months. I am using my home, you see, because...well, you see...why don't we go into the living room and I can explain a little further." He gestured to the room open from the hallway. The long room featured white walls with black furniture, and along the walls hung several recognizable paintings.

Julia held her breath, but kept her face passive. She recognized two by Matisse and leaned closer to read the titles, *Oriental Woman*

Seated on Floor and *Woman Seated in Armchair.* Then she saw Toulouse-Lautrec, even a Picasso, *Standing Nude.* The last painting appeared to be Manet, but she wasn't sure. She walked along the wall. Then she turned to Karl. "And these paintings are for sale, Mr. Eppl, is that correct?"

He stepped forward next to her. "You seem surprised, Mrs. Stuart."

"Yes, I am. But because Mr. Seifert didn't tell us that you had work of such great painters. We expected to find art of less distinction."

"Oh, yes, of course, I do have many such paintings. I'm sure you would find them acceptable. I have lesser impressionists, some post-impressionists, then abstract expressionists, and other modern art, too. It's...you see, I want to display my most important works first for people to see. I have to know where your interest lies. There is always the matter of the size of the financial engagement you wish to make."

"Karl," Hans broke in. "you must not be such a salesman. Mr. and Mrs. Stuart are here at my invitation, and you should not treat them as buyers. Mrs. Stuart is an artist herself and...."

Hugh raised his hand. "Not at all. Not about being an artist, I mean. Julia is a good artist. No, I mean we are indeed here to purchase art. But, I grant you this, we are not accustomed to choosing between lesser and greater art." He put his hand on Julia's arm. "Isn't that right, Darling?"

Julia felt uncomfortable with this display of possession, but she didn't want to react in front of the others. "I think what my husband means, if I may be frank, we have not discussed how much we are prepared to spend, and further, we have not researched the current art market. That, you of course understand, is an important element."

"But on the other hand," Hugh said, "we do know great art when we see it. I think my wife's opinion will be helpful in choosing among some other works of art you may have. I myself would be proud to hang one of these magnificent pieces in my office."

Karl turned to Hans, but his expression said nothing. Then he spoke. "Since you have been so frank, Mr. Stuart, let me be forthright. Are you interested in one particular piece?"

Hugh said, "Yes, as a matter of fact. It's the...." he leaned forward, "...Degas, *Portrait of Gabrielle Diot.*" He straightened up, one arm across his chest, the other resting on it and holding his chin up, studying the pastel drawing. "It's the one I like, I'm afraid, among all these. I would like to have it up on my wall." He turned to Karl in anticipation.

Karl nodded. "I see. It's my most recent acquisition. I won't pretend I am favoring you. This drawing is available for $40,000."

"Let me talk to my wife for a few moments, if you don't mind."

"We'll be in the back." Karl took Hans out of the room.

When they were gone, Hugh said, "That doesn't seem too much."

"You can afford it. I don't know if you're paying too much. To me, that's not the question. It's not a huge sum. It is, after all, a Degas and it's clear you want it. That's what you have to think about. Do you want to try and get a Degas for less? Or go somewhere else?"

"Yes, you have it right," Hugh said. His face relaxed. "I know what I want. Let's call them back." He raised his voice. "We're ready out here."

Karl and Hans returned, Karl watching Hugh's face as he entered.

"We are interested in this Degas drawing," Hugh said. "My wife agrees with me. I will leave the details of provenance and authenticity to her. For myself, I feel that the authority of Mr. Seifert in bringing us to meet you is authority enough."

"Thank you for your confidence. It's true, you are also showing confidence in Zurich International Bank. Their reputation is on the line as much as mine. But as far as the price is concerned, may I bring to your attention that there is much talk of war in Europe. If that does happen, the art market will come to a complete stop. In that case, the price of everything will go up substantially."

"Yes," Hugh said, "I am aware of that. But I am buying art for my own pleasure, not as a business proposition."

"I shall arrange for this drawing to be delivered tomorrow to your house, and if you wish, we shall assist you in placing it in your desired location."

"Thank you."

"Now," Karl continued, "if you would like to follow me, I have work from other artists to show you."

Karl led them out of the room and up the stairs to the next floor, to a room empty of furniture but with walls covered with paintings of all the categories Karl had mentioned before. Hugh watched as Julia went around the room observing every painting with a careful eye.

When she had finished, she talked with Hugh, then selected paintings by André, Michel and Reinhold, along with several drawings. They returned downstairs and prepared to leave, but Hugh insisted on one last tour of the living room. He walked up and down and then stopped to examine *The Letter* by Toulouse-Lautrec. He stepped back, his face showing admiration, then he turned to Julia and said, "This one, also."

Karl walked up to Hugh and Julia. "I can see you appreciate this piece."

"Yes," said Hugh, "it reminds me of my grandmother. I did not expect to feel this way about Toulouse-Lautrec, but, there you have it. How much, Mr. Eppl?"

Karl did not hesitate. "It's not a Degas, of course. To me, it is worth $20,000."

Hugh smiled. "Fine. I am prepared. I will write you a check now. And you say, delivery and installation tomorrow?"

Karl nodded.

A few minutes later, Hugh walked with pride out the door, Julia holding on to his arm.

HUGH STOOD IN the center of his office as Wolfgang Zinsli, the assistant from Karl Eppl, unpacked the paintings and drawings. Hugh opened an envelope and found the documents. He handed it to Julia.

She opened it, and sat in a chair to examine them. "You know, we should have done this yesterday," she said.

"Nonsense. As they said, we have the full faith and credit of the Zurich International Bank. Hans Seifert recommended Eppl. Everything's fine."

"What if we discover something's fake?"

He smiled in condescension. "Hans will make sure it's taken care of. Stop worrying."

The art works were unpacked and displayed on the floor along the wall.

"I am ready to hang them, sir."

"Yes, well," Hugh turned to Julia. "Where do you think?"

Julia turned around the room once, first moving her head down to the paintings, then up at the French chalked wood paneling. "Your Degas, it should go next to the door."

Hugh wrinkled his brow. "Next to the door?"

"Not because it's next to the door. Because it's directly across from your desk."

He smiled. "Yes, you're right about that." He turned left to face the fireplace. "And over there?"

"I think the Toulouse-Lautrec. You?"

He thought for a moment, then said, "I agree. You're good at this." Turning to Wolfgang Zinsli, he continued, "So, you have two pieces to start with." To his wife he said, "Why don't you stay here and finish the hanging. I'll be in the library. Call me when it's done." Without waiting for a reply, he left the room.

Julia smiled at the assistant. "Fine, hang the Toulouse-Lautrec over the fireplace." She went to the row of paintings and picked up the Degas, sat in the leather sofa, and studied it. She turned it over and tensed up. In the right hand lower corner she saw a piece of paper with writing that appeared to be German, she wasn't sure. But she was sure that below the writing was the stamp of a swastika.

"Wait," she said.

The assistant stopped.

"Let me see that, the Toulouse-Lautrec please, the back of it."

He held it up so she could see the back. She searched the back of the painting, but there was no swastika on it. "Thank you. Please hang it up." She went to the other pieces and examined each one, but none of them had a similar stamp. "You may hang the others where you find a space. Make them...no, never mind, I'll supervise as required. I'll place the paintings under the panels where you can hang them."

"Yes, Madam. May I make a suggestion, Madam?"

"Of course. I'll be happy to listen to it."

"The lighting is not good for all these paintings. I suggest you call in a lighting expert to make the paintings visible to their best potential."

"Thank you, Mr. Zinsli, we shall take your suggestion under advisement." She turned around the room. "I see your point, however."

Julia was still unsettled, but she placed each painting as she thought appropriate. Then she picked up the envelope with the documents and took them out. She sat at Hugh's desk and organized them before her. She noted the names of the Swiss art dealers from whom Karl Eppl had purchased the art.

The assistant's voice interrupted her. "I am finished with the hanging. Would you please give your approval?"

Julia put the papers down and surveyed the room. "Yes, they are all beautiful. Thank you, Mr. Zinsli."

He bowed to her, picked up his tools, and left the room.

She went back to the desk scanned the papers. And then, she saw the names of the previous owners of all these works. There were three: Paul Rosenberg, Solomon Blumenkranz, and Moshe Fleishmann. She knew what this meant. She held two documents in her hand when she opened the door to the library found Hugh. He sat in his usual red leather wingback chair, reading the paper.

"Hugh!" The shrillness of her voice startled her, but it came from the dread she felt.

He turned and dropped the paper on his lap. "Why are you so loud? I can hear you. Has he finished?"

"Yes, he's finished, all right. That's not why I'm here. Did you know this was art stolen from the Jews by the Nazis? Is that why Mr. Seifert introduced us to Karl Eppl, because he has the connections to Nazis?"

Hugh stood, his back stiff, the paper dropped to the floor. "My god, Julia. What do you take me for?" His lips tightened into a straight line. His voice was even but hard. "We went there to buy art. We both studied the art. You agreed to the best art and you yourself chose the secondary art. Together, we bought this art from a reputable dealer in New York. What is this nonsense about Nazis?"

Julia put her hands on her hips. "Your Degas has a swastika stamped on the back of it. The document is even signed below the words 'Heil Hitler'. Don't 'my god' me, Hugh. That's about as Nazi as it gets."

Hugh cocked his head and frowned in disdain. "Must I repeat myself, I bought this from a reputable Swiss dealer in New York, not from some German in Munich. My transaction is backed by the Zurich International Bank. This is not about the Nazis."

She furrowed her brow. "Are you being obtuse? The previous owners of this art are all people with Jewish names. Isn't it clear to you what's gone on?"

Hugh opened his eyes wide and extended his arms. "But of course. The Jews have always been big supporters of art. My god, think of Rothschild. Music, painting, sculpture, architecture. What's so surprising here? Julia, they buy and sell art all the time. So some of that ends up in New York. There's nothing unusual about it. Stop this hysterical nonsense."

"No, I will not stop it. We have to investigate this. We must demand a full accounting of the provenance of this art."

"Don't you understand? What if it's true? What if it is all art that Jews sold because they were leaving the country? The point is, they sold the art, they received a fair price, the market price. That's all you or I need to know. You cannot see sinister designs in everything."

"I will not let up on this."

"Listen to me. We have the provenance. The provenance does not tell you if someone sold their art for less. It does not tell you their intentions. We have acquired beautiful art. You of all people should be happy about it. We have purchased art from a reputable dealer with reputable support from an international bank. That is all we need to know. Now that is the end of it."

Julia folded her arms across her chest.

He noted that and said, "Let's go see. Now I am proud of my office. It is every bit as good as Father's library." He went off, not waiting for Julia.

She stood still, defeated. She imagined going back to Eppl, or even Seifert, to complain. But she knew what they would say. They would defend their own purchases. No one had stolen these. Heil Hitler just means an over-patriotic customs agent. Maybe one or two had been sold under duress, but that happens all the time. Businesses fail, family fortunes dwindle, and art is sold for less. She could hear Karl Eppl saying, in any case, our works of art did not change ownership at a loss in Europe. He himself would give her his personal word on that. And, of course, he could vouch for the personal word of the Zurich International Bank and Hans Seifert, whom she could call upon to verify this. Seifert and Eppl. The two of them.

Chapter 13

ELIZABETH'S SCREAMING VOICE came from her room. "My pony! My pony! It's here!" Grace stood at the top of the entrance hall stairway and watched the little girl bound down the steps and strain to open the front door. She set her feet, leaned back, and pulled with all her strength.

"No, Elizabeth you mustn't...."

The little girl slipped through the door and disappeared. Mary and Mrs. Willow appeared from the kitchen door, staring at Grace with eyes full of fear.

"What happened?" Mary said.

"Go get her," Grace said, "she's outside. She ran outside."

Mary ran to the door, pulled it open, and Grace saw Elizabeth jumping up and down, about to cross the street where a white horse with flowers stood waiting with a red carriage.

"My pony! A princess cart!" She screamed and jumped up and down.

Mary caught her as she put her foot out in the street.

Elizabeth sat on the sidewalk and kicked at Mary. "It's my pony, go away."

Mary grabbed hold of her arms and held her tight, while Elizabeth kept kicking at the sidewalk. Mrs. Willow came down the steps and helped Mary keep the child controlled, but she broke away and turned toward the street. Elizabeth ran out, a car screeched to a halt ten yards away, and Elizabeth screamed again and ran back to the sidewalk, rushed by the two women and ran into the house and up to her room.

She ran back out to the hallway and into her father's office, but he wasn't there. "Daddy! Daddy!" she screamed.

Grace came into the room, and Elizabeth stopped screaming, then ran behind the desk, watching her grandmother. Grace stopped, smiled, and stood silent for several seconds. She took a step left, but Elizabeth moved in the opposite direction behind the desk, ready to be chased, so Grace stood where she was.

"Elizabeth, my child, that horse across the street is not yours. If you want to go for a ride in it, we can do it. Would you like that?"

Elizabeth wiped tears from her eyes and shook her head. "It's my pony. Daddy put it there."

"Your father isn't here, is he? What are we going to do, you and me?"

Elizabeth stared at her grandmother. She had no idea what they were going to do, she and her grandmother. That much was clear to Grace, who had no idea, either.

"Your mother isn't here. Your father isn't here. So I'm going to have Mary take you to your room and take care of you until your parents come home. Now, give me your hand." Grace moved toward the desk, smiling.

Elizabeth stayed where she was, shifting on her feet, ready to run. Grace backed away, then walked out to the hallway and scanned the hallway to call Mary, but stopped with a slight jump when she found her right outside the door. She motioned her in. "You go around the right, I'll go around the left." The two women began walking around the desk, but Elizabeth moved the chair and crawled underneath the desk.

"Oh my heavens," Grace sighed. "Mary, get her out of there."

Mary got on her hands and knees and approached the cubbyhole. Elizabeth screamed "I want my Daddy!"

Mary pulled back and sat facing Elizabeth, shaking her head back and forth. "Come on, Lizzie, we'll go play, do something nice."

Silence from under the desk.

Grace sighed again and swiveled around, as if help were coming from somewhere. Mrs. Willow craned her head in the door. Grace motioned her in and pointed to Mary sitting on the floor, waving Mrs. Willow to go over there and help out.

Mrs. Willow bent over Mary, smiled down at Elizabeth, but with a hard, forced smile, that told the child she wished she didn't have to be in this position. "Now, Elizabeth, as soon as Mr. Stuart is home, we'll have him talk to you. He can explain everything. Why don't you let Mary take you to your room?" She held out her hand down to Elizabeth's hiding place.

Elizabeth's shoes pounded on the floor, her hands or head slammed against the wood of the desk, and her voice, growing hoarse, yelled "Daddy! Daddy! Daddy!"

Grace watched this from the hallway. "Mrs. Willow," she called, "Mary!"

The two women waited silently for her. Grace waved them to come to her, and they followed her out of the room. She whispered, "She'll get tired of this. Let's go on with our day. I must tell Gibbons to childproof that door."

Grace walked back to her room to wait for one of Elizabeth's parents to return home and discuss how to improve the child and keep her safe.

She went into her bathroom and took four aspirin, downed with a large glass of water. Then she sat on the toilet and got her breath back. Her hands were shaking. These headaches were becoming more frequent.

She went back into her room and stretched out on her chaise longue and felt the relief of the quiet. Then she heard quick footsteps in the hallway, Mary's voice calling after Elizabeth, a scream from the child, then muffled noise. She put her hand on her forehead, sighed and went to the hallway and heard the noise louder coming from the library.

When she opened the door to the library, she saw Mary move toward Elizabeth and the child run in a blur behind the library table and knock over the antique Oriental vase Grace had received from her mother. It crashed to the floor and broke into pieces. Mary followed her, eyes wide open at the broken vase, trying to keep her balance, stealing a glance at Grace, then away, holding on to the table and then the chair. The child did not stop, but ran past Grace out the door, Mary stepping fast to keep up.

Grace clenched her fists and put her hands on her head as she stared at the precious black and white pieces, the flowers now separated in the shards. This child is out of control, she thought. Out of control. My head aches, my eyes hurt. I cannot go on like this.

She went back to her room and rested, or tried to rest, for half an hour, then called Beatrice in Montreal.

"HELLO?"

Grace felt relieved when she heard her daughter's voice. Someone she could commiserate with. "Beatrice, I can't stand this any longer."

"What's the matter, Mother?"

"It's Elizabeth. She broke my Meiping vase, you know, that my mother gave to me, and before that she ran into the street and was nearly run over. Her mother pays no attention to her." Grace wiped her hand across her brow.

There was a short silence on the other end of the phone. "Have you talked to Julia about this?"

"My Dear, you have no idea how difficult she is. Julia is so defensive about her little girl. Elizabeth has no direction. She doesn't know what's right because her mother won't let anyone else help the child. And now Hugh has stepped in and made a mess of it."

Beatrice sighed. "Oh-oh, what happened?"

"You won't believe this. He promised Elizabeth she could have her own pony, and now she's throwing tantrums until she gets what she wants. She saw a horse and carriage across the street and insisted it was hers. She was almost killed. Who is going to watch over that child?"

"Mother, calm down. Isn't that what Mary is supposed to do?"

Footsteps ran outside her doorway again.

"Oh, if only that were true. Mary can't control her. They're running around out there now. It's giving me a headache."

"What do you want me to do?" Beatrice couldn't hide the exasperation in her voice.

Grace put the phone down on her knee, bent over, and listened to herself breathing. She brought the phone back up, but waited before speaking. "I don't know, Beatrice. I'm at my wit's end."

"Mother," Beatrice said in a soft voice. "Isn't it time you thought of having them live in their own house?"

Grace let out a low grunting sound. "Oh my god, you don't mean that. How could you say such a thing? Hugh was born in this house, and I want him here when I die. Then that woman will have won if she takes my son and granddaughter away from me."

She put the phone down and rubbed her forehead. "You have to help me. I can't take this much longer. What am I going to do?"

No answer came from the other end of the line.

"Beatrice? Did you hear me?"

Beatrice's quiet voice came back. "It's hard to see how this ends, Mother, until you have talked to Hugh and Julia about it. I'm not the child's mother. What do you want from me? I've given you my advice."

"Perhaps if you came down to visit for a while, you could talk some sense into them. You're Julia's age, or at least close to her age, you could make her understand."

"I don't know her," Beatrice said. "We're not friends. I met her at the wedding, that was all. We have never had a private conversation." She was quiet several seconds. "I'm not even sure she likes me. Her whole relationship with Hugh happened so fast. Didn't you think so?"

"Yes," Grace said, "I suppose it did. I don't know what he ever saw in her. Do you?"

"Well, yes, I think I do, Mother. She's beautiful and she's probably great in bed."

"Oh, oh, don't talk like that, please."

"I'm sorry to be blunt, but that's the answer to your question, isn't it, why he married her? It sure wasn't for the money. Except maybe on her part. And anyway, they're doing fine, aren't they?"

"I'm not so sure," Grace said. "They can't seem to agree on the child, and Julia was horrible to our attorney, and now she's unhappy about some art that Hugh bought. No, to tell you the truth, I don't think they are doing fine. And then today, I tell you, this child is uncontrollable. This house isn't safe." Grace sat for a moment to take in with satisfaction that she had identified the problems with Julia.

Beatrice spoke sympathetically. "They can find a brownstone on the West Side. Hugh could keep his office at home there with you. And then you could see Elizabeth whenever you wanted, and on your own terms."

"I don't know. What if Hugh wants an office over there?"

"All right, please stop now. Hugh will be happy to have an office near you, and besides it will be a place away from home. It's perfect."

Grace brought her hand up to her face and then put it down on her knee. It was a dangerous idea. The mother and child are the problem. Not her son. "I understand. How are you doing, Darling?"

"Mother, I'm fine. I love it in Montreal. I'm even getting interested in hockey, if you can believe that."

Grace laughed, and felt relief in laughing. "Oh, my, no I don't believe that. I'm sure that's Pierre's influence."

"You may be right, but it's nice to be interested in something with him. In fact I think that's him now. I have to go. I love you."

"I love you, too." Grace hung up the phone with reluctance and once again the stomping of feet brought her headache to her attention. She closed her eyes and rubbed her temples, then wondered if she needed to intervene. The memory of her broken vase invaded her moment and she stood and went out to the hallway. "Mary!"

No answer. She went to Elizabeth's bedroom and opened the door. "Didn't you...?" She stood in horror at the destruction of the room. Crayons, paints and teddy bears littered the floor. Elizabeth sat on the bed, eyes wide with fear, shaking.

Mary sat next to her, holding her hand. "I can't control her, Mrs. Stuart. I can't."

"Stay with her," Grace said, her voice calm but hard. "Until her mother or father returns. We will discuss it further then. Something will have to change. We cannot go on like this." Grace left the room.

At the library door she hesitated, afraid to see her vase still in pieces on the floor. But she straightened up and went in.

Mrs. Willow swept the last pieces into a long-handled dustpan. She turned and waited, then said, "Do you want to try and save it?"

Tears came to Grace's eyes. She spoke with resignation. "No, it's no use. It's been destroyed. Throw it away."

She went back to her room, opened her bathroom cabinet, and took out a bottle of Valium. Then she lay down and observed the plaster medallions in her ceiling. At least they were safe from the child, she thought. But they meant nothing. They were not a precious vase, a wedding gift from her mother. Insurance was not going to make up for that. So Mary says she cannot control the child. And Julia is not going to control the child. And Hugh? He wants to please

Elizabeth. No, it's up to me. I will take the steps to control the child. And I will do it alone.

Grace turned on her side. She fell asleep as she remembered the arms of George Stuart around her, the man who gave strength to his house and his family.

Chapter 14

HUGH OPENED THE door with unneeded energy and jumped up the steps to the hallway. He went first to the library and saw his mother at the table poring over a fashion magazine. When she saw him she smiled at her son. Hugh smiled back but kept an eye on the portrait of his father, gray hair on the temples, hand on the chair, back ramrod straight.

"Mother," he said, "you're looking beautiful today. I love your dress."

Grace was wearing a dramatic black silk crepe swing dress with chartreuse coloring on the shoulder. She put her finger on the page to hold her place and said to him, "My, you're in a good mood today."

He nodded, and said "Yes I am. I've been midtown to our real estate office and things are going well with that unfortunate apartment fire. The fire marshal is no longer breathing down our necks, the tenants have found lodgings elsewhere, and Elmer is repairing the damage. So that's good news. One less hassle." He put his hands in his pockets and turned his gaze slowly around the room, observing his parents' creation, as if he were appraising it. Then he stopped when he faced his mother again. "You know, Mother, you and father have made a beautiful room. But if I may say so, I have done as well in my office."

Grace spoke with a voice full of irony. "Yes, Darling, but none of ours was stolen from others." She put her face down to the magazine to hide the smirk.

Hugh tightened the muscles on his forehead. "I don't think that's funny."

His mother leaned back in her chair and folded her hands on her lap. "No, I suppose you're right, but I couldn't resist."

He knew she could care less whether her son bought the art from people who had to sell or people who took it without asking. He moved away from her and sat in his red wingback chair. "I also went to Irving Trust and put my bullion certificates in the safety deposit box. I am sure it will be joined by many others in the future."

"I know you will be successful, Hugh. You are every bit as good as your father, and you are standing on his shoulders. The thing I will dare say is that he married somewhat better than you did."

"Well, since we are on a first name basis now, Grace," he said, the irony in his voice matching hers. "Let me say that I don't think it is your prerogative to pass judgment on my marriage." He stood and twirled to face her. "It's not your prerogative. As you say, I have done well handling my own affairs, and that includes my relationship with my wife." He put his hands on the chair and stared at her in defiance.

"And let me tell you, I have spoken to Hans Seifert and I am going to buy some more paintings and drawings. I am going to put them all over this house and perhaps you may see your home turned into something equal to the Frick."

"Why, I think that's wonderful. As long as you don't turn my room into a public museum." She closed her magazine and stood to face him, then she moved around the table. "I always knew you would come into your own, Son. You are so much like your father. Now, if you can control your wife...."

His eyes flared. "Mother...." He stopped at that, sure she would catch the hardness in his voice. He knew he had to control his mother first. But his father's eyes in his father's face stared at him. He changed his voice to a softer tone. "Mother, did something happen today? Is there some reason why you bring up the subject?"

Grace sighed. "It's Elizabeth."

"What about Elizabeth?"

"She's uncontrollable and she's giving me headaches."

"Did you talk to Julia about it?"

Grace stared at him in wonderment. "Didn't you tell me a few minutes ago not to mess with your marriage?"

"All right," he said, " tell me what this is about. Why is Elizabeth giving you headaches?"

"She's giving me headaches because she is wild."

"I still don't see why you can't talk to Julia about it. She's her mother."

"I see," Grace said, "and where is Elizabeth's mother?"

"You don't know?"

Grace's voice rose. "I can well imagine, Hugh, where your wife is. What's she's doing there I have no idea."

The painting of George Randolph Stuart bore down on his son.

Grace continued. "The problem is, you don't know where she is or what she's doing. That's the problem."

Hugh nodded. The room became close, a choking feeling weighed him, his breathing faltered

Grace walked to him and put her hands on his chest. "You should go over there and see for yourself. It would be good for her to know that you are taking an interest. Maybe then she would take more interest in what's happening in this house."

HUGH GOT OUT of the car at the Art Students League on West 57th, telling Timothy to wait for him. He went in under the blue canopy to the lobby. The absence of a receptionist frustrated him. A tall woman with messy long black hair studied him, then turned away. He went to her and asked...he wasn't sure how to phrase it...asked if she knew where he might find Julia Stuart.

"Oh, Julia," she said. "Most likely on the second floor. In the gallery. Everyone's in there for Carlo De Luca's exhibition."

Hugh flinched. An Italian name. There was only one Italian name that meant anything to him. He didn't remember what it was, but he remembered that he heard it from his wife. And he remembered that his mother told him it had something to do with Harlem. He went up the stairs prepared for a shock. He saw the door to the gallery and inside bright lights and white walls below semicircular windows and people who were art students talking in loud voices, pointing, laughing.

Julia was nowhere to be seen. The people who might have been Italian were too young. A young woman in dirty beige slacks approached him with a tray of wine. He waved her away with a sneer and kept on going, peering at each panel, not seeing any art, nothing but possible targets of his search.

He saw her. His heart beat faster. She was not alone. The man, the obvious Italian man, was standing next to her gesturing toward some stupidly obscene abstract nonsense. The man put his filthy arm on Julia's shoulder. She backed away and opened her eyes in alarm. But Hugh knew better. Of course she would back away. This is a public event. Other eyes were on her. She had no choice but to make a show of rejection. This was not some place in private. This was not some apartment in the Village.

HUGH RETURNED HOME. In his office, he lit a cigar and poured a glass of brandy. He turned around to tour the art in his room. He nodded in satisfaction. From his childhood appeared the memory of not being able to see the top of the desk and his father sitting in his chair, a cigar in his mouth, like a god.

He crossed the hallway to the library and stood before the painting of his father. He was grateful his mother wasn't there. But his father was always there. No, if his father was there he didn't care whether his mother was there. He determined that he would wait for Julia.

He took the cigar out of his mouth and walked down to Elizabeth's room. She was on the floor, Mary beside her. He went down on one knee and smiled at Elizabeth. "You know what, Darling, I heard today that your pony is getting closer. I have not forgotten that, no siree. It's stuck in Pennsylvania, but it is coming. Now give me a hug."

Elizabeth dropped her crayons and went to her daddy with a beaming face. "My pony."

"Your pony, that's right." Hugh patted her on the head and went back to the library for his lonely vigil.

As he waited he toured the room, noting the combination of pieces of art along the walls. Then he went to his office and made a similar tour. Back in the library, he sat in his red wingback chair, puffed his cigar and waited. Images from the Art Students League floated in his troubled consciousness and he fought them away with gestures. The phone rang in his office and he started to jump up but held himself back.

The front door opened and he started to jump up again. He calmed himself down with controlled breathing. If Julia did not come in, he would go find her.

The library door opened, he turned, and faced his mother. Her face made clear that she understood his disappointment.

"So she's not back," she said, shaking her head. "You did go over there didn't you?"

Hugh spoke loudly. "Don't start with me. If you have any sense, you'll go to your room."

Grace stared at him with wide eyes but then she nodded and left the room, closing the door with as little noise as possible.

The intrusion made Hugh tire of waiting in the library. Instead, he went to his office and started to pick up the phone, not knowing who he was going to call, and then he put it down. It would be bad to be on the phone when she came. He picked up the fire marshal's report, opened the folder, and then instead slammed it back down on the table. Cigar ashes followed. He blew them off. Turning, he went to the window and watched the endless line of cabs in both directions on Park Avenue. One of them stopped in front of the house and he peered down to the street but could not see who was getting out of the cab. The front door opened again. He listened for the identifying sound of the footsteps. Julia's quick steps came up the stairs in a hurry.

Of course, she was coming back from an exciting rendezvous with her lover. He intertwined his fingers until the knuckles turned white. She was walking toward their room. He followed her.

Inside, she stopped while removing her jacket, turned, and smiled when she saw him. "Hello, Darling, I'm glad to see you. I'm glad that you came in here to see me." Even as she spoke, her voice changed from happy to fearful. Rage shone dark in his eyes. She folded her hands in front of her and waited.

"Where were you just now?"

Julia frowned. "You know where I was."

Hugh raised his eyebrows. "Oh, did you see me?"

"See you? No. I was at the art students' league and you never go there so how can I see you? I didn't go anyplace else."

"Well, I was there and I saw you." He pursed his lips, then drew it in a straight line before he continued. "I saw you there with him and I saw him put his arm around you."

Julia's eyes opened in disbelief. "You saw no such thing."

Hughes voice rose in anger. "Don't lie to me. I was there. I saw it."

She put her hand on her temples and shook her head. "There was nothing to see. I was not there with him or anyone else. I went by myself and saw the gallery by myself." She focused on his eyes. "You're making this up."

"You're telling me he did not touch you at all?"

The pleading in her eyes showed how much she felt caught. "Yes, he did put his arm on my shoulder once. But if you were there then you would have seen that I drew away and I left him standing there. It angered me."

"Of course," he said, "that's what I expect from you. Denial. You could not be seen in public so you had to make a display of leaving him. But the real question is, why he felt free to put his hands on you like that in public."

She sat on the bed and turned to face him. "I can't control the actions of other people. The truth is, he's ugly and obnoxious. I left his painting class, and I have nothing to do with him. This was a public gallery. I had no choice but to walk away from him in that situation. Can't you understand this, Hugh?"

Hugh stood with his hands on his hips. "I understand this, Julia... you cannot go there anymore."

"You don't tell me where I can and cannot go. "

"I can and I do. You're not living alone, you have a husband and a daughter. You have obligations. You are skating on thin ice in this family and you have to change."

He stood facing her in silence.

Then she said, her voice asking for understanding, "If you don't trust me, what am I supposed to do? I have nowhere to go. I have no life but my life with you and Elizabeth."

"You know what, I can trust you onlyas far as I can see you. And right now that isn't far. The way you can convince me that you're not having an affair, an affair that would be devastating for this family and your child, is to give up going to that art league. You can study at home if you want."

Julia sat on the bed and stared at the floor. She was thinking.

Hugh moved to the door and opened it. He held his hand on it and said to her, "I see you don't want to commit to me. I am willing to give you time to get used to it."

Julia remained silent on the bed, her hands folded on her lap, her mind somewhere on the corner of the room.

Hugh saw an opportunity to change the subject in a way that would help her come to an understanding of the problem they were facing. "Will you look at me please?"

She turned and her eyes disappointed because they showed no tears forming. He closed the door and sat on the other side of the bed.

"You know Elizabeth is hard to deal with."

"She's a child."

"That, in itself, is beside the point," he said. "She's uncontrollable, she gives Mother headaches."

Julia stood silent in disbelief, then said, "If your mother would ignore her and let Mary and myself take care of her, she wouldn't get any headaches."

"She broke Mother's Oriental vase, and then she almost got herself killed running into the street after the pony."

"Well perhaps you shouldn't have told her she was going to get a pony and then dumped the problem on the rest of us."

"You can go on as long as you want, Julia, I am telling you there are problems at home and you are not here to attend to them."

"So you want me to be her mother and nothing else in my life."

"Listen to me, something has got to be done about Elizabeth's behavior. I've talked to Mother about this, and we feel that it is in the child's interest to be away for a few days to calm down. To get out of the pressure cooker so to speak."

"And when were you going to tell me about this?"

"I did now. You may think the timing was not good, but in my view this is the perfect time to talk about it. Then you and I will have a few days to work out our relationship and the future."

"You aren't giving me any say in this."

"If you want a say in this, all you have to do is agree to it."

Julia let her shoulders droop in resignation. "When do you want all this to happen?"

"Sever your relationship with the art students' league over the phone. Talk to Elizabeth about our plans. You and I can be together again, Julia. In a few days, when it's all arranged. Mother will go with her, so that Elizabeth doesn't feel alone."

Chapter 15

THE NEXT MORNING when Julia awoke, Hugh had already left again so she went out in her pajamas to the dining room, hoping to find him there, but found it empty. The door to Hugh's office stood open and she saw his vacant chair. She tried the library, but only Hugh's father stared from the wall in disapproval. When she opened the door to Lizzie's room, her heart sank to see that the bed was made, the teddy bear gone, and the closet door gaped open with a hole telling her that she was too late. Lizzie's clothes had been removed.

So they had done it. Without letting Lizzie say goodbye to her mother. Hugh had disappeared so he didn't have to face his wife.

She launched herself forward one step but stopped in exasperation. Grace was not there to hit. Julia shook and a cry escaped in the twitching silence.

She turned back into the library to call Philadelphia and had the phone in her hand ready to dial when she realized she didn't know the number. She had never wanted to. Not until now and now it was too late.

She walked to her workroom and picked up her valise and took three new brushes out of a paper bag but then she broke them in half. She sat on a chair feeling empty. She went for a long walk in Central Park.

Late in the afternoon, she returned to find the house still empty. She waited in the library for Hugh to return. When she heard his loud footsteps climbing the stairs, she stood and walked over to open the door. When she put her hand on the knob, she felt a strong pull and backed away. She walked to the center of the room and turned to face her husband.

He smiled at her.

"Where is Elizabeth?"

"You know very well, Darling. She's with Mother, visiting our relatives in Philadelphia. You knew that."

She stared at him waiting for an epiphany about how to proceed, but none came. "You kidnapped her."

He laughed and put the newspaper down on the library table before speaking to her. "Well, that won't hold up in court will it? You knew all about it, in fact you agreed to it. So don't start acting like you've been kept in the dark."

Julia's eyes narrowed and her lips formed a straight line, then she bit her lip, and then said, "You took her away from me this morning. Or last night for all I know."

Hugh put his hands in his pocket and maintained his amused composure. "As a matter of fact it was last night. I thought it much better to avoid a scene with you this morning. Much better for Elizabeth."

"Better for Elizabeth? To go away without saying goodbye to her mother?"

Hugh shook his head. He turned and read the headlines in the newspaper, thinking for a moment before responding. "It was for the best, Julia. And it's for a short period of time. By the way," he said, turning back to her, "have you called to cancel your courses?"

"I don't have to cancel the courses. I can do whatever I please."

"Yes of course that's right, you can. You can wait until they contact you and then we will see what happens."

"For now," she said, "I'll do my work here."

ONE WEEK LATER, Julia waited at the top of the stairs for the door to open. When she had talked to Lizzie on the phone from Philadelphia, the child seemed distant, but she took it to be a sign that her little daughter was not alone in the room.

The door opened and Mary came in the house, followed by Lizzie and Grace. Julia stared at Grace, who refused pay attention to her, so she held out her hands to Lizzie, but her daughter did not come running up the stairs. She followed behind Mary, turning once to make sure she didn't interfere with Grace's progress up the steps. When she arrived at the top, she came to Julia and waited for her mother to give her a hug.

"Mommy." Then she stood still and waited until Grace stood next to her on one side and Mary on the other.

Julia crouched down until she was at Lizzie's level, gave her daughter a big smile, and kissed her on the cheek.

Elizabeth turned her head up toward Grace and then, and only then, smiled at her mother. "Mommy, I brought something for you." She reached into her pocket and pulled out a tiny wrapped package. She handed it to Julia and waited for her mother's reaction.

Julia stood and unwrapped the little package with great excitement. "Oh, thank you, Darling, I can't wait to see what it is." When she saw the little bronze Liberty Bell, she crouched down again and hugged her daughter. "It's beautiful, I'll keep it by my bedside."

Chapter 16

JULIA GOT OUT of bed in the gray light of dawn the next morning to make breakfast for Lizzie. She dressed in her navy blue dress with pockets that Lizzie loved to hide little things in. As she passed by the library, she saw the door open, and heard voices inside. Hugh and Grace. She stopped and listened to Hugh's voice.

"Mother, are you sure?"

"No, it's not whether I'm sure, Hugh. Are you sure?"

"Yes, of course, I think it will work out fine. I will deal with her."

Deal with her? Julia's heart froze when she heard this domineering tone.

Grace's voice became conspiratorial. "We will have to do this with the utmost care, Hugh. It's the best for Elizabeth and it's the one possible way. As long as she's with her mother, she will never be able to control herself. She will end up hurting herself." Her voice softened as she appealed to Hugh. "You do see that, don't you?"

"Of course I see that, Mother. It has to be done. How soon can you make the arrangements?"

It has to be done? Hugh's words rippled with pain down Julia's spine.

"The arrangements, as you call them, are already made." Grace said it as if she had called the undertaker.

"You know, Mother," Hugh said, "Elizabeth will be happier away from Julia. We've already seen it. She's a much more well-behaved child. No more tantrums." A satisfied smile crept over his face.

"She will adjust, I'm sure."

"She will love having a pony nearby," Hugh crowed.

Julia's legs gave way, she fell to the floor and she sat still, surrounded by a blurry hallway. After a second, she cleared her head and pulled herself up and went to their bedroom. In the second dresser drawer she found her and Lizzie's passports and her checkbook. She put them in her purse and left the house.

INSIDE MANUFACTURER'S TRUST bank, Julia bought $50,000 in various denominations of American Express travelers checks plus a few hundred dollars in French francs, and took the subway to Algonquin Travel near the passenger ship terminal on the West Side.

Surprised to see the lobby full of people, she waited two hours on a hard chair beneath a poster for the United States Lines, showing prices of $127 and up for tourist and $186 and up for cabin class. A huge photo of the S.S. Manhattan arriving in New York harbor was next to it. When she made it to the desk she sat before a man who was wearing a gray suit with a black tie that had been loosened, showing sweat on his neck and dirt on the inside of the collar. Papers of all colors and sizes covered his desk.

He smiled but he was making an effort to do his job. He pushed his glasses back on his nose. "May I help you?"

"Yes, thank you, I wish to buy passage to France."

"Yes, doesn't everybody. Except everybody else is French. Oh, excuse me, you must be French as well." He closed his lips tight and waited for her.

"No, I'm not French. I want to go there."

"Let me explain to you, Miss…"

"Mrs."

"You are aware that the US Ambassador in Paris has advised all Americans to leave the country?"

"That doesn't concern me. I want to book passage."

"As you wish. I must do as instructed. I can't promise you anything. The SS Washington is leaving in three days and I can book you passage on that ship but it will be expensive. "

"Expensive? Why is that?" Julia wondered if he had a bribe in mind.

114

"What is available is cabin class staterooms, with living room and bedroom, the bedside telephone, and personal valet service. That will cost you $300." He sat back and waited for her rejection as he stared into her eyes."

"That's twice what's up there on your wall."

"And it will be three times tomorrow. You decide."

Julia didn't hesitate. Her instinct for preservation dictated her response. "There are two of us," she said, "myself and my little girl."

The man nodded. "And how old is your little girl, if I may ask?"

"She's two years old."

"That should not be a problem. You can arrange for a crib or even a small bed once you are on board. The room is large enough to accommodate that."

"You said…you said…", Julia's confidence was leaving her, "the ship is leaving in three days. What about after that?"

He leaned forward and assumed an exasperated tone. "Do you know why you had to wait so long to see me?" He stared at her and when she did not respond he continued. "This may be the last ship leaving to go to Europe. Without a doubt, nothing will be leaving for France."

Julia felt the tension rise up. She sat still, her hand holding hard to her purse. She thought of Lizzie back in her room playing in silence and following every suggestion that Mary made.

"This is it," he said, "if you want to go to France now you need to book passage on the SS Washington. We don't know when another ship will across the Atlantic. There are none scheduled. In case you didn't know, Britain and France have declared war on Germany. It may be called a phony war, but steamship companies cannot afford to take chances."

"But there are other ships arriving." Her voice carried a note of panic.

He raised his eyebrows. "Arriving from Europe is one thing. You want to depart. I cannot book passage beyond the Washington. If you want to take your chances, that's up to you. But I point out to you, if you will, that all these people are here today because they don't want to take a chance. "

"Yes I will buy passage for two of us."

"Yes, alright, I will need to see your passports."

Relief flooded over Julia and she opened her purse.

JULIA OPENED THE door to Lizzie's room and found her little girl listening to Mary read her *The Poky Little Puppy*.

She sat next to them on the bed. "Listen, honey, I want you to go out with me, for a walk. Okay?"

Lizzie waited for help from Mary, but Mary was waiting for Julia. Lizzie nodded.

"Let's get your coat on." Julia helped her put on her coat, then smoothed it out, and said, "Why don't you take your teddy bear? It can keep you company while I shop?"

Lizzie picked up her bear, but then hesitated. She picked up her Raggedy Ann and held it, too.

"Oh, my, that's a lot to carry," Mary said.

"No, that's fine," Julia said. "I'll help her. It'll be fun."

Lizzie smiled and hugged the dolls tight.

Julia led her out of the room. "We'll be back in…"

Mrs. Willow came up the stairs. "Mrs. Stuart…" she stopped, surprised, as if she caught them, "there's a man on the phone, from a travel agency. He needs to speak to you. In the library."

Julia's heart almost stopped. At first she thought it was Grace. She feared her face gave her away. But she smiled and said, "Oh…" and motioned Mary to come closer. She whispered, "It's a surprise for my husband. I'm planning a trip for us. Please don't tell him, it will ruin the surprise." She waited, moving her gaze back and forth between the two women.

Mary smiled and nodded. Mrs. Willow said without whispering, "I understand."

Julia smiled at Lizzie. "sweetheart, stay her for a minute. I won't be long." She walked slowly into the library and picked up the phone.

"Hello?"

"Mrs. Stuart?"

"Speaking."

"This is Mr. Halliday, from Algonquin Travel."

"Yes, what is it about? I'm ready to go out the door."

"Well, you know, the SS Washington is leaving today…."

Julia whispered into the phone. "It leaves in three days. What are you talking about?"

"No, it's been changed. That's why I'm calling you. We didn't hear back from you, and there is an opportunity to sell your stateroom if you are not going to make the trip. It's possible her sister ship, the SS Manhattan, will be leaving next week or so, although not guaranteed, but, you see, I'm under some pressure from my management here, there are many people who…"

"No, you may not." She caught herself before she said 'sell my stateroom.' "As I said, I'm about to go out the door. Thank you." She hung up and went back out in the hallway.

Lizzie stood between Mary and Mrs. Willow, quite unhappy, with pleading in her eyes.

"Come on, Darling, we've got shopping to do. Give me one of those to carry."

Lizzie compared the two and handed her mother the teddy bear. Together they went out the door and turned left toward 77th.

"We're going down the street a couple of blocks, honey."

Lizzie said nothing.

When they reached 77th, Julia turned right and they walked down to Madison, where they got in a cab.

"Pier 86." Julia turned to Lizzie and handed her back the bear. "Darling, guess what. I decided to go for a ride on a boat. Would you like that?"

Lizzie smiled and repeated, "Boat," and jumped up and down.

THEY ENTERED THE cavernous Pier through a large door. Julia took the teddy bear and held on to Lizzie and warned her to not move away. "I can't carry you…you need to hold on to me. You'll get lost." She pulled Lizzie close and forced her to pay attention. "Do you understand me?"

Lizzie nodded, unhappy at a dark forest of coats and legs pressing in on her. She moved in closer to her mother, facing her, making it hard for Julia to move. Julia took hold of the sleeve of Lizzie's coat.

They raised their heads as a voice came over a loudspeaker. "Passengers who have purchased passage please move to your left and through the gate."

Julia pulled Lizzie along with the group of people moving to the left. Her heart beat faster in the hope they would soon be on the ship. They arrived at a picket fence, with people moving inside a gate and others crowded outside it. Once inside the gate, Julia gave their passenger voucher to a man in a maritime uniform under the sign of "Bursar".

"Your luggage, Madam? Did you send it on ahead?"

Julia held Lizzie's hand tighter and she prepared to lie. "Yes, it's already on board, they tell me."

"Oh, I see, you have a luxury cabin. Of course. Please, follow this gentleman."

"Come on, Lizzie, it's a big boat, you'll see. We're going on board now."

Lizzie frowned. "What about Daddy?"

Julia understood that Lizzie could tell this was not a little boat around the East River. It loomed huge and black above them.

"He's coming later, sweetheart, when he's done with work. Let's get on board first." They followed the man up to the edge of the pier.

"You have a choice," he said, "people like to walk up the gangplank, or you can go inside here and take an elevator."

Julia smiled at Lizzie. "Oh, let's walk up the gangplank, it's not high up there."

They walked up hand in hand, Lizzie staring down at the water and out at the crowds in the pier.

At the top, a young man in a white uniform smiled and held out his hand. "May I see your voucher, please?"

Julia handed him her voucher. She spoke down to Lizzie. "Nice uniform on the man, huh?"

"I see, please follow me along the Boat Deck. It's not far for your accommodations."

They followed him a few feet and he opened a door and ushered them in. Inside the hallway, he opened another door, and held it open for them to enter the stateroom. "Your luggage, Madam? It does not appear to have arrived."

She waved him off. "Oh no, that's fine. We'll get whatever we need on the ship or in France." She turned to Lizzie, but the little girl was trying to reach up to the porthole.

The steward picked up a small table and brought it over to Lizzie. "Here you are, Miss, you can use this to see out the porthole." Then he turned back to Julia. "If you'd like me to point out the amenities on the ship...."

"No, that won't be necessary. I've read the brochure, and we do have plenty of time."

"Thank you, Madam. I'll be available on the intercom anytime during the voyage."

"Well, maybe one thing. Lizzie, shall we have a treat?"

Lizzie stepped down from the table and nodded.

"Okay, how about a chocolate soda? Or would you like strawberry? Oh, I know, we'll get both and we can have some of each." She turned to the steward. "If you wouldn't mind?"

"Certainly, Madam, I'll be back in a minute."

"Lizzie, Darling, why don't we go out on the deck and watch when the ship leaves the pier for the trip around New York? Lots of people are there, and we can try out the deck chairs. And, they have a pool, that would be great to see. And...."

A knock on the door interrupted her.

"Wow, that was fast, wasn't it, Darling." Then she spoke louder. "Please come in."

The response was a louder knock. Julia went to the door and opened it. A man in a uniform with gold braid on the cuffs and shining ornaments on his shoulder stood outside.

"Mrs. Stuart?"

"Yes."

"Mrs. Julia Stuart?" The man peeked around her, and smiled when he saw Lizzie. "I'm First Officer Allen. Would you please remain here for...."

Before the man could finish his sentence, Hugh appeared behind him. "That's her, that's my little girl."

"Daddy! Daddy!" Lizzie ran to Hugh and he picked her up.

Behind him two uniformed policemen, one with blue sergeant's stripes, stood with their arms across their chests.

"This is my daughter. As you can see, my wife has attempted kidnapping." He glared at Julia. "I'm leaving now with Elizabeth."

Julia moved forward, but the first officer blocked her way. "I'm sorry, but they have a warrant."

"But I'm not going to leave my daughter," she said in panic.

"We can't keep you on this ship, Ma'am, but you will have to pick up your belongings before you...."

Hugh appeared again behind the officer. "Please, let me talk to my wife alone."

The officer nodded and backed out of the way.

Hugh closed the door. He opened his eyes wide in anger at Julia and maintained the intensity of his gaze, not moving his head as he spoke, eyes fixed on her. "You stay on this ship. If you attempt to leave, as soon as you are onshore, I will have you arrested and then I will have you declared insane and you will be locked up for the rest of your life. Stay in this room. Don't cross me, Julia. You know I will do it."

Not giving her a chance to reply, Hugh turned around and left, banging the door behind him.

Julia turned the knob, and intended to pull the door open, but then let it go and fell back on a chair in hysterical tears. Her head in her hands, she rocked back and forth, sick and heavy with the knowledge of what she had done. Would she see her little Lizzie ever again?

She wiped the tears from her face and searched the room. Nothing. They had left nothing of Lizzie's. Everything that would remind Julia of her little daughter had been removed.

From outside, the sound of a crowd grew. The ship was getting ready to leave. She stood, wiped her face again, and went to the porthole and she saw the pier below where people were waving to the ship.

She left her stateroom and went out to the Boat Deck filled with passengers waving, but Julia could not get close to the railing and could not see anything beyond them except the high windows of the pier. She fought through to get a glimpse of her Lizzie.

The passengers were saying goodbye, people everywhere, but there was no cheering and exaggerated screaming, no people leaning over the railing to wave a handkerchief or throw a roll of bright red confetti. No band on the pier playing jazzy music.

She remembered when she and Hugh had left on their honeymoon on the *Normandie*, bound for Paris then, too. She felt him at her side, smiling, waving to his sister and parents. Then she shook the image away.

Standing between two people, Julia stood on her toes to see the pier, and caught sight of the policemen and Hugh, carrying Lizzie out beyond the white picket fence. She had a glimpse for one second and then they disappeared around a wall and took Julia's world with them.

Her world now became dizzy, as it seemed the whole wall of the pier shifted to her right, then she understood it was the ship pushing back from the pier. She stood high again, knowing it was in vain, that she would not see anyone down below waving to her. The ship moved past the pier and towards the channel. She stepped out of the way of people leaving the railing and let them pass, then went back and leaned on it, holding the rail tight with both hands, taking in the skyline floating past as in a bad dream, falling ever far away until the Statue of Liberty appeared small, then larger. People gathered again around her, pointing and exclaiming, as they passed the statue, waving to people on the island. Then they broke up in different directions, leaving her, once again, alone.

Julia walked along the railing of the Boat Deck until she reached the end of it, stopped by a gate with a sign that read "Danger: Ship Personnel Only." Beyond the gate were several sailors putting things into a large, square hold using giant cranes that leaned out from a mast. Beyond them lay the open sea, and there was nothing beyond the open sea. She let out a long sigh and all her energy left her.

She walked back along the Boat Deck, lost in her thoughts, oblivious to the people she passed, and entered her stateroom. In the middle of the sitting room on a coffee table was a dish with two sodas on it, one light brown, one pink, with outsized straws sticking out the top, neat white napkins next to them. Julia picked up the chocolate soda and sipped, imagining Elizabeth enjoying the taste. Then she sat in a chair and put her head down, putting her hands over her eyes so that everything was black. After a moment, she sat back up and felt the loneliness creep into her bones.

Next to her on a side table was a telephone and a brochure. She opened it and noted the number for the Communications Office and a short paragraph. How to send a cable.

Chapter 17

Carolyn, Beatrice, New York, 1980

THE TWIN TOWERS of the World Trade Center dominate the lower Manhattan skyline outside Carolyn Stuart's window as the huge DC-10 jetliner circles and then floats down to Idlewild airport. She tells the cab driver to take her to Park Avenue and 85th Street in Manhattan, but then says to go slow along Bushwick and across the Williamsburg Bridge. At first, she sees images of her last days in San Francisco, Marc Silver at the Art Institute, Damian, her mother's severe expression, but then the views of Brooklyn and the first streets of lower Manhattan excite her. As the driver expresses his frustration at the slow mid-town traffic, Carolyn enjoys the beautiful shop windows and the old buildings. The more cars, the more people, the more buildings, the happier she becomes.

On Park and 85th she raised her head up at the red brick building with its high Dutch windows and roof, and wonders why she had never been here in the past. So many times in New York but never in this house.

And there is one other place in New York she will visit this time: her grandmother's grave in the New York City Marble Cemetery on 2nd Street. It is the one personal thing her mother asked her to do. It is the only intimate thing she feels between her mother and herself.

But for now, she gazes up at the tall house, standing by itself on the corner surrounded by huge apartment buildings. Dark green drapes block the windows facing the street. Carolyn hopes to see Beatrice's face peering out, welcoming her. But she doesn't wait, she puts her hand up to knock and the door opens. A smiling face with lustrous green-blue eyes beneath soft, straight, salt and pepper hair greets her.

Beatrice Corbeil holds her arms out and embraces Carolyn, then kisses her on both cheeks and smiles while studying her. "Hello, it has been too long." Beatrice is small, her hair pulled tight behind her head, and her skin smooth and with almost invisible wrinkles around the eyes. A charcoal sweater and a green and brown tartan skirt fit well on her athletically thin body. She steps back for a moment with a little nervous laugh. "You are Carolyn, right?"

Carolyn feels emotions pouring over her that she is unprepared for. She isn't going to cry, but warmth flushes through her body. She didn't know her grandmother or grandfather, and now she's meeting her great aunt. "Of course," she says. "Aunt Beatrice, it's so nice to see you. I feel like I've waited forever."

"You and me both." Beatrice reaches out and takes Carolyn's suitcase. "Oh, here, let me take that for you."

"Oh, no, I can do it."

"I'm stronger than you think, young lady. I get my exercise. We New Yorkers have to walk a lot."

"Thank you." Carolyn feels the warmth of the sympathy Beatrice extends to her.

"Come on, let's use the elevator."

Carolyn smirks. "Oh, I thought we were going to get our exercise."

Beatrice laughs as she closes the elevator door. "Yeah, well, that's for outside. In here, it's the quickest way. Hugh put it in for Mother after her heart attack. I use it when I get lazy." She laughs once more. "Or when I need to haul something upstairs."

At the top, Beatrice drags the suitcase out and lets it stand in the second floor hallway. "Let's leave it here for now and go into the library and eat. When you called from the airport, I ran out to the deli and got a whole bunch of stuff. Can't have you going hungry on your first day in New York."

"That's so very nice of you."

"Oh, no, I'm so excited. Let me see you again. You are beautiful." Beatrice then changes her mind and shakes her head. "You know what, I don't want to stay here. Let's go out to eat."

"But…you said you ran out to the deli already."

"I know, I did, but now that you're here, standing right before me, I'd rather go out with you. *La Donna e mobile*. We'll have so much more fun, and the food will keep."

Carolyn smiles at the reference to opera. "It's fine with me. Either way, I don't want to put you out."

Beatrice puts her hands on Carolyn's shoulders and stares into her eyes. "I'm thrilled you're here. I'm happy to have someone to eat out with as much as I want. So no party pooping from you, okay?"

Carolyn grins. She looks around the hallway as if she expects someone new to come out from a door. "You live here alone?"

"Yes. It's fine with me. For now. I think I'll sell it at some point and make a killing, but for now, with you here, I'm happy where I am. Maybe it's a big house, but it was my childhood home, my father's house, and my grandfather's house. So it has a lot of ghosts. Maybe you will get to know them, too."

"You're kidding, right?"

Beatrice laughs and observes Carolyn with mock intensity. "Kidding? Did your mother say I was eccentric or something?"

"No." Carolyn understands the error of her statement. "But then, maybe there are noises at night."

Beatrice shakes her head. "My grandmother saw ghosts, but then nobody treated her seriously. I mean that it's a house with history. I think your mother's still here and…." Beatrice hesitates and becomes serious. "Her mother, too, but that's a whole other story. Right now my stomach's growling. I haven't time for ghosts. And I have so much to talk to you about. There's a great delicatessen a couple blocks over. A nice short walk."

IN THE DELI on Madison, they sit next to the window with an outsized pastrami sandwich to share.

"I've never been to San Francisco. I'm sure they have good delicatessens." Beatrice takes a large bite and wipes her mouth with her napkin, leaning over the table to keep the crumbs on her plate.

"They're like a sampling of New York delicatessens. David's on Geary is about a quarter of the size of this." Carolyn observes the wall of menu items and the salamis hanging below. "But we have Chicago delicatessens, too, so perhaps more variety."

"I know this one well, being so close to home, but I don't eat much of this stuff, good as it is." Beatrice takes another bite, then continues, "So, tell me, do you know the city?"

Carolyn sits back and stares out the window. An indistinct reflection of the two of them puzzles her, but then a young man with tight jeans and a red tie walks past, and Carolyn sees him as a friendly neighborhood guy. A New Yorker like herself. At least that's what she wants. And hopes she can soon become. She turns back to face Beatrice across the table. "No. I don't. The museums and the theaters. I guess I'm a West Coast person. I know L.A. better."

Beatrice smiles to herself, then says, "That's good for me so I can show you around. I haven't been here long, but I've learned to love this city."

"You grew up here, didn't you? And then you came back?"

Beatrice reaches out and covers the top of Carolyn's hand. "Yes, I did. From Montreal. And there's so much to tell you. Anything you want to know. Ask."

Carolyn turns her hand up and wraps her fingers around her aunt's hand. "I suppose the number one thing is why you and Mother haven't kept in contact."

Beatrice puts her head down and moves her napkin around before she replies. She obviously is wondering how much Carolyn knows of the family history. "You're asking a hard question. There's so much to go over. You know what, you're done, right? It's not a quiet place to talk. Let's go find a charming bar where we can have a little drink and start our long, long conversation."

"Yes, that sounds nice. Thank you for the sandwich." A long, long conversation. Carolyn has waited a long, long time for it.

A SHORT CAB ride later, they sit in a booth in JBird, surrounded by maroon leather and dark wood. No sports screens. When the waiter comes, Beatrice orders single-malt Scotch whiskey for both of them. She notices a slight frown on Carolyn's forehead. "What?"

"It's nothing. My mother likes to drink that."

"Is it a problem?"

"No, but...I'm starting a new life in New York. How about something more... do you have a house specialty?"

He smiles. "Too many to count. May I suggest a quintessential Upper East Side drink? The Manhattan."

"Hmm." Carolyn purses her lips, intently feels the presence of Beatrice, realizing her aunt is at a higher level of sophistication. "Yes, that's about as local as you can get. That would be fine."

"Wait," Beatrice says. "Not a house Manhattan. What do you use?"

"That depends on the customer. I suggest McKenzie Rye. It's from New York, the Finger Lakes region. But you could request Old Overholt, or even Jim Beam rye. If you want a real Manhattan. None of that Canadian stuff."

Beatrice stiffens and feigns annoyance.

The bartender smiles at her. "No offense. Canadian whiskey isn't rye. You can have whatever you want."

Beatrice waits for Carolyn, then says, "It's your decision."

"McKenzie, that sounds right."

The waiter nods in polite deference and leaves the table.

"Well," Carolyn continues, "that was more complicated than I expected."

Beatrice raises her eyebrows, cocks her head and speaks in a conspiratorial tone. "Yes, but you've now become a New Yorker. Everything's more complicated here. And now it's your drink."

Carolyn moves her head from side to side. "I don't think I want to have my own drink. Although it is nice to be able to order something my friends back home never drink." *Back home. I can't wait to say that about New York City.*

"No, you don't have to have your own drink. But you can have one if you want. You know what's nice?" Beatrice didn't wait for Carolyn to answer. "It makes you local already. I didn't know rye was so important for a Manhattan."

The waiter brings their drinks and they each take a sip. Carolyn likes that. Beatrice is treating her like an independent adult. The first person ever to do that. She settles back against the leather and savors the rye whiskey and sweet vermouth. Yes, she thinks, as she watches Beatrice take a drink, a local. East Coast, not West. That's what I want.

"I asked Mother why she never talked to you, but she didn't have an answer."

Beatrice is sympathetic. "I don't think either of us has an answer. For me, you know I lived in Montreal for twenty years, and stayed there even after my husband died five years ago. Then shortly after that, Hugh died and left me the house."

"Mother won't talk to me about it," Carolyn says. She notices once again the bar, the low lights, the mirror, the quietness of it all. As if they were in a protective cocoon. A flush begins in her cheeks from the Manhattan and she feels snug and far away from home but yet beginning to feel like she *is* at home.

"I understand." Beatrice twists her glass, stares into the dark liquid and speaks. "Her father disowned her."

"Do you know why?" Carolyn sees the bartender walk under a bright light. His face reminds her of Damian and a memory intrudes but she sighs and pushes the feeling away.

Beatrice now looks at Carolyn and pauses a moment, to bring her back to the conversation. "Do you not know why?"

A brief sense of embarrassment warms Carolyn at being absent for a second. But the question unearths something else. That her mother has not told her the truth. Or, maybe it's that she, Carolyn, doesn't care enough.

When she replies, her voice is defensive. "Well, yeah, I know she was pregnant with me. Girls get pregnant, but they don't get thrown out. That's kind of old country isn't it? She's a financial wizard like him, you'd think he would appreciate that. Did you ever ask him why?"

Beatrice's face shows that she hears Carolyn's voice as pain and she lowers her own voice and sighs before speaking. "I started to, once. But as soon as I said 'Elizabeth' he became angry and told me never to mention that name again. I did talk to Mrs. Willow, the cook. She said he had never gotten over his wife's...your grandmother's... infidelity. So he took it out on his daughter. Elizabeth's pregnancy—to him it was a bastard child. He despised her for that because to him, Elizabeth did the same thing as Julia."

Carolyn lets those words sink in, then purses her lips for a moment. The word that stands out for her is 'bastard,' but she doesn't feel she can ask about it. It would be too embarrassing again. So she changes the subject from her mother to Beatrice. She leans forward to emphasize her intimacy with her aunt.

"But...you...weren't you friends with her? My grandmother, I mean." Carolyn finds herself drawn in to this web of relations. Friends, mother, grandmother. New York, great aunt. It slowly dawns on her that she has a family she's never known or cared about. She moves her hand toward Beatrice.

Beatrice observes Carolyn's hand and shrugs, but her voice softens more. She is also learning to adapt to a new relationship. For a second time she puts her hand on Carolyn's. "I can't say I knew her well. I had left for Montreal before Hugh married her."

"Hugh...my grandfather?"

Beatrice frowns. "Yes, Hugh. Did you not know much about him? Apart from finance, I mean."

"No, of course, yes, I was sort of repeating after you. That's all I know, he was rich. I don't know anything personal about him."

Beatrice widens her eyes and cocks her head. "I was beginning to wonder how much Elizabeth has told you. You can indeed learn some things about your family from me. I'm sorry it has to be this way, sorry for you, but it'll help you and me become closer. So, for now, it's good."

"See, I'm asking about my mother and her father, and a minute ago you were talking about my grandmother. She's to me...a blank. My mother was three or four when her mother died. She didn't know her at all." Carolyn shrinks back against the booth and inside herself.

"What is it?" Beatrice whispers.

Carolyn speaks as if to herself or to someone far away. "Oh, it's that I'm supposed to see my grandmother's grave while I'm here. My mother says it's the one thing she has left of herself in New York."

Beatrice smiles and raises her voice to get Carolyn's attention. "Hey, not any more. Now she's got two of us."

Carolyn stifles a yawn, but feels guilty interrupting the conversation.

"Mon Dieu," Beatrice says. "Come on. I'm keeping you up."

"No, it's okay, I'm on West Coast time."

"Maybe, but you've had a long day." Beatrice widens her eyes. "You need a rest. Let's get you home."

Home. The word bypasses Carolyn's brain and goes straight to her heart. She's been thinking of this as home, but now she hears it out loud. She watches Beatrice as she says in a quiet voice, "Home. Wow."

WHEN THEY ARRIVE back, Beatrice opens the door. "Come on, it's getting chilly out there."

"Aren't you kind of lonely here? This whole house all by yourself?"

Beatrice moves her head around the foyer, turns her mouth down and shakes her head a little in thought before she smiles at Carolyn. "Oh, no. I like being by myself at night. I have a lady, Anna, who is here every other day. And I pay the doorman at the building next door to watch this house. Fred. A big bruiser. He'll stroll down the street every once in a while." She puts her arm around Carolyn. "Let's go up and I'll show you to your room. I'll show you the whole house tomorrow, after you've had a good night's rest."

They walk up the stairs to the hallway and into a room. "This was my mother's room."

"Grace?"

"Yes. Hugh didn't change anything, and I've left it that way, too." Beatrice turns to leave. "I don't want to keep you up. We have so much time to talk about all this." She puts both hands on her cheeks. "Oh, you know what, you should phone your mother and let her know you got in all right."

Carolyn waves it off. "She's fine. I'll call her sometime tomorrow. There's no rush."

Beatrice frowns. "You sure? It's a phone call."

"No, thank you, it can wait." My mother can wait a long time.

"All right, well, I'm next door if you need anything."

"I'll ask any passing ghost."

Beatrice laughs. "There are no noises in this house. You'll sleep like a baby." She embraces Carolyn, pulls her in tight, and hugs her for several seconds. Then she steps back and lays the back of her hand on Carolyn's cheek. "Welcome to New York. Welcome to your home."

"Thank you," Carolyn calls as Beatrice walks out the door.

Beatrice stops and turns back. "Your mother loves you deeply, you know."

Carolyn hesitates and puts her arms across her chest. "I appreciate what you say, Aunt Beatrice. But sometimes people have to show their love." She walks to her aunt and kisses her on the cheek. "Maybe like you do."

"We have a lot to talk about, Young Lady. Good night. And skip the aunt stuff. I've always been Beatrice. Maybe because in Montréal it was always Béatrice," she says, emphasizing the French accent as she closes the door.

Carolyn empties her suitcase and sits on the bed. She eyes the elegant white French-looking telephone on the ornate desk and senses a pull to call her mother. But she resists. Not yet. When I'm settled in, I know a bit more about this house, and I'm more in control. When I'm…but she lets it go and goes to bed and imagines the deli and the bistro until she falls asleep.

Chapter 18

THE NEXT MORNING, Carolyn awakes to a quiet house. She gets out of bed, puts on a beautiful white terrycloth bathrobe she finds in the closet, and goes out to the hallway. She knows only her own room, the hallway immediately outside it, and the stairway down to the front door. In contrast to the evening before, the doors on this floor are open, inviting her to explore. She turns left and glances in the first door.

A library with light wood paneling and a grand fireplace invites her in. A man who might have been J.P. Morgan or Andrew Carnegie hangs in majesty over the mantelpiece. Carolyn steps in to see the painting, to see the name, assuming it was one of the Stuart ancestors, but there isn't any. She studies the face, wanting to find herself, but can't see a resemblance. A sense of being lost comes over her, as if she were entering a maze with no hope of finding a way to get out the other side. Or of finding her way back. For a moment, she's lost in this room in her new home.

The background of the portrait doesn't tell her if it might be her grandfather or great-grandfather. The look isn't of something older than that. Her mother's father? The one who threw her out of this house?

Books line the walls of the room. Some have gilt lettering and designs, and might be first editions. Carolyn is very impressed that someone in this house was interested in more than stock markets and art as investment. She leaves them for later inspection. Rectangular empty spaces on the wall glare at her. Art that was worth too much to keep. A small blond Baldwin grand piano stands in the corner.

"Good morning." Beatrice's voice comes from behind. "I hope you slept well. "

"Yes, I did, thank you, Aunt…," Carolyn stops when Beatrice cocks her head, although she keeps smiling, "sorry…Beatrice…I'll get the hang of it."

Beatrice carries a tray of coffee with small pastries on it. "Here's something to wake you up. Then we'll go downtown. I have two treats for you. We'll have lunch at Windows on the World at the top of the World Trade Center, and then we'll descend to the 4th basement of the Empire State Building for a choral rehearsal."

"Oh, that sounds marvelous. You're going all out for me."

"Because you're going all out for me, Carolyn. You've travelled across the country. Sit down and have some coffee. You do drink coffee, don't you? I never asked whether you're one of those, ah, natural type of people."

"Oh, no, not me. I have my own drink, remember."

Beatrice laughs. "That's right. With New York rye. That's not quite vegan."

Carolyn gestures to the painting. "Who is that?"

Beatrice puts the tray down and hands Carolyn a cup of coffee. She points to the pastries. "If you're hungry. Myself, I'll wait for lunch." Then she remembers that Carolyn doesn't know the painting on the wall. "That is my father, and Hugh's, of course, George Randolph Stuart." Turning to Carolyn, she continues, "Your great-grandfather. He started the family fortune back at the turn of the century. Some kind of commodities baron. I guess. I never cared to know. He was never home. Not for me. Not even for a birthday."

Carolyn feels the pain in Beatrice's voice. "I'm sorry."

"Well, he was home every day, in the morning, at the table, reading the paper, not even noticing me, and then once in a while he'd come back long after I'd been shuffled off to bed." Beatrice sighs and waves her thoughts away. "But that's all in the past. Life goes on. What's important is that we don't know what the future holds."

"I'm sorry you had a childhood like that. But also, I'm sorry I never met your husband," Carolyn says. "I know that's in the past, too, but I wish I could have known him."

"Thank you. I'm grateful for what we had. We couldn't have children, but I have known true love in this life, and that's all I ask for. It more than makes up for my father."

"Will you tell me about him? Your husband, I mean."

Beatrice withdraws for a moment, inside, remembering, her eyes starting to mist. "Pierre was so handsome. And fun. We did everything together. A man who will go shopping with you, that's a treasure. He worked for the CBC."

"The CBC?"

"Oh, my dear, you *are* from the West Coast. Canadian Broadcasting Company. He was a producer."

"Can I ask you what happened?"

"Yes. But I don't want to go into it. It was quick. He went to the doctor and three months later he was gone."

"I'm so sorry. So fast. But you had forty years with him."

"Almost that many. Carolyn, I'm grateful for all the years we had. That's all anyone can ever ask. I mourned for him. I will always mourn for him. I think he will always be with me. And I'm so grateful now that I have you. And Elizabeth. You know, my husband died five years ago. I would have stayed in Montreal if my brother hadn't left me this house. I rent out our place up there."

"You still have a home in Montreal?"

"An apartment, not a house. On the Ile des Soeurs. It's on the St. Lawrence River." Beatrice pauses in reverie, then comes back.

"I used to go for wonderful long walks. I sold our home on the Plateau. It was too big for me alone."

"You must've had a lot of friends up there. It must be lonely coming here."

"Yes, you're right. But I had to come here to kind of relive everything. Even the ghosts. I've lived in two worlds."

"Beatrice, this house, it must be bigger than the one you had in Montreal."

Beatrice laughs. "That's true, yes. And I won't stay here. Someday, I will sell it and find someplace...I was going to say smaller, but I don't care about that. Maybe a neighborhood that has less money and more character. That's my project for the next few months. To explore this city and find my neighborhood. Maybe you could help me."

Carolyn nods in agreement, but not with enthusiasm.

Beatrice waves her hand. "Oh, I didn't mean to drag you wholesale into my world."

"No, I didn't mean to sound like...I mean I don't know the city so I wouldn't be any help to you."

"And you have your own agenda." Beatrice stood. "Why don't we talk about that downtown?" She picked up her dishes and says, "Have you called your mother?"

Carolyn remains quiet.

"Oh, okay, I'll let it go."

They put the dishes away and left for the World Trade Center.

ON THE 106TH FLOOR, the young waiter with black hair combed back on his head seated them in the small table next to the huge window.

"Have you been here before?" Beatrice asks as she unfolds her napkin.

"No, I haven't. It's a real thrill for me. We did, a bunch of us from school, go up to the observation platform. But to sit down to lunch with a view of the two bridges...that's Williamsburg and the Brooklyn Bridge, right?"

Beatrice scans the world below. "Uh-huh. Another view of your new world."

"My new world." Carolyn studies the world down below and wonders where her new world will finally be. "I don't even know where I will live."

"Oh, no, you will live with me. The longer you stay with me, the longer I delay selling it." Beatrice hesitates, to get Carolyn's attention. "The real question is what you are going to do now."

"Now."

"Yes, of course. Your next move in New York. Your first move. I understand you're here to interview at NYU. That's what your mother told me. Is that what you have in mind?"

The question forces Carolyn to glance out the window once more, as if that will anchor her response in the real world. But nothing down there tells her what to say. "My mother. Yes. I have the name of someone at the NYU School of Business."

"Graduate school, I presume. You already have a BFA, don't you?"

The waiter comes by to deliver water and bread and take their orders. They haven't thought about it. "Is this your first time here?"

Beatrice answers for them. "No."

"May I suggest the World View of Seafood? Oysters, lobster, periwinkles?"

"Oysters...from where?" Beatrice says.

"Any coast you like. Chesapeake, Long Island, Puget Sound."

"Chesapeake," she says.

"What are periwinkles?" Carolyn says.

"They are sea snails. Delicious. I recommend them."

Carolyn and Beatrice exchange glances and agree.

"Sounds great," Beatrice says.

"And wine?"

"We'll take your suggestion," she says.

"I can call the sommelier if you like."

"Oh no," she says, "no need to get complicated. Why don't you bring us a couple of glasses of good white wine?"

The waiter nods condescendingly, even though he doesn't know who they are. "Chenin blanc or pinot grigio? A Riesling perhaps?" Trying to ferret out their ignorance.

Beatrice defers to Carolyn, who says, "I'd like the pinot." Knowing enough to not have to say 'grigio', she waits for a reaction from Beatrice, who just smiles and gives a little wiggle of her head. "Two glasses of that."

"I'll be right back."

Beatrice continues their conversation. "So, where were we before he interrupted us? Ah...NYU."

"NYU. My mother knows someone there. I have to set up a meeting. I have a name, but as you can tell, I'm not in a big hurry."

Beatrice tightens her lips. "It's not me that needs you to be in a hurry. A meeting. With whom?"

Carolyn sits, quiet, not knowing what to say. "To be honest, I don't know. Somebody. Somebody in their admissions office, or...I don't know."

"You must have some sort of expectation."

"That's it. I know I can't breeze into an MBA program. God that would be awful anyway. So, I guess they've worked out something. Mother's been a big enough contributor, or at least she is now, that they'll find a spot for me. Some special program. Whether I like it or not."

"It sounds as if you don't like it."

The words struck home. "Yes, that's it in a nutshell." She doesn't say that it's been a long time since she'd given it any thought at all.

The wine arrives. Beatrice holds up her glass for a toast. "No matter what, here's to you being in New York."

Carolyn clinks her glass against Beatrice's. "Thank you. Here's to meeting you. And here's to the future."

They drink their first sips of wine in silence.

"To the future," Beatrice says. "To yours. You're young, Carolyn. You don't know what life is about. You don't know what you want."

That stings. Carolyn puts her glass down. It sounds too much like words she's heard from her mother. "I do know what I want."

"Well, yes, you wanted to get an MFA at Berkeley, I know that much. But that path isn't open to you now."

Carolyn can't believe...or won't accept...what she hears. She has an instantaneous desire to stand and leave, but she catches herself and takes a deep breath.

Beatrice holds a hand up and frowns. "Sorry, you're pretty sensitive about it. I don't want to butt in where I'm not wanted."

Carolyn sighs. "No, I don't...."

The waiter appears with a plate of shellfish and salad, red, green, yellow pieces. He clears a place and puts it down between them and gives them each a plate.

Beatrice takes a small oyster fork and makes a delicate stab at one of the oysters. "Umm, look, it's fresh." She picks up the oyster, opens her mouth and lets it slide down her throat. "Delicious. Come on, dive in."

Carolyn, grateful for the interruption, takes a piece of lobster and dips it in clarified butter.

"I think we'll eat off the big plate," Beatrice says, speaking in a low voice, inviting Carolyn to be conspiratorial.

"Suits me. I agree it's delicious. I think I'm brave enough to eat a periwinkle." She takes one of the small snails and uses her oyster fork to pick it out of the shell. "More butter." She dips the snail in the butter and puts it in her mouth, then closes her eyes and chews and swallows in a hurry. "Okay," she says. "Not bad. Better than escargot, I think."

136

They finish their lunch, talking only about the quality of the seafood, pay, and leave for their next appointment.

CAROLYN MARVELS at the huge aluminum and gold mural in the lobby of the Empire State Building. Beatrice arranges for their passes and they take the elevator four floors down.

Outside the elevator Carolyn laughs and points to the exposed pipes and wiring of the hallway ceiling. "Oh, that doesn't give me a comfortable feeling."

They stand before doors labeled "King's College."

"It's in here," Beatrice says. She opens the door and ushers Carolyn inside a large musical practice space with a dozen folding chairs. A low stage with two narrow elevated platforms stands empty with several music stands haphazardly strewn about.

They sit in the chairs in the middle of the room and wait.

Carolyn frowns at Beatrice, who leans over and whispers, "Be patient."

Carolyn is patient and her reward is a full hour of rehearsal for an American folk song recital later in the month. No one else comes in to hear the choir. After hearing *Shenandoah*, *Deep River*, and John Corigliano's *Dylan Thomas Trilogy*, they applaud, sounding foolish with their meager sound.

The conductor turns around. "Thank you," he says, as he half smiles half grins at them. "And you are…."

"My friends," comes a woman's voice from the back of the choir.

"So, Jenny, why don't you introduce them?"

Jenny stands. She has a huge head of light brown hair. "This is my friend Beatrice, from Montreal, on the right. The other person is…."

Beatrice puts her arm around Carolyn's shoulder. "My niece, Carolyn, from San Francisco."

A whoop sounds from somewhere else in the choir.

The conductor laughs. "They're coming out of the woodwork."

Jenny moves in little snake steps around the choir members and comes over and shakes Beatrice's hand, then twists to Carolyn. "It's nice to meet you. Maybe we'll get together again. But right now, I've got to get back to work."

"Oh, sure," Carolyn says.

"We're off," Beatrice says. "And thanks for the invitation."

"Sorry you have to leave," Jenny says.

Beatrice and Carolyn make their way up to the lobby.

"Thank you so much," Carolyn says. "Two treats in a row. You sure know how to show a girl a good time."

"We're not done yet." Beatrice hails a cab. "We're off again to uptown."

"The cloistersum," she says to the cab driver.

As they make their way north, Carolyn says to Beatrice, "You don't have to do all this for me, you know."

"Do you object to me doing it?" Beatrice touches Carolyn's forearm.

Carolyn feels ashamed of her mistake. "No, it's wonderful. I'm having a great time. It's all a whirlwind on my second day in New York."

"That's right. For me, too. Because you are my family, now, Carolyn." Beatrice moves her hand to Carolyn's upper arm, holds it there for a second as she says, "Do you know how amazing that is?"

Carolyn folds her hands together and holds them up in a gesture of joy. "Yes, I do. It's a total surprise for me. A month ago I was...it's that...at this rate...we'll have done all of New York in a week."

"No, I'm starting you off. We have one more thing to do today."

"What's that?"

"We're going to see a marvelous tapestry, *The Hunt of the Unicorn*."

"Oh, I've never seen that. How did you know?"

"Maybe your mother knows a bit more about you than you think."

Mother. Carolyn pulls her arms in tight.

"Oh-oh, there I go again," Beatrice says. "I suppose you still haven't called her yet?"

"And when did I have time to do that?" Carolyn laughs.

"I thought you might have done it before you came in for breakfast this morning."

"No. And she hasn't called yet, either. It suits me fine." Carolyn stares out the window at the gray waters of the Hudson River.

"Gee, I keep getting on your wrong side."

Carolyn shows a serious face. "It's not my wrong side." She keeps to herself for a moment, then says, "Yeah, it is. But it's because I haven't figured out my right side yet." She raises her eyebrows. "Maybe you'll help me do that."

Beatrice's eyes sparkle at the last few words, and her mouth widens a little. "Help you? Do you mean that?"

"I do, yes."

Beatrice turns to face Carolyn and put her hand back on her arm. "Okay, I think we're on our way."

AT THE CLOISTERS, a young man meets them as they put their coats away and introduces himself with a Scottish accent as Gillian Macdonald, a graduate student working on *The Hunt of the Unicorn*. He spends an hour with them, explaining the heritage of the tapestries, the intricacies of the weaving, the connections with Stirling Castle in Scotland and *The Lady and the Unicorn* at the Cluny Museum in Paris. At the end, he presents each of them a foot-high porcelain unicorn made by Royal Doulton.

Chapter 19

WHEN THEY ARRIVE home, exhausted, they put both their unicorns on the mantelpiece in the library and admire them, impressed with their good fortune.

Carolyn plops down on the brown leather sofa in an exaggerated display of tiredness. "I can't thank you enough. You are amazing, Beatrice."

"Let's not take this too far. I haven't enjoyed myself this much since…," she glances up at the ceiling, "you know, since I left Montreal. How about a drink before dinner?" Beatrice walks over to the corner cabinet. "Can't make your own Manhattan, but anything else I've got." She pulls a panel door open and flicks a switch to reveal backlit cabinet shelves with bottles of red, green, yellow, light brown, and dark brown liquid.

"You know what, maybe something pretty light. I'm hungry right now."

"Yeah," Beatrice says, "how about we bring up yesterday's deli stuff?"

"Sounds great to me."

They go downstairs, heat the platters of paninis and vegetables and bring them up to the library table. "Why don't you look in the small refrigerator," Beatrice says as she walks toward the door. "Find some good beer. I'll get plates."

"Terrific," Carolyn says, jumping up with renewed energy. She opens the door of the refrigerator and finds several bottles of Péché

Mortel. They make her laugh. "What? Mortal Sin?" She takes two and opens them.

When Beatrice comes back with plates, Carolyn holds up the beer bottles and makes a funny face. "Where'd you get this?"

"Oh, I have a whole case of it. From Montreal. Makes me feel close to Phillip."

They both sit on the sofa and eat their dinner.

"This is good," Carolyn says. "Especially for leftovers."

"More like day old donuts, but it's still good."

"Oh no, not like day old donuts at all. It's too high class for that. It's more like the day after Thanksgiving to me. And a Montreal beer!"

Beatrice smiles awkwardly as she chews, then says, "Still good, I agree. This food makes me think of the delis in Montreal."

"Montreal, that doesn't seem like a deli kind of city."

"Oh, but it is, because it's a mix of Quebec and Ontario, French and English, and a great Jewish population."

"Yeah, like New York," Carolyn says. "Speaking of which, I think this has been the most cultured day of my life."

Beatrice sits back and sighs, wipes food particles off her hands, and sips her beer. "For me, too. I wanted you to see what I like about New York, Carolyn. It's the city that never stops. I miss Montreal, but there isn't the music, the art, the films...the everything. Not like New York. You couldn't have chosen a better place to land and try your luck."

Carolyn sighs. "My luck. I'm not in a big hurry to try for it. Not yet." She stands and walks around the room. "Not to change the subject, but it kind of seems like there are empty places on the wall for paintings."

Beatrice's voice carries a strong note of sadness. "I remember paintings. Here, and in father's office. And in Elizabeth's room down the hall."

Carolyn turns her head when she hears her mother's name. "Elizabeth? My mother?" She knows when she says it that she's showing Beatrice how ambivalent she is about her mother.

Beatrice stood. "Come with me," she says as she walks out to the hallway. "I promised to give you a tour and I forgot."

Carolyn follows her to the next door and walks in when Beatrice holds the door open for her. The paneled room is dark, the curtains closed. Beatrice flicks the light switch and the rich dark wood of the walls, the chairs and the desk blend into a wave of browns as the room comes into focus.

"See," Beatrice says, "this was his office. There were paintings here, too. But, in the last days, they were all gone. Sold. He had cash flow problems. I think it's what killed him." She runs her hand over the desk. "Mother said he put all his and her money into gold, then made real estate mistakes, then he couldn't sell the gold fast enough. Because of the war. It was in Switzerland."

"But that was long before he disowned my mother because of me."

Beatrice faces Carolyn and speaks with a sharp tone, shaking her head. "He didn't disown your mother because of you. It was because of your grandmother. To him, Elizabeth betrayed him as her mother had."

Carolyn's voice becomes sheepish. "I know what you're saying, but still…."

"You're changing the subject. We were talking about money."

"Sorry."

"That's okay, we need to talk more about that, too. I think I'm going to be your family historian. Anyway, it's true, his financial problems started way before you came along. It meant he didn't have enough to fall back on. He lost the real estate and began speculating in the stock market." Beatrice stops for a moment, puts her arms across her chest, absorbed. When she speaks again, her eyes are moist. "He did well for a long time, but he lost so much in the downturn of 1960. That's when he began selling the paintings."

"He had valuable paintings?"

"Oh yes. How about Degas. Toulouse-Lautrec. Ostade."

Carolyn remembers back to her last art history class at Mills. "Ostade? That wouldn't be so valuable, would it?"

"Oh, don't get all art-dealer on me. They lasted a year maybe, and then they were all gone, sold. My point is, the empty spaces on the wall show you where they were, his last chance, and then, not long after your mother went back to California, he kind of gave up. Mother had died a year before, and then Elizabeth broke his heart."

"Broke his heart?"

Beatrice sits in the chair behind the desk. "I see I'm going to have a hard time with you. When he talked to me, yes, his heart was broken."

Carolyn takes one of the ornate chairs in front of the desk. "A broken heart. I never heard that from Mother."

"Look," Beatrice says, leaning forward and putting her arms on the desk, "your mother, as far as I know, went back to Stanford and made her own way in the world. She is successful. She did it on her own. And you're right, it wasn't she who broke my brother's heart. It was her mother. But Elizabeth, she, well, yes, she kind of broke it again. I'm just telling you what I saw happen from Hugh's perspective. I'm not blaming or defending."

Carolyn stands, puts her hands behind her back, and turns to survey the room, taking time to let it all sink in, then says, "You're saying my grandmother, Julia, broke his heart."

"Oh, Carolyn, I'm saying that when he talked to me, after Elizabeth left, his heart was broken. Do we care to try and think through all the details? I don't want to. Sure, I want to help you understand, but I don't want to relive all that heartbreak. It was terrible talking to my mother and brother all those years. Pierre used to tell me I was fortunate to be living in Canada, away from all this."

Carolyn purses her lips and thinks for a moment. "You and I have different views on all this. I was always on the outside and far away. But you, you were here."

Beatrice shakes her head. "No, you're wrong. I wasn't here. I was in Montreal, married, living a different life. For me, everything happened on the phone. After the fact. Come on, let me show you Elizabeth's room."

They walk down the hall. When they enter, the room disappoints Carolyn. It's a large room but there's only a simple bed and a nightstand with a plain lamp on it, a small desk with a chair and another plain lamp.

"What's wrong?" Beatrice asks.

"Oh, I don't know. Funny, I was expecting a little girls' room, but that's not what it is at all. It's a...a... college girl, maybe a high school girl's room. You know, might not even be a girl's room. A big room with little in it. Not like the other rooms I've seen." She opens the drawer in the desk, and finds a cup with a Trinity School logo. She picks it up and turns it around.

Beatrice smiles. "Ah, Trinity School. We all went there, Hugh, myself, Elizabeth."

"Where is it?"

"Upper West Side."

"It's still there?"

Beatrice laughs. "What do you mean? Of course it's still here. Why would you ever ask that?"

Carolyn laughs, too. "Sorry. It's that I automatically think that about my mother...that there's nothing to relate to. You know, like Gertrude Stein, there's no there there."

"Yeah, I understand, more than you know. You know what I think? When Elizabeth left, she of course took anything that made it personal to her, and the room hasn't been used since. Nobody has paid any attention to it."

Carolyn thinks to herself for half a minute as she surveys the room. She slides gracefully to the window and pulls back the dark red drapes. "A nice view of Park Avenue," she says.

"Yes. This was my room before it was Elizabeth's. I remember waiting, staring out this window, waiting for a ticker tape parade. But it never came. It was two blocks over on Fifth Avenue." She chuckles to herself.

"Beatrice," Carolyn stops for a moment, then says, "Do you think he kept it this way for my mother, for Elizabeth his daughter?" That's what Carolyn wants to believe. Something that seems to make her mother and grandfather closer together.

"To be honest, I don't know. If you want to think of it that way, that's fine with me."

"But you don't think so."

"I would say I never thought about it. It's pure speculation. Or wishful thinking."

"Thank you, Beatrice, anyway, for showing me this. Remember, yesterday, you spoke of this being my home. Now I'm beginning to feel a little bit like it's...um...like I *am* at home." She puts her arms around Beatrice and holds her tight. "Thank you for welcoming me."

Beatrice's eyes gleam. "I'm so happy you came. I think we both are going to gain from this. And speaking of your mother..." She raises her eyebrows.

Carolyn frowns. "No. Not yet."

"You're so conflicted. You seem to want to know all about your mother...and the rest of your family...but you don't want to call home. She's the closest family you've got."

"I know, but, I'm not ready to call her yet. This is my new home."

"You know what I mean, Carolyn. You have to call her up at some point. Don't you think she's worried about you?"

"Worried? No, I don't. She's worried about J. P. Morgan and Goldman Sachs."

"Oh, come on, that can't be true. The reason you're here is because she sent you. That makes her pretty wonderful in my estimation."

"All right, yes, I see that side of it. And I haven't forgotten it, either. But I'm not ready. I don't want to talk to her when all I've learned is that there's a cup in a drawer from high school."

Beatrice sighs. "Hey, it's your second day in town. I don't mean to rush you."

"Thank you." Carolyn yawns.

"Know what," Beatrice says, "I kind of assumed you'd have something lined up like your mother spoke of, some interview at NYU or...but you don't seem in a hurry. Which is fine with me, and I won't push the point. Why don't you settle down for the night, and I'll put the dishes away."

"Thank you again. But I'll help you with the dishes. I'd rather, if you don't mind."

"Good."

THE NEXT MORNING, Carolyn awakes, takes a shower, and steps lightly down the stairs when she hears familiar sounds coming from a room she'd seen when she first entered the house. Beatrice is finishing a table setting for the two of them.

Beatrice smiles when she sees Carolyn turn the corner around the banister and come toward the room. "Good Morning! I thought we'd have a couple of croissants and then be off."

"Be off? Again? Really?"

"Yeah, can't stay home when I've got a traveling companion with me. I had a friend sneak us a couple of free tickets to a rehearsal at the Met. *Lulu*, with Julia Migenes. I could have told you all this in advance, but it's more fun this way."

"*Lulu?*"

"You don't know it? Oh, I'm sorry. I didn't mean to talk that way. You're into art, not music. I've heard it once. But I don't want to pass up a chance. Not when it's for free, and fits for our time together, you and me. It's Alban Berg. Pretty modern, I hope you don't mind."

"Mind? Of course, I don't mind. But you're right. I don't know opera well. And not modern pieces. I get the feeling you're not going to quit until I'm educated."

"Oh, don't think of it that way. It's not education, it's you and me in New York. Anybody can go see Puccini, but this is challenging."

"I'm up for it. I think."

"It's modern music, not that saccharin Italian stuff."

"You don't like Italian opera? How can that be?"

Beatrice rolls her eyes. "I can see, it's good you left the small town and came to a metropolis. You need to hone your satirical skills. Of course, I love Puccini, Rossini, and Donizetti. I cry every time I hear the fat girl dying in *La Bohème*, or that poor Japanese girl having the lieutenant's baby. I'm surprised you've never heard of *Lulu*, though."

"No, I did. I've heard of it. I'm sure in one of my classes. But I haven't gone much to the opera. I did see *La Bohème* with some friends at the Orpheum in San Francisco. And, yeah, we went to *Madame Butterfly* at the San Francisco Opera. That's about it. I'm not the crying kind, I think. Got that from my mother. The problem is, you have to wait too long between arias."

"Right. But this is different. *Lulu*, wow! It's degenerate. It's like punk rock for opera. You may not like it, but it'll up your sophistication for sure."

Chapter 20

FOUR HOURS LATER, Beatrice and Carolyn arrive home from Lincoln Center.

Relaxing on the sofa in the library with a Coke, Carolyn waves her head back and forth. "Amazing. What an opera! Death at the hand of Jack the Ripper. That's better than the devil."

"I see you liked it." Beatrice is happy.

"I'm not sure yet I like the music." She focuses her eyes on nowhere in front of her with a puzzled look. "That may take some time. But the story, it's…it's…more than amazing. It's a movie. A gangster movie. I never thought that music…an opera…could…convey the same thing. I think it showed her feeling more than any classical opera could." She wrinkles up her face in a sneer. "It kind of makes me sick." Carolyn leans back as if exhausted.

Beatrice stares at this transformation. She lets her hands fall on her lap.

Carolyn turns to Beatrice with a smile. "I think I can't thank you enough. This has been a learning experience I didn't think I would ever have."

"I'm not sure what you mean." Her eyes squint, with an impish gleam.

Carolyn stands and moves with the drink in one hand and gestures with the other, as if she's lecturing. "What I mean is…." She stops moving. "That…I didn't expect…." She turns to Beatrice and catches her attention. "I didn't expect to learn so much from music."

She sits in an easy chair and places a hand on one of the arms, balances the drink with the other. "This was a nasty story, you know."

Beatrice nods and smiles knowingly. "Uh-huh."

"Well, it meant I paid more attention. I've seen bloody Shakespeare, but I've always avoided chainsaw massacre movies. This was so different. The high art kind of sucked up the blood and guts and made them…I don't know what. I'm not sure what I know any more."

Carolyn's eyes become heavy. She puts the drink down on the table and returns to the chair, feels comfortable, and warm, and lets herself fall into an easy blank state.

WHEN SHE OPENS her eyes, a green and brown afghan covers her, dark yellow light bathes the room, and everything is quiet. Through the open door, she sees it is late afternoon or evening. She remains in the moment of the silence and the stillness and then drifts off again into sleep.

A nudge on her shoulder wakens her, still in the chair, still warm. Beatrice's face hovers over her. "How're you doing, sweetheart?"

Sweetheart? Carolyn stares with sleepy eyes at Beatrice.

"Oh, sorry, didn't mean to get sentimental. That came out from the past, I'm sure." Beatrice smiles. "But you were so peaceful. Beautiful. Like a little girl."

Carolyn pushes the afghan off and rubs her eyes. "No, I'm sorry. I didn't mean to doze off."

"Do you want to sleep some more?"

Carolyn searches the room, trying to figure out what she feels like. "No. Not at all. That was…what I needed…I think."

"Good. Then go freshen up. We're going to Madison Square Garden."

Carolyn sits up at the news then stands. "What? Tonight?"

"We don't have to, if you don't want to."

"Are you kidding? I'm up for anything. I meant…oh, I don't know what I meant. Still sleepy. It won't take long. Let me get ready."

"Good. We'll eat there. You'll like it. I hope."

"Oh, yes, anything, you've been marvelous Aunt… oops, sorry. Beatrice. I'm still in a daze, I think. I've been here one day, and already

I feel like a New Yorker. And I didn't think there was anything more to see in the city. But I trust you. It'll be fun."

AN HOUR LATER, Carolyn steps out of the cab in front of the Garden and sees the marquee and laughs. "Oh my god. Hockey? I've never seen a hockey game. This is a surprise."

"Yeah, I know. I'm not a great hockey fan, but...my husband was... so I kind of like to go when the Canadiens are here. And I pay for good seats, I can't stand sitting way up high."

They muscle their way into the arena and down to their seats close to the glass. Carolyn finds herself facing huge men in front of the glass and people surrounding her speaking French. "Wow!" she says, laughing, to Beatrice. "Big guys. And we need that glass?" She can barely hear herself speak with the noise of the arena.

Beatrice leans over. "Yeah," she says, cupping her hands over Carolyn's ears. "Hockey players have to be brutal. The puck would kill you if it hit you in the head."

"Oh my gosh!"

"Don't worry, we're safe."

A large man with a full day's beard leans in and in slow motion bumps Beatrice on the shoulder. "'Allo, ma Cherie. C'est longtemps."

Beatrice stands and hugs the man. They carry on an animated conversation in French, then Beatrice introduces Carolyn.

"This is my niece from San Francisco."

"Okay, mes amis," he says, "why don't you join us after the game. We're going to go to Frontenac, down in the Village. It's been a long time, Béatrice. I didn't know you were in New York. Did you come down for the game? We could have come together, you know."

"No, I live here now, Alain."

"Well, I see they are getting ready to play. Will you come down to the Village with us?"

"I know the Frontenac. We'll be there."

"Bien alors. Au revoir."

"Au revoir," says Carolyn.

When he has left, Beatrice turns to Carolyn. "How's your French?"

"Not bad. I did spend half a year in Paris in school. But it's been a while and I haven't had a chance to speak it."

"Not to worry, these guys all half speak English anyway. Montreal is not like Quebec. Oh!"

The crowd roars as the puck misses the goal. Two players grapple with each other inside the window and cries erupt around them of "Allez! Frappez!"

One of the Montreal players slams into the window in front of them and Carolyn jumps and holds on tight to Beatrice. "My god, they're killing him."

Beatrice laughs. "Exciting, no?"

"Do you go often?"

"No, like I said, when the Canadiens are in town and I'm not busy. It keeps Pierre close to me. We had season tickets in Montreal. I suppose you like football?"

"Me? No. Nothing about sports. Mills didn't do much. Tennis and swimming, but I'm not athletic. So this is my first professional game and it's...well, it's...gruesome."

"Yeah, hockey is an acquired taste."

TWO HOURS LATER, they step out of a taxi in the West Village and enter Chateau Frontenac. An oversized black and white photo of the chateau above Quebec City dominates the room. An animated conversation in French comes from one corner of the room, attracting Carolyn's attention, and she recognizes Alain from the game.

He sees them and motions them over, then introduces them to the small group. Carolyn stands next to a young man who appears to be the same age. She is impressed with how well her French holds up, how easy it flows.

"You are all from Quebec?" she says to the man who had introduced himself as Robert.

Robert has a dazzling smile underneath his unruly black hair. His eyes are a clear light lustrous brown. "Quebec is a big place. I don't know everyone. I know Alain. He works for a Canadian film company."

"Are you in films? I almost said 'the movies' in English."

"Sort of. I am a filmmaker, yes. But I am making my own small film here in New York. Alain is helping me with production ideas. He invited me here tonight, and then he shows up with all these hockey fans, so I haven't had a chance to talk to him."

"You weren't at the game?"

"Me? Hockey? I'm not into ice sports, or any sports particularly. Are you?"

"No, I've never been to a game. My aunt invited me. It is exciting, for sure. But to be honest, I don't mind the violence, I was surprised at myself. It's hard to follow the action, it all happens so fast."

"I agree with you." He picks up his drink and motions her to follow him to a table away from the group.

Carolyn follows him and sits down, taking her coat off. "What kind of film are you making?"

"Do you know the film *The Last Metro*? It's the latest film by François Truffaut?"

"No, I don't. But I know Truffaut. Maybe that's too strong. *Day For Night*, I've seen. We studied it in film class. And *Jules and Jim*, that's pretty famous. And don't forget *Fahrenheit 451*."

"Of course, but there you see, *Fahrenheit 451* is a book from Ray Bradbury, and Truffaut didn't write the book, just the screenplay. I want to write and direct."

"You are going way beyond me, Robert. I see your point about creating everything from scratch…."

"No, I don't think so. I mean, not beyond you, Carolyn. In fact, I'm impressed. You had a film class? Where?"

"At school. Mills College. It wasn't a whole course, part of the French classes. A week on French cinema. So your film is…what?"

Robert purses his lips. "It is set in New York, but I'm filming in Montreal. I'm down here in Manhattan setting up the exteriors."

"That I don't get." Carolyn frowns. But Robert is very interesting. She is thrilled to have a conversation on a contemporary topic and be able to learn something.

"It's too expensive to film here. The actors, the crew, the permissions. Do you know how much they charge in New York to block off a street for a couple of hours? It's astronomical. In Montreal they do it for nothing."

"Wow, I wonder why New York discourages making movies here. But then, why are you here if it costs so much?"

"As I said, I'm just shooting exteriors. Just one cameraman, myself, I can get away with that. Trains coming and going into the station, over the bridges. Stuff like that."

"Anyway, what is your film about?"

"It's about two people searching for each other in the subways."

"Doesn't Montreal have subways?"

"Yes, of course, but it has 3 lines, and New York, I think the subway here it's infinite. So I found it easier to imagine complications for my story. And you, Carolyn, what do you do in New York?"

"Now that's a good question. I've been here two days."

He laughs. "Oh, now I see. Where did you come from?"

"San Francisco."

"I've never been there. But, of course, the famous *Vertigo*, Hitchcock, that was filmed there, am I not correct?"

"Yes, that's true."

"A great film. Ah, but nothing like *The Conversation*, Gene Hackman, that's almost French. It's damn good."

"You are up on your films."

"You are right, Carolyn. It's my life, you see. We in Quebec are sort of caught between America and France. But you can think of it in another way. We are the convergence of two great filmmaking worlds. Steve McQueen and Alain Delon. It's a great time and a great place. But I don't mean to bore you with movie details. You didn't tell me what you are doing here."

Carolyn is at a loss. She doesn't know what to say because she doesn't know herself what she is doing here. At least not anything that she could tell someone in total command of his life and his plans.

Robert's face showed that he'd asked the wrong question. "You don't have to tell me what you are doing here. I didn't mean to pry."

Carolyn nodded. "No, you aren't prying. I didn't reply because I'm not sure what I'm doing here. I haven't made any definite plans."

"Okay, you are mysterious. But you speak excellent French, and you're accent, it's good. Where did that come from?"

"Thank you, you're nice to say so. I spent a semester in Paris. At the Louvre, as a matter of fact. I remember, there were many students in Paris from the University of Quebec."

"And what did you study there?"

"Art history. But it was studying the paintings in the Louvre. An infinite resource. We got to study with the people who work in the Louvre. We even got to work alongside them."

"What," he laughs, "you restored the Mona Lisa?"

Now Carolyn, for the first time, laughs with ease. "Is it that obvious? I tried to sign my name alongside Da Vinci's but they wouldn't let me." She notices him staring. "I'm kidding, you know that, huh?"

"Maybe I'm just noticing that you have a nice Mona Lisa smile."

She waves him off. "We did get to catalog recent research. But now I'm thinking the whole thing was a mistake."

"A mistake?"

"They didn't do modern art."

"No, you're right. For that there's Musée d'Orsay and le Pompidou. But still, why was it a mistake?"

"Because I worked on old paintings, I didn't get a sense of what artists are doing in Paris now. Art that I would like to do."

Robert's eyes widened in surprise. "Ah. Now there's the first interesting thing you've said all evening. Your art. Tell me about your art."

Carolyn feels pressure for the first time in New York. She hasn't given any thought to what had happened to her art career. Images flash in her mind of the rejection at the Art Institute, of Damian in bed with the woman, of the restless sea below Sea Cliff.

A hand touches her shoulder and she sees Robert up close, who holds her attention with sympathetic but intense eyes.

She lets out a long breath and speaks to the floor. "My art is in shambles right now. No, the Louvre was wonderful, educational, interesting. But it was the Northern Renaissance, van Eyck, Memling, and Weyden."

He nods as if he understands the references. "And your art is what?" He waits for her with his eyes wide open.

His intense stare, the aggressiveness of it, and the pressure to respond unsettle her. "My art is nothing." She takes a long drink of light creamy wine.

"Nothing. That's not believable. You sound like you can't take what someone's said about your art. I hope it wasn't you yourself. Tell me what you mean."

"I mean, I'm disappointed."

"With your work? Tell me...tell me, what is your work?"

Carolyn looks over to Beatrice, who is laughing in response to something Alain has told her. Then she wants to be honest with Robert. "That's it. I don't know what my work is."

"You mean, you don't know the medium, or you don't know the style?"

"Or, I don't know what it's all about. Medium. Style. Content."

"That all sounds very academic. Painting isn't a theory, painting is action."

"Oh yes, I can pick up a brush and put some color on a canvas. I...."

He doesn't let her finish. "Right, it's an image, something to see. Same as in filmmaking. The problem is you don't like what you see."

She shakes her head. "No, the problem is not me. Others don't like what I paint."

"Who? Please, I'd like to know."

She doesn't want to tell him that a major school has dismissed her work. That her hoped-for mentor has given her a mediocre review. That a lesser painter was accepted.

"Okay," he says. "I can see you want to keep that to yourself. But you must remember, you yourself are the important art critic."

The wine starts to work on her. "Ah, there you go. You're more academic than I am. What kind of movies do you make? Are they cartoons?"

He draws his lips in a tight line and spills a little drop of whiskey on the table. "No. You have a thin skin, mademoiselle." He stands and walks to the bar and motions for more whiskey.

Carolyn turns and sees Beatrice watching her with some concern. *Now I have another minder.*

Chapter 21

BEATRICE EXCUSES HERSELF to her friends with a gesture and comes to Carolyn. She glances to the bar and then back. "I don't mean to intrude. I hope you're having a good time. We can go whenever you like. I don't know the guy you're with."

Carolyn, patient, smiles at Beatrice. "No, don't worry. I can take care of myself. I'm having a good time, I promise you."

Beatrice nods with the same exaggerated impatience. "That's great. But, if you find out he's...."

"I'm okay, thanks." This time irritation comes out in her voice.

Beatrice pats Carolyn on the shoulder and walks back to her table.

Robert returns with his whiskey. And a dark red drink for Carolyn.

"What's this?"

"It's your favorite. A Manhattan."

"What's it made with?"

He frowns and cocks his head. "What?"

"My drink. The Manhattan. What's in it?"

"I don't know. Whiskey and...some other stuff."

"I don't want it." Carolyn pushes the drink away, spilling some.

"Oh. And why not?"

"Let me tell you why not, Robert. I didn't ask for it and I don't want it. Is that hard for you to understand?"

"Well, now you are not being very polite."

Carolyn pinches her lips tight and holds them for a second, then says, "Who are you to tell me what to drink? Is that some kind of French-Canadian macho crap?"

He smiles to himself, then sparks at her. "You know what this is? It's some kind of American spoiled child crap. You don't know what your art is so you reject my friendly offer of a drink."

She contemplates picking the whisky glass up and throwing it in his face, but doesn't want to do it in front of Beatrice. "Why did you get me a Manhattan anyway? I'm curious."

"Okay, so I asked Beatrice if there was something special you like to drink. What's wrong with that?"

She laughs but her laughter is dismissive. "If you don't mind, next time, ask me if I want something to drink. I don't need my aunt to do it for me."

Robert holds up both hands in defense. "All right, Carolyn, I get the picture. You're a big girl in a big city with a big problem. Sorry. I didn't mean to offend you." Then he glances to his right.

Beatrice, Alain, and the others have stopped talking and are watching them.

Carolyn hesitates, and then walks over to her aunt. She smiles and says, "What do you think? I'd like to go back. Could you give me a key to the house? I think travel fatigue has set in. If it's all right."

Alain nods, saying, "Beatrice, I think you should take her home. You and I can catch up some other time."

Carolyn feels a sudden hot rush of embarrassment. "No," she says in a loud voice that startles even herself. "Let me have the key. As Robert said, I'm a big girl. I can take care of myself. You should stay here and continue your conversation." She stops, almost out of breath and waits for Beatrice.

Beatrice takes a quick sip of her drink, puts her coat on, and says good-bye to them all. She leads Carolyn out the door.

Carolyn breathes in and then lets it out with an exaggerated sigh. She feels pressure behind her eyes as she speaks to her aunt. "You could have given me the key."

Beatrice stops and makes Carolyn pay attention to her. She speaks with a soft voice. "I should have given you a key, sure. Sorry I didn't think of it. But I couldn't stay very long anyway. It wouldn't be fair to wake you up."

"Oh, I would have let you in."

"Yes, I know, you and I are good friends. We should have worked this out before. But we didn't. I didn't want to have to go to the doorman next door and ask for the spare key."

Carolyn studies the sidewalk.

"So," Beatrice says, "you should show a little patience."

Carolyn shrugs. "Yeah, I'm sorry, I was so irritated by that jerk, and I didn't want to bother you."

Beatrice starts walking. "Let's take the subway home. It'll be fun. It's on up to 96th and a short walk."

Carolyn feels sheepish. "I'm sorry, Beatrice. I didn't mean to take you away from your friends."

"I know you are. It was nice to connect with Alain again, but at the moment, I'm kind of like you. I'm not interested in men from Quebec. Alain is married, and he's a little too friendly to me right now. He thinks maybe he's the grieving widow's answer. So you gave me the perfect excuse."

"But Alain said you should take me home."

"He did. But he wasn't sincere. He expected me to give you the key."

"Anyway, thank you once more."

LEAVING THE SUBWAY, they walk in silence two blocks over to Park and down to the house.

Beatrice twists out of her coat and says, "Now, it's late and we're both tired and we've gone nonstop for a couple of days. Tomorrow is R&R for us. Taking it easy."

"You know what I'd like to do, is go see grandmother's grave. I promised Mother I would do it. It's not hard to get to, is it?"

Beatrice hugs Carolyn. "You know, I haven't ever been there. Mom wrote to me that Hugh had her buried somewhere, without any ceremony. I thought it was awful and I did try to ask him about it once, but he wouldn't talk about it. I don't know the name of the place."

Carolyn's face brightens. "Did you know Mother visits the grave when she comes to New York?"

Beatrice winces. "I do now. But all these years I didn't. There's so much that's going to change. So, that's settled for tomorrow. We'll go and it will be a joyful discovery for both of us." She puts her hands up to her face. "I'm sorry. It's not joy."

Carolyn comes to Beatrice and pulls her close, then holds her at arm's length and says, "It is joy. I think you're right. I have to learn to trust your instincts. I haven't learned yet to trust my own, but you, my Aunt Beatrice, you are someone I can trust."

She pulls away and says, "Until tomorrow," and walks to her room.

"Good night." Beatrice says, smiling.

The phone rings in the room as Carolyn is undressing. She waits for Beatrice to answer it somewhere else in the house, but it keeps on ringing. A knock on the door indicates that isn't going to happen.

"Come in," she says, putting on her bathrobe. The phone rings again.

Beatrice's head appears inside the door. "Mom had her own phone line in here. I think this call is for you."

The phone continues ringing.

"I am very sure it's for you. And you know who's calling."

Carolyn sighs and droops her head in defeat. "I see. She's going to let it ring all night. I wonder how she found out I have this phone number in my room?"

Beatrice smiles and raises her eyebrows. "How hard can it be?" She pulls her head back out and closes the door.

The phone rings more insistently.

Carolyn slow-steps to the ornate desk and stares at the phone, a beautiful ivory-and-silver ornate piece. She picks it up and cups the earpiece while her subconscious mind makes its decision. When she speaks, she has no thought of how she wants the conversation to go, then, as soon as she says, "Mother?" she knows she'll talk about the plans for tomorrow.

"Carolyn? Is that you? I thought maybe Beatrice was making you up."

That cool monotone voice. With its sarcastic tone. At this distance across the country Carolyn thinks of the woman on the phone as Elizabeth, not as Mother.

"Yes, it's me. Who did you think it was?"

Silence on the other end, broken by, "I know you're avoiding me, but I don't think I should have to hear all the news secondhand."

Carolyn wonders about "news". "What news? I've been here two days. There is no news."

Elizabeth's voice comes back with a sharpened tone. "Then that is the news, isn't it. Have you forgotten why you went to New York?"

Carolyn puts one leg on top of another, settling in, making a gesture to herself, having to endure her mother's intrusion. "No, Mother. I haven't forgotten why I came here. As I said, it's two days. Why are you so impatient with me? Should I run down to Goldman Sachs and apply tonight?" Carolyn bounces her leg up and down in frustration.

"Carolyn, can you please be serious with me?"

"Serious? Serious about what? Why do I have to be in such a hurry? Beatrice has been wonderful to me. I've been to the Metropolitan museum and opera. I've been to a hockey game, for god's sake. And I met a French-Canadian filmmaker."

Elizabeth sighs on the other end of the line. "You met whom? You think what you need right now is another boyfriend? Didn't you learn anything in Berkeley?"

Carolyn holds the phone in her hand away from her head. She searches the room as if something could jump out at her to respond to her mother.

Her mother's voice comes from the phone. "Carolyn?"

Silence. Carolyn waits, unable to reply.

"Are you there?"

She bites her lip, then puts the phone back up to her head. "Yes, I'm still here."

"Then why won't you answer me?"

"Mother, I didn't say a word about a boyfriend. Why do you have to misinterpret what I say?"

"I don't think it's a misinterpretation at all. It's too soon for you to start up with someone else. It takes time to get over these things. You should be thinking of your career."

"For the last time, I don't have a boyfriend."

"Then who were you meeting in a bar?"

"God. This is unbelievable. I didn't meet anybody in a bar. I went with Beatrice and her friends."

"One of whom makes films and is going to make you a star."

Carolyn wants to slam the receiver down. She makes her voice low and calm. "Mother...we're going to do something different tomorrow. We're going to grandmother's grave."

Elizabeth remains silent for a time on the other end of the line, as if it's some new revelation. "Where are you going?"

What is this, a test? "What do you mean? It's where you told me. The New York City Marble Cemetery on 2nd Street."

"Who is the we?"

Carolyn's voice rises and becomes sharp. "Who? Your mother's sister-in-law Beatrice and me. Mother!"

"Well, thank you, Carolyn. Be sure you don't mix it up with the other one."

A line forms between Carolyn's brows. She wishes this didn't have to be so difficult. It's just like everything else with her mother. "What other one?"

"The one on 2nd Avenue. It's around the corner. You want the one that has a long iron fence on the street. And has "City" in its name. And Carolyn...."

Carolyn waits for her mother to continue, curious about what more she might have to say.

"Thank you."

"You're welcome."

"And Carolyn, for me, will you kneel down on the ground and lay your palm flat on the stone. I know, you're a modern child. It's not fair of me to ask."

Carolyn sighs. "Sure, Mother. Of course I will."

Carolyn hangs up the phone and goes to her bed, takes off the robe, and lays back, exhausted. She lays still, watches her chest go up and down in slow rhythm. Images of New York float through her consciousness until she falls asleep.

Chapter 22

THE NEXT MORNING, Carolyn and Beatrice walk up out of the Bleecker Street station, head across Bowery and along 2nd Street. When they reach 2nd Avenue, Carolyn stops, confused.

"I think it's here. 2nd Street. Or Avenue. I'm not sure which. Let's go up here." She turns left on 2nd Avenue and walks along, searching for anything that she could recognize as a cemetery. "These are apartments," she says, frustrated. "And that's an Italian restaurant. You would think we could see headstones. Mother said there was an iron fence, but I don't see anything like that...wait, that plaque, there...well, that's a gate, not a fence." She walks up to the gate and reads out loud, "New York Marble Cemetery."

Beatrice comes up behind her. "You said the name had "City" in it."

"I know, but this gate could be a fence."

"This isn't it, Carolyn. Let's go back down to 2nd Street and go down at least a block, and if there's nothing there, we'll come back here." Beatrice scans the street, but says nothing more.

Carolyn follows her gaze and says, "Wait, let me go in here, first. Maybe somebody can help us. There are flowers on the gate, must be recent."

She reads the brass plaque. "It says the names are on the walls. It's funny, that's not what Mother said." She enters the gate and follows the narrow alleyway along the old brick walls. At the end is a large green expanse with trees and bushes, the whole thing surrounded by modern New York apartment buildings.

161

An old woman sits on a green lawn chair in the middle, knitting something in the early stages. Carolyn approaches her. "Hello."

The woman puts her knitting needle and red yarn down, sorry to be interrupted. She shades her face with her hand and says, "Yes, can I help you?"

"I thought this was the New York City Marble Cemetery, but it is something different out front."

The woman laughed. "Yes," she says, with half a sigh. "A common mistake. The other one is what you want. Across the street on 2nd Street."

"There are two of them?"

"Yes. Like twins, but not identical."

"I'm looking for my grandmother, but my mother says the gravestone is on the ground."

"Yes, that would certainly be the other one. You can see them from the sidewalk over there."

Carolyn feels a rush of sympathy for the woman. "Do you have someone buried here?"

"Oh no," the woman says, smiling. "It's a very lovely park to me. No one's ever in here. It's been so long since anyone has been buried here. I so enjoy the peace and quiet during the day, if the weather's fine."

"Thank you for your help."

The woman concentrates on her yarn and pays no attention to Carolyn's remark.

Carolyn and Beatrice leave the cemetery and walk to 2nd Street.

"This has to be it," Beatrice says.

They walk along 2nd past nondescript buildings and a fat couple walking their little lap dogs, until halfway down the tree-lined street they see the iron fence with a cemetery behind it.

"Must be somewhere here," Carolyn says. "Let's keep going." Inside the fence a few gravestones are scattered on the lawn, along with several obelisks, some seeming to be twelve feet high. "I can see why the old lady liked the other one. This one is much more public."

Beatrice laughs. "I don't think I'd like to spend my time knitting in either one of them."

In the middle of the block, opposite a gray stone church, they find the entrance.

"New York City Marble Cemetery. This has got to be it," Beatrice says.

She pushes the gates open. "Did Elizabeth say where the gravestone was?"

"Yes. She said it was on the left as you go in, toward the end, under a tree."

They walk along the grass between gravestones and obelisks. A bright yellow cab goes by, then another, and two loud hipsters stroll by, reminding Carolyn of the quiet for the knitting lady in the other Marble cemetery.

"Not very old for around here," Beatrice says. "1888, 1854. That's almost modern. Maybe another section is older. Oh, here's 1958."

Carolyn walks ahead of her, not listening. She nears a tree made up of several trunks grown together. On the ground ten feet in front of this tree she sees the gravestone, Julia Marie Stuart, and the image of her mother jumps into her mind, she feels a small thrill in her abdomen and, for the first time she can remember, she thinks about her mother with some sympathy. She kneels and lays her hand on the gravestone and holds it there. It is warm from the sun. Then she stands.

She turns and calls, "Beatrice," but is startled to find her aunt a few feet away, as if she has just appeared out of a dream and Carolyn is surprised how she could slip into a kind of daydream state for a few moments.

"Is that it?"

"Yes." Carolyn reads it out loud. "Julia Marie Stuart. May 23, 1920, Lewiston, Maine - September 4, 1943, Versailles, France. Wow. That's amazing. Mother didn't say she died in France."

Beatrice doesn't say anything, waiting for more reaction from her niece.

"France? How did she get to France? Why did she go there?" Questions swirl around in Carolyn's mind. They tug at her, but she doesn't know which way they lead. She turns to Beatrice, then back to the gravestone. "Did you know she died in France?"

Beatrice shakes her head. "I'm not the one you should ask."

Carolyn feels a sudden distance from her aunt. "But you were here, she was your brother's wife, you must have known something."

There's a sudden sense of urgency in Carolyn's own voice. It shocks her. First the daydream, now this emotion poking out of nowhere.

"No, remember, I wasn't here. I was in Canada. And I wasn't close to my brother, or, to tell the truth, not with my mother either." Beatrice gazes at Carolyn with caring eyes.

The situation begins to focus for Carolyn with his information, the knowledge that it isn't just her mother Elizabeth who seems alienated from the New York Stuart family. She wants to think about it, but there is too much she doesn't know about her grandparents, her great aunt, her mother.

She moves back from the gravestone and takes her aunt's arm. Together they walk to the exit of the New York City Marble Cemetery. Carolyn turns back and feels the gravestone receding and drawing her back at the same time.

As they close the gate behind them, Carolyn stands for a moment and puts her hand on the iron grill. Then they walk toward Second Avenue. When they arrive at the end of the cemetery fence, Carolyn stops again and focuses on the grave a few feet away, inside. Julia pulls on her from the past. Then she aces Beatrice in silence as if more magical information will appear, and then continues walking.

Her voice, when she speaks, has a quality of pleading to it which surprises her once more. "Beatrice, tell me what you did know."

Beatrice has intense sympathy in her eyes, or maybe Carolyn just sees her aunt more intensely. "I knew that Julia had left Hugh and her daughter and went off on her own. She disappeared. My mother told me that she believed that Julia ran off with an Italian man." Beatrice leans into Carolyn. "You have to remember something else, my dear. Canadians were in the war before the Americans were. This was 1940, we were in the war alongside the British. They called my husband up and sent him overseas. That's all I cared about. Not what happened to my brother and his failed marriage."

Shame burns Carolyn's cheeks. "I do understand. I don't mean to be unsympathetic to what happened to you during the war. There is so much more I want to learn about it, about you, about Pierre. See, this is something you didn't tell me before. Now I have learned about your suffering, and it helps me to feel closer to you. I came here to get away from my mother, but now I'm finding there is more here for me than I ever thought possible."

They cross Second Avenue on their way to the Bleecker Street subway station. Carolyn says, "look there," pointing down the street. "There's the other Marble cemetery. We almost lost our way. I almost lost my way."

They continue walking in silence but Carolyn holds on tighter to Beatrice's arm to the subway and back home.

ONCE IN THE HOUSE, they enter the library together and sit on the armchairs facing the cold fireplace.

A long minute of silence hangs between them and then Carolyn says, "Your husband was in the war in Europe?" Now she knew something of how her aunt had suffered. Her mother Elizabeth had never talked of suffering—she had always been too tough for that.

"Yes," Beatrice says, placing her arms on her knee. "He was gone for five long years. I went to England to visit him and spent five years there, and wanted to volunteer for the ambulance corps, but he objected. He said it made it tougher on him if I was also in the war. I believed him." She stands and walks around the room. "You know, everything of his and mine is still back up in Montréal. That tells you something doesn't it. I haven't made up my mind where I'm going to live." She sits back down and leans forward toward Carolyn. "That is, until now. You have helped me make up my mind. My future is here, whether in this house or not."

Carolyn shifts in her chair. She has a new interest in learning about her grandmother and why she went to France, but now that leads to learning about Beatrice's life. Her own loneliness merges with that of her aunt. "Tell me about Pierre. What did he do in the war?"

"He was in the infantry for the invasion of Sicily and he fought through to the capture of Rome. I felt he was lucky, because he worked for division headquarters doing reporting back to the war office. The office work disappointed him, and he volunteered for patrols, but they wouldn't let him go. That's what he said in his letters. I never knew if he was lying to protect me, but after the war he said he had never fired a gun."

The idea of the letters hits home with Carolyn. Something tangible, to hold in your hands. To read and understand. "You have those letters?"

Beatrice thinks for a moment. "Somewhere, I'm sure. Back home. In the attic." She beams as if she has made a discovery, and her eyes brighten.

"What is it?" Carolyn's own spirits lift in response to Beatrice's eyes.

"The attic. I've never been in the attic."

"But you said that's where your letters are."

Beatrice shakes her head. "I'm confusing you about New York and Montreal. No, I mean I've never been up in the attic in this house since I returned to New York. Who knows what's up there. I've no idea. When I arrived this place was full of furniture, but all the personal things were gone, all the clothes, the paintings on the wall, the paperwork. For the most part. I have never wanted to explore the house."

Carolyn stands and pushes her hair back, biting her lip, waiting, her heart beating a little faster.

Beatrice, seeing Carolyn ready and excited, stands too. "What are we waiting for?"

"Will we need a key?"

Beatrice says, "Oh-oh. I don't know. Let's find out. I doubt it." She starts to walk, then stops. "You know, honestly, I've never gone through all the drawers in here or in Hugh's office." She puts her head in her hands and says, "My god, I've not moved in at all. It's like it's been a hotel for me." She motions Carolyn to follow her and goes out the library door.

Carolyn follows her to the end of the hall. They pass Hugh's office on the right, and before they arrive at Elizabeth's room at the end, Beatrice turns left into a small alcove and opens a door.

"Here we go, no key," Beatrice says, as she places one foot on the stairway, which leads up to a small landing and door at the top. "We'll see. I've never been up here. Alice, my cleaning lady, said she went up here once and didn't think it was out of the ordinary. I think she was hoping the paintings were all stored here." She peers up at the small window on the landing and grasps the handrail.

At the top, Beatrice opens the door. "Oh, see, not to worry."

Carolyn follows behind her. "Oh, my," she says. "This isn't an attic, it's the top floor."

"Yes," Beatrice says. "Alice has kept this perfectly clean. I must thank her for that. It's a room." She turns left and points. "And there's another hallway with a couple of doors. Well, this is a surprise. I'm sorry I didn't come up here sooner."

Carolyn glances left where Beatrice pointed, then back to the room they had entered. The room seems long, the empty walls a faded white, almost becoming gray. No signs of anything ever hanging there. Two large quarter-circle windows at the end of the house look out across Park Avenue.

"I remember those from the outside when I arrived. They were beautiful. You can see the world from here." On their right are two dormer windows. Carolyn walks over to them and pulls one up. It slides easily. She peeks out to the street. "A nice view." She closes the window and steps back to take in the whole room. "But the room is empty. What was it when you were a child?"

"Oh, we weren't allowed up here. It was always Grandfather's room, and then Dad's room, and I did come up here a couple of times, there were bookshelves, and a table and chairs. I remember at the time I thought it was kind of like a dining room, but it would have been a place for them to be alone."

Carolyn inhales. "It smells like disinfectant. Your housekeeper does a thorough job."

"Yeah, I kind of wished she hadn't. It's my fault for telling her to come up here. But it takes away...I don't know...." Beatrice puts her fingers up to her lips. "...I wish I could have smelled it, the history, whatever it was like up here."

"It would be a great place for kids up here. So high, they could put a train up here, or have a room full of doll furniture." Carolyn laughs. "Or ghosts. Lots of room for them."

She stands quiet. "Listen. The wind. You can hear it up here. It's like you're closer to nature up here at the top of the house than you are near the ground. I love it."

Beatrice walks to the other half of the room, to the hallway. There are doors on either side. She opens the door on the right.

"Well," Beatrice says, "nothing in here. Wait, a trunk, kind of hidden behind the door."

Carolyn, her interest heightened, walks behind Beatrice into the room. Beatrice opens the lid of the trunk.

"Women's clothes," she says.

"Let me see," Carolyn says, her eyes widening. "Oh, there's that mothball smell. At least something up here has a smell to it."

Beatrice lifts clothes out of the box. "All dresses. All very nice." She holds one up to herself. A black velvet and lace dress. "About my size. Let me see you." She holds it up against Carolyn. "Yes, would work for you, too. And the label is...Anna Miller. Don't know that. But this is nice. I'm impressed. See if you can find one." Beatrice twirls herself around the room near the windows to let the light show off the dress.

Carolyn picks up several dresses, then takes one out. "Oh, my, this is beautiful." It's a black dress with bright red ribbon designs accented with red and white stylized chrysanthemums. "Look, the shoulders, so 1930s, the three-quarter arms. I've got to try it on." She lays the dress back on top of the trunk, takes her sweater and jeans off, and puts the dress on. "Hey, I'm Debbie Harry before she was rich. The original Blondie. I'll have to get cowboy boots to go along with it." She laughs. "I'm kidding. What a treasure this all is."

Beatrice says, "Well, I'm not going to go that far." She holds up the black dress again. "Oh, how beautiful. It's a sweetheart bodice. Amazing. And this," she removes a lace train from the trunk, "this lace, and the velvet." She holds the dress against her body as she runs her hand over her thigh, luxuriating in the material.

Carolyn shakes her head and smiles. "This gives a whole different view of Julia. If it's Julia's clothes."

"Oh, it must be. Mother would not have worn these things. I wonder who kept these? We'll have to go through the whole trunk and pick out a couple of things to keep. Well, leave them all here for now. These are so marvelous. I never thought I could feel like a runway model, but I do today. I think I'll have my cleaning lady put them all on hangers to all air out. I bet a vintage clothing store somewhere in the Village would love to have these."

"Oh, great idea." Carolyn studies the dress, feeling herself in it, moving around, noticing the way the skirt of the dress moves with her. "This is the woman that went to France. I feel like I'm her. So somebody kept all this, the beautiful dresses. Somebody who cared about her. Do you have any idea?"

Beatrice thinks for a moment. "No. There was Mrs. Willow, and then Mary, the girl who watched after Elizabeth. Hugh had left Mrs. Willow some money. After his funeral, she went away. We never corresponded. There was something, later on, a few months after Hugh died, a letter to her, and returned no forwarding address, so I never pursued it. And Carolyn, don't get your hopes up about Julia. I mean, we don't know the whole story, but, maybe she's an angel, and maybe she's not." She rubs her hands on the dress. "We may never know."

Carolyn moves her eyes around the room, as if searching for an answer. "No, I know, I'm looking for something…" she stops at the trunk, "someone who's not here. But, do you understand, until now, I had my mother, and we didn't get along at all, and now I have you, and so I want Julia, too, even if it's fantasy for now."

Beatrice carefully lays the black velvet dress back in the trunk and closes the lid.

Carolyn feels sheepish still wearing her chrysanthemum dress, so she takes it off and gently returns it to the trunk.

"You don't have to do that," Beatrice says.

"It's okay, maybe later. Let's wait until they're all hanging up, then try them again. Like our own vintage store."

"Right. Well, we have another room left. Still a chance for the ghosts to show up."

"I think we found a pretty nice ghost right in this room. We should stay up here some night and see if the trunk lid opens and someone floats around the room."

Beatrice laughs. They go out and across the hall.

"Oh. Wow." Beatrice says as she leans into the room.

"What?" Carolyn rests her arm on Beatrice's back as she comes up close to see the room.

"This is something special."

A huge skylight in the roof floods the room with light.

"Yeah," Carolyn says, "you can't even see this from the street. And my god, do you see that?" She feels a strange flush through her body. She puts her hands up on her cheeks.

Chapter 23

IN THE CORNER, opposite the two dormer windows that face the building across the street, is a painting. It is a man, the head and shoulders, with a background of vague paintings on a wall. The man observes the viewer with sympathetic eyes but his body ghosts out into an uncompleted white canvas.

"Oh my god!" Beatrice gasps. "It's Hugh."

Carolyn stands silent, shocked. "Hugh. My grandfather? Him? This must be a painting by my grandmother? Unbelievable." She examines the painting, her heartbeat racing. "And it's oil, too." She stands back and stares at it for a moment. "Nice brushwork. I'm impressed. With her work, not the subject by itself."

Beatrice nods, keeping her eyes on the painting. "Yes. Him. What a surprise. I'm afraid I don't know much about the details of painting."

"This is amazing," Carolyn says. "You said all the paintings had been sold, but not this one. It's not finished, of course, so they wouldn't try to sell it. Do you think my grandmother did it?"

"This," Beatrice studies the painting, hoping for a signature but not finding one, "yes, this is Julia. I'm sure of it. I'll bet you Hugh didn't even know this was up here, or he would have had it destroyed."

Carolyn's heartbeat slows down, and she breathes deeply the spirit of the room and the painting. "I must ask Mother if she knew about this."

"That's an interesting question. Your mother was in this house for eighteen years before…," Beatrice slumps into herself…," before she went away to school."

"You mean when my grandfather threw her out."

Beatrice stops moving, focuses on Carolyn, her eyes misting up as she surveys the room. "Yes. That."

"But Mother would have come up here and seen this. All those years, her whole childhood."

"I presume she didn't mention it to you...or you'd know."

Carolyn shakes her head. "All she ever had from here was the picture of herself as a child with her parents. She never mentioned anything at all about this house. Of course, she wouldn't talk about any of it. She didn't even tell me where this house was."

Carolyn scans the small room. It's empty except behind the easel is a wooden box on the floor. "Oh, wow, it's...a box of paints, I think." She steps around the easel and picks the box up. "It's heavy enough, I think the paints must still be in it. All dried up, I'm sure." She holds the box in one arm and opens it. "Oh, oh, yes, the paints are, but there are some letters or something."

She turns and shows Beatrice the box. Beatrice lifts the letters out of the box. Carolyn glances at the rest of the contents in the box and then sets it down to see what Beatrice is holding. There are several light blue aerogramme letters, wrinkled and folded, a telegram yellow with age, and a ragged piece of notepaper with gray lines that have been torn off, maybe torn off in haste.

"Letters? Whose letters would they be?" Carolyn wishes they'll be letters home from her mother, but knows that's too much to hope for.

"Let's see," Beatrice says. "There's a note. From Mrs. Willow."

"Who's that again?"

"It says...she was the housekeeper, remember, the one who I last saw at the funeral...it says, 'I wanted to save these. I took them from the trash bin.' It's signed 'Margaret Willow.' Funny, I never knew what her first name was, until Hugh's death, I saw it on a few documents."

She sorts through the letters. "There are four of them. One's a telegram, from the SS Washington, and three letters, see, aerogrammes. All addressed to Hugh. Come on, let's go down to the library and see what we have here."

When they are in the library, they sit at the table. Beatrice lays the four envelopes down in order by postmark date.

Carolyn's excitement builds. "The telegram, what does it say?"

Beatrice flushes in anticipation and turns to the yellow piece of paper and leans close to Carolyn so they can see it together:

SS WASHINGTON URGENT=
HUGH STUART 40 E 85th ST NY NY
Hugh I'm sorry I've made a huge mistake will return as soon as possible stop
cable me on board ship STOP
love julia

The two women stare at the telegram in silence.

Carolyn feels a surge of pain run through her chest as she faces Beatrice. "Can you imagine? Sending a telegram like that? How old was she?"

"Well, let me think, I don't know, but she was very young when she married Hugh, around twenty, I remember Mother was dead set against it. She thought Julia was a gold digger. But then she didn't like my Phillip, either."

"It says she made a huge mistake? What was that? It must mean going away, don't you think?"

"Yes, you're right. Let's read the other letters." Beatrice spreads the three letters on the table. "They're all in 1940. May, then June, then August." She turns to Carolyn. "That's all there were in the box?"

"Yes, I'm sure, I was very thorough."

"I'm almost afraid to read them."

"I can't wait, read the first one."

Beatrice unfolds the first aerogramme and reads it out loud.

My dear Hugh, during my time on the ship, I've come to see what a mistake I've made. I miss you and Lizzie so much.

I was upset and not thinking straight. If I can I will take a plane home, from Lisbon, or a ship if I have to.

You know I love you and Lizzie and I want us to be together as a family. She needs a mother and you need a wife.

I will do anything to make that possible. I know what I did was wrong. I misunderstood and thought you were going to take Lizzie away

from me, but I was terribly wrong to think that. I will be home as soon as I can, Darling. I'll send you a cable when I've made arrangements.
With all my love - your Julia

"How sad. And she called Mother 'Lizzie,' isn't that something. I bet mother never knew that. She said her mother was, to her, just someone in a picture." Carolyn's heart beats fast and her eyes mist. Elizabeth didn't know her own mother the way Carolyn doesn't know her own father.

Beatrice touches Carolyn's arm. "Ready for another one?"

Dear Hugh, I'm so terrified. I beg of you to get me home. I had a ticket for Lisbon but on the way we were bombed by German planes. I escaped, but some others didn't. Now my exit visa is no good

Could you please send a letter, or better yet a telegram to the American Embassy in Paris so they will know who I am and can expedite my exit visa? I know, it seems crazy to get a visa to go home, but the Germans have taken over Paris and are making everything difficult.

I can't call or cable. I'm so scared, Hugh. Please do this right away.
Here is a picture for Lizzie.
Love, Julia

"A picture? Oh no. There wasn't a picture?" Carolyn's voice rises.

Beatrice shuffles through the papers. "No. Maybe in the box still?"

Carolyn stands, saying, "I'm going to find out" and runs out the door to the hallway. In the attic room she picks up the box and goes through it, picking up each tube of paint, disappointment making her hot. She goes back down and Beatrice then shows her the third letter.

Dear Hugh, I can't believe what has happened. I don't understand why you haven't contacted the embassy. They don't believe me because I said you would write them and then you haven't. Some Americans are being placed in a camp outside of Paris.

Hugh, it's a camp run by the Germans. They have interrogated me. They want to know who my parents are. Even my grandparents and where they came from. I have nowhere to turn. You can't forget how much I love you and Lizzie. Hugh, you are my only chance for survival. Please help me, if not for me, Then for our poor daughter. With all my love -Please-Julia

Carolyn stares at Beatrice in disbelief and speaks in a rush. "She died, in 1943, in France. Maybe it wasn't France. My grandmother could have died in a concentration camp. I saw documentary film about it at school. It was so awful, it made me sick. But she is buried here. Hugh must have had the body brought back after the war. There would be records...."

Beatrice puts her hands around Carolyn. "No, I can tell you that, whatever papers Hugh had, there weren't many and I went through all of them. There was nothing about Julia's burial."

"So we're left with nothing at all?" Carolyn feels a world opening and closing at the same time. A flush permeates her whole body.

"We have these letters, and the picture, and the painting and clothes upstairs."

Carolyn's voice rises in panic. "Letters? Clothes? That's not my grandmother!"

"Carolyn, listen to me. This was during the war. Millions of people died. Millions of other people don't know what happened to their families."

Carolyn calms down. "I know, I know, but this is all such a sudden shock."

"At least, now, maybe you have something to tell your mother. Something to help you understand her a little. Something to bring you closer together."

Carolyn stares at the picture, then stands. "I could go over to France. Try and find out what happened. They have records."

Beatrice nods. "Yes, they do. And perhaps you could find out. But perhaps not. My husband lost a cousin and they never knew. He was missing and there was never anything more after that. You don't have to go over there right now. You should finish what you came here to do."

"For now, I'm going to go upstairs. I want to see her paints, study the painting. That will make me feel close to her."

Aunt Beatrice blinked a couple of times, then nodded. "All right, if that's what you want to do."

"It is."

Carolyn leaves the room and returns to the attic. Standing inside, she notes the broad light from the ceiling skylights combined with the side lights from the dormer windows. Perfect, she thinks. You can have as much or as little light as you want. And all alone up here on top of the world.

She moves toward the half-finished painting. As she studies the colors, dominated by brown and blue, she bends down to the box and picks up the combinations of tube colors and whites that make these particular hues, and plans in her mind the composition, how the figure of the man stands out against the background. She feels almost faint, she is so close and yet so far. She becomes weak, she falls to the floor and sits there, her legs pulled up close, and sees the light on the painting and now she smells the familiar scent of oil paint from the box.

She picks the box up and concentrates on the brushes and tubes of paint. Some have never been opened, but the brown, blue, green, yellow, white and red, the colors used in the painting, these tubes, Julia Stuart herself had pressed them inward. The same kind of impression that Carolyn's fingers made on her own paint tubes.

There are four brushes of varying width in the box. Someone has cleaned them. They are still supple. She picks one up and moves her finger back and forth over the bristle and imagines it's Julia's hand. Standing up, she takes the brush and moves it over the painting, seeing the striations that reveals to her trained eye how the brush has been moved on the canvas, and she repaints the canvas, seeing the hand of Julia in front of her creating the original painting.

Why had Julia stopped? Was she interrupted? Did she have to drop everything and run away? Why did she think they would take her child away from her? Why did she have to go to such desperate lengths? And why wasn't the child, Elizabeth, Carolyn's mother, why wasn't she with Julia? Is this the reason Elizabeth was never sympathetic to Carolyn's art?

Will the questions never end? Does her mother know more than she was letting on? Over those more than twenty years with her father Hugh, Elizabeth would have asked many times about her mother.

175

What about Margaret Willow? She saved the letters, she saved the painting. She wanted someone to see them.

Carolyn goes back down to the library, where she finds Beatrice sitting at the table, rereading the letters.

When Carolyn enters the room, Beatrice turns her head. "How did you feel up there?"

"Different from down here. These letters, I know they have some amazing story contained in them. But it's the paper, it's so thin, it's like tissue paper. Upstairs, the paint, the painting, they're all so substantial compared to paper. So I feel closer to her up there. I feel her presence with me. The letters, they're frightening. But they speak to me, too, Beatrice. They tell me something else. That the answer is somewhere in Europe."

"What could you expect to find out?" Beatrice's voice shows exasperation. "She didn't leave any legacy over there. Her legacy, what there is, is here, in this house, upstairs."

"But I can find out what happened."

The phone interrupts her. The sound of the ring pierces the air as an unwanted intruder. Beatrice and Carolyn glance at each other, but Beatrice answers the call.

"Hello?" She listens a long time in silence.

Carolyn shifts in her chair.

Beatrice cups her hand over the black phone's receiver.

Carolyn wonders if it's her mother, but then dismisses that. Just some business thing.

"Carolyn, it's a Mrs. Devlin. She says she's from the NYU business school. She wants to talk to you." Beatrice holds the phone out to Carolyn.

Carolyn hesitates and frowns, startled to realize she hoped it was Robert, but takes the phone from Beatrice.

"Hello?"

"Carolyn Stuart?"

"Yes."

"I'm Sharon Devlin from NYU. I'm calling to talk to you about your program here at NYU. Is this a convenient time?"

Carolyn's brows are furrowed, she doesn't want to interrupt their conversation about Julia. "What is this about?"

"I've been talking to your mother, Elizabeth. We have worked out a program for you. It's a combination of art and business. If you could come down here, I'd like to discuss it with you."

"A program? What kind of program?"

"We in the department, we've been able to put together an individual study program for you between the Tisch art department and the business school. It would lead to a Professional Certificate in Art Dealership. It's quite unique."

"My mother worked this out with you?"

"Well, now, I wouldn't put it that way. Your mother has been a generous supporter of NYU for many years. In essence, she has saved you a great deal of time by laying the groundwork, so to speak."

"But my mother made these arrangements with you, is that right?"

"Are you not aware of this? Your mother informed us that you would be calling us to work out details of your program. Since we have not heard from you, and since your mother is interested in working this out, we decided to call you and get things moving. There's a class starting, which would be a good introduction for you."

Carolyn takes the phone away from her ear and grips it tight, as if the machine were the source of her frustration, then she sighs and puts it back up to her ear. "My mother and I have different expectations about the timeline for this. I'm not ready to start classes now. I've been in New York only a few days."

"Ms. Stuart, that's up to you. It's that…it's not a private study program, a tutorial or something. You have a large opportunity to design the program, but some classes would be required, minimal perhaps, but still it has to start sometime. And the professional certificate is a valuable educational achievement."

"A certificate? That's what the achievement is?"

"Well, it's not a degree program."

"No, I can see that. If you will excuse me, I appreciate your calling. I have some details to work out and then, then I will call you back. I might not be able to fit in with your class structure right now. I will have to think about it."

"That's understandable. I wanted to let you know that the University has requirements it must adhere to, and to help you fit within that structure."

Carolyn rolls her eyes. "I understand. Thank you for your call. Good-bye." Carolyn puts the phone down and shakes her head at Beatrice. "So. Mother has worked it all out and given them a ton of money no doubt so I can go back to school and fit right in with their curriculum. And do you know what I get out of this?"

Beatrice waits.

"A certificate. A damn certificate. I have a BFA and now I'm going to get a certificate."

"It's not for me to say, Carolyn, but it does look like your mother has gone to some trouble, and some expense, to try and help you out. Can't you see at it that way?"

Carolyn sits down. "Yes. I can. But today I discovered my grandmother. I'm not interested in going to school."

"I honestly don't see why the two are incompatible."

"But I want to go to over there now. I want to find out about my grandmother now. Mother will have to give me the money. I'll do that first, and do my art later."

"That's a funny way to talk."

"Why do you say that?"

"Your mother giving you the money. Why don't you use your own trust fund?"

"Trust fund? What trust fund? What are you talking about?"

"The trust fund that Hugh left for you."

"For me? My grandfather left me a trust fund?"

"Why of course. Oh god, don't you know about it? Didn't Elizabeth ever…?"

Carolyn's chest tightens. "Tell me? Oh, hell, do you mean my mother didn't tell me?" The indignation and disappointment in Carolyn's voice comes from deep within. "Considering she's never told me much of anything, why should I be surprised? Oh, wow! I need to find out where my money is and I'm out of here."

One week later, Carolyn sits in the front row window seat of the Air France Concorde and watches the screen at the front of the airplane as the speed of the plane changes to Mach 2.0. The passengers applaud, but Carolyn doesn't join them. Thoughts filled her mind of landing in Paris and being free to find her own way in life without having to cater to anyone else's wishes.

Chapter 24

Julia, France, 1940

JULIA SENT HER CABLE to Hugh and asked the Communications Officer if she could be notified when they received the reply. His light blue eyes, underneath black hair cut short like the military, seemed sympathetic and kind.

He noted that her stateroom was not far, and he was sure she would want to see the cable right away, so he would make sure to bring it to her the moment it arrived.

She left the window believing that this man held the possibility of her happiness in his hands for the next six days until they reached the other side of the Atlantic. No, not six days. Hugh would be home in an hour, the telegram would arrive in the afternoon, and he could reply right away. She would receive his reply this very day. She had the six days across the Atlantic, and then she would have six more days on the return voyage. People said the ocean was desolate, but no one knew how lonely it would be for her. But then she would be reunited with her beloved Lizzie. Maybe Hugh would arrange for a flight back and she could see them in two or three days instead of almost two weeks.

SHE PASSED A WINDOW to a lounge with several people sitting around the table drinking wine. Two women, two men. None of them laughed, but an elderly gentleman with a white mustache and a pipe billowing smoke above him winked at her and smiled. Feeling invited by both his smile and his age, she went inside and over to the table. There was an empty chair, so she stood beside it and asked them if she could join in. Anything to keep her from thinking about what she had lost.

"Yes, of course," said the gentleman with a deep, sympathetic voice in a French accent. "And I'm sure a waiter will come by and get you something to drink."

Julia glances around the large room dominated by a mural of Christopher Columbus standing at the front of one of his ships. Groups of people at other tables seemed to know each other. Julia wondered if she was the sole person alone. Very few were her age.

As they introduced themselves, Julia came to realize that all the others had French accents. And when she spoke, they all stopped drinking, or smoking or watching others, and paid close attention to her.

A woman, the one close to Julia's age, but maybe ten years older at 30 or so, sitting on Julia's right, took her round glasses off and asked Julia why she was going to Europe.

The question surprised Julia. Of course, it was an obvious question for a ship crossing the ocean, but it seemed so direct, and the woman's voice had a low pitch to it, too, and that unnerved her. "Why I'm going? To tell you the truth, I don't know. Could I ask you the same question? You all seem to know each other."

The elderly gentleman took his pipe out of his mouth and observed each member of the little group before he spoke. "Well, then, perhaps when you have heard our stories, young lady, you will know what your story is. We're always nervous about someone who has a secret to hide. My name, by the way is Roger."

Each of them moved a little in their chairs and to Julia it seemed odd that they seemed reticent to answer her question. A man on her left, dressed in a gray suit with a black tie, with a large head and strong features, flicked ashes from his cigarette off his trousers, then spoke.

"I am André." He reached over to shake her hand.

Julia was unsure what to do, but then realized she appeared foolish to the others so she took the man's hand and responded with a feeble handshake.

"We don't know each other at all. Except that we may all be sailing the wrong way." He watched the others to see if anyone was going to contradict him. "There are four of us you see here, excluding yourself, and two are Swiss and two are French. We have begun to ask that very question among ourselves and now I think we don't know what we are going back to. This isn't a vacation for us. I will speak for myself. I am going back to France to join the French army to keep Hitler out of our country. He will not get past the Maginot Line, but last time he went through Belgium, and we have to be there to stop him. I am an artillery officer, which is what is needed."

The elderly man raised his eyebrows. "You are an officer? And you are not in the army now?" He leaned forward and made his question serious with his voice. "Are you a deserter?"

André laughed and shook his head. "No, I am not a deserter, Monsieur. I don't believe I would have gotten on this ship if that were the case."

The elderly man leaned forward to make his point. "You can get off the ship before we get to France. In Ireland or England." He leaned back again, satisfied that all the others would know that the artillery officer was not to be trusted.

André ignored him. "I meant that as my previous rank. I am sure I will have no trouble joining the fight once I announce my presence to the military authorities." He glared at the elderly gentleman with an air of defiance, adjusting his jacket to announce he had finished.

The elderly man did not give up. "Why aren't you in uniform then?" He glared at André.

André sighed, weary of the argument. "You aren't that ignorant. I must first reach Paris and then make contact with my old regiment, and from there I will make my way to the front, once they have reinstated me with my old rank. Captain, if you must know."

The elderly man snapped back. "Don't call me ignorant. I am Swiss and we stay out of wars."

Julia nodded and studied the others as they all remained silent. To join the army. Putting your life on the line.

The woman on her right, with blond hair bangs rolled back over the head, and big soft curls down to the neck, wore bright red lipstick. Her black long-sleeve blouse had oversized shoulder pads. She turned to Julia and looked at her with sympathetic hazel eyes when she spoke. "I'm not going to join the army, I can tell you that." She leaned forward and laughed, but her laughter did not seem sincere. Her deep-set eyes did not laugh, and the others did not change their serious expressions. "I live in Paris, I was visiting family in New Jersey when Hitler invaded Poland. So now France is at war with Germany, and I have family in Paris. I'm going back to them to face the future with all of them." She looked André in the eye. "Maginot Line or not."

Julia felt sympathetic to the woman. Not for her view of the military, but for her bravery in going home to face danger. She realized she had never thought of this in her life. For herself. Even the paintings that Hugh had bought, from Jews fleeing for their life, she felt the deep immorality of this thievery, and it had made her heart beat fast in anger, but it didn't make her feel like she was in danger. A quick shot of pain ran through her chest as she realized what she was hearing. She had put herself and Lizzie in danger without even thinking about it. She wanted to leave, but was unable to move.

Julia felt she should wait to hear the other two, one a large man, young but much older than she, and the final person, a woman of middle age with no makeup and a wrinkled gray suit speckled with dust or hair or debris of some sort.

The woman , whose light brown hair was parted in the middle and fell on either side, spoke up. "I tell you, this is a voyage of the damned. We are going back to Europe that is on fire. I am Swiss, but my husband is Jewish." She stopped and waited, for effect. "So I don't care if all of you are Gestapo already. He has been interned, but I am going to go back and get him out. If any of you can help me, please let me know. I am a member of the International Red Cross. I have connections." She shook her head and seemed to be talking to herself or whomever she had in mind in Paris or Berlin or Zurich. "I told him to come with me, but he wouldn't and now I have to go back and get him out of those Nazi clutches. And after that I'm through with him." She sat forward and her voice rose. "I don't care who knows it."

Julia wished at that moment that she had not brought the subject up. She thought she should speak up but she didn't have any idea what to say. How could she tell them, she was a few years beyond her teens, and she had done the most foolish thing imaginable. It didn't take any Nazis to lose her daughter. What should she say? That she was running away from home into a war zone?

Before she could speak, the remaining man spoke with the voice of caution, but his voice was tired. "I see. There are deep emotions here. Well, first of all I don't think you should have to worry about any of us being members of the Gestapo, Mademoiselle. We are all poor lost souls going back home. I'm not in the military, and I'm not in the Red Cross. I'm a businessman, a *négociant* trying to arrange the purchase of French wines in America. But I made a rather unfortunate error in timing. Now that France has declared war on Germany, even if there is no fighting, even if France is protected by the Maginot Line, even if there's a Red Cross, it's going to be impossible to ship wines across the ocean. There will be U-Boats everywhere stalking French cargo ships, and the insurance has gone sky high, and we had better drink up all the wine before those Bosch take it all away."

Terror gripped Julia as they all turned in silence to watch her, waiting patiently with cigarette and pipe smoke and upturned glasses of dark red wine. Not one of their faces was sympathetic.

"I'm going to Paris to study art," she said as it popped into her head unprepared. What could she say? I've run away from home and now have lost my child and I don't know what to do and I hope that Hugh will forgive me and send me a telegram back today? She smiled as if it were the most natural thing in the world.

The woman on her right, the one with the bright red lipstick who was returning home to be with her family became sympathetic. "Well, I admit that is a rather ambitious plan for these times. But we all know there is no better place to study art than Paris."

The elderly man put out his view. "But, of course, there is also Florence, they have a little art there." He exhaled smoke and coughed, giving himself a small thump on the chest. One of the Swiss with no army but willing to fight battles with everyone.

The woman sighed and said, "Listen, I didn't mean to get into competition with anybody. This…, " she turned to Julia and placed her hand as if she were about to make contact, but kept it an inch away, "what did you say your name is?"

"I didn't," Julia said, happy to have someone make this a little bit more personal. "It's Julia."

"Julia," the woman said, "I'm Isabelle. Pleased to meet you." Isabelle turned back to the elderly man. "Let's be a little more gracious, shall we? Anyone who wants to study art while the Germans are destroying art is somebody we should respect."

André said, "Germans may destroy their own art, but they will never destroy French art. The French military is the strongest in the world. We are not weak like the Poles. Julia, you will be able to study art in Paris as long as you like." He turned to the elderly man. "As for Florence, you are correct as far as it goes. But Mussolini has joined with Hitler, so it's not going to be a good place for foreigners to study." He nodded his head in a little triumphant debating point.

The elderly man did not want to give up. He nodded at Julia again and said, "You are very young. Are your parents not on this ship? Nor your husband?" then he directed his gaze to the ring on her finger so that everyone could see what caught his attention, "Madam?"

Julia felt caught. "My husband?" She covered the ring with her right hand. "No, my husband is not on this ship. He has business to take care of. He will be coming over later." She thought of André's statement. "He's not in the wine business. Real estate, in New York, so he won't be affected by what happens in France." She knew by the their eyes that she had closed one box and opened another.

"What will he do while you study art?" the elderly man said, sounding like a prosecutor.

Julia realized that she was in a den of Europeans who would not stop until they forced her to admit something. At the very least, that she should not be on this ship with the real people who are going to where they belong.

She stood. "I'm sorry, I don't feel comfortable discussing my career plans with you." She turned to the elderly gentleman. "Thank you, sir, for inviting me to sit with you. If you'll excuse me, I have something important to do."

The woman in the dirty gray suit said, "I'm sure you do, my dear, and it's better than listening to us tear each other apart. I wish you luck. You will need it."

Julia started to smile, but stopped and felt her mouth straighten and close. She turned, but felt a touch on her arm, and turning back she saw Isabelle's friendly face.

"Julia, let me go with you. I think there are many things to do on this ship." She stood and moved close to Julia, but waited until Julia moved away from the chairs.

"Thank you," Julia said. "I didn't want to be rude."

"Oh no, not at all." Isabelle's voice was conspiratorial. "That old man had found a convenient group to show off with."

They left the lounge for the Sun Deck and Isabelle held out her hand. "Perhaps we can see each other again. We have a long way to go."

Julia shook Isabelle's hand, then waved and turned into the hall leading to her cabin. But she stopped, retreated back out onto the deck as Isabelle was passing by. "I would like that." Julia leaned back to catch Isabelle's attention.

Isabelle smiled. "Well, then, at least you see we are not all devastated by events."

Julia kept her gaze on the woman while she opened the door again, then said, "We should walk together," and went back inside. But one more time she came back out.

Isabelle was walking farther along on the deck.

"Let's meet for dinner," Julia called out. "In fact, why don't you come to my cabin around five?"

Julia turned back and laughed. "Sure. What cabin is it?"

"Oh. I don't know. Wait." Julia opened her purse and took out her ticket. "It's on A-Deck, A100."

"Oh my, that's the deck with suites. I can't wait to see it. See you then."

Julia turned once again and waved good-bye and smiled to see Isabelle waiting for her to make sure she had left this time. But once inside, her mind turned to the telegram she hoped, believed, was waiting for her in her cabin.

When she opened the door, her heart sank to see nothing had been slipped into the room. The diamond watch on her hand, a gift from Hugh during their honeymoon, from Hermès on Rue George V in Paris, told her that she had a long enough time before Isabelle returned for dinner. And dinner reminded her that she had no clothes except what she was wearing. She opened the brochure on the coffee table and found the location of the small shopping arcade.

The arcade consisted of a jewelry store, bookstore with postcards and other souvenirs, a drugstore, and the clothing store, and then several cosmetic parlors. Inside the clothing store the selection disappointed her and then she felt disappointed with herself for thinking she would have more to choose from. This was the North

Atlantic and heavy outdoor clothes dominated the room. But she did find two decent blouses, one white and the other light blue, and was grateful to find two pair of slacks, gray and brown, but the brown pair did not fit her. The young woman who managed the store told Julia they had a seamstress on board and she could have the pair of slacks dropped to her cabin tomorrow at noon. Julia said she appreciated that and took her clothes back to her room. Studying her tired dress in the mirror, she realized that she had nothing elegant to wear for dinner in first-class and that she didn't give a damn. She was certain that Isabelle would feel the same way.

For a moment, she thought back to the strange set of people in the lounge. Her group of art students were different from these people. Maybe they had worries like these people, whose fear of war dominated their lives, but they didn't let politics become their veneer.

The stateroom surrounded her in emptiness. The sofa, the two over-cushioned armchairs, the empty coffee table and side tables, they made her feel shrunk to the size of little Lizzie. Lizzie, who was now alone with Hugh and Grace and nursemaids who couldn't give her the love she could get from her mother. Julia put her head down and cradled it in her hands and felt the gentle rocking of the ship.

Chapter 25

FOOTSTEPS FELL OUTSIDE her door and she sat up, startled, waiting for the knock. None came. The footsteps took her hope with them down the hall. She sighed and went into the bathroom to clean up and remembered that she had come on board with nothing. She had lost her daughter and she knew every day there would be some reminder that she had lost everything else, too.

Back to the arcade she went, and purchased a toothbrush and paste and some soap. When she arrived back in her stateroom, she took her dress off and filled the tub with hot water.

As she tried to relax in the tub, the water rolled in a long gentle wave over her but it didn't help. Her mind filled with the contrast between New York and Park Avenue, the large house, and this isolation in a small room out in the center of the ocean. Knowing she would not get the soothing help she wanted from the bath, she got out of the tub and dried herself off, searching for a bathrobe, saw she didn't have one, and put on the light blue blouse and gray slacks.

Her shoes were ridiculous medium heels, suitable for a dress, but not for slacks on a ship. So, once again, she put them on and went back to the shopping arcade and found herself once again limited by the options available to her. The woman behind the counter pointed out that they had a limited selection because it's what they sell. People don't bring dance shoes, and they don't bring walking shoes, so they buy them on board the ship.

Julia tried on some white peep-toe mesh shoes, but they seemed too glamorous or happy, so she selected a pair of black oxfords, thinking they'll last until she gets back to New York. The woman told her she'll enjoy dancing in those, great for swing, and Julia gave her a face that made it clear she wasn't going to be doing any dancing. The woman made change for Julia and gave her the shoes without looking at her.

Julia noticed something on a table along the back wall. It was a travel wallet. The mere sight of it reminded her that she had a huge amount of cash in her room. With a sigh of relief, she purchased the wallet, and back in her room she put her money inside, ready to carry next to her body when she left the ship.

The two clocks on the far wall told her the time in New York and Paris, the real time for her, not this ship's time.

It was close enough to dinner and Isabelle would arrive soon. She picked up her purse to check her lipstick and saw the envelope with close to $50,000 in it, minus the few small purchases she had made on board. It wasn't safe to carry that kind of money around with her on the ship. She hurried down the hallway again and found the bursar's office, where she deposited almost all the money in a safe deposit box, keeping 100 dollars for the trip. Until the next time she found what it was that was essential and she had ignored.

She hurried back to her stateroom to wait for Isabelle. She had not been gone long and she was sure that Isabelle would have waited for her. Once inside, she left the door open to make it more inviting for her friend.

It did not take long and the knock on the door announced Isabelle's arrival.

"Please come in."

Isabelle smiled and her face told Julia that the size of the room impressed her. "These rooms are even nicer than I thought, "she said as she caught herself and put her hand up to her mouth, "I'm sorry, it's none of my business how you cross the ocean."

Julia smiled. "It's not what I would have taken for myself, but I bought my passage very late." She sensed that Isabelle was being polite but was indeed in awe of Julia's accommodations. Something else that hadn't occurred to Julia, that a new found friend on board a ship heading to Europe could feel like some of the students at the art league who made it clear they didn't care for the beautiful rich girl playing at art. She saw that Isabelle nodded at the remark. "Yes, it's much too big for me, but I'm out the money, so there's nothing to do. They were going to give it to someone else if I didn't pay for it right away. They even called me at home."

Isabelle waved her off, "No, I'm sorry, you just caught me off guard. Where I'm staying is small, but it's very nice, too."

Julia picked up her coat. "Yes, I'm going on too much as well. Shall we go to dinner? I admit to being very hungry."

The two women went out on their way to dinner, but as they reached the stairwell Julia turned left to go out to the deck and Isabelle turned right to go down the stairs.

"Isabelle, where you going?"

"Oh, I see, I didn't think about it, I guess my hunger got the better of me and I was going down to dinner on our deck."

Julia beckoned her to come out. "That's nonsense, you're coming to dinner as my guest. That's it."

"Thank you , that's very kind of you."

Julia held the door open for Isabelle and the two walked down to the Mayflower Café. Inside they found a table beneath a huge mural of the landing at Plymouth rock.

After they ordered, Isabelle sat back in her chair and studied Julia for a moment. Then she leaned forward and spoke in a conspiratorial tone. "Julia..." then she hesitated a moment and moved her head down and back up before continuing to speak, "I have to ask you something, if you don't mind."

The intimacy of Isabelle's manner surprised Julia. "No, I don't mind." She gave out a little laugh. "I'll have to wait to hear what your question is, I suppose."

Isabelle smiled and said, "It's none of my business but you've been very kind to me. But when you came on board ship I saw you and a little girl...."

The heat of embarrassment ran up Julia's back and flushed her cheeks. What was Isabelle doing, watching her come on board?

Isabelle said, "I'm sorry, I have upset you and I didn't mean to do that. I had no right, please forgive me." She put her napkin on the table and pushed her chair back.

Julia touched Isabelle's arm. "No, don't go. You didn't upset me, that's not what it is, I mean I'm already upset and I'm glad to have somebody to talk to." Julia picked up her wine and took a small sip but kept the glass in her lips as she tasted the burgundy. "I don't know what to say. It's you who have been kind to me." She glanced at Isabel's eyes and saw the mixture of sympathy and curiosity in the gunmetal gray. "I did come on board with my little daughter. We were going to Paris together." Julia wanted to be careful, she didn't want to tell Isabelle, who was after all a stranger, everything that happened to her. She didn't know herself how she should explain this to somebody. "My husband came and took her back at the last minute."

Isabelle nodded. "I'm sorry, Julia. I am. This must be hard for you. If there's anything at all I can do to help you, I would.'"

"Yes, thank you. But we are out on the ocean now, and there is nothing anybody can do." She noted the people coming in and out and in various stages of eating and was glad that none of them paid any attention to her. "I'll have to wait until the ship arrives in France, and then see what I can do. I mean, see how fast I can get back."

"So you're not going to study art in Paris?"

"You don't know me, Isabelle, of course, but my little girl was everything to me. It was a complete surprise when my husband took her away. It was supposed to be a vacation, for me and Lizzie, but it didn't turn out that way."

"Lizzie?" Isabelle seemed much more interested when she heard the name of the little girl. "Your little girl? How old is she?"

"She's two years old, going on 10." Julia laughed for the first time in a week.

"I'm sorry that you don't have your little girl with you. I would have taken care of her while you were in school."

"Yes, I know you're that kind of person. I wasn't going to go to school full-time, I thought I would find somebody to take care of her for an hour or two. The concierge, most likely would know someone. I figured I could work that out when we got there." When she heard herself say the word "we", Julia felt her eyes well up. She put her head down and spent a longer time than necessary adjusting her napkin.

"Have you tried to contact them, your husband I mean?"

Julia decided to find a way to talk about something else, although she wanted to talk about nothing at all. "Yes as a matter of fact, I have sent a cable and I'm hoping to hear back soon. But you know my daughter is no doubt upset now and he can very well have taken her on a trip somewhere or even to the park and who knows when they will get back home. Now, if you don't mind I would like to change the subject. I have to wait and I have to wait by myself and no one can help me."

Isabelle nodded. "All right, perhaps now it is time for me to go. I think I've overstayed my welcome in your generosity."

Julia shook her head. "No. I still don't want you to go, Isabelle. I don't want to go on talking about something beyond my control."

"I think I am finished, but you might want some dessert."

"No, I'm done, too." Julia stood up and turned to leave the table, but waited for Isabelle to come with her. "Shall we explore the ship?" Julia was very glad now to have someone to talk to. She didn't want to be by herself while she waited for the telegram from Hugh. She knew she could not wish it into happening. It might never come. And she would then be on her own on the other side of the Atlantic, and after what she heard from the group in the lounge earlier, she faced an uncertain arrival. Isabelle could help her understand what was going on. She didn't think there was going to be a war.

Julia went out to the deck, followed by Isabelle. A strong wind blew Julia's hair up. She held it down with her hands, then decided to let it go. She laughed at Isabelle, who seemed unconcerned about the sea air and what it did to her appearance. Julia took notice of that. Isabelle didn't seem to care about such things. She was attractive enough, but her dress was very ordinary. At that moment, Julia realized it didn't matter to her, either. They walked along the deck past people in chairs, a mother standing over a basket with a little baby in it, two men in their maritime uniforms walking toward them. One of the men tipped his hat to Julia.

"Well you won't be ignored on board ship, Julia," Isabelle said, with an impish smile on her face.

Julia wasn't interested in whether sailors paid attention to her. "Isabelle, tell me about your family. You said you were visiting New Jersey?"

Isabelle nodded, her face lighting up when asked. "Yes, New Jersey, my brother is there. He has a wife and two children. He's been there a long time. It's not my first trip."

"So you were there to see them?"

"Yes, you might say that. To tell you the truth, I'm not so sure that everything will be okay in Europe. So I decided to go see Daniel before anything happens."

"But you left your family behind in France?"

"Yes, but I'm not married. I have my mother. My father died in the Great War."

Julia touched Isabelle on the arm. "I'm sorry. I'm sorry you're not…" Julia hesitated, then thought better of it as she saw that Isabelle knew what she was going to say, "married, I was going to say. Please now forgive me for my indiscretion."

Isabelle smiled at her and leaned in closer. "No, not at all. I think it's very sympathetic of you. But no, I've never been married. I'm not sure why. Maybe it's French men. If they could all be as nice as Daniel, maybe. But, to tell you the truth, I don't miss it."

"I understand," Julia said, her voice carrying her concern. "You noticed my daughter, so to me that meant you liked children."

"Ah, that, yes, it's true. I adore Daniel's children. But for me, I think it will never happen. Now it's too late for me." Isabelle turned and focused on Julia's eyes as she continued. "I must stay home and take care of my mother. She is not well."

Julia stepped away for a moment, a small shiver going through her. "Oh, but how could you leave her?"

"That was my feeling, too. But she was the one who insisted on it. Julia, you see, she lived through the war once, it was terrible. She lost the man who gave meaning to her life. There was nothing left for her except Daniel and me. She was the one who told Daniel to get out of France. He was going to try to live in Switzerland, but she forbade even that. My mother told him to go to America, where there's no war. That was ten years ago. But now, when Germany attacked Poland, that terrified her. She said I must go to America to see Daniel and give him her love."

"But who took care of her?"

"She has friends around her. You know, people in France, they have been suffering together for a long time."

"But you must be worried about her?" Julia had for a few moments forgotten about her absent daughter. Here was a woman who had loyalty divided between her brother and her mother. She thought of her own mother, now long dead, living her short life in peaceful upstate Maine without the world turning everything upside down.

"Yes, of course I am, Julia. As you are worried about your little Lizzie. And that is why I am going back home. I have seen Daniel, and now I will go back to my mother."

Julia stepped out past the end of the covered deck and into an area with people playing shuffleboard while dressed in long overcoats. Ahead of them were cranes tied down and a huge anchor up against the outside wall. A steel fence prevented them from going that far. She pulled her coat tight against the cold.

"Isabelle, why don't you bring your mother back with you to New Jersey? Then she can be with both you and Daniel."

Isabelle thought for a long moment, which seemed strange to Julia, who thought it was a simple straightforward idea.

"I have tried. I argued with her. Daniel wants her to come and live with him, too. But she's so stubborn, Julia. She doesn't want to leave her little corner of Paris. She won't find friends, she says, or won't leave her friends. But most of all, I think, she wants to go to the cemetery on Toussaint, All Saints Day, and put flowers down for her husband, and her cousin's husband and her friends' husbands. They all go."

"I think I understand that," Julia said. "For her, that's what her life has been all about. But that's not the way I would be. I love my family more than my friends."

"Ah, but my mother, she loves my father. The Germans gassed him in the war, you know, and my mother took care of him for months until he died. To tell the truth, she died with him. And that's why I think she kind of thought I would stay in America. But I love her, too. Maybe she doesn't understand that well enough."

Julia frowned at Isabelle. "Oh, come on, you know she understands that. But she has terrible choices. Your mother has been afraid for a long time. She wants you and Daniel to have a life she could not."

"So, do you think I should stay on the ship and come back, like you?" Isabelle's voice betrayed a change in her feeling. Now she seemed to be drawing away from Julia.

Julia worried she might lose a friendship she had made on the ship. "Please don't look at it that way."

"But what would you do if you were me, Julia? Tell me, I would like to hear it." There was more of a sincere pleading in her voice now.

Julia stopped and sat in an empty deck chair. She waited for Isabelle to join her.

"To be honest, I would do what you would do."

"Well, that's not a good answer."

Julia shrugged. "Of course, because you can answer your question. Now you are going back, and there's no way you're going to stay on this ship and turn around with it. Think of it, already you're on the way to your mother. First make it to Paris, then see your mother, then make up your mind. And now I know the answer to that."

"What is it?" Isabelle appeared to be surprised.

"It's obvious, isn't it? And you've already said it. Once you are there with your mother, you are not going to leave her while there's a war going on, even if it's a phony one."

Isabelle sat up. "You must come with me and meet my mother."

Julia shook her head. "You know that's impossible. I have to go home. If I don't get a telegram from Hugh, my husband, I will go back on my own." She leaned toward Isabelle. "Wait, no, you're right. I will go to Paris and fly back home from there. That's faster than the ship anyway. So, it's settled. For both of us. For now."

Isabelle for a few moments didn't quite comprehend what had been settled. She nodded and said, "For now. That's not a long time. But I am happy you will meet my mother. Oh, she's a wonderful cook. She will make you boeuf bourguignon, and champignons, we shall go pick them ourselves in the Bois de Boulogne and...."

"Wow, that sounds wonderful, Isabelle. But remember, I'm staying long enough to get a flight out. No, I do want to meet your mother, maybe I can convince her to go to New York with us, and we'll all go to New Jersey." Isabelle couldn't believe the lighthearted way she said all that. "But, let's not get ahead of ourselves."

That evening, Julia turned out the lights in her cabin and listened to the humming of the ship as it rolled across the ocean. She wondered what Lizzie was hearing as she lay in her bed. Was she thinking about her mom? Have they already moved her out of the house and to Philadelphia.

She believed that tomorrow was still a possibility. It was a new day for Hugh and Grace. They would realize what they had done, they would notice little Lizzie and see how sullen she was, crying, refusing to come out of her room.

She focused her attention on Lizzie's face, at the intense fear in the little child's eyes when they carried her out of the cabin and out to the deck. As she lay in the dark, she told the little girl to not give up hope, wait for me and your mother will come back to you and we will be together as a family. She repeated that several times each time with more intensity, and each time she felt the relief that passed over her.

Chapter 26

IN THE MORNING, Julia walked down to the communications room and asked, with soft politeness in her voice, if a telegram arrived, saying she knew that if you had one you would bring it to me, but I'm waiting and this helps me wait. The officer showed great sympathy but he had nothing to show her. She thanked him and left, trying to pretend to him that it wasn't so important. But she couldn't hide the pain inside from herself.

At the end of the day, she knew she had to go home on her own, but she had to believe that once she arrived there would be a happy reunion because Hugh and Grace did not want Lizzie to suffer without her mother. She had to believe that. Had to. This became her mantra.

As the ship sailed closer to France Julia came closer to realizing that it was Lizzie who was the glue that held her marriage together. It was the family that made the marriage possible. When she returned, the three of them would start over. Make it work. She had to make it work.

When the ship was on its last day of the cold voyage across the North Atlantic, Julia hurried to the bursar's office. Inside sat a young officer organizing paperwork, preparing for the end of the crossing. He was intent at making notes. When she came in he smiled, knowing she was happy to be nearing land again.

"How can I help you?" He leaned back in his chair and pointed to a wall of safety deposit boxes. "You must be the last person to pick up your belongings."

Julia realized she hadn't even thought about her money. That wasn't why she had come to the bursar's office. "Why yes you're right."

He didn't wait for her to speak any further. "Julia Stuart isn't it? Everyone else came in early. Do you have your key?"

Julia felt foolish and opened her purse and found the key. "Here it is," she said, as if she had to make the announcement to overcome her lack of preparation. She waited until the young man had given her money back in its envelope. She had an impulse to count it but she couldn't do that in front of him. "Well, I'm here about something else as well." She composed herself and thought about what she was going to say. "I'm here to inquire about passage back to New York." She surprised herself with this impulse. She remembered telling Isabelle she would return from Paris. But now, so close to Le Havre, she wanted desperately to stay on the ship and return to America with it.

He seemed surprised. "I have to tell you, I'm sorry," he said and then pretended to search his desk as if to find her name again. "That's not possible. We have not been informed by the United States Line where we are to go from here."

Julia's heart sank. "Oh, I had no idea. Aren't you going back?"

The young man nodded, his face showing consternation. "We shall stay here for a day or two because we need to refuel and take on supplies for the crew only. I am not prepared to accept new passengers. Normally at this point we would have a cable with the number of passengers boarding here, and whether we're moving on to Hamburg or Southampton."

Julia couldn't let it go. "Don't people ever go back?"

He smiled with sympathy. "Of course they do," he said. "People always arrive and then have many reasons why they have to go back right away. There were others who wanted to go back with us just like you. The situation here, you know..." and then he intertwined his fingers in front of him as if he were going to pray. "It doesn't matter. It's not up to me."

Julia shrunk inside herself. She held up her hand in a meek wave of goodbye and left the room. And as she walked back to her cabin she felt disappointed and guilty, as if she had betrayed Isabelle. Now she had no choice but to go to Paris. At first she had thought she had to wait until the ship had docked and then she could go on shore and book passage in the ship company's offices. But it was clear from what the bursar had said, that it would be a waste of time.

There was nothing for her to do until they arrived in port. Isabelle was somewhere and she couldn't leave the ship without finding her. Beyond walking down the gangplank, Julia had no plans for her arrival. She walked once around the deck. There were half as many people as usual, and no one was playing shuffleboard or any of the other activities she saw every day. Of course, they were all packing their suitcases and putting dresses back into trunks. She went down to the C deck and found Isabelle in her small cabin, with the door open, closing the lid on a large suitcase.

Isabelle straightened when she heard Julia's voice saying hello. She stood and smiled, then said, "Oh I'm so glad you came down here. I'm afraid I waited too long to start packing, and then I was going to go find you. But you saved me the trouble."

Julia waved off the apology. "I must admit the thought occurred to me that maybe it would work for us to go to Paris together, and I hadn't made any arrangements for myself. And then of course I wanted to say goodbye if things didn't work out."

Isabelle appeared hurt for a moment and then said, "Oh no, it's all set. I sent my mother a telegram, and so she's waiting for us and knows you're coming. One thing about Christine, she loves company. She knows you're an American and that excites her I'm sure. She'll hope you'll know Daniel."

"Well, that sets my mind at rest."

"Julia," Isabelle said, frowning, "you didn't think I was going to leave you at the dock, did you?"

"You know, it's the way I am. When the ship arrives then the voyage is over and I start a new voyage. I'm nervous, you know my real goal is to get back to my little Lizzie. They aren't taking on passengers now. I can't just sail back. I'm… I'm so… worried"

Isabelle came over to her and put her hands on her shoulders and held them there for a moment before letting them fall at her side. "Of course, you are, of course. As soon as we are at home and you're settled in I will go with you to the airline office and we'll arrange for your tickets home."

Julia let out a sigh of relief, and felt tears behind her eyes. "I want to stay and get to know you and your mother and Paris, but of course I also want to go home and be with my family."

Isabelle smiled. "I'll meet you on the dock. Stay as close as you can to the gangplank and I'll be able to find you. I'll find you so don't you go searching for me."

"No, I have a better idea, Isabelle. I'll have a porter bring your baggage up to my cabin, and they'll carry all our luggage down for us. I only have one small purse, so it will be fine."

Julia took the stairs back to her cabin and picked the few things that she had and put them into the sacks that she had received at the store. She arranged for Isabelle's things to be brought up and then went out. When she arrived at the deck for departure, she found it jammed full of exasperated people, some of them with luggage on the deck, all leaning left and right like penguins, to see why the line was not making any progress.

Julia asked the woman in front of her, who was holding the arm of a man on one side and a small boy on the other, "Do you know what's happened?"

The woman smiled, irritated that Julia had chosen her to solve the problem. "I believe it's because they're searching everyone's luggage. There are police down there alongside the customs officials."

Julia frowned, "They didn't tell us this would happen."

"I'm afraid they did. That's what the bursar told me. No one took it seriously."

"I don't think so. I didn't hear about it."

The woman smiled again and turned away from Julia. Moments later Isabelle came through the door out to the deck and pushed her way next to Julia.

"Oh, there you are," Julia said. "I didn't expect this."

Isabelle sighed. "First of all, thank you for your generous help. I guess I should have told you. Some people know it and some don't."

"But why are they taking so long?"

"It's customs."

"Yes, I know that, but it went quickly last time I was here."

"My dear," Isabelle said, "have you forgotten? There's a war now."

"They are going through everyone's luggage."

"I am not surprised," Isabelle said, with a weary face. "You know who they're doing?"

"Me? Trying to find German spies I should guess."

"Ah, yes, that, too, but they are searching for communists, for people smuggling weapons into the country. You know, from an neutral country like the United States."

"I see," Julia said, "that makes sense, now I feel foolish. We're going to have to wait. I think it's going to take a long time."

Isabelle excused herself as she pushed past people near them, making her way to the railing. She scanned a long while, surveying the whole scene, becoming more serious the longer she inspected the wharf. Back at Julia's side, she said, "There aren't many inspectors, so this is going to take a long time. Listen, you aren't in a hurry are you?"

Julia glanced at her in surprise. "Yeah, I think I am. I want to get to Paris so I can go back home."

Isabelle laughed, "Oh, you're thinking more long term. I mean, why don't we go back inside and sit down in the lounge and wait for the line to become smaller?"

"All right."

They went back inside and sat down in the Mayflower Café. To their chagrin, service had been discontinued, but there were glasses of water made available by some thoughtful staff, so they sat down next to the windows. Soon other people filled the tables around them. But the line started to move and then eventually there was no one outside the window. Isabelle stood and surveyed the deck and motioned Julia to go with her. They made their slow way down the gangplank and onto the wharf and at last stood before a table with a customs officer seated behind it and a police officer behind him. Behind them stood a third man in an overcoat who surveyed the scene with suspicious eyes.

The customs officer motioned them forward. "Bonjour. Welcome to France. Your passports, please. Are you traveling together?"

Julia said no and Isabelle said yes, and they frowned at each other in surprise. The officer raised his eyebrows in an exaggerated manner and peered back and forth between them, then leaned back as if to bring the police officer into the situation. The third man adjusted his stance and narrowed his field of vision to Julia and Isabelle.

"Well, now, which is it, ladies. Are you together or not."

Isabelle spoke up first. "We're both right, sir. She said no because we did not come on the ship together. I said yes because we met on the ship and now she's coming to Paris with me to meet my mother."

The customs officer kept his lips tight as he thought of the proper reaction. Then he nodded, "I see." He took Julia's passport, but gave the Isabelle's to the policeman. Switching his eyes between Julia and her passport he flipped through the pages. "Madame, do you speak French."

"Oui, Monsieur." Then Julia decided to give a longer answer to impress on him that she knew more than was in a guide book. "You can see that I have been to France before."

The policeman motioned for Isabelle to follow him off to the side. She smiled at Julia and said, "I'll be right back."

Julia nodded, but frowned.

The customs officer noticed it and said, "Don't worry, it's routine. She's French, you are not. So, where is your luggage?"

Julia had forgotten that she had none. She felt foolish, not having any luggage and not having any reason. "I don't have any."

The officer sat back in his chair and seemed to worry, as if they were making a fool of him. "I see. You come all the way across the ocean, here you are, and you have no clothes. And do you expect me to believe that?"

"It's the truth. That's all I can tell you." She lifted a paper bag with her new clothes in it and held it out to him.

He snickered and pushed it away. "And why should I believe you?"

"I have no other answer."

He stood up and glowered at her. "Well, you had better come up with a better answer than that or you are in serious trouble young lady." He stood, leaning on the table, close to her face.

Julia stepped back. "I'm sorry. The fact is I ran away from home and I did it in a hurry and I couldn't give myself away by packing my suitcase. I had my little girl with me...."

"Your little girl?" The man almost shouted out. He feigned searching around and under the table. "And where is she, your little girl?" He opened his eyes wide to make sure she understood he was losing patience with her.

"Here," she said, opening her purse, and handing him her ticket. "It says right on the ticket. But my husband came and took her away.

You can ask the crew, there was an officer on the ship who was with him. You can ask them." Once more, Julia understood the seriousness of the situation. She motioned to the police officer talking to Isabelle. "You can ask her, too, Monsieur, she saw it. I mean she saw me come on with my daughter. You must ask the ship's officer about my husband."

The customs officer appeared satisfied with this response. He had someone he could give the problem to. "One moment," he said, his voice more sympathetic. He went to the police officer and talked to him and Isabelle for a moment. Then he came back and nodded to Julia. "She corroborates your story. Or at least part of it. You wait here. I will find someone on the ship who can help me with the other part of it." He pointed to the chair.

Julia sat and watched him walk away to the ship and up the gangplank, disappearing on the deck. Isabelle came back and joined her.

"Are you all right?" Isabelle said, touching Julia's arm. "Where's he going?"

"He's going to ask an officer on the ship to verify that my husband took my daughter away. Are you all right, Isabelle?"

"Yes, the police were suspicious because we gave contrary answers at first. But it's all right. They asked me to tell them all I knew about you on the boat, and if you were alone, and when I told them about little Lizzie, the customs officer was satisfied, and so they, I think they stopped worrying about us. But now we're in their little book."

"Oh?"

"As I said, Julia, it's wartime, even if it's a phony war. They have noted that we came off the boat together, and whatever else they want. That fact will make its way to Paris and we will be famous. In a way." Isabelle reacted to Julia's concern at the last remark. "Oh don't worry, they're not going to remember us. There are so many people coming and going. It's good, you see. All the information goes to Paris and then nobody can ever find it. Thank god for Napoleon, at least this once."

The customs officer returned and became his normal perfunctory self. He stamped her passport, checked that Isabelle's travel permit had been stamped by the police, then returned the documents to them. The police officer then stepped forward and produced two more documents and handed them to the customs officer, who handed one each to the two women. He held on to the pieces of paper, saying, "You may go now, ladies. These permits will allow you to travel to Paris, but you will of course, report to the district office in your arrondissement within two days, won't you?" He then let the pieces of paper go.

"Yes, sir," Julia said. She put her hand out to him.

He was surprised, but then smiled and shook her hand. "Madame. Enjoy Paris. While you can."

"Thank you," Julia said, but her shoulders suddenly felt tight.

Isabelle moved from the table without saying a word. Julia followed her and, a few feet away, she turned back and saw the three men laughing among themselves, the police officer pointing at her and Isabelle, making a hand gesture that could have been lewd. Welcome to France.

They moved out from the pier and into the bus station outside on Quai Atlantique. At the Le Havre train station, they had a short wait for the train to Paris. As they traveled south, Isabelle reassured Julia that their interviews back on the pier were nothing to be worried about.

"Julia, is everything all right? Are you still concerned about what happened back there?"

"No, not…yes…but not because they asked us those questions. It's, you know, oh, I don't know. Oh, yes I do. There I was in front of customs and I had no luggage. It must have been suspicious to them."

"Okay, Julia, maybe at first. I tell you what's a good sign. The customs officer went himself up to the ship to find out. That means that he trusted you. You're in trouble when the police do the searching. There's nothing going on. So don't be worried. Let's go to the snack car and get something to eat, and enjoy our couple of hours to Paris."

Julia nodded and felt better, but still not secure. She knew she would not feel that until she arrived home in New York and was playing with Lizzie in Central Park.

Chapter 27

JULIA AND ISABELLE arrived in Paris as the sun set golden beyond the city. Julia offered to take one of Isabelle's two small suitcases. Isabelle was happy to let her share the burden and they set off to her mother's house in Montmartre. As they walked up Rue Lamarck to Rue du Mont-Cenis, Isabelle pointed up to the steps leading up the hill to the top of Montmartre.

"We'll walk up there soon. It's a challenging exercise mounting those steps. You can see the whole city of Paris in front of Sacré-Coeur, everything, Notre Dame, Eiffel Tower. You'll love it, Julia. And Place du Tertre, ah, the best crepes in the world." She thought for a moment, glanced sideways at Julia with a twist of the mouth, then said, "Oh, but you've been there."

Julia nodded, but smiled, "Yeah, but this is different with you. You live here. You're Parisian."

Isabelle's face lit up. "But, here we are, 32, where my mother lives. Can you believe it? Home." She pressed on the black button on the doorframe.

They waited and a tiny voice came from above. "*O là là.* Un moment!" They both moved their heads up in response, and the window was still open on the second floor, but no one was visible. One second later a buzzer sounded and Isabelle pushed open the door and held it for Julia to enter.

Julia picked the suitcase up and carried it inside the building. In the small foyer, she struggled to move without hitting Isabelle. It was dark and the walls were dirty and pockmarked. She stood still and let

Isabelle pass her by, and followed her on the wooden staircase as it wound up to the second floor.

The tiny voice could be heard up above. "Isabelle. Ma fille. Enfin." At the landing Isabelle stopped, dropped her suitcase and hugged the petite woman standing outside the doorway.

Julia continued up the last few stairs. As she, too, let the suitcase fall, and her bag of clothes, Isabelle stepped away from the woman. She was very short, with hunched shoulders on a small frame. Her plain gray dress hung on her body as if it were a set of rags and her skinny legs ended in plain black shoes with scrapes all over them.

Isabelle continued in French. "Julia, this is my mother, Christine."

Julia saw Isabelle with a genuine wide happy smile for the first time since she'd met her.

The older woman grinned more than smiled, showing a missing tooth on the side, and came to Julia, raising herself up to kiss Julia on both cheeks, then turning to Isabelle, "Ma petite chérie, I see your friend is a beautiful American. And so young." Christine switched her eyes back and forth between the two of them, her eyes the color of amethyst, brilliant, ecstatic. "But come in, please." She hurried back into the apartment and held the door open for the two of them.

"Isabelle, you can put your friend Julia in Daniel's room." Christine performed a short little dance of joy. "Oh, this is a surprise. An American. Let me go make a pot of coffee. I have wonderful cake from Boulanger Albert, your favorite, a tart aux pommes, they have the best apples from Normandy, you know," she said, then turned to face the newcomer in her house, "Julia, my favorite tarte, too. Oh...." she put her hands on her cheeks, "and some Calvados, Albert got it from his cousins. From the farm. Amazing. Beautiful." She laughed at herself and disappeared around a corner, her elbows moving back and forth like a puppet.

"She's an amazing woman," Julia said, her eyes wide open in surprise at this small dynamo. "You didn't tell me about her."

"No, maybe I'm used to it. She has more energy than little kids. C'mon, follow me."

Julia followed Isabelle into a small room with an old bed covered in a gray blanket. It used to be white but over time had lost all its brightness. Above the bed hung a small wooden crucifix, and behind it a dry palm branch. Julia thought how long it's been since she had been to Palm Sunday services. Not since childhood. The room felt empty, despite the small varnished table with many scratches on its surface, a chair and a three-drawer dresser against one wall. But the furniture in the bedroom, like the furniture when they entered the house, was of very good quality. It appeared old. Not antique as such, but old, well-made, with hand-made carved ornaments. "Isabelle, you have very nice furniture here."

"You think so? I didn't notice it." Isabelle's eyes swept the room. "Maybe. Someone made it, I guess. But it doesn't have gold, or inlays."

Julia shook her head in disbelief. "Okay, so it's not Louis XVI or something. I think it's wonderful handmade furniture. By a real craftsman. You are spoiled here in Paris and don't appreciate what you've got."

Isabelle pursed her lips. "Well, I bet you have some real antiques back in New York in your apartment."

Julia started to respond, then understood that Isabelle was asking her questions on wealth and decided to stop the direction of this conversation. So she lied. "No, nothing like that. We have good furniture, I'll say that, but I'm certain it came from a factory in North Carolina." Once she heard herself, she went one step further. "One piece we have like yours, my mother bought in Canada. Made by hand by a cabinet maker in Quebec. A beautiful table." Now she could not stop, although her next statement was not an invention. "My house where I grew up, in Maine. We had furniture made by hand by French-Canadians." She saw Isabelle's eyes narrowing. Tired. "But we're here."

"Oh, are you French?"

"Yes, actually, on both sides."

"So your parents spoke French?"

Julia shook her head. "No, my grandmother. I learned it from her."

"And your parents, are they still there, in Maine?"

"No. They're both dead. They died rather young, of Spanish flu, soon after I was born."

"Oh, I'm so sorry."

"I didn't know them."

Isabelle nodded and smiled in sympathy. "So, this is Daniel's room, but he hasn't been in it for a longtime. I'm right next door."

Then she saw Julia's bag. "Ah, I forgot, you have what you purchased on the ship. Well, we have some lovely shops in Montmartre, I'm sure you can find something nice to wear."

"Thank you," Julia said, "but I only need enough to fly back to New York. Maybe a dress. Maybe."

"But, while you're here...in Paris, Julia," Isabelle said, frowning.

"To be honest with you, I don't want to be here very long. I'm very happy to be here with your mother, and I'm going to adore the tarte aux pommes...." then Julia stopped and laughed. "I don't know about the Calvados."

Isabelle touched her on the shoulder and turned to leave the room. "Well, then, I will unpack later. I promise you we will go find the airline office first thing in the morning." She smiled and left without closing the door. But a moment later she came back and peeked in the room, eyebrows raised, and said, "We have our own bathroom here, Julia," sounding as if she had to make at least one point in defense of her mother's apartment. "I'll show you."

When they sat at the table, Julia asked Christine to tell her the story of the picture of a thin man in a double-breasted suit and tie with a turned-up collar.

Christine stopped eating and put her fork on her plate. She studied the photo as if her whole life were contained within the glass, then turned to Julia. "That's my husband. The Germans gassed him in 1918, you know." She threw a glance at her daughter, then back to Julia. "I'm sure Isabelle has told you that. He died for France. He was a hero. And he died in my arms, in this house." She was going to cry but then seized some courage from within and made a long sigh and said, "He is always with me. He is buried not far from here, in the Montmartre cemetery. If you have time, I could take you."

Isabelle touched her mother's arm, but cut her off with, "Mama, Julia needs to get back to New York. Her daughter is there, I don't think she has time."

Julia smiled at Christine. "No, Isabelle is right. I do want to see his grave." She held back tears, "but I must get back to my little girl."

Christine frowned. "I don't understand, why are you here without your little girl?"

"Mama!" Isabelle's eyes widened at her mother's question.

Julia shook her head at Isabelle. "I understand your mother's question. It's not my fault that my daughter…."

The muscles in Christine's face tightened. "Oh, I didn't mean that the way it sounded, Julia, please. Please excuse me. You are so young." She put her napkin up to her face as if to hide her tears.

Isabelle raised her hands up. "Maybe we're carrying this a little too far?"

Christine said to Julia, "Of course, you must go home to your little daughter." Then her face lit up in a smile, although her eyes did not agree. "And you can bring her back to Paris if you want. We will keep you safe here."

Isabelle smiled at that remark. "I think Julia needs to go home, Mama."

Julia put her hand out on the table toward Isabelle's mother. "I appreciate your kindness. My little Elizabeth wanted to come to Paris and I know she'd love tarte aux pommes."

Christine laughed at that, but her eyes were still moist.

"Tomorrow Isabelle will take me to the airline office and I will buy my ticket. When I get home, Christine, will it be all right for me to send you a letter, and maybe a picture of my little girl in the park?"

"Yes, of course, I'd love it."

Isabelle's stood and picked her dishes up and took them to the kitchen.

Julia, alone at the table with Christine, spoke in a quiet voice. "You have a son in New Jersey?"

Christine smiled, the same warm smile she showed when she saw Isabelle come up the stairs. "Daniel, yes, I want him where he is safe. I could not accept that I have to go visit him in the cemetery, too. Do you live in New Jersey?"

Julia shook her head. "No, I live in New York, but I could walk to where I can see New Jersey. What town is he in?"

"He lives in Guttenberg. He said he can see New York, too, at night. That must be a famous view, no?"

Julia had no idea what was on the other side of the Hudson River if you followed 85th west. "Yes, the New York skyline. But I don't know the town your son is in."

Christine waved the idea away. "Oh, never mind, but you know, it's very nice that you live near him. I wanted Isabelle to…" she waited while her daughter came back and picked up more dishes. She watched her, then continued when Isabelle had disappeared. "I wanted her to stay there."

Isabelle stopped, holding a dish in each hand, and turned back toward the table, her face a window of mixed emotions. "I put a stop to that. She won't go with me, and I won't leave her. So there you are." She continued through the small door into the kitchen.

Julia saw a row of gleaming copper pans hanging above a small stove.

Christine wiped her hands on her dress and shook her head, determined to keep ahead of her daughter. "You know, my father, Victor, he was alive in the Franco-Prussian war. People were killing each other here. You have seen our Sacré-Coeur at the top?"

Julia nodded, but kept her lips closed, wanting to know what this intriguing woman had to tell her.

"They built that after the war. My father told me when I was a child that Parisians were killing each other, they killed the archbishop…" Christine made a sign of the cross, "and priests, and he said people ate rats. I do not want my son and daughter to go through that when the Germans come here. Thank god Daniel is safe. But this foolish girl!"

"Mama, don't talk like that. We are safe." Isabelle came back in the room and her voice rose. "We have the Maginot line and the Ardennes to protects us. We have the largest army in the world. France can never fall!" Isabelle turned to Julia with a stare that told her the speech was for her mother's benefit.

Christine shifted in her chair. "Oh my, my daughter, I don't want to argue politics with you. I love you too much. My life is over, anyway. My father suffered so much, my husband gassed, what do I care about the Ardennes? I have you and Daniel."

"Daniel? There it is, that's the problem. Mama, why won't you come with me. I will be happy to leave all of France behind if you come with me to America. We can be there with Daniel."

Christine sat back in her chair and seemed to fold into herself. "No. I will never leave my husband. Never."

"Fine," Isabelle said, "that's your decision. I'm staying with you. Paris is for lovers and rats."

They shared a glance, and then both faced at the same time to Julia, who sat with her eyes wide open.

"I'm sorry," Julia said. "I didn't mean for this to happen." She ran her fingers through her hair. Nothing mattered to her except going home to Lizzie. Nothing. "Perhaps I will find a hotel for tonight, and tomorrow I will go to Pan American Airlines."

Christine stood and walked to Julia and put her arms around her. "No, my child, tonight, tonight you must stay with us and Isabelle can take you tomorrow." She walked to Isabelle and put her arms around her. Then she stood back. "This beautiful young girl, she is here without her husband and her daughter." Her eyes misted. "I thought I was tough, having seen so much." She wiped her eyes with her apron. "Let's all go tomorrow, huh? To the airline office. Who knows, maybe there I will be closer to Daniel than to the dead." She smiled, but it was not a happy smile, it was the smile of defeat. "Maybe we can all go to America."

Isabelle stood in shock, waiting and breathing before she spoke. "Mama, do you mean it?" She put her fingers up to her lips as if in prayer. "Really?"

Christine held her hands up. "Yes, my daughter, you know I mean what I say. I don't know what I will tell my husband when I say goodbye to him. But you, Isabelle, do you mean what you say?"

Isabelle was worried. "Mama, what do you mean? Why are you asking that?"

"You know very well what I am asking. You think I don't know what you are doing? Where you go in the evening? You think I don't see you meeting with your so-called friends on the street there below the steps. We know who they are."

"We? We?"

"Yes, I know, from Madame Sequin, and Madame Hermel. They know more than I do. You tell me nothing."

Isabelle shot Julia a quick glance, then spoke to her mother. "Mama, I do what I do for France. As papa did, as grandpapa did. But I am not sure what France does for us. So, we are going to America. Did I not hear you say that?"

Christine nodded and sighed. "We both said it. And now I must thank this wonderful girl for helping us. Let's finish the dishes and walk up to Place du Tertre and have some crepes and sweet wine, what do you say? To celebrate. Tomorrow we all start a new life. I will see my Daniel, and you," she turned to face Julia with a radiant smile but eyes near tears, "you will see your darling daughter." She pulled Isabelle and Julia closer, this small trembling woman, and put her arms around their necks. Then she pulled back. "Let me get my shawl."

The three women went out to the street and turned left up Rue du Mont-Cenis. As they arrived a few steps later to Rue Lamarck, arm in arm, Christine pointed across the street to the Au Relais restaurant. "Wonderful. You must eat there. I've eaten there all my life. I love Madame Roussard. You will like her too. If she likes you back, she will always make something special for you. And, she has a first class wine cellar, with wines from Montmartre. Not every restaurant has that. I must show you that, too. Clos de Montmartre. Every bit as good as pinot noir or Bordeaux that they all go crazy for. And, my dear, the Lapin Agile, you know that?"

Julia shook her head, amazed at this old woman's energy and spirit.

"Ah, that's where, it's a few blocks away, Picasso, see that's a famous painter I know, he went there in the evening with his friends. Well, he wasn't famous then."

Christine stopped before crossing the empty street. She pointed again, up the hill toward Sacré-Coeur. "See, you see all those stairs. I'm not going up there. That's for tourists." Then she laughed. "I use them for coming home. Come on, follow me." She took them across the street and turned left and led them one more street uphill to Rue Becquerel. She stopped and pointed once again to the right in triumph and excitement. "See, right up there, a few steps past the park, where the old men play petanque, ha, there it is."

Julia was surprised to see the top of Sacré-Coeur, so close, with no effort at all to reach it.

"I always laugh," Christine said, "when I see people trudging so hard up those stairs on Mont-Cenis, when the easy answer is around the corner. Of course, the really smart people take the bus." She laughed at her own little joke.

Isabelle turned to Julia, amazed at her mother's new found sense of humor. She touched Julia on the shoulder and whispered to her, "Thank you."

A few short quick minutes and they came up along the back end of Sacré-Coeur. An open gate before them led underneath a passageway,

211

a greensward visible beyond it, and some misty part of Paris beyond that in the distance and below them.

"See, no one here. Tourists are all on the right."

Isabelle pulled her mother close. "Mama, don't speak like that. Julia can hear you."

Christine laughed, and turned to Julia. "Ah, but you, my dear, you are one of us, you are not a tourist."

"Thank you, Madame," Julia said in appreciation. But inside was the burning fear of being a tourist and not at home with her daughter.

They wound their way around to the front of the basilica and out to the space overlooking the city. Julia gasped at the view of the Eiffel Tower shooting far up above the horizon.

Christine came next to her and had Julia follow her pointing finger to the left. "See, over there, you can see it. Our Notre Dame de Paris cathedral. It's so majestic."

Julia searched hard in the distance and found the twin square towers of Notre Dame among all the buildings before them.

"Come now, girls," Christine said, as she moved away from the banister overlooking the city. "Let's go to Place du Tertre and have our crepes."

"And sweet wine you said, Mama."

"Oh, of course."

They followed the street around to the right, turned left and found the open Place with tents and lights and artist stands. And a magical glow.

"Oh," Julia exclaimed, pointing, "I remember that. All the art." She laughed as she stopped at an artist sitting in a chair drawing a caricature of a young man seated opposite him.

Isabelle pulled on her. "Let's go to Chez Eugène. I'm hungry."

For two hours, the three women ate their crepes, drank some sweet Riesling from Alsace, toured the Place, chatted with artists, and left the rest of the world out of it.

Julia ate her crepes suzettes, but didn't drink her wine. She spent most of the time watching the little children run around the restaurant. "Isn't this beautiful," she said. "It's so marvelous for children. So many. So happy. The way they play."

A little girl in a red dress came running by and tripped. She held on to Julia's knee to keep from falling, then looked up in shock at the stranger so big before her. But Julia laughed and caressed the little girl's head. The girl smiled at Christine and Isabelle, and Julia's eyes misted up. "She's like my little girl. Now you know empty my heart is. What a mistake I have made. I must get home as soon as I can."

"I see," Christine said, "I know in my own heart that you are a wonderful mother. My heart goes out to you. You do not belong in France. You belong in New Jersey." She laughed and put her hand up to her face. "*O là là*, no, I mean New York."

Christine enjoyed her wine, and watching the tourists, but then tired out. "Come on, now, take me home. At least the steps downhill are easy for me. Hold on to me so I don't tumble all the way down."

THE NEXT MORNING Isabelle and Julia ate their croissants and drank their wide bowls of coffee and milk, then set off for the Montmartre city hall to surrender their travel permits from Le Havre.

Once inside the building, Julia saw with resignation the number of people milling around inside. She waited a full hour before she and Isabelle could speak to someone at a window.

"Ah," the man said. He studied them over his glasses. The ceiling light reflected off the top of his bald head. His white stubble rustled as it scraped against his dirty collar. "I saw that you came off the ship at Le Havre." He shook his head back and forth as he stared at Isabelle. "Yes, I know that already. You are stupid. You were in America and you come back? I know you Isabelle. I know your mother...and your father, bless his soul. We went to first communion together. What's wrong with you?"

"Monsieur Ducasse," Isabelle replied, "I know you, too. Your daughter Clémentine went to school with me." She turned to Julia. "We're saying all this for your benefit." Then she turned back to the man and said, "Monsieur, this is my friend Julia. She is staying with me and my mother for a few days. She needs a residence permit, too. And then a new travel permit."

They both pushed their temporary travel permits into the booth.

He nodded and pushed his glasses up on the top of his head and settled back, ready to make a grand pronouncement from behind the counter. "Of course, I can give you a residence permit, and I do so because I know you, Isabelle and your mother. Let me do that. He stamped Isabelle's card and gave it back to her. "Now, young lady," he continued, turning to Julia. "You need a residence permit, of course. Please give me your photograph."

Isabelle put her hand up to her mouth and opened her eyes wide. "Oh, merde, we forgot all that. Oh, Monsieur, what a mistake. Please forgive us. We will go out and do that right away. I know a photographer, well you know him, too, Monsieur Margulis." She tapped Julia on the arm. "I'm sorry, I should have remembered that you don't have a residence permit." She turned back to the man. "Monsieur, please return my friend's travel permit. She will need it for another day, until we can get the photograph.

The man smiled as he pushed Julia's travel permit back to her. "My advice, Isabelle, is to come back tomorrow, in the morning before the rush. Then I can help you myself. You won't have to explain yourself again. Please say hello to your mother from me."

Isabelle and Julia left the city hall and walked a few hundred meters to the photography shop of Jacques Margulis. Inside, Julia saw that it was a complete photo shop, with film, cameras, frames for pictures, and large developing equipment. One enlarger took up most of the display window facing the street.

Monsieur Margulis came out from the back through a dark gray curtain. He was tall, with broad shoulders. A dark brown cardigan sweater hung open over a light brown shirt. His black hair stood high on his head, swept back from his face. He did not smile.

"How may I help you, Isabelle?" He stared at her with an intensity that Julia found disconcerting.

"Jacques, well, we are here because my friend here needs a residence permit."

"A residence permit? You can't get that from me, Isabelle. You know that."

Isabelle let out a sigh. "No, but she needs a picture of herself to take to city hall so she can get a residence permit there. You know that, Jacques." Isabelle's voice conveyed familiarity.

Julia wondered, were they lovers? Or were they connected some other way? There seemed to be an air of tension between them.

He shook his head. "Of course, that's most of my business these days." He motioned to Julia. "If you would come with me, please. I can take your picture, and if you return in an hour, I will have several copies of your photo."

"Oh, thank you," Julia said, smiling. "That's very nice of you to do it so fast. And to make copies." This man was for the moment the most important person in the world to her.

"Yes, you will need to have more than one copy of your photo if you are to survive the government's requirements, young lady. Please come with me."

When he had taken her picture, Julia walked to the front next to Isabelle and looked at the cameras in the case.

"That's interesting," Isabelle said, "cameras. Mama has a camera. I can take pictures of the house and neighborhood for Mama to have when she's with us in America." Isabelle frowned and screwed up her face as she realized that she didn't want to say that. She glanced sideways at Jacques.

"If she means it," Julia said, trying to give Isabelle an out if that would help her with the photographer

"Oh, don't remind me, Julia. I know she could change her mind at the last minute. But I'm for anything that makes it easier for her to leave France before the Germans come pouring across the border with their panzers."

"Your mother is going to America?" Jacques' voice came from behind them.

Isabelle opened her eyes wide and raised her eyebrows to show how she felt about her mother's intentions. "That's what she says. She seems quite serious about it."

Jacques seemed worried. He folded his arms across his chest and stared pointedly at Isabelle. "And you? Are you going to go with her?"

Isabelle nodded as she waited for his reaction.

He hesitated again and slowly shook his head with fear in his eyes. "Are you here to take her with you? Do you have some connection with Daniel? What's going on here? Are you leaving us?"

"Don't start that, Jacques." For the first time Isabelle showed fire in her eyes.

Julia turned to go out the door but stopped. She sensed the tension between Jacques and Isabelle, but she didn't want to add to the drama because she wasn't sure it was anything important. Her movement caused them to stop their conversation. This worried her and she turned back. "I think it might be better if I waited outside."

Isabelle moved to where Julia stood and said, "No, it's all right, Jacques and I can talk some other time." She pushed Julia to the door and before shutting it she leaned back in and said, "Thank you so much for helping us out. We'll be back in a couple of hours for the pictures." She continued to push Julia past the store window. Then they walked together down the street. "Now it's time to go to the Champs Élysées and see about getting an airline ticket back to the United States." She sighed and put her arm around Julia's waste. "For all of us I hope."

Chapter 28

WHEN THEY SURFACED from the subway on to the Champs Élysées they were opposite a large window that read All Airlines, with logos for Air France, Lufthansa, Pan American, and Swissair.

Inside the building, lit by bright sunlight through the large picture windows, were a long series of counters with airline names behind them. Lufthansa was empty, as they could see. No one even sat behind the counter. But most of the other counters were also empty of people, even though sad clerks sat waiting for some relief from the boredom.

Julia and Isabelle frowned in disappointment when they saw there must have been at least half a dozen people jockeying for position in front of the Pan American counter. They went closer to see whether they had a chance of talking to someone, when a young man stood up from his desk and walked over to where they stood, as if he thought he had to come to their rescue. Smoke from a cigarette with long ashes still on the end made him blink. His grey suit was wrinkled as if he had been in it all night.

"Excuse me," he said, "I think that you are here to book a flight on Pan American." He said this in English with an American accent. "Or perhaps you need information." He smiled, but appeared weary of answering questions.

Julia smiled. Here was someone who could help her get back home to be with little Lizzie. He was tall and thin with a narrow mustache on his upper lip. His hazel eyes switched between her and Isabelle undue intensity.

217

"My name is Peter Smyth. You'll spend all day waiting to see somebody at that counter. I have a better method. I can give you an appointment and you won't have to wait in line."

Julia breathed a sigh of relief. "That would be wonderful. I have my passport here and I am ready to fly." She patted Isabelle on the shoulder. "This is my friend, Isabelle, who is ready to fly back with me, she and her mother."

Peter turned to Isabelle and said, "There is no reason we cannot get you all on the same flight." He turned to Julia and then moved back to be able to talk to both of them at the same time. "Forgive me for being presumptuous," he said with a little bow. "You are both American, is that right? And you have your travel permits? That's all you need and we can proceed. Of course, you will have to get your own train ticket for Lisbon, but we can issue you your ticket for the Clipper flight from Lisbon to Miami."

Julia stood there for a moment in shock. She had expected it was simple, you could fly from Paris straight to New York. Get on the plane and go home she'd thought but it wasn't so easy now. Lizzie seemed so far away now. "Lisbon? I thought you could fly straight to New York."

"I must tell you, never straight to New York, uh, I would like to be a little more personal and helpful. Your name is?" Peter inched closer to Julia, then blinked again at the smoke twirling up from his cigarette. He twisted away to put it out on a chrome ashtray on a dark wooden table behind him. Then he returned his gaze to her.

"Julia. Julia Stuart. Thank you, Peter. We appreciate all you can do for us, believe me." She smiled, or tried to appear smiling to him, but inside she felt her life disappearing.

"Well," Peter said, "since France declared war on Germany, airlines based in the United States don't fly here anymore. We fly out of Lisbon. Unless you have a way to get to England, then you could take British Overseas to Ireland and Newfoundland."

Isabelle interrupted him. "Yes I understand," she said, "Julia is American. I am French, and my mother is going with us, she is French, but I have a brother who lives in New Jersey. I came back from a visit with him. It will be no problem for us to get the necessary travel permit. I am well known to a man in the Montmartre City Hall."

Peter frowned and made it clear that he was doubtful about her connections with municipal officials. Or maybe he was doubtful that her connections would make any difference.

"No, it's true, I don't mean to say that I have relationships high up, but I've known this man all my life and so that is what gives me confidence that he will be able to help us out."

Peter shook his head sympathetically. "Julia should have no trouble getting her travel permit from the police, assuming everything is in order. She is going to go home and that's routine. But you, you are leaving France in wartime, and your travel permit will not be so easy to get."

"Yes, yes," Isabelle said, "we understand all that. I have returned from the United States and I am clear on all the requirements. It is because I have received permission to travel to the United States and have been gone for two months, so I have gone through this process and nothing's changed and the permit process will be the same for me. We appreciate your help."

Peter moved his gaze between the two women and smiled with great sympathy. "In any case, we will not be able to schedule a flight until we have your travel permits in our hands."

Julia turned to Isabelle, her heart sinking. She had sent her cable and gotten no response. Now she had to wait even longer go home. And, she thought to herself, Christine, she couldn't drop everything and run off to Lisbon. She had to be careful to keep her trip home separate from Isabelle and her mother. I have one goal, she thought, and that's to get myself home to Lizzie.

Peter waited for Julia to pay attention. "And you do know that it is a two-week delay at the very least before you will receive your permits. It is not city hall anymore but also the police, and not in the district but at the Paris police headquarters. I wish I could give you an answer that would make you feel better."

Julia felt the need to push this young man, who knew how bureaucracies worked. "But there must be some way we can speed this up. Is there no one we can talk to?" The idea formed in her mind that Hugh could be of decisive help in getting her out of this mess. If he had not responded to her telegram, or maybe not even have gotten it, then she would send him an urgent letter. She would do it as soon as she finished here, before she even picked up her photographs and went back to city hall for her travel permit.

Peter turned to face Isabelle. "And I am not one to tell you about getting your permits, Mademoiselle, but you need your travel permits, both of you, and I hope you can get them soon." As soon as he said this, his face darkened.

"But then you are travelling to Portugal, so you will need your exit visa from France, and your transit visa for Spain and another transit visa for Portugal. And then your train ticket. I'm sorry to go on like this, but you need to know the whole situation. Once you arrive in Lisbon, and believe me, I understand you might have no problem getting all these documents, I must tell you also, once you are in Lisbon, you can be bumped from the flight by people with diplomatic passports. I can say, I have been doing this job for a month and there are always complications when there is a war."

Isabelle became indignant. "Thank you, Monsieur, we are not ignorant of what's going on. You came over to see if you could help us, but in the end you are listing complications. People are getting out and city hall is helpful. I think we should be on our way."

Julia felt a touch of panic at Isabelle's criticism. "No, no, Peter, I thank you for your clarification. I have learned much that I didn't know, and I…and…Isabelle, too." She lightly rubbed Isabelle's arm as she turned for a moment toward her. "We both thank you. These are difficult times." Then her fear of not seeing Lizzie for a long time prompted her to continue. "I have a little girl back in New York. I'm trying to get back to her as soon as I can. Anything you can do to help us, you know, it would mean everything."

Peter smiled, but said, "You must do everything I said. It is up to you to get your paperwork. You must dedicate yourselves to getting that done. That's the key to leaving France as soon as possible."

He held out his hand to Julia, then after shaking her hand, turned to Isabelle and held out his hand, his smiling face showing that he didn't want to antagonize her more than he already had. Isabelle took his hand, but did not smile in return.

"Come on," she said to Julia. "Thank you," she said to Peter, in her most businesslike voice.

"You're welcome," he said, in a voice loud enough to catch their attention before they moved too far away. "One more thing. Let me preface this by saying I don't know either of you. But keep in mind that Lisbon is full of Gestapo agents."

Julia and Isabelle froze.

"Yes," Peter said as he nodded, confident he had made an impression on them. "As I said, I don't know you, but people do arrive in Lisbon and are then whisked away by the Gestapo into Spain and then disappear."

Isabelle spoke with indignation. "And why do you think this applies to us?"

"I don't know that it does. But in a way it applies to everybody. I don't want you to go off thinking that agents of Germany are restricted to German soil. There are too many stories. And, if you don't mind my saying so, it's because I think the two of you are very innocent that I offer this advice. Sorry if I offended you." Peter turned away from them and walked to the crowd of people still pushing each other at the Pan American counter.

The two women walked back on to the Champs Élysées and stood for a moment in the wind.

"That was very frightening," Julia said. She stepped closer to Isabelle in hope of hearing something reassuring. "But you must have known all that."

"No," Isabelle said, slowly shaking her head. "At least not all of it. I did not know that Le Bourget was closed."

"Le Bourget?"

"The Paris airport."

"He didn't say anything about airports being closed."

"Not in so many words. But he said we have to take the train to Lisbon. This is more serious than I thought. This phony war has changed French transportation. I know we don't concern you directly, but you know, I fear Mama will never leave Paris if she has to do all this."

Julia nodded, concerned for her friend, but unable to think of how to help her.

Isabelle leaned in close to Julia. "I see you understand the situation. Then we must change plans. We will get you out of the country first thing. As soon as possible."

Julia's heart jumped at this offer from Isabelle to ignore her own situation to help her get back to Lizzie.

"Be careful what you say at home. We don't need to get Mama excited. Once she knows how long it's going to take to get an exit permit, that will be enough for her to forget her own plans. All we need to tell her is that it's easy for you because you're going home. Ah!" Isabelle lifted her head back and then hit herself on the forehead. "There you go. He didn't mention the most important thing."

Julia was now insecure and puzzled. "What?"

"America. We need a visa to enter the United States. He didn't even mention that. He was so worried about the French police and the Gestapo, he forgot about that important thing. But, then, it's what will make Mama patient enough. I will tell her that, and she and I will work on getting to the embassy. Meanwhile we'll get you out of the country."

"That's gracious of you," Julia said. For the first time, she felt her stomach settle down. Now she had to concentrate on getting home to Lizzie without having to worry about someone else first.

"For now, let's pick up your permit photographs and go back to city hall, and then we'll figure out the exact wording for Mama. I think when it comes to finally leaving, it may break her heart." Then she sped up. "Let's keep moving."

As they walked to the subway station, Julia said, "One quick thing. I want to make a phone call to New York. I don't want them to worry about me."

"Fine," Isabelle said, "it's not a problem, even in this wartime country. The post office will have phone booths where you can place a call, if that's what you want. There's one of those in Montmartre, too. Nearby."

"No, I don't want to wait. It will be late in New York, but someone will answer the phone. We have to do this now." Her pulse quickened as she imagined hearing Hugh's voice, and then Lizzie's.

They walked the short trip to La Poste on Rue Colisée. Inside, people lined up at the counters for mailing, but the phone booths were empty. Julia went up to the phone counter. "Bonjour. I want to place a phone call to the United States, please."

The woman behind the counter took a piece of paper without smiling or acknowledging Julia. She wore large round glasses that made her appear like a child underneath a huge volume of wavy hair. She waited and fidgeted with her pen before paying attention to Julia.

"The number please?" She said it in a way that made her displeasure clear, as if Julia interrupted her boredom.

Julia told her the number, and the woman wrote it down, then said, again without moving her head up, "Sit over there. I will call you when the connection has been made."

Isabelle pulled at Julia, and they sat along the wall opposite the phone booths. The child-woman behind the counter turned around and handed the piece of paper to someone inside a small window. She stared at Julia and Isabelle to make sure they were still there, then resumed her position behind the counter and attended her desk.

Julia walked to the woman. "Do you have any idea how long it will take?"

The woman opened her eyes in surprise. "I beg your pardon? How would I know this? Do you see the clocks on the wall behind me? Do you see Montréal? Is that not the same time as New York? I cannot promise you anything, Mademoiselle. There are connections to be made and…oh, what difference does it make. Please take your seat and wait."

Julia returned to sit by Isabelle. The woman lit a cigarette and sat back in her chair.

Isabelle raised her hand toward Julia, then took it back, as if conscious that others were studying them. "Julia, you can't do anything about it. And neither can she. I know how much you want to talk to your family. I called Daniel once in New Jersey, and I had to wait an hour, even though he has his own phone. You will have to be patient."

Julia sank down in the chair, defeated. But her spirits rose when the woman came out from behind the counter and walked to where they were sitting.

"I am sorry, Mademoiselle." She hesitated when she saw the ring on Julia's finger. "Excuse me, Madame. But no one answers the phone at this number."

Julia spoke in a shrill voice. "But it's morning there. They are six hours behind Paris. Someone…."

Isabelle interrupted her. "Thank you, Mademoiselle. We will try another time."

Julia turned to her. "They can try again," she said, her voice breaking.

"No, they…."

The counter woman interrupted Isabelle. "Oh, yes, if you wish, we will try again." She smiled at Julia. "As you can see, no one is using the phones now. No one comes in any more. Not since the war started. Let me try once more."

But once more no one answered. The woman came back with sorrow in her eyes. "I'm sorry. Sometimes the calls do not go through, and we do not know the reason why. This time, Alphonse asked the New York operator to make sure, but then the New York operator didn't respond. I'm afraid it's hopeless. They think the German U-boats are trying to destroy the undersea cable. Sometimes it works, sometimes it doesn't."

"What about sending a telegram?"

"Yes, you can do that, but I must tell you, they have to wait for the police to read them before they go out, and that could be weeks. And we have to take down all your personal information. You might try the embassy. Or a consulate." The woman pulled her blue sweater tight as if she had become cold.

Puzzled, Julia said, "I...I'm not sure what you mean."

The woman's face showed sympathy, but a feeling of superiority. "I understand their telegrams are not censored. So if you can convince someone there, if you know someone." She raised her eyebrows in anticipation.

Julia understood. She could be an American with connections. Well, if that were true, she would be out of the country already. "Thank you. I have to go there and I will try."

Julia thanked the woman and shook her hand, and went to the mailing counter. She said to Isabelle, "Then I will have to send an aerogramme." She bought the aerogramme and they sat at a café while she composed her letter to Hugh. At the post office she paid for first class expedited delivery of the letter. She asked the clerk, a fat man with graying hair and charcoal eyes that seemed to peer into nothing, about delivery time, and he shrugged his shoulders and shook his head.

Isabelle stood next to her and pulled her away after the clerk had stamped the aerogramme and flung it in a pile with his other mail. "Julia, he can only put your letter in with the others. Don't worry so much. They will expedite delivery and it will be faster than you think. Remember what Peter said. First your residence permit, then your travel permit, then your two transit visas. Then you can get an airline ticket."

Julia sighed. "Yes, I'm not going to see my Lizzie as soon as I thought." And she burst out with a cynical laugh. "And maybe at the end the Gestapo will stop me."

Isabelle waved the idea away. "Don't be silly. He thought he was going to play the big man and scare us because he had nothing better to do. Wait a minute." She turned back to face the clerk and asked him how the post office could expedite delivery when she knew there weren't even any planes leaving Paris."

He gave her a forced smile, as if he were weary of children's questions. "Madame, if you please, your letter will go from here by boat to London and by aeroplane to Newfoundland, and from there it will arrive in the United States. Are you satisfied?" He shook his head the smallest amount as if to keep his annoyance to himself.

"Oui, Monsieur." Isabelle gave her best imitation of happiness. She turned back to Julia. "Come on, we have to pick up your photographs."

THEY WALKED ALONG Rue Courtine until they stood before the Jacques Margulis photography shop. The bell on top of the door clanged as they entered. The shop was empty.

"Hello?" Julia spoke with a soprano voice. When he did not respond, she continued. "Jacques? It's us. We're back."

Still nothing, but then a door opened beyond the curtains and footsteps coming down a stairway announced his arrival. Jacques came through the curtains with his arm raised almost as if in defiance. "All right, I know. I was coming." He shook his head. "Isabelle, you should show more patience."

"Oh, Jacques, please," Isabelle said, showing the mildest irritation. "You said a couple of hours, so we're here. Julia is the one who's impatient, not me. And she has reason to be, doesn't she? Anyway, may we have the pictures?"

"Of course. Let me get them for you." He spoke as if his feelings had been hurt, or maybe too much had been demanded of him. Or some plans had been disrupted.

It didn't make any sense to Julia. Why this tension between them, the same as before when he took their photos? She felt Isabelle's presence, standing closer to assure her.

"Here they are," Jacques said, "ready to go. I made three copies. I of course will keep the negative for you, if you like. But maybe if you are leaving you will want to take it with you. Either way. It's up to you." He threw an envelope down on the counter as if throwing it away.

Despite his rudeness, Julia smiled and picked up the envelope. Reading the cost of the pictures, she opened her purse and gave him three francs.

Isabelle sucked in her breath when she saw the amount. "Jacques. That is not your usual price."

Julia stopped Isabelle. "It's fine. We asked for expedited service. It is reasonable. These are not school pictures. You worry too much." She smiled again at Jacques. "Thank you. I appreciate it. You are helping me to get home to see my little daughter, and that means everything to me." She gave Isabelle another frown of disapproval. "But now I want to see something different."

Isabelle started for the door. "Ah, Julia, we want to make it to Montmartre city hall today, we don't want to be late for that. Come on."

THEY ARRIVED AT CITY HALL and Monsieur Ducasse's office. He was at his window alone, bored. He perked up when the two women appeared before him.

"Ah, hello, you are back, Isabelle. So quick."

"Not so quick," she said, "my friend Julia has today to get her residence permit. And she has the pictures."

Julia handed the pictures to him.

He smiled, almost in nostalgia. "Jacques Margulis. Good. You used our neighborhood photographer. Very wise. If anything happens, he is close by. That is important."

"Happens?" Julia grabbed Isabelle's arm.

Monsieur Ducasse peered over his glasses like a professor. "I'm sorry. I didn't mean to frighten you. You Americans have it too easy. In Europe, in France even, things are always changing. Don't be upset young lady, it was my experience. Those of us who have been through the war, and now our little sitting war with Germany, we always overreact. I worry. You don't have to." Then he smiled, but he forced it.

Julia became nervous. "I would like to believe you, Monsieur, but I am anxious to get back to my little girl, and your words do upset me."

"Your little girl? Is she here, with you in your hotel?"

He was prying now, Julia thought. "No, she's in America. That's why I want to go home."

"Oh, that is sad. You came here without your little girl? All alone?"

Julia thought for a moment, started to turn to Isabelle, then decided to keep it to herself. "No, it should have been different. They were coming in a little while, but then when the boat arrived, they said there wouldn't be any more. Because of the stupid war. So now I have to go back home. We were going to go on a grand tour. You know, Paris, London, Rome. I was going to get us a pied á terre in Paris at first. But everything's turned upside down and...."

Isabelle touched Julia on the hand, out of sight of the clerk.

Monsieur Ducasse nodded in a solemn gesture of wisdom. "Yes, I understand. So many vacations ruined, so much travel disrupted by this stupid war, as you call it. But you mustn't worry, Madame, we are safe in Paris. And so is London and so is Rome. France has the largest army in the world. Hitler will never cross the Rhine, I promise you that... Ah, but I see you are nervous despite what I say. Here, I have put your photograph on your residence permit. All you have to do is come back next week and present yourself. Here, or the police station, it doesn't matter."

Julia began to worry. "Police station? Whatever for?"

He shook his head. "No, no, you can come here. I meant whatever is convenient. You know, Madame, you worry too much. They want to keep track of you. They try to keep track of everybody these days."

"But I haven't done anything wrong," Julia said with indignation. But then she realized he'd heard this many times.

Ducasse nodded again and sighed. "That is not for you to decide." He searched documents on his desk. "Madame Stuart, it has been decided for you by the Germans. You have been noted by the customs officer and the French National Police upon your arrival." He now felt that he had become his natural self, the lecturer. "You came in this country without any luggage. Do you know what that means?"

"Monsieur Ducasse," Isabelle said, "I think we have what we came for. We will go home now."

He acted as if he didn't hear her. He leaned forward into the window frame. "It means they believe you are here to meet somebody who will take care of you." His eyes bulged.

"Oh là là," Isabelle said, her voice raised. "Nobody is here to take care of her. She is staying with us until she can go back home."

At that, he stood up, his eyes burning. "You? You, Isabelle? With your mother? Don't you think you are already enough trouble for your poor old mother? Now you have to take this stranger on? You socialists, you don't know when to stop. Beware, I tell you. Beware." He turned his fierce gaze on Julia. "And you, you American, do you have any idea what you are getting into? You go back home as soon as you can. That's my advice. The police may be coming for this lady. I have told her mother that already. You are making a big mistake." With that, he sat down and closed his window and put up a sign that read "Closed."

Julia turned away from the window, and from Isabelle, trying to understand what Monsieur Ducasse had said. The police coming for Isabelle? Images flashed in her mind of Isabelle talking to the police at Le Havre, of strange glances passing between Isabelle and Jacques, of Christine complaining about her daughter going out at night. Now she had no one to trust. She put her arm out and touched the wall to keep her steady.

"Julia," Isabelle said, as she touched her on the arm. "Don't listen to what he says."

Julia backed away and wanted to run but she had nowhere to run. The hallway became small and stifling. Huge men in uniforms and shirts stained with sweat passed her by. Nausea swept over her as the stench wafted in her face. She became dizzy and held her hand up to her forehead, trying to think, but nothing came to her. She had nowhere to go, and the full powerful dread from her folly settled on her. Isabelle's voice came at her as if from a distance.

"Julia? Julia?"

Julia swung her arms out to push Isabelle away. Two men stopped as they were going by. One of them put his hands on Julia's shoulders. She screamed and fell backwards. The man's strong hands held her up. She felt she might vomit, but Isabelle's voice became stronger.

"Julia, you're okay. Wake up. Look at me."

Julia opened her eyes and saw Isabelle's face in front of her, intense, worried, her eyebrows close together, skin flushed.

"Julia, come on, we've got to get some air."

Bewildered, Julia found herself surrounded by the two men and Isabelle in the middle. She nodded and took Isabelle's arm, and let herself be led down the hallway and outside. The cool wind blew her hair up and stopped the nausea. Standing before the ornate wrought iron in front of city hall, she focused on the small merry-go-round across the street. A little girl the same age as Lizzie was holding tight on to the brass pole as her pony went around. Julia relaxed and breathed in and out in a slow rhythm. She thought the little girl smiled at her and felt better. Turning to Isabelle, she said, "What was that man saying about the police?"

Isabelle thought for a moment. When she spoke, her voice had a hard edge. "What he meant was that he is a fascist and I am a worker. That's why he wants me to think the police are coming for me." She shook her head back and forth to make her point. "But they're not. He's saying that to scare you. That's what he does, you know. He scares people so he can be a big man. But he doesn't know anything."

Julia spoke in a low voice. "But he scares me." She opened her eyes wide.

"Sure, because you have not been long in the country. He doesn't know you, so he thinks he can be tough. Remember, now you have your residence permit, and we can go get your travel permit. Think about it, Julia. That's all he meant. You want to go home as soon as you can. That's what we should be doing." She stepped back and studied Julia. "Are you all right? Maybe we should go home first."

Chapter 29

JULIA AND ISABELLE were soon at the base of the steps up Rue du Mont-Cenis that led to Christine's apartment. Julia strained her neck to see if Christine was looking out her second-floor apartment, but the dark green leaves of a tree blocked her view. On the right was a small restaurant with bright yellow walls and a red overhanging canopy. Two white chairs and a table were on the street.

Isabelle leaned toward the restaurant and pulled Julia toward the table. "Let's go into Chez Francis and have something to drink. It will make you feel better."

"Oh, no, I need to go back to your apartment and get some rest. That's what I need, if you don't mind." Julia couldn't stand the thought of being in public in Paris any longer. She wasn't sure she wanted to go home with Isabelle, but then she felt that Christine would help her sort out the situation. Isabelle, she wasn't sure of, but Isabelle's mother was somebody she could trust. Somebody who made her feel at home and safe.

Inside the apartment, Julia went to Christine, who was at the kitchen sink, washing small dishes. Christine turned when she heard them come in, and smiled, but then seemed alarmed when she saw Julia.

"*Ma fille*, what happened? Are you all right? Come, sit down. Sit, here in this chair." She pulled a chair out from the kitchen table and led Julia to it, then hovered close to her, touching her forehead. Christine's light blue eyes almost filled with tears. "Hmm. You don't have a fever. But you are flushed." She raised herself up and her eyes locked on Isabelle with anger. "What happened to her, Isabelle. I thought you would have watched out for her."

Isabelle sighed. "Mother, she's fine. Monsieur Ducasse at city hall said some stupid things. Julia didn't understand. He mentioned the police and...."

"Police?" Christine put her hands up to her face. The anger in her eyes changed to fear. "Oh my god, what do you mean?"

"Mother, please, he didn't mean anything. He was spouting off like he always does. You remember when you had to get your residence permit when the war started? How he treated you?"

Christine sighed and nodded, then put her hands on Julia's head. "Oh, I see. Yes, my dear, Isabelle is right. You shouldn't worry about what that man Ducasse says. He thinks he runs the city. He's so arrogant. My husband didn't like him at all, even when they were in the army together. You see, he didn't get hurt at all in the Great War, and so he's tried to lord it over all of us ever since."

"Maybe I should drink something," Julia said, with a weary voice.

"Oh, I'm so sorry." Christine went to the cabinet and brought out a bottle of cognac.

"Oh, no, not that," Julia said. "It'll make me sick."

"Please, do as I say," Christine said. "A sip, it will make you feel better. And I will make you a tartine with some cheese, and then you will settle down." She poured a little cognac into a small liqueur glass and handed it to Julia.

Julia smelled the strong cognac and resisted drinking it, but couldn't resist Christine's frowning face over her. She closed her eyes and let the warm liquid fall into her throat and burn down and rest in her stomach. A quiet peace came over her. She put the glass on the table, put one arm up on the table next to it, and rested her head. She breathed three times, then responded to Christine's smiling face. "Thank you, Madame."

Christine's face showed sympathy and a small triumph in calming the situation. She spoke in a warm whisper. "Now, my dear, you have your residence permit, is that right?"

Julia sighed and said, "Yes."

"Well, then, you go in and take a nap. Then we'll figure out what to do. I'll bring your tartine in to you in a minute."

Julia went to her room and lay down on the bed, now feeling a little dizzy from the cognac that still burned. A sharp pain ran down both legs. She closed her eyes and let the world fade away. She heard Christine and Isabelle in the next room.

"Mama, she's all right. Make her the tartine and I'll tell you what happened. It was too much for all at once. She has to go to the American embassy and get an exit visa."

Christine took a loaf of bread and began cutting a slice, but then interrupted her. "A visa? To go home?"

"Yes, well, you know, they're playing at war. It's not for the American government, they don't care, I'm sure. It's for everybody else. She has to get a visa from America, then she has to get a transit visa from Portugal to take the plane from Lisbon."

"Lisbon? Why not Paris?" Christine put butter on the bread and a piece of camembert on top.

"Because there are no flights from Paris. We can't help that. Then she has to get a transit visa from the Spanish embassy to take the train for Portugal."

Christine shrugged her shoulders and moved her head back and forth. "I don't like that. Spain is now fascist. It makes me nervous. And then is she done?"

"No," Isabelle poured a glass of wine and began drinking it. "When she has all that, she goes to the Paris police prefecture and gets her travel permit for France. But Mama, it's all a formality. She's not in any kind of trouble, so it will take time to go around, but we will be able to do all of it tomorrow, and then we go down to the train station and get her a ticket and see her off."

Julia dozed off hearing those words, telling her that everything was all right and she was on her way home to Lizzy.

When she awoke, it was dark and the house was quiet. Someone had put a blanket on her, she felt warm and comfortable, and she went back to sleep.

When Julia woke again, it was light, the house was quiet, but outside a truck moved along the street. Someone yelled "Bonjour." She pushed the blankets off and took a step out toward the hallway, then felt her blue linen nightshirt rustle against her legs, and stopped. Was she familiar enough to Christine and Isabelle to come out like this, she wondered. Instead, she put on a dress, and took her little night bag out with her to the bathroom. No one else was visible, so she washed her face and combed her hair, then went out to the kitchen.

Christine sat at the kitchen table peeling apples, but smiled with cheer in her eyes when she saw Julia. Her voice showed enthusiasm. "Good morning, my dear. Come, have some coffee and a croissant. You must be starving."

Julia tried to match Christine's voice. "Not that hungry but I'd love it. Thank you." She surveyed the room. "Isabelle isn't up yet?"

Christine waved her hand and said, "Isabelle. No, she's already out this morning. She said she had to go see Jacques, you know, the photographer. I have no control over her."

The remark surprised Julia. "I don't want to intrude, Madame."

Christine slowly turned to Julia, her eyes demanding attention. "You are not intruding, my little girl. Isabelle has an excellent opinion of you. And so do I. It's wonderful, you know, to have an American friend who speaks French so well." She put a large bowl of coffee in front of Julia and put a small pitcher of milk next to it, along with a croissant. "But Isabelle, well…," Christine seemed to be studying the table, but it was obvious she was thinking over how much she should tell Julia. "She is a communist, you know." When she said it, Christine stood still, nodding in finality, and her eyes begged Julia for understanding.

"I'm afraid I don't know what you mean." Julia frowned in a deliberate way, trying to show sympathy. "What's wrong with that? In America, France is well known for having many communists. We have communists, too."

"Yes, of course, you can vote communist, that's not so bad, it's foolhardy. But she's doing more than that. I don't know what, but she should be trying to find a job."

Julia took a sip of coffee. "It's delicious. I don't want to ruin it with milk." She was going home as soon as she could. There were no communists on Park Avenue and she didn't care about it. "Isabelle has been very kind to me, and so have you, Madame."

"Oh, please, don't call me Madame." Christine leaned on a chair and bent forward to emphasize her statement. "My name is Christine. Please call me that."

Julia hugged her and said, "Merci beaucoup, Christine."

At that, Christine was happy and returned to the other side of the table and pushed strawberry jam and butter over to Julia's plate, then returned to peeling apples.

"So," Christine said, "I don't know how long Isabelle will be. I think she promised to go around with you today."

Julia was glad Isabelle wasn't there, so she could make the rounds of the embassies today by herself. She was worried that Isabelle would want to spend time at the American embassy asking questions about getting her mother out of the country. She dipped her croissant in the coffee and ate it in quick bites. "Thank you, Christine. She doesn't need to go with me."

"You can find everything yourself?"

Julia smiled and almost laughed. "No, but I think a taxi can. I saw a stand on the street below." She returned to her room and picked up her purse, then came back to the kitchen and bent down and hugged Christine at the table. "May I say something?"

"Yes?" Christine was puzzled.

"You've been so nice. May I say I'll be home for lunch? Maybe the three of us can go down below for something? My treat."

"Ah, yes, that would be very nice. I wish you every success today. You are getting closer to seeing your little girl. I know everything will go well for you."

"Thank you," Julia said, as she left.

HALF AN HOUR LATER, she stepped out of the taxi on Avenue Gabriel before the ornate United States Embassy. Her heart speeded up as she walked through a stand of trees in white bloom and up to the gate.

A tall young man in a Marine uniform put his hand up. "May I help you, Miss?" he said, smiling but reserved.

"Yes, thank you, I'm here to get an exit visa to go back home."

He nodded. "I see. Yes, of course. Let me point the way to you." He stepped out of the way and pointed in to the grey marble building. "You see that door, the one with another Marine in front of it?"

"Yes," she said, getting excited.

"You tell him what you want to do and he will direct you inside."

"Thank you." She smiled at him with all her heart.

He gave her a small salute.

Inside the building, a guard directed her to a room off a corridor with the word "Visa" in gold lettering over a door. A young woman in a formal blue suit sat behind a desk filled with paperwork. The woman stood when Julia entered the room.

"Good day. May I be of assistance?" the young woman said. Her lustrous dark brown hair lay around her face and on her shoulders. Another smile.

"Yes, I'm here for an exit visa to go back home."

"Glad to help," the woman said, in a perfunctory way. "In preparation, may I ask you, you have your passport with you? And your name, please?"

Julia nodded. "Julia Stewart."

The woman waved her hand to indicate she didn't want to have the passport herself. "Thank you, you will need it for your interview. If you would have a seat, please, over here." She wrote Julia's name on a small piece of paper, and some word below it. She extended her arm to the left with another smile.

Julia turned and stopped in disappointment to see what she thought was a group of 20 people, at least, seated in chairs on both sides of the wall leading down the hallway to a door with no description on it.

"Oh, don't worry," the woman said, her voice now sympathetic, "they're not all here for exit visas. You won't have to wait, too long. Well, unless someone has a problem, but today it's gone rather fast. And you're here in the morning. It's the afternoon when things start slowing down."

She took Julia by the arm, softly, and led her over to an empty chair, then said, "I'll be right back." She walked with her piece of paper inside the door and disappeared.

Julia studied the people seated next to her and on the opposite side. All of them appeared somber, afraid, or maybe worried. Were these all people with visa problems? Were they Jews, perhaps? But then she heard someone laughing on her side of the hallway and she felt better.

The woman came back in and as she passed Julia, she said, "They'll call for you in a few minutes." She returned to her desk and to moving paperwork around and stamping it and putting it in neat piles.

None of the others waiting with her in the hallway talked. She thought they must all be here as individuals and not know each other, except for the laughing lady a few chairs away on her right. She felt relaxed. This was the first real progress she had made since she arrived. She hadn't been in Paris a week even and she was so close to going home. Her hands itched. She wanted to scratch them, but didn't want to appear odd to all these people or the young woman. Instead, she put them together and moved them back and forth over each other in a slow, gentle movement. It didn't stop the itching, and she felt hot and sweaty.

The door opened and a middle-aged man with graying black matted hair came out. He was wearing a three-piece blue pinstripe suit, wrinkled at the elbows, with a wilted white shirt and a perfect red and black paisley bow tie that was too neat for the rest of his clothes. "Julia Stuart," he called out, swiveling his head up and down the rows of chairs, then stopping at Julia. The young woman from the desk must have described her to the man.

She jumped at the sound of her name, but her hands stopped itching, and she felt cool again as she stood and walked to him.

"Please, come in." He escorted her through the door. He led her past two doors down the hallway, then pointed to a small room with a photo of President Roosevelt, and other photos of people she did not recognize, except for this man posing in several of them, shaking hands with other men. "Please, take a seat."

She sat in a hard chair in front of the desk. The room was claustrophobic, the walls dusty, the light dim. The man moved around the desk and sat down, then leaned forward. "Jim Stansfield," he said, smiling and showing tobacco-stained teeth. He put out his hand to her, and she noticed the tobacco on his fingers as well. "I'm happy to meet you. You may be surprised, but we don't get many exit visas these days. Americans that wanted to go have left."

Julia's head jerked a little at this and she felt herself blushing and getting hot.

"I didn't mean to scare you. I deal with it every day." He waved the thought away. "A lot of bureaucratic crap, if you ask me."

"But all those people out in the hallway…" Julia felt guilty being chosen ahead of them.

"Well, yes," he said as he leaned back in his chair. "But it's not what you think. They're not here for me. I do exit visas. They have other ordinary visa problems, you know, they get married, or they get into a little trouble with the law, or they need us to certify something." He shook his head and his jowls wiggled back and forth. "But I don't want to bore you with that. What is it I can do for you?"

"I need an exit visa." He wasn't boring her, but she didn't like that he was now going out of his way to be reassuring.

"Yes. Yes. That's what Marlene said."

"Marlene? The woman at the desk?"

"Yes. That's her." This time he gave a slow exaggerated nod, to let her know that he was on top of this, no doubt to try and keep her calm. "You want to go back home. It's stupid, isn't this, needing an exit visa to go home. It's not us, you know."

Julia did know, from Peter at Pan American. Everything pointed to the possibility of a complication and delay in getting home to Lizzy. "I don't know what you mean."

"Well, you are an American and…would you let me see your passport? Might as well do things in the right order."

She handed it to him and he flipped through the pages.

"Oh, my. You have been here less than a week. And going back so soon? That is unusual." He frowned at her and then stared at the open passport.

"Is there a problem," Julia said, nervousness creeping into her voice.

"No, no. Not at all. It's unusual, that's all. It's a long way to come for such a short stay."

"Yes, I know," she said. She felt he was staring at her in order to see whether she was hiding something. "My family should have come over after me, but then my father became ill, so now it's the other way and I have to go back." She smiled at him, relieved for the moment that she was able to think of an answer to the predicament. She hadn't thought they might question her intentions.

"Oh, I see. Yes, that can happen. I hope your father is all right?"

"Well, I don't know. I won't know until I get home." She now felt comfortable with her lies. And ashamed that she had brought herself to this.

"Yes, quite so, until you arrive home. In any case, this is not a big problem. Look, I will take care of this right now." He opened a drawer, and with a small flourish took a stamp out, stamped her passport, and put the stamp back, giving her the passport, all with one smooth movement. "Here you are. I am sorry about your father. If there is anything else we can do to help you?" He raised his eyebrows and waited for her response."

"I don't think so," she said with a little shake of her head, then put her lips together for a second and continued. "Yes, actually."

"Of course, anything. Well, anything within my power."

"I need to get on the plane from Lisbon. That's the fastest way home. And now with my exit visa, I can get a Pan American ticket. But I need a transit visa from both Spain and Portugal. And a travel visa from the French police."

He frowned in sympathy. "Sometimes it amazes me. Here we are, we can picnic on the grass in Paris, but have to move heaven and earth to get out of here. But you shouldn't worry. You're not in trouble, so it should go without a problem. The Portuguese don't care at all. I haven't heard of trouble with them. The Spanish, oh, they can be a little difficult themselves. After all, they did have a war. But you didn't have anything to do with that. So you shouldn't worry. My advice to you is to go to the bank and get some pesetas and escudos. Have them ready at the border. It will be easy."

"Oh, I hadn't thought of that." His advice made her feel more comfortable. "How much are we talking about here?" She had more than enough money to take care of it, but she didn't want be stupid about getting to Lisbon.

"Yes, I think..." He leaned back in his chair and put his hands together. "A hundred dollars in each."

"A hundred dollars?"

"Oh, if you don't have that...."

"No, it's not that, it's, I'm surprised, is all. It's a lot for a little greasing of the palm on the border."

"You might think," he said, "but these days people are leaving Germany in a hurry and they want to be sure, so I hear there's, um, let's say it's wartime inflation."

"Yes, I see." Julia had not expected to have an education on bribery while she was here.

"Now, you don't have to, you know. Your papers are fine, you're not a refugee."

Julia shook her head in a wide arc. "No, no, I appreciate your advice. My goal is to get home, not save on travel expenses. Besides, I can use the money I had expected to spend here."

"One more thing," he said, "that I can do for you. I have a friend with the police downtown. If I call him and let him know you are coming, it will help."

"Oh, thank you, sir. It means everything to my father."

"You make a big deal about your father when you're there, and they'll be sympathetic."

"Can you tell me his name, your friend?"

"Oh no, I can't do that. Anyway, you won't see him. But he will see your application, and it's then that he'll think of my intervention." He stood and offered his hand. "I hope you have a safe and swift voyage home, Mrs. Stuart."

JULIA'S VISIT TO the Spanish and Portuguese embassies went as Jim Stanfield had predicted. They, too, weren't much interested in her, and they, too, were very sympathetic to her need to get home to an ailing father. The officer at the Spanish embassy volunteered that he was happy to meet someone so attractive who was not a refugee. Again, she learned that it was the French who wanted to place such heavy burdens on normal travelers, and they were glad to be helpful.

She left the Portuguese embassy in a cab for Pan American with a light heart. And she left the airline with a lighter heart still, holding a ticket on the Pan Am Clipper from Lisbon to the Azores to Miami.

On the advice of Peter Smyth, she had also bought a ticket on the Clipper from Marseille to Lisbon. Yes, he had said, you have a Spanish permit, but why not just fly over the country and save a step?

He told her that her documents were impeccable, but you never know when you reach the border. You don't know who's standing in line with you. They get in trouble and you are suspicious by being next to them.

Why not eliminate one unnecessary leg of her journey? She observed that there were no dates on the tickets. Peter replied that these were extraordinary times, that she will be able to get out in a few days at the latest, and she should not worry about it. He said they couldn't put a date on the tickets because diplomatic travel dominated these routes and there were heavy days and light days.

Julia left Pan Am overwhelmed with information and hurried out the door to find a cab.

The cab driver waited on the Champs Élysées, fingers tapping on the steering wheel, while she figured out where to go. Her final stop was the Prefecture of Police, near Notre Dame, down the street and across the Seine. She had spent several hours going through embassies and airlines and had no trouble at all.

In fact, everyone she met was sympathetic and helpful. But the police were a different matter altogether. They held her fate in their hands. She needed that travel permit, she needed it now to get home to her daughter and her husband. But the thought of an interrogation, however mild, terrified her.

"Madame?" the taxi driver now became impatient. "Where to?"

"Montmartre," she said, making the decision that gave her the least fear. Home, as it were, as she felt, to Christine and Isabelle. Because she knew that Isabelle would have to go with her.

She didn't have the courage to face the police alone. She remembered the fear and humiliation she had felt at the dock when she arrived in France and the police interviewed her there. Yes, she needed Isabelle.

She found the street door on Rue du Mont-Cenis open, as it often was. On the second floor, she pushed the buzzer to the apartment and waited. The door opened.

"Julia!" Isabelle said, in an angry voice. But her face did not show any anger.

"May I come in, I'm exhausted."

"Of course, but I'm still upset with you."

Christine's voice came from within. "Julia, is that you? You're in time for tea."

"Tea?" Isabelle frowned but her voice didn't show this, either.

"Yes. Of course, why not. The British have tea. I don't know what Americans have, so I did the next best thing." Christine laughed at her witty idea.

"Thanks, that's very nice," Julia said. And she meant it. "I'm exhausted, and tea is the right thing right now."

"And scones," Christine added.

"Scones? Oh my, you have gone all out today. Are they French, scones?"

"Oh no, but you know, everybody eats everybody else's food today. I did have to ask around for a recipe, and Marianne Desjardin around the corner knew this one. So I can't vouch for it, it's not a family tradition or anything, but I took a bite of one and I liked it. So I hope you enjoy it."

"I'm sure I will. Let me put my things away."

Isabelle followed Julia into her room. "I missed you today. I'm sorry you ran off without me. Did everything go well?" She noted the envelopes Julia had taken out of her purse.

Julia hesitated, not sure what to do with the envelopes and not wanting to go over everything about the day. "Yes, actually, everything—except the police."

Isabelle folded her arms across her chest, now serious. "The police?"

"Oh, no," Julia said as she sighed, "I didn't make it to the police today, that's all. I have my exit visa, my transit visas, and my airplane tickets for Marseille and Lisbon."

"Marseille, too?"

"Yes, Peter, you remember him, at Pan Am, he suggested it. We'll see how it goes, but he said it would eliminate having to travel to Madrid and deal with more border guards. And he's right, you know, guards at the French border, and then again crossing into Portugal. So I think I'll take his advice. I'll fly over Spain and not have to worry about it. And save a hundred dollars, as well."

"A hundred dollars? For what?"

"Oh, he said at the Spanish border, a hundred dollars would make sure there I get across easily."

"Yes, I understand," Isabelle said. "But a hundred dollars. I would think twenty would be more than enough. I wouldn't give them more than ten."

Julia thought for a moment about Isabelle's reaction. This was the first time she had given any indication to Isabelle that she had a lot of money.

Isabelle interrupted her thoughts. "That's right, you were in first class on the boat coming over. You have a different idea of what's expensive."

"No, I don't," Julia said, eager to eliminate whatever suspicion Isabelle was harboring. "The man at the visa office said that. I was as surprised as you are. He said there are so many refugees who pay a lot of money, and everyone else has to live with that."

Isabelle smiled and changed the subject. "So, you are all set except for the police."

Julia moved a step closer to Isabelle. "Yes, so, I could have gone today, but I wanted you to go with me."

Isabelle smiled. "Of course, I will. I think it's a good idea. I haven't been there, you know." She hunched over in a bit of laughter. "Not that I want to. But they're quite busy now. We are under martial law. So I will help you find your way around that labyrinth. But come, Mama is waiting with our tea. And scones!"

At the table, as Christine poured their tea from a teapot with purple flowers and gold ornamental leaf, Julia said, "Oh, you do have a nice teapot."

"Isn't it beautiful? It's Belclair. My sister," she blessed herself, "gave it to me for a wedding present. We don't drink much tea, so it's stayed perfect. My husband was a coffee drinker. Turkish coffee and Egyptian cigarettes. Until…" Tears filled her eyes. She held the teapot away from the table while she wiped the tears from her face.

Isabelle stood and took the teapot away from her. Christine went to the kitchen counter and cleaned her face with a towel. Then she came back, smiling, or, rather, attempting to maintain a smile. "Yes, let's finish our tea."

Chapter 30

THE NEXT DAY, with the dawn lighting the streets in bare gray, Julia and Isabelle arrived at the Prefecture of Police.

"Let me do the talking at first," Isabelle said, keeping Julia back by standing in front of her.

"No, that isn't right." Julia stepped around her. "They will think it's something funny."

"I am trying to help you."

"And I thank you for it. Anyway, we're here, let's go in."

There was a long line in front of the Travel Permits door. They were there first thing in the morning, but many others had been even more ambitious. Julia wondered what happened once you got inside the door.

"Isabelle," Julia said, "He's going to ask me where I'm staying. It's better if you're there with me."

"You might be right. If you need me, then you can come get me."

She arrived at the head of the line in a dingy room with a man behind the desk who paid no attention to her. He was young and bored, and swept his view of his desk from left to right as if he would do anything rather than talk to her. She switched from left to right foot and back but he still paid no attention to her. Sweat dripped down his forehead. He removed his rimless glasses and cleaned them with a dirty handkerchief. He wiped his forehead, then pinched the ridge of his nose with his eyes closed. Then he put his glasses back on. He said, "Next."

Julia, startled, thought for a moment there was someone standing next to her whose place she had taken. "Me? "

"Yes, I think you are the one standing in front of me." His voice had the character of a machine.

She was glad to stand before him in the morning and not in the late afternoon. "I am here to get a transit visa."

"A transit visa? I don't think so. You are in the wrong office, then. Is that what you want? Or do you even know what you want?"

Heat began to run down Julia's spine. "I'm sorry. I don't know what to call it."

"I see. Then tell me what it is you want to do?"

"I am here to get papers I need to travel to Portugal."

"Oh. Now I see. You want a travel permit, do you?"

"Yes, thank you, that's it. Thank you for helping me." She had learned by now that patience and politeness were her two best friends when dealing with bureaucrats.

He held out his hand again without giving her any attention. She handed him her passport, her residence permit from the Montmartre city hall, her exit visa from the American embassy, and her transit visas for Spain and Portugal. She hesitated and then handed him her airline ticket.

He read the documents before him, his mouth formed a thin line and then he began to frown and then he raised his eyebrows. He lifted his head up and lowered it again.

A loud thump from the left startled her. Her body twitched. The man behind the desk sighed and let out a little laugh. Now he raised his head up to her and smiled, then said, "We're not being bombed yet Mademoiselle." And then he laughed at his own cleverness. Now more relaxed, he continued, "Your papers all seem in order, that's a relief. There are a couple of minor details to clear up."

Seeing the man more relaxed, Julia smiled at him but then felt foolish because he was ignoring her. "What is it?"

He sighed, breathed in and out slowly several times, then observed her now with a serious face as if the preliminaries were over and trouble had begun. "You are staying at an address on Rue du Mont-Cenis?"

"Yes."

"That's the street that that leads up to Sacré-Coeur. There are no hotels on that street." Now he eyed her like a predator. "So, what do you have to say to that?" Then he gave a sidelong glance at his neighbor as if to let him know that he was being tough.

Rolling nervousness fluttered inside her. "I don't believe I said I was staying at a hotel. I'm staying with friends."

"Ah." He nodded and chewed on his lip. "Friends. Who are your friends?"

Julia let out a great sigh of relief. "My friend," she said as she turned and pointed out to the hallway, "Isabelle is out in the hallway."

"Well then," he said with impatience, "I suppose you had better go and get her, hadn't you?" He opened his brown eyes wide to emphasize his point.

Julia nodded and went and brought Isabelle back with her.

The man sized Isabelle up. Isabelle smiled at Julia and then at the man.

"And you are you?"

"My name is Isabelle Valin. Here are my papers."

Julia had an impulse to reach out to Isabelle but thought of the man seeing that and felt foolish. He peered over Isabelle's residence permit and her identity card and then picked up Julia's residence permit and studied the three of them. He nodded to himself and thought for a moment then said, "All right, so I see your residence is in order. But I noticed that both of you came into the country not too long ago. How is that?" He shifted his gaze between them, but lingered a longer time on Julia's face and managed a brief glance at her chest.

Isabelle said, "We came on the same ship from America. I was returning home from a visit with my brother there. I met Julia on the ship."

"I see, but why are you staying with this lady?"

Julia said without hesitation, "Because she became my friend on this ship. I offered to stay at a hotel but her mother…"

"Her mother? Now we have a new person in this story." He motioned for Isabelle to follow him over to the corner of the room. They spoke for a few seconds, then he motioned for her to stay there and he came back to Julia. "What is her mother's name?" He raised his eyebrows and stared at her in an attempt at intimidation.

"Christine."

He sat down and motioned for Isabelle to come forward.

"I approve your travel permit. There!" He picked up a stamp and brought it down on her residence permit, then took another piece of paper, wrote several words and dates on it, then signed it. "One small detail, and you will be ready to go to Lisbon." He shook his head to himself as he said, "A beautiful city. I took my wife there once. So different. Wonderful, friendly people."

Julia glanced quickly at Isabelle. Was this man playing with her?

"I see your worry. The final authority always rests with the criminal division. You will come back here in one week. Your permit will be available in the central lobby." He turned to Isabelle. "You know, perhaps where that is?"

Isabelle nodded.

He returned his gaze to Julia, making sure she understood he meant to be serious. "Will there be a problem with the criminal division, Mademoiselle?"

"No, Sir. I want to be back home with my father."

"Fine, then." He stood and offered them his hand again.

Isabelle offered her hand and held his hand as she shook it while smiling.

Julia also offered her hand, but in a weak grip, touching his fingertips. She turned to leave the room but then realized that she had made a serious mistake with a man who held her future in his hands. She became terrified that he would not approve her travel permit at all and that she would never see Lizzie. So she turned back and smiled, looking at the man in the eyes with her head held high while she said, "Thank you, Monsieur, I appreciate everything you are doing to help me to get home to see my father before it is too late." She inclined her head to him and waited for his response.

He nodded and said, "As I said, Mademoiselle, provided everything is in order...."

Julia's heart was pounding. She smiled with her mouth closed and then hurried out of the room. She waited in the corridor for Isabelle to catch up to her.

"Julia, I think you can take him at his word. We will come back in a week and everything will be waiting for you. What we need to do now is get your train tickets and you will feel much better."

Julia's heart was no longer beating at a rapid pace, and her breathing became normal. "But I don't trust that man," she said, holding her forehead with her hand.

Isabelle stepped in close to Julia and forced her to pay attention. "No, you are merely nervous. You want this all resolved now and it's not going to be. It's something routine, something we'll deal with next week. In the meantime, how about you and me go have a nice long visit to a café?" Isabelle nodded and smiled and added with a whisper, "One that serves spirits."

"Listen," Julia said. "I want to go and get the camera. Can we do that?"

"Of course, we'll stop on the way back home. Let's go. You're right, it's the best thing to do. It will keep us busy this afternoon."

TWO HOURS LATER the three of them stood above the city of Paris from the terrace in front of Sacré-Coeur. The city below them began to glow with millions of small lights turned on for the evening.

Julia turned to Christine, and said, "This is the most beautiful city in the world. I will always love this city more than any other, knowing I will soon see my daughter because you and Isabelle have made it possible."

Christine took Julia's hand and studied her eyes with great sympathy. "You have made it possible, my dear. And that is a happy thought, so let's walk over to Chez Eugène and have some crepes and wine."

AT PLACE DU TERTRE, Julia stopped at a painting of the window with a green frame and red and yellow flowers in the window box below it. Next to it sat a man in a black beret and black sweater, with a gray mustache and a gray beard cut into a triangle. He waited with a sparkle in his eye, his head cocked.

"You are not like most people. You seem to be studying and not observing. Am I right?"

Julia nodded. "Perhaps you are right, and perhaps people study your painting more than you think. It is beautiful and it's very natural. Very Parisian."

"And you, do you paint?"

"Yes, I do paint, but I don't do scenes like this. This is a form of landscape, with somebody's house instead of mountains."

"You understand painting." He thought to himself for a moment. "I have no pretense. My work is not going to be shown in the Louvre."

Julia laughed. "Your work does not have to be shown in a great museum in order to be very good. If it were me I would be happy if someone would buy it. So far I have not been that fortunate."

"Yes, you are right again."

"Thank you for talking to me," she said as she walked to the entrance to the restaurant.

"It's all right," he replied. "I'm waiting for the Germans. They love little paintings like this. I shall make lots of money from the Bosch."

Julia felt a rush of air and heard Christine's voice behind her in outrage.

"Monsieur, you are one of the rats left over from the last time the Prussians were here. You should be ashamed of yourself. The Germans will never reach Paris. Never! We have the world's largest army and the Maginot Line. You will starve if you wait to sell your worthless paintings to Germans."

The man shrugged his shoulders. "Don't get so excited, Madame. Maybe I am mistaken. Maybe France will be strong. I myself was at Verdun in the last war, so I know what we can do. But you must read the papers. The Germans are already massing on the Belgian border. It will not be long. And this time France has been weakened by the communists."

A second loud, outraged voice, that of Isabelle, made Julia's ear ring. "Ah, I see, I supposed you are some kind of fascist, Monsieur. That's why you love Germans. You are a stupid street painter, you should be happy what the Popular Front has been trying to do for the people."

He laughed and nodded in pretense of showing how wise he was. "Yes, I know you, I have seen you giving out your communist newspapers up here. You are the problem, young lady. It's because of you that I will be able to sell my paintings to the Germans." Hatred now blazed in his light green eyes.

A large crowd gathered around them. People started shouting, some saying, "Fascist!", others, "Communist!"

Julia put herself in between the painter and the two women. "Please," she said, "can we go have our dessert?"

Christine took Julia and Isabelle through the crowd into the restaurant and ordered expensive wine and two kinds of crepes for each of them.

"But it still galls me," Christine said. "That man. He is a traitor to his country." She turned to Isabelle. "And he's been spying on you."

Isabelle's eyes glared in disgust. "That man? I don't think so. Anyway, it doesn't matter. We are going to America, Mama, and the Germans can be somebody else's problem."

Christine shifted in her seat, then drank an entire glass of wine and filled it up again.

"Mama," Isabelle said, amazed. "Be careful. You won't be able to make it down the stairs to our house. What are you doing?"

Christine waved her away. "It makes me so god damn mad. Who does he think he is? I'll bet all he did at Verdun was to clean out the latrines." She sighed at Julia, then smiled at Isabelle. "Yes. We must think of Daniel. We shall soon see him and leave Montmartre to all the rats up here. *Garçon*," she yelled, "a bottle of champagne, if you please."

"Mama, I think you're going too far."

"No, you two can carry me home if I can't walk. Listen to them out there, they're still yelling about us. That's hilarious. Tonight I celebrate America and distance from Germany."

Julia sat, quiet, relaxed, then stood and took her new camera out of her bag. "Come on, let's start with pictures here tonight."

Christine sat up straight and ran her fingers through her hair. "Oh, my, I didn't know I was having my portrait taken."

"Isabelle," Julia said, "sit next to your mother. This will be my first picture."

Julia took the leather cover off her camera and held the viewfinder up to her eye.

"But the light meter," Isabelle said.

"Oh, well, yes, the light meter," Julia said. "I don't need that. It's for photography, you know." She smirked as she emphasized the word. "I'm taking pictures. If I can see, I can snap. She took a glass of water and put the camera on top of it. As she squatted to peer through the viewfinder she said, "But to be safe, I'll make it stable." She squinted for a moment, then said, "Okay, ready, smile." She pressed the shutter, then took the camera off the glass and stood. "Tomorrow, we shall photograph all of Paris. And I will have so much to show Lizzie."

"No, wait," she continued. "I need to use a couple of different shutter speeds, to make sure." And she made them wait for two more portraits, before they made their way back down from the top of Montmartre on Rue du Mont-Cenis, holding Christine and the railings and each other down the steps too treacherous for those who've had both wine and champagne.

Chapter 31

THE NEXT MORNING, when Julia walked out to the main room, feeling heavy and sick but having made an effort to fix her hair and put on some makeup, Christine and Isabelle were silent, staring at *Le Monde* lying flat on the table. They didn't even react to the sound of her footsteps, which was unusual for them.

"Do you have any aspirin?" Julia said, feeling her forehead.

Christine looked up at her, her face contorted into a grimace, her forehead wrinkled into a frown, her mouth turned downward. "You're going to need more than aspirin. The Germans have broken through the Ardennes." She wagged her head back and forth. She stood and touched Julia as she went by, trying to smile but not pulling it off. "Of course, we have aspirin. That and a strong black coffee will make you feel better, at least as far as your hangover."

She brought Julia the aspirin, then sat down again. "We are crazy. I went out this morning for the croissants, and down on Rue Custine all the shops were full. People were talking like it was a holiday. I heard them. They went to the theatre, they went to the park." She sat back and folded her arms across her chest. Her head was still, but her eyes flicked back and forth between Julia and Isabelle. She laughed, then settled her gaze on Isabelle. "Did you tell her?"

Isabelle shook her head.

"Well," Christine continued her voice carrying a note of triumph and satisfaction, "we have our visas and cards and passports and papers and everything. Bet that's a surprise. We're ready before you are."

The news shocked Julia and she rubbed the back of her neck. How can this be possible? Are they going to fly to Lisbon, too? She became worried, thinking of all three of them stuck on the border because Christine or Isabelle's papers were not in order. She hoped they did not see her reaction. "I think that's wonderful. How did you manage it so fast?"

Isabelle's face seemed like she had engineered a coup. "You're surprised, Julia. So was I yesterday. Monsieur Ducasse, you remember him, he did it. I thought Mama was being too coy with me, because I didn't ever believe she would leave her home. It turns out the whole time she was working with Ducasse to get the papers."

Julia felt relief that Isabelle didn't notice her reaction. She turned to Christine. "And I believed Isabelle. I thought it would be harder for you to get your papers. Well, I must say, I'm not sure what all this means. Are you going to go to Lisbon? Do you have airline tickets?"

Christine wagged her finger. "No, not so fast young lady. We know we wouldn't have a good chance in Lisbon, but we're not sure yet. Perhaps we'll go to Bordeaux, or most likely, we will go to Marseille with you, and from there take a boat to Algiers."

Julia frowned. "That's a big difference, Bordeaux or Marseille."

Christine nodded. "Yes, but we don't have to decide this minute. We will wait until next week when you have your papers. It depends on whether ships are arriving in Bordeaux or not. If the navy controls the port, and doesn't let any passenger ships dock, then it's a waste of time."

Julia watched Isabelle give a conspiratorial glance to her mother. "Isabelle, are you sure this is the right thing to do, now? Travel, I mean, without any real destination?"

Isabelle had a serious face. "I have papers for my mother to leave this country. It is the right thing to do, no question about it."

Christine put her hands up, stern. "No more arguing. Remember, I am doing this for Daniel and Isabelle, not for myself. Don't make me think twice about it. We will go to Orleans with you in any case, and then we will decide whether to go south with you to Marseille or west to Bordeaux."

"Yes," Isabelle said, as she stood up and took her dishes to the sink. "That sounds crazy to me, too. We're not going to learn anything in Orleans. Have your coffee and croissant, Julia, and then let's go take the pictures you're so determined to do."

"Oh, of course, I'd forgotten. With this headache, anyway." She picked up the bowl and drank all her coffee, then took her croissant with her to her room. "Let me get my camera, and we're off."

ONE HOUR LATER they were standing in front of Notre Dame. Isabelle posed in front of the doors while Julia took a photo of her friend dwarfed by the arched door and the giant Romanesque rose window above it. They reversed positions after Julia made sure that Isabelle kept the settings on the camera.

"I think Hugh will like this picture," Julia said, wondering in her heart if he would even look at it. She wanted to compare it to one taken when they were here on their honeymoon. Most of all she wanted to show both photographs to Lizzie and tell her that one day all three of them would have their picture taken here.

"Mama is right," Isabelle said. "All these people, no one is worried at all. They are all so gay and carefree."

"So maybe she's overreacting. Maybe the Germans will be thrown back."

"It doesn't matter," Isabelle said, "she's afraid of being a rat. She's not going to take a chance. In her mind, she's already moved to America. It may be hard for her to change her mind, but once she does, she's unmovable." She pointed to the arched doorway. "Let's go inside and take some pictures of the stained glass windows."

Julia shook her head. "No, let's not. I haven't figured out how to work this thing inside a room. I can do daylight for now. Let's go take a picture of the American Embassy, the Seine, the Tuileries, the Louvre. See, over us, the beautiful blue sky, we can walk along the Seine and create memories for me to take back."

"And we can remember them when we meet again in New Jersey."

"Oh, yes," Julia said, "I will introduce you to Lizzie. That will be something." She wanted to imagine them all together in Central Park, but that familiar knot in her stomach told her to be wary. She needed to get home on her own. Lizzie needed her. "Okay, but let's go over there and take a picture, facing the other way, toward those trees."

"As you like," Isabelle said, smiling. "It's your time."

"Oh, and Shakespeare and Company, that's near here, too. I want that. Maybe a famous writer will be there."

"Shakespeare? In Paris?" Isabelle was bewildered.

"Oh, you wouldn't know. I read about it in the New York Times. A bookstore. Lots of Americans go there. We're on a long walk, aren't we?"

"Wherever you want. All of Paris is at your feet. You have your very expensive camera, so take advantage of it."

Julia didn't notice jealousy in Isabelle's voice, but she studied Isabelle as she moved her eyes around the square in front of the cathedral, her blond curls jumping in the breeze. Isabelle's hazel eyes betrayed no animosity. Still, Julia felt uncomfortable. She wished at the moment that she had bought a less expensive camera.

"So where to now?" Isabelle turned to face Julia with expressionless eyes.

Julia strained to see up the towers of the cathedral. "Can we go up there?"

Isabelle laughed. "I think the question is, can we make it up there. That's a lot of steps."

"Have you ever done it?"

"Yes, once in school a long time ago. When I was young and strong."

"Then we must do it," Julia said as she walked to the entrance, gesturing for Isabelle to follow her.

They headed up the narrow spiral stairway, holding on to the sides because the stone steps were worn away in the center. Exhausted halfway up, they stopped at the souvenir store.

"Here," Isabelle said, "the plaque, Quasimodo and Esmeralda."

"It's so historical. Victor Hugo, *The Hunchback of Notre Dame*. I read that in high school," Julia said, and then she smiled in amusement. "It wasn't too long ago, I saw the movie, very sad." She narrowed her eyes and remained inside herself for a moment. "I remember, Hugh didn't want to come up here." Julia pursed her lips and drew a long breath. "Thank you for coming up with me. I feel rested now, let's finish the climb so I can take more pictures."

At the top, Julia marveled at a gargoyle, took a picture of Isabelle next to one leaning out over Paris, its head resting on its hands, its hands on the banister. She stood for a full minute taking in the view before she took a picture of Sacré-Coeur gleaming white on top of Montmartre in the distance. "There, that will be a reminder for us all of where you used to live." She looked at Isabelle to make sure she followed her pointing. "From here, knowing the picture's from the tower of Notre Dame, it's a real story of Paris for all time."

Julia waited for a reaction from Isabelle.

Isabelle came close and put her hands on Julia's shoulders. Her hazel eyes opened wide. "Julia." She waited a moment. "Julia, do you realize what you have done?" She waved her head back and forth. "It's because of you that my mother is coming with us to New Jersey. Daniel and I owe you a huge debt of gratitude." She took her hands away. "I don't think you understand how much this means to me, Julia." She gestured at the city below them, down to the gray green waters of the Seine. "Being up here, alone with you, you, me and this ugly gargoyle. Above Paris. It's made me realize how important you are to us." Now Isabelle's eyes focused on Julia. "But, whatever happens, you have one goal, to get back to your daughter. I haven't forgotten that."

Julia felt close to tears. "Thank you. I appreciate it. I feel so close to you at this moment. You are like my sister, Isabelle."

Isabelle hugged her, then said, "All right, then, let's go take the rest of the pictures."

At the bottom of the stairs, Julia stopped Isabelle. "Wait. I want to light a candle." She walked to the North Rose Window, underneath it's stained glass art of the Virgin Mary holding her Christ Child. "A mother holding her baby," Julia said. She lit a candle and stood for a moment with her hands clasped on her chest. Then she nodded and walked back toward the cathedral doors.

As they walked out from the cathedral, pushing their way past tourists speaking Spanish and Italian and English, Julia led Isabelle across to the far side of the plaza to the corner with dark green trees. She pointed to the intersection of the corner.

"So stand over there, Isabelle and…." Julia searched the vicinity, then asked a young man in a blue beret with a cigarette hanging out of his mouth to take their picture.

"Oh, that's a Leica. I'm afraid I couldn't." He shook his head, took a step back and held his hands up as he tried to smile without losing a cigarette.

"Yes, you can," Julia said in a reassuring voice. "I've already focused on my friend. You only have to click the shutter, on top, here."

He nodded, threw his cigarette away and took the camera. "If you wish, but I'm not responsible." He bent over a little and moved back and forth in his imitation of a photographer.

"No, you're not," she said as she put her arm around Isabelle's waist and felt Isabelle's hand pulling her close.

The man took the picture and first turned the camera around in his hand, then handed it back to her.

"*Merci, Monsieur,*" Isabelle said, with wary eyes.

He gave them a little salute and walked away, pulling a pack of cigarettes out of his pocket.

"You shouldn't have done that, you know," Isabelle said with a frown. "He could have run away with it."

"Yes, you're right, maybe, but there are gendarmes over there, and we could have screamed."

"You think so."

"Oh come on, everything's all right. Don't be such a worry wart."

"Sure. I don't want to be a worry...wart, is that it? Where to next?"

They used up the two rolls of film at the Eiffel Tower, the American Embassy, the Tuileries, the Louvre, the Seine. They didn't make it to Shakespeare & Co. bookstore, but Julia didn't care. She had her souvenirs. Taking the pictures, thinking of showing them to Lizzie gave her a sense of relief. Of knowing that she would be home soon, and this horror of separation would be over. In a few days. With one more piece of paper.

"Come on," Julia said as they walked down the steps to the metro. "I want to get these pictures to Jacques today."

THEY DROPPED THE pictures off at the photographer's shop and went home to see what Christine had made for them. And they were very pleased to find her waiting with the table full of delicacies.

"*O là là,*" Isabelle said. "That's wonderful. Beef bourguignon, chocolate mousse." She waited for Julia in expectation of a similar response.

Julia smiled as she eyed the table, at the beautiful dishes with blue patterns. "Oh, it's beautiful, it's Delft isn't it?"

The response thrilled Christine. "I'm so happy you recognize it. It's from my grandmother. We couldn't afford that by ourselves, but she left it to me, and she told me herself that I would get it. So I bring it out for special occasions. I am not going to take it with me when we leave, so now is a good time to set it out."

"You know what," Julia said, "when we are all together in the United States and we can wave to each other across the Hudson River, then I will see that you get a replacement set of dishes."

"Wait," Isabelle said, laughing, "I don't think you can see each other across the river."

What a stickler, Julia thought to herself. "Oh, some places you can, you can see little tiny people, and you have to know who it is." Then she waved the idea away. "It doesn't matter anyway, because we will be close enough."

"Well, I'm starving," Isabelle said, "and I'm not going to wait that long." She sat without waiting for the others and unfolded her white linen napkin.

Julia and Christine joined her.

They ate in silence for a long time, then Christine said, "What was it like today out there? Did you see any refugees? Are people still going out like nothing is happening?"

Julia swallowed the bit of potato that was in her mouth and said, "You're right. There was nothing special about today. No matter where we went there were people having a good time, as if there were nothing to worry about."

"And maybe they're smarter than my mother," Isabelle said as she viewed the table with worry in her eyes. "Maybe the French Army is as good as they say it is."

Isabelle nodded, "I think you're right Mama, they all believe that France cannot be defeated." She studied her lap, thinking for a moment. "I wonder how you will feel when we arrive in America," she said as she raised her head, "and nothing has happened. You have lost your apartment and everything in it, including these beautiful heirloom dishes, and you have nothing and France is still standing, glorious as ever."

Christine laughed and shook her head at Isabelle. "I don't care about the glory of France anymore. The glory of France," she continued, fire in her eyes, "is lying dead in the cemetery down the street. The glory of France didn't do my husband any good when he suffered all the years from being gassed." She threw her napkin down on the table. "I don't want all this. I want you and Daniel safe in America. To hell with the glory of France. I can't wait to apply for American citizenship." She sat, hunched over, wringing her hands, still agitated, moving about in her seat. "Yes," she said as she glared at Isabelle, "it's true. I've changed because I choose life, the love of my family. You and Daniel. To hell with my friends. I'm not going to sit here for the rest of my life scared whether the Germans are going to come pouring across the Meuse River and destroy glorious France. I want peace." She stood and raised her voice. "Do you hear me? Do you understand me, Isabelle?"

Isabelle sat mute, staring in shock at her mother, her eyes wide, her face long.

"Do you?"

Isabelle nodded.

"Then don't question my resolve any more." She sat back down and sighed. "Sometimes I think I am stronger than you." She waved her hands around in wild gesticulation. "You go around and deliver your communist newspaper, and I think you are in danger, I worry about you, but you are too careless and you think you are safe."

"Mama…"

"No more, Isabelle." Christine pointed her finger at her daughter. "Let's enjoy our dinner. And then, I have something special for you. To remember our last nights in beautiful Paris."

Isabelle glanced at Julia, then back to her mother. Her lips were tight together in submission.

"I have something arranged. To celebrate going to America. I wasn't going to tell you until later, but now I think we need something to calm us all down. Wait a minute." She stood and went to a dark wooden cabinet in the corner. "Let's have some cognac." She brought the bottle and three small snifters and put them on the table. After she poured some of the cognac into each glass, "Vive la France," she said in a low voice. Then she raised her voice very loud, "Vive l'Amerique."

Julia and Isabelle repeated the words in unison, the three of them clinked their glasses together, and then they sipped in silence.

"What's the surprise," Julia said, peeking sideways at Isabelle.

"Well," Christine said with a self-satisfied smile, "I've arranged for us to go, tonight, to the Folies Bergère."

"You're joking," Isabelle said.

"No, we're going to see Josephine Baker doing the Danse Sauvage."

"Mama," Isabelle said, her hands over her face. "She's half naked in that."

"I don't care. It'll be fun. It will make us feel like we're already in America."

"I'm game if you are," Julia said to Isabelle.

"Come on, help me with the dishes," Christine said, "and we'll make the first show."

They were down the steps and on the subway in five minutes, and it seemed almost that fast and they were standing in line on Rue Richer for the Folies. They were not disappointed. Josephine Baker was at her best, the jazz was exciting, the champagne very good, and the crowd lost and away from the idea of refugees, Germans, and police. For a couple of hours.

And then, on the way home they talked of tomorrow, when Julia would go down to the Prefecture of Police and pick up her travel permit.

Chapter 32

IN THE MORNING, Julia was up when Paris was still dark. She opened the window to the street, and looked down past the steps to Rue Courtine, where a waiter in Café Bruxelles was opening the door and putting out tables and chairs in the ghostly light of the street lamps. He then transformed it into a yellow stage when the café lights came on. Turning her head left, up the hill toward Sacré-Coeur, she saw the steps leading nowhere, except to heaven. Up there, beyond that hill and down again lay her destination. And her heart. Julia stayed at the window and watched Montmartre wake up. Across the street, the lights came on at Au Relais, down the hill they came on at Chez Francis. People walked below toward the subway and work. From somewhere the sweet smell of baked goods made her inhale, close her eyes, and smell and hear Paris. A child's footsteps brought her to home, New York, and Lizzie. She opened her eyes and morning light changed the sky to light gray.

Julia closed the window. The house was still quiet. She went to her room and arranged her few possessions, for something to do. Slippers slouched along the hallway, the bathroom door opened and closed. She walked on tiptoes to the door and left the house for the police station.

On the subway, the people were different. More of them appeared tired, their clothes dirty, their eyes furtive. As she left the metro and walked to the police station, she seemed to be joining lines of people as if drawn by some magnetic lines of force, until she entered the building, and found herself unable to find the window that held the papers of her freedom.

A long time she jostled, pushed, waited, moved ahead, and she stood before a frustrated man with a dark shaven face and haggard eyes who listened to her and turned to his left and opened a drawer and removed a paper, and told her to sign at the bottom. Then he stamped it, shoved it to her, and turned away from the window and ignored her.

SHE FOUND CHRISTINE and Isabelle sitting at the kitchen table, waiting to hear.

"I have it."

They both sighed.

"Have some coffee." Christine poured dark coffee into the bowl that was waiting in front of the third chair at the table.

"Thank you." Julia drank from the bowl, wiped her lip, and put the bowl down on the table.

"Did they give you any trouble?" Isabelle stared into her bowl.

"No."

"We are ready." Christine's voice sounded solemn, determined.

"You have your train tickets, I see." Julia touched the envelope from the French National Railway Company, on the table. "Where's your luggage?"

"It's in the bedroom. There's not much." Isabelle answered.

"I don't want to wait," Christine said, "I don't want to stay any longer than I have to. As long as I have my picture of my husband."

"We're all going to Marseille?" Julia's voice hung in the air with finality.

Christine and Isabelle stood and pushed their chairs in to the table.

"To Marseille." Christine picked the tickets up from the table and put them in her purse. "We each have one piece of luggage. Enough for the trip."

"Wait," Isabelle said. "Sit down." She smiled with an impish frown.

Isabelle went to her room and came back out. She was holding fingernail polish and lipstick. "Sorry for the last minute delay, but I'm going out in style."

Christine and Julia gave in and joined her and all three soon wore bright red lipstick and fingernails.

"Are you going to leave all this here?" Julia said. "I'm going home. I have nothing to take with me except what's in my small suitcase. You have your whole life here in these rooms."

Christine stood and turned around to survey the room. She went to the china cabinet and opened the door. Holding up a piece of her grandmother's fine porcelain, she said, "This?" She went into the kitchen and banged on a shining copper pot above the stove. "This?" She came back and sat in a plush chair near the window to the street. The velvet on the arms had been rubbed down, and the seat cushion depressed. "This?"

Julia's voice betrayed her fear. "What about your family pictures? The one on the wall of you and your husband in front of the Eiffel Tower?"

Christine nodded. "Yes I understand that. I have a picture that I am taking with me of our marriage. That was the happiest time of my life. Of course, I am taking that with me. But Daniel has pictures that we gave him when he left. Those will do for me. I don't have time to sell this. We're at war. I made a decision in a hurry so I'm going to leave in a hurry and leave all this."

Isabelle went to the window and searched up and down the street.

"What's going on?" Julia became nervous. She didn't understand how this was going to proceed and that made her insecure.

Isabelle spoke with her head still out the window. "See the beautiful flowers down at the bottom on Rue Courtine. You would think this was an ordinary beautiful spring day. Monsieur Calvert, there he is on his bicycle bringing home his long baguette."

Her voice carried the nostalgia that seemed to creep over her, thinking about all the ordinary things that French people do every day. "I don't see him, Mama."

"Don't worry, darling, he will be here. He's not going to be down there, he's going to be up on Rue Lamarck. He will ring the buzzer."

"Julia," Isabelle said, "I think we should tell you now."

Julia waited, biting her lip. Her eyes began to sting. Are they going to leave her behind? Are they going to send her out on her own? She had always wanted to leave without them, but now she had no control over her destiny.

Christine came and took Julia aside. "I see you are worried, my second daughter, but please don't be."

The words did not reassure Julia. All she had done since she had arrived in France was plan for a way to get back to New York and Fifth Avenue and Lizzie. The last few days were an exhausting whirlwind of bureaucratic complications. It had all been done. They seemed set to go. But something was holding them up and she had no idea what. She put on a brave face. "Are you waiting for a taxi? I thought we were going to take the subway. We don't have much to carry. What's going on?"

"Not the train," Isabelle said while continuing to watch the street. "There's a better solution. Monsieur Ducasse is going to take us all in his car."

Julia became even more worried. The car? Why was that better? The idea of a train, a big long heavy train full of people, was much more secure to her than a little car. "Why is he taking us?"

Christine, sympathy in her eyes, came to Julia and held her hand. "My darling, my second daughter, do not worry. This is much better than taking the train."

"I don't understand," Julia said, "I have my tickets. You have your tickets. Why did you change? Why do you trust this man? I'm confused. I'm…," she pulled her hand away from Christine.

Christine sighed and tears began to well up in her eyes. "Oh please do not talk like that. Believe me I understand your fear. If it is what you want we will of course take you to the Gare de Lyon and you can get on your train to Marseille. We would never do anything to interfere with you getting home to your daughter, Julia." Christine stared into Julia's eyes. Her eyes were no longer filling with tears but with cold determination. "But believe me we had to accept his offer. There are so many more options with the car. We can go where we want."

That remark sent Julia into a tailspin. "We have one place to go. I still don't see why we need a car."

Isabelle closed the window and came next to Julia. "Mama is not telling you everything. Monsieur Ducasse has another advantage."

Julia frowned. "I can get to the Gare de Lyon by myself." She stood and went to pick up her suitcase.

The buzzer sounded. Julia put her suitcase down, feeling trapped.

Christine went to the window, pushed it open, and searched below. "You are here. Thank god. We're coming right down." She came back and addressed Julia. "We will take you to the train station. It's not out of our way. Jules, Monsieur Ducasse, can explain it all to you on the way. If you want to get out and take the train, you will make me cry. But I'm going to cry anyway when we separate at Marseille." She touched Julia on the face. "I want to be with you as long as I can."

"Mama," Isabelle interjected, impatience in her voice.

Christine nodded, picked up her suitcase, took in the room one last time, and walked toward the door.

ON THE STREET, Jules Ducasse was waiting, his black Simca 8 Berline idling by the curb. On the street and not behind a window, he was thinner and taller than Julia expected. He tipped his black hat. He was wearing an impeccably pressed black suit, a clean white shirt and a plain gray tie. "Good morning, ladies. Thank you for being punctual. Here, let's figure out how to get all this luggage on the car." A luggage rack had been installed on the top with belts that were hooked on to the door frames. One suitcase had already been tied down. He put the women's suitcases on the rack and tied them down with rope. "Après vous, Mesdames," he said with a slight bow. He opened the front passenger door for Christine, while Isabelle and Julia hunched over to climb into the back seat. Ducasse got in, started the car, adjusted the throttle, waited for the motor to calm down, then pushed the throttle back in. Then he turned around in the car and said, smiling, "Are we all ready?"

They all answered yes in unison.

"You have a nice car, Monsieur," Isabelle said.

"Thank you", he said as he backed uphill to Rue Lamarck and made a three point turn to go downhill. "It's really a Fiat. The French government doesn't want you to know that. For me it's been a reliable car." He let out the clutch and moved downhill past Au Relais. "So. Where are we going?"

Isabelle laughed. "We thought you had that already figured out."

"Oh, I have," he said, "for me. And also, for you and your mother. We are all going to the south of France, and from there we will see.

I have family in Provence. You want to go to North Africa. No, my question is for the young lady so quiet in the back."

"Yes?" Julia said, biting her lip. She held her arms tight across her lap, and moved her eyes to Monsieur Ducasse but kept her head straight.

"I understand you want to go to Gare de Lyon. You intend to take the train to Marseille. Is that right?"

Julia nodded to his image in the rear-view mirror. The car turned the corner on to Rue Custine.

"Ah, well. First of all, we are going in that direction before we leave Paris and head to Orleans. So it is not a problem. But I must tell you, Mademoiselle, that you are making a grave error."

Christine turned to Julia, who sat still and quiet, hunched down in the back.

"Let me explain it to you," he continued, "you will simply not get on the train."

"But I have tickets," Julia said, fear stabbing her heart.

"So do thousands of others," he said, looking at her still in the mirror with cold brown eyes. "Someone will already be in your place. All these refugees, more than the Belgians now, there are French from the northeast. And they are all going the same way."

Julia reached forward and touched him on the shoulder. "But Monsieur, you, you work in the mayor's office, you…"

"Oh no, not now, not with this madness. I cannot do anything."

Julia's voice rose in panic. "But you must have contacts?" She turned to Isabelle, who touched her on the arm, but said nothing.

Ducasse shook his head. "Those are railroad people. I work in city hall. I'm sorry."

Christine twisted around, holding the back of her seat to face Julia. Her eyes were full of compassion. "Now you see, my dear, why you must come with us. You have no choice. This is the right decision."

Isabelle pulled at Julia's arm. "You must come with us."

These three people overwhelmed Julia. She sat back and gave in. Her only chance to see Lizzie again. "Yes. I understand. I will go with you."

Ducasse nodded with satisfaction. "Let me tell you, all three of you, the advantages of coming with me. First, I will be honest. For me, it would be impossible to drive alone. There are soldiers coming this way. The first colonel we see would get off his horse and take it for himself. So, the three of you, you are now my family. I will tell you something else. If you must be my family, I have papers for all of us."

"What?" Julia said, in total surprise.

"Mama? Were you aware of this?" Isabelle said, leaning forward.

Christine smiled. "Yes, I plead guilty. I'm not going to leave everything I ever had behind and then go unprepared."

"But I can't pass as your family," Julia said, her voice choked with emotion.

Ducasse waved her concern away. "Don't worry. You won't have to act as my daughter. No one will question you. Trust me."

Julia took Isabelle's hand.

"But that's not all," Ducasse said, "I also am prepared to use my office along the way if need be. All the villages farther out are setting up roadblocks, and that is where I can be of some help. I have documents, and hand stamps I can use to intimidate stupid country people." He let out a quick laugh. "I brought my office with me! They will understand that I have powerful allies in Paris. We shall have no trouble at all. I have thought of everything. There in the trunk, I even have a placard that says Red Cross. If we have to. Trust me, Mademoiselle, you are in safe hands. Ah, there we are." He pointed to the right. "It's the road to Orleans. We are on our way. We'll go on the Boulevard de la Bastille." He turned to Julia. "Very famous, no?" He swerved in time to avoid a collision with a three-wheeled black delivery truck stopped to pick up baguettes from a bakery. "We'll be out of Paris sooner than you think. And you understand we take a route out of Paris that is not well known. Down the Rue des Archives to get to the bridge across the Seine."

"Faster than the Germans, I hope," Christine said, fear stalking her voice. She turned around to study Isabelle, who leaned forward to touch her on the shoulder. Christine turned back, but kept her hand on top of her daughter's.

"And faster than the refugees," Ducasse replied, "I promise."

In the back, Julia watched Isabelle and Christine, shook her head and ran a hand through her hair. Hot air blew over her and she undid the top button of her brown dress as Paris slid by outside her window.

Chapter 33

THREE HOURS OUT OF PARIS they headed south toward Marseille, caught in the stream of traffic ahead and behind them, which had grown with every village they passed. West to Orleans was out of the question. Ducasse had told them they would head to Dijon, and from there straight south to Lyon, and from there to Marseille.

In the beginning, they had maintained a steady forty kilometers an hour, but three hours later that had slowed to half with the growing column of refugees.

Julia sat cramped in the back seat, watching out the window as other cars and trucks joined them from each of the roads they crossed. Some flowed in from the right, from the west, but the huge influx came from any road that fed in on the left, from the east, fleeing the oncoming German army.

The traffic became a two-lane road south, because no one was coming back toward them. No one was coming to Paris. When they passed Auxerre, on a clear bright morning, the refugees joining them were no longer long streams of automobiles. Now there were stragglers on foot, on horseback, whole families walking beside a cart. The cars still maintained a column in the center of the road, but the two lanes had merged into one.

Julia hunched down in the back seat, her arms folded across her lap. She was dragged along in a maelstrom of poor people fleeing for their life. Ducasse, Christine, Isabelle, they were quiet, all in a shock at what this escape from Paris had become.

Ducasse pounded his hand on the steering wheel as if he could slam people out of the way. Cars were starting to pull over to the side of the road as they ran out of gas. Christine sat with her hand over her mouth as if that would protect her. She turned to Ducasse, who looked forward, put the car in first gear, then put it in neutral and waited, put on the brakes, then put it in first gear again as they moved forward, but had to stop again after a few moments.

Now horses were jamming the road and people who were leading cattle, the cattle pulling carts loaded with all their belongings.

A horn blared at them from behind. All four of them turned around to see who it was that thought they had some sort of priority. It was a military car with an officer in the back. The car stopped and the colonel or general got out and yelled at them. "Let me through," he said, emphasizing the word 'through'. He raised his fist in the air to show his authority. "I must get through."

"My God," Ducasse said, "who the hell does he think he is?" He turned around and shook his fist at the man, who couldn't see him. "He's running away from the battle and we're supposed to help him?"

Ducasse ignored the man and tried to move forward again, but this time they were stuck behind a military ambulance with a big red cross on it. Like all the other military they saw, it was going away from the enemy. Now they started to see soldiers walking on the side of the road. Their uniforms were in tatters and they had no weapons. They kept their head down and put one foot in front of the other with no purpose. They didn't even appear to be running away, they seemed to be poor homeless beggars walking along the road.

The staggering column of refugees thinned out as people disappeared into farms or small towns. Then they made faster progress south. They saw a sign for the first time that said Dijon, but the next road was filled with new refugees merging in with them.

The slow column became slower. The car began to sputter, filling Julia with dread. Isabelle, who had been silent the whole time, took Julia's hand.

"Damn," Ducasse said. "We're out of gas. I have three liters in the trunk. After that we're out of luck."

"What are we going to do?" Christine said, panic in her voice.

"Don't worry," Ducasse said, "this will get us to Dijon."

"But we can't get to Dijon," Isabelle said, "we can't make a left turn with all these...." she hesitated, saw the carts, the bicycles, the horses, the people on foot. Then, more soldiers, all moving in a solid sludge of despair on the side of the road. They avoided a bicyclist, then brushed past a stationary car. They were like dirty ragged ghosts. "All these people," she ended with despair in her voice.

"You're right," Ducasse said. "Let me put what I have in the tank, and we'll have to see how far we get."

Three liters got them nowhere. The road procession began to slow down and then stopped. Ducasse got out of the car and stood on the running board to see what was ahead.

He stuck his head in the window. "I can't see anything. I don't know what's blocking the road."

The refugees all around them began to leave the road and go into the fields, climbing over fences, knocking them over, going into houses and barns, under trees. But it did not seem to reduce the number of people and animals on the road.

Christine opened the door. "We might as well get out and stretch."

Ducasse and Christine stood in front of the car leaning back on the headlights. Julia and Isabelle got out of the car. They went to the side of the road and sat on the grass. Others were doing the same on either side of them. To their left, a few meters back, a horse lay on its side as two men tried in vain to get it to stand up. One of the men said, "Shit," pulled out a gun and shot the horse. Everyone jumped, several women screamed. Then everyone was quiet again.

The sky was clear, a few clouds in the West moving across the sky in no hurry, and the breeze pushed the treetops back and forth as if this were any normal beautiful afternoon. The ground was warm to Julia.

A rumbling sound began, coming from no direction. It grew louder and then they looked in the sky, everyone on the earth below, and saw two or three airplanes circling above them. Then the planes flew into a formation higher up into the sky, flew away from them in a circle. They felt the sigh of relief coming from around them. Julia moved closer to Isabelle, who touched her on the shoulder and then relaxed.

In a second the roaring became louder, and a great screech of a siren blasted their ears. Julia put her hands over her head. The siren grew louder and louder and then a bomb exploded. It was close.

Julia and Isabelle hugged each other and fell to the ground in the drainage ditch by the side of the road. Another siren came screeching down at them, piercing their ears. The plane came in low a hundred yards ahead of them, machine guns slamming the earth with bullets. Julia yelled at herself, everything blended together in the horrible sound of screaming Stuka sirens, people wailing in pain, bombs whistling and cracking, then explosions ripping the distance. When it had flown away her heart's pounding kept up the massacre.

They got up. Some people were screaming, others were holding bloodied corpses in their arms and yelling for help.

"Mama!" Isabelle ran to the front of the car and picked up her mother's lifeless body, blood covering Christine's chest and legs. Next to her Ducasse's still body lay in the road. Julia stood frozen by the side of the road her hands covering her face. She let her arms down and watched Isabelle rocking Christine back and forth.

Isabelle kept saying, "Mama, Mama," and running her hand over her mother's hair, her other arm covering Christine's chest as blood ran down her arm.

Julia ran to Ducasse's side, his body at a grotesque angle, his eyes staring up. There was no wound on the top of his body, but blood oozed into the dust underneath him. She knelt there, ears ringing, heart pounding, and then she saw her own blood running down her legs. Little pieces of glass stuck out from her shin. Forgetting Ducasse, forgetting Christine, Julia put her leg out straight and removed twenty or so pieces of glass from her right leg. Her dress served as a cleaning towel, and she was left with many small red spots and pink smear up and down her leg. But she was grateful nothing had gone deep into the leg.

Next to her, the car started rocking. She saw two men and a woman in the car. Julia jumped up and yelled at them, and they ran away with suitcases and purses. She started to run after them, but one movement of her leg brought her up short. They were gone into trees and nowhere to be seen. She turned back to Isabelle, still cradling her mother in her arms, dazed, thinking of what she was holding.

Several soldiers came up to them. One, with stripes on his arm, with round fogged up glasses, said, "We cannot let you stay here. We must move the bodies off the road."

Isabelle screamed at them. "She's not a body. She's my mother."

"I am sorry, Mademoiselle. I know what you are feeling. But we have to free up the road."

"They've stolen everything from us," Julia said, her arms out wide in outrage.

"I'm sorry for that, too, Mademoiselle. We are not the police. If it was up to me I would be several miles down the road by now. But we have our orders."

Isabelle put her arm around Julia. "Where will we go? What will we do?"

The soldier looked sympathetic, but he shook his head and motioned to others to come to take away the bodies.

Isabelle began screaming in panic. "What are you going to do? You can't dump them by the side of the road?"

The soldier's eyes blazed in impatience. "No. We won't. We have to bury them in the field. Then we will be on our way."

ONE HOUR LATER, Julia and Isabelle stood over two mounds of dirt in a field to the side of the road. They had found a small notebook in the car, and noted the location of the burials.

"Do you know where we are?" Julia said.

Isabelle took Julia by the hand and started walking back against the flow of refugees. "Yes, more or less. I know what road we are on, I know how to read the signs. We will have to walk back to the next road sign, and write it down."

"But what will we do? We have no papers. All my money was in my purse."

"I don't worry about papers. Jacques will get us papers when we get back. As for money, well, walking is free. We will have to beg at farmhouses like everyone else. And steal if we have to. We'll worry about the rest when we get back."

They found a sympathetic farmer two miles north, glad to find someone who wasn't afraid to go back to Paris. He gave them some bread and cheese, and some fruit to take with them in the morning, and said he would pray for them.

They walked all day and into the evening, turning into the town of Avallon. On the church steps, they found a group of refugees who had gathered straw for the night. An elderly man and his wife made room for them. Isabelle and Julia found a huge pile of straw around the corner of the church. "Left by a farmer," said the old man. "And over there," he pointed to a table across the plaza, "they will give you something to eat. You'd better hurry, or it will be all gone."

Isabelle said that Julia should stay and watch over their magnificent hotel room. She brought back bread and ham and a bottle of wine.

The old man shivered. "We're lucky it's not going to rain tonight."

His wife shook her head. "No, we should go into the church. They wouldn't keep us out then."

The next morning the sound of a truck coming close jolted them awake. Julia and Isabelle were the last ones up. Everyone else moved as one to surround the truck. It was an army truck, heading north, toward the fighting, rare as that was.

"Where are you going?" a woman asked, her voice raised in anger. "What are you soldiers waiting for to stop this war? It has got to stop."

Others in the small group of refugees yelled in support of the woman.

A man shoved forward close to the driver's door. "Do you want them to massacre us all with our children? Have you seen what they did in Belgium? They are murdering us on the road. Why don't you seek peace?"

This change in the attitude of the refugees shocked Julia. A day before the soldiers were fleeing faster than civilians. Now the people were trying to get the soldiers to surrender.

"Bastards," Isabelle said. Several people turned in horror when they heard her. She grabbed Julia by the arm and led her out of there and out to the road north to Paris. When they were out of earshot, she said, "Did you hear them? They have given up. Thousands dead, our soldiers killed." Tears filled her eyes, but she did not stop. "My mother dead. Monsieur Ducasse dead. And these traitors want to surrender? When we get back, Julia, we will find the communists who are still willing to fight the Germans."

Julia stopped and looked with fright at Isabelle. "What are we going to do? Isabelle, I am not a communist. I am an American who wants to go home to her family."

Isabelle nodded, but took Julia's arm again and kept on walking. "No, of course, I understand. Nothing has changed for you. Except one thing, you have no money, you have no identity card, you have no ticket, you have no travel permit. Where do you think you will get one?"

"But I will go back to the embassy, I will start there. They will remember me."

"Oh, yes, of course," Isabelle said, rolling her eyes. "The embassy. Of course. But then what about the police? And what if the Germans are there? I sympathize with you, my friend, but things are more difficult than you think."

Julia's head spun, her throat was dry, and her leg ached. Lizzie? Will I ever see Lizzie again?

RUMORS SPREAD THROUGHOUT the day that an armistice was coming. The phony war became real and France had lost. People joined them now, walking back to Paris. They found two abandoned bicycles and moved faster on bicycles than they did in the car. Soon they were in Fontainebleau forest. In two days, they saw the city rising up in the mist before them.

As they rode through Paris, they seemed to be alone. Few people were on the streets. It was dusk, and no lights were on. The city was for all practical purposes deserted.

On their way across the city, they saw something impossible. The Champs Élysées, the most elegant street in the world, was a ghost town. They pedaled across the middle of the traffic circle around the Arc de Triomphe by themselves. The few people who had begun returning with them had stopped at cities and villages before Paris. They made it, alone, along Rue Caulaincourt to the base of the steps of the back end of Montmartre, where they put the bicycles down and climbed up the steps to 32 Rue Mont-Cenis.

Isabelle opened the door to the apartment and entered it with caution. Nothing had been touched. Their coffee cups were there where they had been left. She collapsed on the floor and sat looking down, her arms at her sides like an abandoned puppet. Julia went to her and put her arms around her friend, and they stayed that way, unable to move, unable to think, unable to feel.

"It's all my fault," Isabelle said, covering her head with her hands. "I made her go. It's me. I killed her."

"No you didn't," Julia said, "don't you remember? She decided on her own."

"She wouldn't have left if I stayed home." Isabelle moved her head from side to side, trying to shake off the reality of what had happened.

Julia wanted to comfort her, but she felt so heavy, so tired, exhausted beyond relief. She lay down on the floor, and Isabelle fell down next to her and they lay there, together, breathing, hearing the silence all around them, watching the darkness take over the room, and enveloping them in oblivion.

JULIA AWOKE in the middle of the night. She pulled Isabelle up and led her to her bedroom, let her down on the bed, and returned to her own room. She tried to think about what she could do, but there was nothing that came into her mind. Sleep came again to her.

In the morning, she heard a noise out in the kitchen. She went out and saw Isabelle writing at the table.

"What are you doing?" The weakness of her own voice frightened Julia.

Isabelle was clearly determined as she continued writing. "I'm writing down the information Jacques will need to get us new identity papers. And transit visas and exit visas."

"Jacques, why Jacques?" Julia's fear deepened. She knew what it meant. Jacques was a forger. Isabelle was a communist. They were in it together.

Isabelle put her pen down and pointed for Julia to sit. "What kind of fool are you? You have lost all your money, your papers, your clothes. You are nothing. Soon the Germans will be here, and you will be put on a train to Germany. Or worse, to Poland."

Julia sat, frozen, numb. She had never heard Isabelle talk this way. She had been helpless before the police, before the embassy people. Now she was helpless before the one friend she had in the world. She knew she could not get to Lisbon on her own. Hugh was not responding to her. She could go to the embassy and get a new passport. They would remember her. They had records of her visit. But she couldn't go back to that police station and tell those men that she had lost her papers. They would take forever.

She had no money. She wasn't helpless, she was penniless. All the traveler's checks she had brought with her were now being spent somewhere near Dijon. And no one was going to investigate that with the Germans coming.

Julia found it hard to speak. "What are we going to do?"

Isabelle's mouth narrowed to a grim line. "I'm going to take this to Jacques, it's our personal information, and what I remember from our travel and exit visas. He might be able to get you an American one, I don't know. He doesn't do that every day. It depends on what he has in his stock. But first let's get something to eat. Then I'll tell you what we're going to do."

Isabelle made coffee, and they ate croissants left over from yesterday.

"Now, I know, Julia, you still want to go home. That has not changed. But you cannot get on a train to Marseille until you have your papers and some money."

"But the American embassy, they will help me. I will get word to my husband."

Isabelle looked at Julia and shook her head. "Your husband. He's had a lot of time, and you haven't heard from him. I'm not surprised, either. If I remember, when we met you were leaving the country with his daughter."

Julia shrank deep down inside herself and tears came to her eyes. "He must love me. He must. It's been so hard."

Isabelle stood and strode across the room. "Who are you kidding? You are all alone. You have me. If you work with me, you have a chance. Otherwise they'll find you dead in a gutter somewhere."

Julia stood and tightened her fists. "No," she yelled. "It's not true. I will get home, with your help or without it. Nobody will stop me. I'm going home to Lizzie. I can do it by myself if I have to walk all the way to Lisbon."

Isabelle was taken aback by the fiery accusation in Julia's tone. Her own voice softened in sympathy. "Yes, of course. I want that for you, too. By all means, do go to the embassy. Apply for a visa. Get them to send word to America." She walked to Julia and took her by the arms. "But in the meantime, you will have to wait. You can't sit around. Jacques can get us papers much faster than your embassy. You can use those papers until your good ones come."

Julia hugged Isabelle and laid her head on her chest. "Yes, I understand. I know you are trying to help me. And believe me, I want to help you." She pulled back and peered into Isabelle's eyes. "I'm sorry for your mother." Then, she collapsed on the floor and began sobbing.

Isabelle pulled her up. "What is it?"

Julia slowed her crying, then stopped, then took long breaths and one final sigh. "It's Lizzie. Imagine if she were here with us. She would have gone with us in the car. She would have been killed." At the end, she lost her voice, and held her hands over her mouth as she began crying again.

"All right, all right," Isabelle said, holding her. "But she's safe in New York. Now you have to plan to get back to her. Nothing's changed about that." She made Julia look at her. "Are you with me? Are we going to do this together?"

"Do what? I don't know what we are going to do?"

"Jacques will help us out with a little money until we figure out what we can do. There are things here in the house we can pawn. We don't need much to get by. The first thing is, we have to stock up. There isn't anybody here."

"Here? Where? What do you mean?"

"Paris is deserted. Very few people have come back. We'll go to the stores and stock up on what we need to keep us going until we find a way to keep on going."

"How are we going to do that?"

"Tonight, we'll do it when it gets dark, the later the better."

"But that's stealing."

Isabelle's voice rose and became hard. "My god, Julia, what the hell do you think this is? The Germans bombed and strafed us, killed my mother, people stole everything we have and you are worried about right and wrong." Isabelle stared at Julia with violence in her eyes.

Julia understood. She put her hand on Isabelle's arm. "You can count on me."

"Soon we'll know where we stand and where we can go. I know we can at least get to the south of France, and from there we can go across the Pyrenees, and we'll be in Spain."

Julia nodded, but now she felt that her whole life lay in the hands of this woman.

"Come with me," Isabelle said, "tonight we must go to Jacques. Once you have talked to him, you will feel much better. Because you will have a purpose, and someone else who can help you. Remember this, if anything ever happens to me, you can always go to Jacques."

Julia smiled for the first time. "And I had forgotten he has my pictures. The ones I want to take home to Lizzie."

Isabelle nodded, seeing Julia as if they were now partners, now that Julia had accepted a mission.

Twenty minutes later, they entered Jacque's photography shop. Julia learned that he had not developed her pictures.

"I'm sorry," he said, in an unsympathetic voice. "You left without coming back for them. I didn't do anything."

Julia felt that familiar sinking feeling, that she was losing control.

"Oh, but Jacques," Isabelle said, trying to help Julia. "You can work on them, can't you? It's important for Julia. So it's important for me."

"Do you know what's going on, Isabelle?" he said, anger now taking over his face.

"Yes, I do, Jacques. My mother has been killed, Mr. Ducasse has been killed. So shut up about your damned knowing what's going on. We're here because we need new papers. That's your job. How long will it take?" She stood, defiant, arms across her chest. "Can you get Julia an American passport?"

He nodded. "Yes, I can. There's no competition for that. British passports, now that's something hard to come by. Everyone wants one of those."

"When can we have ours?"

"Let's see, you need your residence permit, your travel visa, your exit visa, your Spanish transit visa and your Portuguese visa. Will that be all, Ladies?" The mocking tone in his voice was unmistakable.

Isabelle stared at him with bulging eyes.

"Yes, well," he said, studying the counter with the papers Isabelle had given him. "I can have all of these for you in three days. But for now, here are your residence permits."

Isabelle and Julia stared at each other.

"Yes, of course, from Monsieur Ducasse, already arranged for your car trip, but I made another copy, too. Now you see how smart I am. The others, as I said, in three days."

"Three days? Are you joking?" Isabelle said, pointing to the papers on the counter. "It used to be two weeks. What are you giving us? Bad stuff?"

Jacques laughed. "No. You see, everyone's gone. The city has been empty. So I have enough to take care of you. But it works both ways. I work on yours, and I will work all night, but you must help someone else."

Julia spoke up with a quiet little voice. "Is it possible to pick up my pictures."

Isabelle turned to Julia, shaking her head, her eyes over-bright. "Not now. Your pictures can wait until we have our papers."

Julia nodded in acceptance, and took a step back, hitting the door, her head down.

"Julia," Jacques said, trying to sound like he cared, "I will try to work on your photos, I will. But when the Germans arrive, people will come in here needing new papers, good ones. The Gestapo does not accept papers that have been created in a hurry."

"And, so?" Isabelle said.

He sighed. "And so, I need you to get me some good documents."

Julia now became frightened. "What do you mean? I thought you had good documents to work from?"

"Calm down," Jacques said, raising his hand, frowning. "Isabelle, you know what I mean. I need you two to work with my sources."

Julia touched Isabelle. "What does he mean? What sources?" The shop became very hot and her heart beat fast.

Isabelle turned to Julia. "Listen, it's not so hard, and it's not dangerous. I'll explain it to you." She turned to Jacques. "She's right, though. What sources?"

"I have two of them now." He glanced at Julia. "They are the ones who do the dangerous work. I need you two to act as drop-offs."

"All right," Isabelle said. "What sources, Jacques? Tell me who?"

"Ah," he said, shaking his head. "Things are different now with Nazis showing up any minute. They say that the Germans will be marching down the Champs Élysées in two days' time. Now, Isabelle,

I cannot tell you who my sources are. You do not need to know that. Tell me that you will help me, and I will give you your instructions."

Isabelle turned to Julia, who waited a long time, then nodded.

"Yes," Julia said, "I will help. Because of what they have done to us."

Isabelle turned back to Jacques. "And?"

"Come closer," he said.

Isabelle and Julia went up to the counter and leaned forward.

"I need documents from people who are coming from the East. The place to find them is on the trains coming into Paris from the East."

"Why the East?" Julia said, puzzled.

"Because that region is now behind German lines. No one will go back there to check the authenticity of the documents."

"I see," Isabelle said. "A good idea."

"So," Jacques continued. "Your part is very simple. You go to the Gare de l'Est every evening."

"Evening?" Julia said.

"Yes," he said, nodding, "every evening, each on your own, each for a different set of hours, until we have two sets of papers."

"Two?" Julia said, now confused.

"You can't both be going together to the train station. People will start to recognize you. Sure, you might each get a set of papers on the first day, and then it will be over for you. But that's not likely to happen. Anyway, I have others who are willing to help the Party. You are merely the first."

"I don't understand," Julia said. What are we supposed to do?"

"Isabelle will tell you," Jacques said.

"You have done this before?" Julia said, turning to Isabelle, fear in her eyes. Then she remembered. "Oh, yes, your mother was angry at you for something, for going out by yourself. So, now I know." She turned to Jacques, stood with her chest out and her head held high. "I will do my part."

Jacques nodded and held out his hand to each of them. "Vive la France!"

"Vive la France," Isabelle replied.

"Vive l'Amerique," Julia said, defiance in her eyes.

"Yes, yes," Jacques said.

Chapter 34

THEY LEFT THE SHOP and turned the corner on their way to Isabelle's apartment on Rue du Mont-Cenis. The streets were not empty now, but there were no cars, only the isolated bicyclist. People they passed on the street, people whose faces Isabelle knew from childhood, kept their eyes down. They had already accepted the same defeat as the French army.

Inside, Isabelle turned on the radio on the table in the living room. She turned the dial until she heard a voice in French. "Listen," she said. "I know that voice. It's de Gaulle. I wonder what he has to say."

The two women listened in silence as de Gaulle explained that the French army would regroup around him, and that all French citizens should show their support.

Isabelle laughed. "Did you hear that? What a hero. He's in London on the BBC and he wants our support. Well, to hell with him. We're here in Paris, the Germans are coming and we'll be on our own."

"Isabelle," Julia said, feeling more confident, but still feeling weak and insecure. "What is it we have to do at the train station?"

"In the evening when the trains arrive, you and I will each have a copy of a newspaper, Le Monde Diplomatique."

"Le Monde Diplomatique? Why that newspaper?"

"Because it's a weekly, but last week. That's an important clue. It's the way they know who we are. And then we face the paper away from us on the table. That paper upside down to us, sitting at a table next to the fast food counter where they sell ham and cheese sandwiches they

280

will recognize that, whoever they are. We sit there for an hour after the train arrives and then leave."

"So, I don't understand," Julia said. "What happens?"

"You and I each buy a sandwich and put it in a paper sack. We eat the sandwich over the hour, maybe have a glass of wine, but we sit there. The paper sack is open on the table. That's where the pickpockets will drop the documents. They walk up to the counter, and as they pass us they drop the documents in the sack and keep on going. It all happens very fast."

"How do they know whom to choose to steal the passports?"

"I don't know myself. It's not something I want to know. That's part of the success. We don't know each other. But it's simple, I think. They choose people who look like they're not Parisians. Clothes, suitcases maybe, ragged or dirty. They're afraid. That's my guess."

Julia nodded in amazement. "Then what?"

"Then we get up and leave."

"Together?"

Isabelle slumped in disbelief. "No, stupid, not together. We don't go in together, either. We have to act like we don't even know each other." She glared at Julia.

Julia wasn't cowed. "You've done this before, Isabelle. I haven't. You know you're brave. I don't."

JACQUES, OR SOMEONE sent by him, knocked on their door two days later. When Isabelle opened the door, the hallway was empty, but an envelope lay at her feet. She picked it up and closed the door.

"Julia, our papers are here," she said, excited, "he did work all night."

Julia took her papers from Isabelle and breathed a deep sigh of relief when she counted them: residence permit, permit to travel to Marseille, transit visas for Spain and Portugal, and a well-worn American passport, with her picture stamped on it, and a recognizable signature from the embassy. She was even more surprised to find beneath that a ticket for Pan American Airlines Clipper Service from Marseille to Lisbon to New York. And a train ticket from Paris to Marseille with enough francs to buy food on the way.

"How is this possible?" she said to Isabelle, going pale and covering her mouth.

"It's Jacques," Isabelle said, smiling. "He's the best there is. Him and Virginie. She's an artist of the first rank, if you ask me. It must be what he said, that everyone has left the city and they have not started back yet in large numbers, and Julia, he works fast, too."

Julia began to shake. "I don't know. If someone asked me to show these papers, I would be so afraid. I would show it, I know, but still…."

"Ah, yes, I understand, my friend. But you have one day before we go out. Now is the chance to test yourself."

"Test myself? How?" Julia brought her nervous hand up to her forehead.

"We'll go out. You show your papers to someone, we'll figure out who, in a store, or maybe a policeman, just for a test, and then you'll feel comfortable."

"Oh, I couldn't do that." Julia turned away and went to the far corner of the room before turning back.

"I understand," Isabelle, said, showing great sympathy in her voice. "Julia, look me in the eyes." When she had Julia's quiet attention, she continued. "You don't have to do it. You are not French and you'll be going home very soon. It is not fair to put you in this position."

But Julia could not accept that. "No. No, I can do it. I was scared at first at the thought of going out." She came back to Isabelle and stood before her. "I am with you. I can't run away now. And anyway, it's two times, isn't it? Isn't that what he said? What's so hard about sitting at a table eating a sandwich?" But she knew that it might be many more than two times.

It wasn't hard. Toward the end of the hour a man, a kid it seemed to Julia, dropped something in the bag on the table. She didn't even see his hand. The bag didn't move, didn't make a sound. It was a blur by the side of her face. She took a bite of her sandwich and a drink of wine, and put the sandwich back in the bag, and doing so she noticed a passport in the bottom of the bag. A Swiss passport. Excited, she left the train station and made her way home. When she arrived at Rue du Mont-Cenis, she saw the light was on in the apartment. Isabelle was waiting for her inside. Julia's eyes burned with pride when she handed the bag to Isabelle.

Isabelle did not take out the document. She took the whole sack and put it next to another one on the table. "Tomorrow I will bring this to Jacques. And we are done for now. Or at least you are. You can plan your trip home, Julia."

Julia sat, exhausted, drained. Relieved, but feeling hot and shaky. "I can go home? Aren't you going with me?"

Isabelle looked at her, shaking her head, her lips tight. "No. I have to pay them back for my mother. For what they have done. Jacques needs my help." She stood and went to Julia. "But you, you have done more than can be expected. And you have your little Lizzie in New York." She smiled in secret to herself. "Across the river from New Jersey."

"That's right, but you," Julia said, "you have your brother, Daniel. You have to think of him, too."

"Daniel? Yes. I think Daniel will do the same as I, the same as millions of other French citizens. I know he is going to come back over here and fight for France. And I sure as hell am not going to go over there to New Jersey and then find out he's not there. He will come here, Julia, to his home. He will find me, and together we will defend our country."

Julia held her hands in front of her face. "I don't know how to get to Lisbon. I need your help."

"Stop it," Isabelle said, her voice angry. "You do know how. Tomorrow morning we will bring the sacks to Jacques, you can pick up your photos, and you will leave on the first train going south."

THE NEXT MORNING, they left the apartment but Isabelle stopped Julia when they arrived at the bottom of the steps. "Now I say goodbye to you, my most cherished friend. Someday, when this is all over, we will meet again. But for now, we must separate. I will go first. I will drop off the sacks and leave. You wait until I've disappeared around the corner. That will provide enough time to separate us. Then you can go into the shop and get your photos."

Without waiting, Isabelle turned and walked away. Julia went to the window of the restaurant and stared at the menu as long as she could, then followed in Isabelle's direction until she came to Jacque's shop. She peered through the window to make sure that Isabelle wasn't inside. Jacques wasn't to be seen either, but she knew he was in the back, putting the documents in a safe hiding place. She entered and walked up to the counter.

"Hello? Is anyone here?"

Two strange men in long black trench coats came out from the back. They both wore black fedoras as well. One was tall, with blue eyes and dark blonde hair, and a black mustache covering the whole of his upper lip. The other was shorter, with black eyes, brown hair, and a round face with pockmarks.

Julia's heart pounded in her chest.

"Who are you?" said the tall man, his voice deep. He did not talk with a native French accent.

"I, I'm here to pick up my photos."

"Ah, I see," he continued. "And your name?"

"Julia Stuart."

The smaller man stepped in front of the other and put his hands on the counter. "Stuart? Hmm. Are you British?"

"No. I'm American." A deep terror began to rise within her as she reached in her pocket to take her documents out. Following Isabelle's instructions, she had put her passport, transit visas, and tickets in her inside pocket, and her documents for France in her outside pocket. She handed them to the man.

He pulled them out of her hand, and studied them. Then he gave them to the taller man almost as if dismissing them. He nodded, his eyes narrowing. "Give me one minute. I will see if I can find them." He went to the back.

"Where's Jacques?" Julia said in a moment of panic. She regretted admitting she knew him.

"Jacques. Oh." The man spoke in a friendly voice, but his face was passive. "He is a friend of yours?"

Julia shook her head. "No, not at all. He's the owner of the shop." She pointed to the name on the window behind her, now backwards from the inside.

He nodded, his eyes penetrating, not believing her, or not caring either way. "Ah, yes, I see. Well, Miss, we will wait for your pictures." He shrugged his overcoat on better, then surveyed the shop before turning back to Julia. "You have very many documents on your person. And it appears you have arrived not too long ago." He stepped around the counter and came closer to her. "You have a residence permit and a travel permit for France. For travel within France? Why do you need to travel within France? You must have a passport. Please show it to me." He spoke in a polite voice to her, but his eyes and his contemptuous mouth continued their accusation. He studied her face, and studied the opening of the top of her coat.

Julia fumbled in her pocket so she could extract the passport without taking her transit visas or tickets out. She handed him the passport. Her heart beat fast, but she controlled her breathing, and forced herself to smile. "Please, I want my pictures. I'm taking them home to my little girl."

"You should not be worried," the tall man said, smiling. "We are here for routine police business, that is all."

The short pockmarked man returned from the back and said, "Your little girl? Where is she?"

Julia held her hand out to receive the pictures, but the man held them back in defiance.

He raised his eyebrows. "Where, did you say?"

"In New York. Back home." Julia felt a sense of relief in saying New York, as if it would protect her from these men, who were not Parisians. And maybe not French.

The tall blue-eyed man took her passport and handed it to the pockmarked man, who put the passport in his pocket and walked to the door.

"My passport!"

"Oh, please, be patient, young lady, and everything will be well."

The short man returned to the shop and brushed past Julia and into the back. The tall man went by her and blocked access to the door.

Julia was shocked to see Isabelle come out the back, followed by Jacques. Isabelle came by, kept her head down and hit Julia on the shoulder as she passed, followed by Jacques, also with his head down.

A screech came from outside. Julia turned to see a large sedan arrive, and then another. She felt a strong hand take her arm and push her out the door. She put both feet down flat and resisted, but then the short man took her other arm and they pushed her into the street. The first car drove off with Isabelle and Jacques in the back seat, and a second car pulled up. She was shoved hard into the back seat. The short man got in next to her and the tall one sat in the front. The engine roared as the car took off. Reaching over Julia, the man locked the door, then he put his hand on her arm and held her immobile.

They drove through the empty streets of Paris until they arrived at Rue de Lauriston, opposite the Passy reservoir. Julia was pulled out of the car by the tall man onto an empty street.

They dragged her up the steps and into the building, then down stairs to a basement and inside a room. Isabelle and Jacques stood alone in a dark room with a small window and dirty concrete walls. Isabelle shook her head at Julia.

In less than a minute the door opened and the short man came in and pulled Julia out with him. They went upstairs to the first floor and into an apartment. There, the tall man stood behind a simple table in an otherwise empty room. Her documents were on the table. The short man lifted her coat, and Julia resisted but he stepped in front of her and stared at her eyes while he continued to take it off.

He gave the coat to the tall man, who rifled through both pockets and took her transit visas and tickets out.

Julia did not wait for him. "You see, I am going home to New York. I am an American. You have no right to hold me."

The tall man laughed. "Mademoiselle, we are not holding you. Don't misread us. We wish to ask you a few questions, and then we will let you go home to see your family in America. Please sit."

Julia studied the simple wooden chair in front of her but did not move. The short pockmarked man came over and led her in front of the chair and pushed her down. She sat, staring at the floor.

"Now," the tall man said, "we see that your residence permit has the same address as your friend Isabelle. But of course, she did not acknowledge you at the photography shop. And now, in the basement we observed how she shook her head at you. What do you say to that?"

Julia's voice choked. "We live at the same address. It is a coincidence."

"So, you do live at the same address, and yet she tells you not to recognize her. What are we supposed to make of that?"

"You have no right to keep me here. I demand to talk to the embassy."

"Of course, of course. All in due time," the tall man continued.

The short man stood in the corner with his hands in his pockets, like a disinterested observer.

"But first," the tall man said, "you must help us understand."

"I don't know who you are. You are not the police," Julia said in defiance. "I don't have to answer your questions. I want to speak to someone in the embassy."

The tall man shook his head but his voice carried sympathy. "So you know Isabelle Desjardins, but you deny it. You pick up your pictures in a shop that works with the communist underground."

"I did not."

"You did not what?"

"I don't know anything about communists. I am an American."

"Once again," the tall man said, in an impatient voice, "here we are. You don't know her, but she shakes her head, you don't know her but you live in the same building, on the same street. And then," he came around the table to stand over her with the pictures in his hand. He pointed to them. "You take pictures of the Paris Police Headquarters. For what? To help the communists, I am sure."

"No. Those pictures are for my little girl. I didn't even know that was a police building."

He waved his head back and forth in mock sympathy. "Even though that's the building where you picked up your travel permit."

Julia's hands shook on her lap. She looked up at him, pleading. "That's a picture outside the US embassy."

His face twisted into a contortion of disgust. "It's a picture of the police building."

The short, ugly pockmarked man walked over to Julia. He took a dark object out of his pocket and hit her knee.

Julia screamed and fell out of the chair. She tried to get up, but the brutal pain in her knee kept her on the floor.

The tall man lifted her up and put her back in the chair. He spoke to her in English in a German accent. "It doesn't matter. We have our evidence. Maybe you are not a communist. But you have helped a communist and I can't help you for that. Tomorrow the German army will enter Paris. Then we will take your friend Isabelle and her collaborator Jacques to police headquarters and extract all the information we want out of them."

Julia rubbed her knee, trying to soothe the pain, but it didn't help.

"As for you, Miss Stuart, you are an enemy alien, and as such you will be put into a camp where you can wait until the Third Reich has conquered all of Europe. And after that, who knows." He leaned over to get close to her, hatred in his eyes. "There, they will have an opportunity to interrogate you about your family background. We don't have the luxury of a long interrogation. They do."

They took Julia outside to a waiting car which brought her to the Rue de l'Odéon. There she was put on a canvas-covered truck and brought to the forest on the outskirts of Paris. She found herself in a warehouse where she waited with other foreign women. The women were dirty, silent, looking at each other with frightened eyes, both old and young, trusting no one.

SHE LINED UP THE next morning for an interview with the German Red Cross. Three stout women in dark gray coats with the red cross emblem on the chest and sleeve, sat at a table in a corner of the warehouse. Julia sat at the end of the table, opposite a woman with gray eyes and hair, and splotchy skin. The two women to her left were speaking in French. The Red Cross woman opened her coat and inside, on her shirt, Julia saw a small swastika.

"I am here to help you," the woman said, her eyes impassive, her face cold."

"I am an American," Julia said, hoping another time that someone would listen to her.

The woman nodded. "I understand. This is not a political interview. I am here to help you contact your relatives and see if you need any other help. We are an international organization, you see."

"So what can you do?" Julia said, but her tone indicated more derision than curiosity.

"If you give me your address, we can contact your family. Also, any friends." The woman poised a pen on top of a sheet of paper with Rotes Kreuz written on top, and an address Julia could not make out.

Julia gave her the information.

The woman smiled. "You have a little girl?"

Julia nodded.

"How old is she?"

"She is two."

"I see," the woman said, puzzled. "Well, then assuredly you will want to do everything you can to be reunited with your little girl."

"Of course," Julia said, her eyes blinking fast.

"Then this is my advice to you." The woman leaned forward to appear sympathetic. "Do as you are told. Stay out of trouble. Then you will see your little girl sooner."

Julia leaned back, away from the woman, and narrowed her eyes, but she did not respond. That was not advice. It was more of a threat.

The woman saw that Julia wasn't accepting her admonition. She nodded and smiled. "Let me tell you. From experience. It's best to help them out."

Now Julia understood. This wasn't the Red Cross, it was a Nazi in disguise, hoping to get information out of her. She decided to accept the threat. "Yes, I understand. That is very helpful advice. Thank you." She stood, and winced from the sudden pain in her knee.

The Red Cross woman stood too, and leaned across the table to help Julia. Julia pulled away.

"Your knee, or leg, what is it?"

Julia glared at the woman. "It's nothing. It will get better."

"But, still, you should be careful of your movements." The woman, as if she were being stealthy, took a small box out of her pocket. "Here, here is some aspirin. It will help. As soon as you get where you are going, you should have a doctor see to your leg." Then, without waiting, she called out, "Next," and pointed for someone behind Julia to come forward.

Julia moved out of the way and limped back into the center of the warehouse. She took some aspirin, and was grateful for it, but she knew it was a ploy to gain her confidence.

Two hours later, a new person told her that the American Embassy was waiting to see her. Julia went back to the same tables used by the Red Cross, and saw a lone woman sitting at the table. Her spirits lifted when she recognized the woman as Marlene, the receptionist from the embassy. She was wearing a dark blue suit, with a card hanging from the breast pocket that identified her as from the American embassy.

"Hello." Julia smiled and offered her hand to the woman. She didn't feel any pain as she sat down, a good sign.

"Hello. I'm Marlene Lindquist, from the embassy." The woman smiled at Julia.

"Yes, I remember you."

"You have a slight limp. You didn't have that when you came to the embassy. Are you all right?"

Julia wanted to tell Marlene what had happened to her, but she wasn't confident that anyone could be trusted. Not in this place. "I'm all right. I think my knee will heel. Thank you."

"Do you know why you are in here?" Marlene's tone changed. No longer friendly. Now serious.

"Know why? No. No, they saw a picture I had taken, and they said it…"

Marlene shook her head. "No there's something else. It's rather serious for you. It's your passport."

When she heard those words, Julia understood and knew there was nothing she could say. But she decided to keep it to herself. "What about it?"

"The French police called us. It seems you gave them a passport, and they called us to verify it. We did say we knew you, that you had been in to get an exit visa. That was fine. But the number on your passport is not the number we had in our records. There was nothing we could do."

Those words, nothing we could do, hit Julia like a knife in her heart. "I, I, I lost my passport."

Marlene's voice became sympathetic, as she raised her hand. "I'm so sorry, Julia. The matter is out of our hands. Why didn't you come to us first?"

"My friend said she could help me. There wasn't time, and the French police wouldn't give me a new travel permit. It wasn't my idea, I was going to go to the embassy, but then the police came."

Marlene's eyes softened and she put her hand on top of Julia's. "I am sorry, believe me. We are not sympathetic to the Gestapo. Do you have anyone who can help you?"

Once again, Julia gave the information about Hugh, and Lizzie. Marlene promised that they would contact her husband. Before she left, she gave Julia a pen, paper and envelope, and waited while Julia wrote a letter.

"I will make sure this is in the next diplomatic pouch, so it can be mailed to New York."

Marlene stood, hugged Julia, and walked away.

On the fourth day, they were all put back on trucks and transported to the Pantin Station, where German soldiers accompanied them for a day and a night to the town of Vittel and internment. They were told they would stay there until Germany had conquered all of Europe. And then their fate would be decided.

Chapter 35

Carolyn, Paris, 1980

THREE AND A HALF hours after taking off from New York, the Air France Concorde supersonic jet lands like a modern pterodactyl at Charles de Gaulle airport not long after noon. Carolyn takes the Roissy bus for the hour-long trip to the Arc de Triomphe at the center of Paris.

She then walks up the avenue de Friedland to the Hotel Napoleon, still within sight of the grand arch and its circular traffic. As she walks into the lobby she remembers why she wants to stay here. A Russian merchant built the hotel as a gift to his new love, an art student.

But now above the bar, to the right of the entrance, hang pictures of Americans, Errol Flynn, Orson Welles and Josephine Baker. She feels already like it is her home away from home, her pied à terre, even if she is going to stay only long enough to find a place to live. And that place will be on the Left Bank near the Sorbonne.

Carolyn relaxes in her room that afternoon. She takes a long hot bath, luxuriating in the French soap. After she is out of the tub and dry, she calls the hotel salon, and is able to get her hair styled. She has them cut her long hair off, then cut it more until she sees herself in the mirror with the Paris gamine look, a part on the left side. Like Jean Seberg in *Breathless*. Very French. Totally not New York and not California.

Back in her room, as the scene outside her window darkens with sunset, she watches the Eiffel Tower light up in the distance. She walks out and down to Restaurant Marie-Suzy for dinner in a warm and intimate setting.

THE NEXT MORNING, she walks back to the Champs Élysées to the Banque National de Paris, where she writes a check for $50,000 from her fund at the Chase Manhattan Bank in New York. She receives 17,280 French francs in cash and a passbook noting 200,000 French francs in her account. And a promise she can pick up her new ParisCard in a week. As she returns to the street, she speaks to herself. *Thanks Mother, you managed so well. That at least you could do for me, now I can do everything for myself in French francs.*

That afternoon she takes her map, her address book, and Le Monde newspaper to a table in front of Shakespeare & Co across the Seine from the magnificent Notre-Dame cathedral. She plans to spend the long afternoon hours on a search for a place to live. As a student, she had lived in the Left Bank near the Sorbonne University, while she worked as a researcher in the Louvre. The area feels like home already because she knows the streets, the buildings, the restaurants, the art and bookstores.

But when she arrives at the first address on her list of possible apartments, and the concierge asks her a barrage of insulting questions, like what school she attends, is her mother taking care of her, does she have noisy boyfriends, her face flushes. She realizes she did not expect to be taken for just another college student among the thousands of Americans in Paris. She thanks the concierge and hopes she sounded dismissive and heads away from the Left Bank.

Feeling very stupid for not remembering what Parisian landlords are like, she walks to the Champs-Élysées and takes her map and address book to Stella Maris near the Arc de Triomphe.

Outside the bar, traffic passing by, elegant men and women walking down the street, Carolyn opens her address book and searches for familiar names from her time as an exchange student. The first name that catches her eye is Nathalie Rameau, the woman who supervised her studies on the Northern Renaissance at the Louvre. Perfect, she thinks. Nathalie was 30 years old, married with children, but still, almost a friend as well as advisor. Carolyn feels that this woman will understand her predicament.

Well, it's not a predicament. She wants to be practical about her decision where to live. She'd like someone to think it through with her as well as give her expert advice as a only Parisian can do.

She drinks a small espresso and walks three blocks back to the Hotel Napoleon. This time as she notes the photos of American actors over the bar she feels the now familiar reminder that she isn't as French as she would like to be.

Yet, as she passes the registration desk dominated by the huge portrait of Napoleon III, and nods to the clerk, she remembers that her accent is so good that no one speaks to her in English, even in a hotel that prides itself on old Hollywood movie stars.

In her room, kneeling on the sofa and looking out the window at the Eiffel Tower in the distance, Carolyn knows this is her new home. An urge to call Beatrice prompts her arm to move to the small table with the phone on it, but she resists. Not yet. Not until she's settled in her new home in Paris, in whatever arrondissement that will be.

The phone number from Carolyn's address book still works and in a few moments she breathes a sigh of relief that she didn't have to go through the maze of departments of the Louvre museum administration to reach Nathalie.

"Bonjour."

"Bonjour, Nathalie, it's me, Carolyn Stuart. Your assistant from two years ago."

"Carolyn…" Nathalie pronounces the name in her favored fashion as car-o-leen, although her English was perfect from her research time at Harvard. "How are you? Where are you calling from? Are you in Paris?"

The charm and warmth of Nathalie's voice brings back memories of laughing among the hidden workrooms of the great museum. Carolyn smiles to herself and feels a confidence she thinks had long escaped her. "Yes, I am, as a matter of fact."

Nathalie does not wait to hear what Carolyn's call is about. "Are you alone? Are you traveling? Tell me, what's going on? I have missed you."

Now Carolyn feels a sense of guilt for not having kept contact with her mentor. "Oh, thank you, Nathalie. Well, actually, I arrived yesterday, and today I went to look for where I'm going to live."

"To live? You are going to live in Paris? But you must have finished college, isn't that true? I thought you wanted to go to Berkeley?"

Now Carolyn crosses her legs in an unconscious defensive posture, and feels the small bite of regret that she is still not much beyond a student. Still, she's relieved knowing that Nathalie doesn't think of her that way.

"Yes, I did graduate. But I'm not going to Berkeley. I need to be somewhere new. That's why I'm in Paris."

"Are you going to study?" Nathalie stops herself. "Listen, Carolyn, you know this isn't a good time for me, this very moment, I'm in the middle of something. Why don't you come to my house for dinner tonight? Bernard will be happy to see you, and the girls, well, I think they may or may not remember you. They're a lot older now. What do you say?"

Carolyn receives Nathalie's invitation as an unburdening. She's glad she phoned Nathalie first and hunches forward with a sigh. "That's so nice of you. So, the girls, when I was there Anne was," she laughs, "there was Anne. Who else do you have?"

"Little Marie is now past her first birthday."

"Oh wow, congratulations. I don't want to put you out. Little kids are a lot of work." Carolyn remembers that Nathalie put in long hours at the Louvre, and now with a family things would be that much harder. And with a French husband, more so.

"Oh don't worry, you don't put us out. You get to eat what we do, and I remember you as a generous girl, so it won't make any difference to you. Shall we say, then, about eight? You're going to have to learn again to eat later in the evening." Natalie gives a short, but light laugh. "Do you remember where we live?"

"Of course I remember where you live. You had me over so many times. Numero 8, Rue Gavarni. Can I bring something?"

"Oh no, come and be with us. I'll take advantage of you to entertain the children while I put dinner together."

"Nathalie, now you make me feel like I'm putting you out, showing up like this."

"Nonsense. Or before then. Why not? The nanny might be there with the children, but you can come in."

"Are you sure I can't bring anything?"

"Carolyn, please. I tell you what, if you feel you must, Bernard loves his brandy. Of course, French brandy for him. Or anything. Don't go out of your way. It's you we are interested in. But, I have to run. See you tonight."

"Thanks. Bye."

Carolyn hangs up the phone and sits back on the sofa and feels a weight lifted off her shoulders. Now she can expect a great French dinner with great French people. She goes to take a shower, then remembers she has to go out and find something special for Bernard. And flowers for Nathalie. And maybe little gifts for the kids.

The tall clerk with round-rimmed glasses at the front desk gives her a strained appearance and in response to her question about buying cognac says the closest store is Nicolas, not far from the hotel, on the corner of Rue Beaujon and Wagram.

At Nicolas, she says she wants cognac, and the man, short and pudgy with pasty skin and a black double breasted suit, and an air of superiority, puts his arm up and shows her a wall with every possible brand and cost. He recommends Cognac, Armagnac or Salignac. She selects Salignac. And soon after she has flowers and toys.

Before long she's out and leaving the metro at the Passy station, up to the street. Rain is falling, more of a light mist that lays a reflective sheen on the street and sidewalk. Two short streets and she's on Rue Gavarni, now becoming familiar with its yellow buildings and narrow streets. As she turns left around the building she knew as number 8, she smiles at the recognition of the small chic Hotel Gavarni across the street from Nathalie's house. And then, beyond the house, the fabulous Sushi Passy, and beyond that Axel Brixe with dark red paint around the windows that display the very expensive, but always fashionable, women's clothes. And then the Auto École that kind of ruined the upper-class appearance of the street.

Oh, she sees Maison de la Presse, she could have bought something for the kids there. And down at the end of the street, the funny hot pink Lollipops sign.

Nathalie's house is much plainer than the rest, a dull grey house whose upper stories have more the look of a cheap New Orleans street rather than this elegant Paris arrondissement.

But, Carolyn sighs, as she adjusts the brandy, flowers, and toys to ring the bell, this is more like the real heart of Paris. Easy to get to, easy to live in. Away from the university, away from students. Most important, away from prying landladies.

"Car-o-leen!" comes the sound of a child's voice from up above.

She sees little Anne peering out of a second-floor window...it had to be her. She doesn't remember Carolyn does she? The girl continues waving to her. Carolyn smiles with pleasure and waves back. "Bonjour Anne."

The little girl squeals and disappears and at the same time the buzzer on the door allows Carolyn to push it open. When she enters the foyer, Anne is already at the bottom of the curved staircase and running toward her.

"Bonjour Car-o-leen."

Carolyn wants to lean down and hug her, but her packages make that impossible. Anne pushes the elevator button and squirms in excitement.

"It's nice to see you again," Carolyn says.

"Merci," Anne says. "I have a little baby sister. Are those flowers for us?"

"Yes they are." The elevator door opens and they squeeze inside the small space. Carolyn manages to get the flowers into Anne's hand. "A baby sister? Isn't that wonderful. How old is she?"

"One year. We had a birthday party for her."

The elevator door opens on the second floor and Anne takes hold of Carolyn's arm and pulls her into the open door to the apartment. "Mama," the little girl cries with a wide smile on her face, "we're here," as if they had been on a long trip.

Nathalie appears holding a little baby in her arms. She brushes her dark brown hair back from her face and puts her arm around Carolyn's neck. "Bonjour." She pulls back and lets Carolyn see the baby. "This is little Marie. Say hello to your Aunt Carolyn." Now she pronounces the name correctly. Nathalie takes the baby's arm and makes a little wave, but the baby turns her head to hide in her mother's neck."

"She's your sister?" Anne said, her blue-green eyes wide in surprise that Carolyn is family.

Nathalie laughs and touches Anne's head, playing with a little strand of hair. "Oh my, you are grown up. No, she's a friend from work, it's a way of making her feel at home. Go find papa, my little girl, and tell him Carolyn is here."

"But the flowers, Mama." Anne waits in hope she can be part of this grown-up scene. She holds up the bouquet of red daylilies and green leaves interspersed with small sunflowers to her mother.

"They are beautiful," Nathalie says, leaning down to smell the bouquet.

"But wait, I have this too," Carolyn says. She hands a small kit of beads to Anne.

Anne takes the flowers and beads, turns to go, then stops to say thank you, then runs out of the room calling, "Papa!"

Carolyn gives Marie a rattle, and the baby warms up to her, then she follows Nathalie down the narrow hallway to the living room. She remembers the back wall behind the sofa full of books. So European, she thinks.

"Oh, you know Anne," Nathalie says, "she's daddy's little girl."

"She's a lucky little girl."

At that moment, a tall thin man enters the room, holding Anne's hand. His smile shows a row of perfect white teeth. He wears his dark Navy uniform and comes to Carolyn and kisses her on both cheeks.

So thin, so French, Carolyn thought. She offers him the bottle of Salignac, saying, "*Oh, mon capitaine*, I see you have more bars on your epaulets."

He laughs, his brown eyes reflecting the lamplight, "And you, I see you pay attention to military rank. Yes, *capitaine de frégate*, two months now. I believe you would say commander." He holds the bottle of brandy out before him and makes a face of appraisal and approval. "This Salignac is fit for an admiral. Thank you. I will take it on board and impress the junior officers."

"Bernard is getting ready to go to sea," Nathalie says. She glances at her husband, and shows perhaps not real worry, but some concern.

"Oh?" Carolyn is unsure how to react. She raises her eyebrows as something noncommittal.

Bernard returns Nathalie's glance. It's clear there has been a conversation about this. "Yes, you know Tito died, and so to help calm international nerves, my ship is going to go tour the Greek isles to show the French flag in the Adriatic sea. There's nothing dangerous about it." He gives his wife reassurance.

Nathalie shows she does not take that reassurance well. "It's never dangerous until it is."

Bernard's voice betrays some irritation. "Come on, now, it's not like there's fighting going on anyplace. And Tito doesn't have a navy, anyway, so the worst that could happen is we have to chase a cruise ship for fun."

Nathalie laughs at the last remark, a sign that she believes Bernard. "And then, after that, he comes home for a few weeks and he's off to the Caribbean. I tell you, the Navy is the best."

Bernard shakes his head, but smiles at Nathalie and takes her hand. "Yes, it's a lovely place. But we're going to bring relief supplies to Guadeloupe and Martinique. They've been hit rather hard by the recent hurricane."

Anne comes running up and holds her father's other hand. "Papa is going to be admiral someday."

Carolyn shows exaggerated happiness as she responds. "Oh, I'm sure that's going to happen soon. You must be very proud."

Anne nods and smiles.

Nathalie gives the baby Marie to Bernard. "Carolyn, come into the kitchen and help me a little with dinner. Bernard is happy with the girls."

"Oh, all right, please excuse me," Carolyn says to Anne and Bernard as she gets up. She pats the baby on the head, and the little girl laughs.

Anne follows them into the kitchen, waiting for attention.

"Oh, of course, my petite, will you help me too? But nothing hot, all right. Will you bring the bread in?"

Anne nods and takes the basket with large pieces of baguette in it, walking with care to make sure nothing falls out.

"There's not much," Nathalie says, "leftover couscous and chicken. If I remember correctly you eat anything."

"That's right. And I'm hungry, so especially tonight I'm an omnivore!"

"Did you have any problems finding the place?"

"Oh, no, it's so easy, across Rue Passy and you're here. I did like seeing the old stores I remember from before."

Nathalie hands Carolyn the bowl of couscous and takes the plate of chicken and a bowl of salad and points to the dining room.

Once they are sitting and have filled their plates with food, Nathalie begins the conversation. "Okay, Carolyn, you must tell us what you are doing here. You graduated not too long ago, right?"

"We did, at school, you know, the big thing in the auditorium." She aligns her silverware a moment, then continues. "My mother came. It was very nice. But afterwards she had something to go to in the City, so she couldn't stay."

Nathalie purses her mouth as if she would say nothing more. She wipes the face of Marie, who is scraping pieces of cookie off her high chair. "You arrived yesterday, Carolyn?"

Carolyn is glad the conversation turns away from European politics. She is aware that she neglected her education in that area and she resolves to start reading *Le Monde* every day and watching *France2* news at night. "It was wonderful. I flew on the Concorde. Amazing. So high up, it's true you can see the curvature of the earth."

"Wow," Bernard said. "That's not cheap."

Carolyn hears his remark as a reminder to be more careful about what she says to other people, since all Europeans think Americans have money to burn. "No, but I splurged on that. So, I have to make up for it in other areas. It will be a while before I can afford a car." She makes that last remark up on the spot, and feels guilty for doing it. "But there's an example of British and French entrepreneurship, if you ask me."

Then she thinks of something she heard a few weeks back that would show them her attention to French history. "I understand Sartre died. Now that's an end to an era."

"Yes, that's right," Nathalie said. "You know, in that respect I think we're all the same. We all read *Being and Nothingness* in college and then forgot about it."

Bernard nods in agreement about this change in tone of the conversation. "Philosophy is still a major subject for the baccalaureate, but once you're out of school, unless you're a professional philosopher, it's not studied. Same as in the States, I suspect."

Carolyn puts her knife and fork on her plate in a sign that she has finished. "I think you're right. It's like music. People used to have a piano in the home and kids used to study it, but now we have the Sony Walkman, and you carry your music with you."

"That's right," Nathalie says, "I see kids now. They are even thinking of a way to bring them into the museum, so you can take one with you and listen to a painter while you study the pictures."

Then she laughs. "Not in my area, though. There's nobody around anymore. Speaking of art, Carolyn, do you know what you are going to do? Are you going to study painting at the Sorbonne?"

Carolyn had wanted to have this conversation in private with Natalie, even though Bernard is sympathetic. She decides to be honest, for herself. "No, I don't know what I'm going to do, I only know I want to do something more than seeing art."

"But it is art you are interested in, then?" Bernard says.

The question puzzles Carolyn.

Bernard senses it, and says, "I mean, you studied art with Nathalie, and you graduated with an arts degree, I think. So, it is logical."

Logical. That's Bernard.

Nathalie shakes her head. "She could be studying business or…." She stops herself. "Or anything. I'm sorry, Carolyn, we shouldn't be pestering you like this."

Carolyn sits back in her chair. She watches Anne playing around with the food on her plate. "I think we're probably pestering Anne."

Anne's head rises up at the mention of her name and she smiles, wondering if the adults expect her to say something. She squirms in her seat and goes back to eating.

Carolyn continues. "No, I called you because I wanted to talk to you. I think you could help me decide on what I want to do." There, she said it, more to herself than them. Back home she sought sympathy. Here she needs cold French logic.

Bernard crosses his arms over his chest and focuses his olive eyes on Carolyn. "You said you don't want to look at art. What did you mean by that?"

"This isn't vacation but I haven't figured everything out yet. Of course, I arrived a few days ago. But I'm not going to visit museums and see the Loire Valley. I plan on living here for the foreseeable future."

Bernard leans forward and puts his elbows on the table. "I take it you have enough money for that?"

"Bernard." Nathalie's voice carries a reprimand.

It seems a strange remark for him to make, but Carolyn reacts with indifference. "No, it's all right. It is why I came here tonight. Yes," she says, nodding, "I do have enough money. For now. For a few months. If I can't find a way to make a living I will have to go home." How easy she speaks this lie, having enough money to last the rest of her life if she's not extravagant. "I can stay in Paris meanwhile. And I know too, that I want to do something with art, but I haven't figured it out yet."

Nathalie touches Bernard's arm, but faces Carolyn. "What about your own art. I remember you did some nice things while you were here. You did a nice watercolor of Notre Dame from across the Seine. And I liked your portraits. Remember the one you did of Anne? I think you are talented."

"Yes," Anne says, sitting up and excited. "You painted me. I remember it. Maman, where is it?"

Nathalie seems embarrassed. "We have it stored away, somewhere. We'll find it and put it up, don't you think?"

Anne nods and opens her eyes wide as she remembers. "Oh, yes, it's in my art gallery."

Carolyn frowns in feigned amusement. "Your gallery?"

"Yes, I have a box with my paintings and I'm sure yours will be in there, too."

"We'll find it first thing tomorrow after school," Nathalie says, laying her hand on her daughter's head.

Carolyn is grateful for Nathalie's personal comment. It is so like her, to think of Carolyn's feelings. But it comes mixed with the painful realization that she failed to get into the school of her choice.

"My own art? My own art is on hold, I'm afraid."

Nathalie's eyes show her inner sympathy. "I don't understand you."

Carolyn sighs. "I mean, I found out that the problem with school is that, well, you're in school. It's more figures, more drawing, more experimenting with all the different media. I need to settle on something that I can develop. That's my own art. And I don't know what that is. That's why I came to Paris, someplace completely different from California."

"But not so different for you," Bernard says. "If I remember, you fit into Paris very well. Your French is almost perfect. You could say you're from Montreal and nobody would question you. And you ate all that stuff we wouldn't touch. I remember andouillette sausage, for example."

"Thank you, Bernard, that's very nice of you. But Paris is different from New York, too, and here I'm not me, I'm not the girl from San Francisco. So I don't know what's in store for me, I only know it's not in school. Which brings me to the question I have for you."

"Oh, for us? That's interesting. Go ahead." Nathalie puts her fork down.

"It's not a big deal. You could help me with where might be a good place to live. I remember so much, but I don't want to be in the Left Bank, because it's full of students. And not in Montmartre because its, oh, it's…trendy or something. Here in the 16th is very nice, but you're here and I don't want to intrude."

Nathalie laughs. "Intrude? I don't think so. I remember you as an excellent and handy baby sitter. That's my point of view."

"Sure, Nathalie, I'll always do that, you can depend on me."

Bernard sits back, thoughtful. "Everywhere is nice in Paris. Everywhere has some, let's say, some less desirable areas. Let me ask you, are you trying to save money, Carolyn?"

"No, that's not it. I'm okay for a year or two, I can get by. I don't want to put out a lot of money. It's more, I'm thinking someplace central, but not near the Sorbonne and not very expensive."

Nathalie shakes her head. "You're still not being very clear. I think you still want to be close to art, so you don't have to make a long train ride, isn't that right?"

"Yes, that's true. But there's so much art in Paris, that anywhere would do. I thought of you, and it would mean so much to me if you'd help me."

Nathalie sits up with an idea. "So, let's be, as Bernard says, logical about this. You are here for art, one way or another. But not museums, and not schools. Well, then, I think there's one answer."

Carolyn waits in anticipation. She knows she made the right phone call. She opens her eyes and smiles while she demonstrates her interest in Nathalie's idea.

"For me, it would be the fourth arrondissement, the Marais, the Centre Pompidou. You remember that?"

"Yes, of course, I do, they finished it when I was here. But it's a museum. I remember the big beautiful lips near the pool." Carolyn laughs at the memory. "Sorry, I remember that as being funny."

Nathalie waves off the humor with her hand. "That's not my point. It's an area with many new galleries. You see, that's what's good for you. Not museums, but galleries. And there's something else."

"What?" Carolyn says, curious, her eyes open wide.

"No students. They have some very upscale apartments, and they don't have any cheap apartments like over the hill in Montmartre. But they have nice apartments you can probably afford and there won't be any students in them."

"Oh, thank you, Nathalie. I knew I could count on you. Well, I didn't mean I should count on you, but thank you all the same."

"So I think I solved your problem, Carolyn. And there are many nice places all over. Where we are, this building isn't very nice, I mean, sure, inside, we have a nice apartment. It's a little small with the children, but it's not expensive like the others in the neighborhood. Bernard inherited it from his parents, so we are lucky to live in the 16th. And there are bound to be many places in the 4th like this. You have to be patient."

Nathalie studies her older daughter, who has fallen asleep in her chair, leaning against her father.

"What do you say we have some chocolate mousse."

Anne awakens, sitting up and stretching, then smiling as if she had fooled her mother.

"Oh, so not too sleepy for dessert, my little girl." Mother and daughter laugh together.

After dinner, with the children put to bed, and feeling like a new person, Carolyn wishes Bernard well on his deployment, and thanks Nathalie several times as they stand in the foyer.

"One more thing," Nathalie says. She holds the door open as she rests one foot on the threshold. "Search around, but when you find something you're interested in, give me a call at work. I'll use my lunch break to see it with you. They still will pay attention to you, Carolyn, you are very young and pretty, and they will try and take advantage of you. Will you do that?"

"You are so helpful, Nathalie. I can't thank you enough."

"Go on," Nathalie says. "You've thanked me enough tonight, Carolyn. I'm happy to do it. Now that Bernard is gone for a while, Anne is in kindergarten, and I can't get home for lunch with my baby, but the 4th is close enough to the Louvre. It'll be fun."

Carolyn embraces Nathalie and kisses her on both cheeks, then walks over to the subway but it is a beautiful night in a beautiful city, and she has all the time in the world. She walks home and takes every opportunity at every corner to see each different view down an avenue toward the amazing lights of the Eiffel Tower.

Chapter 36

CAROLYN WALKS THROUGH the gold and white doors into the lobby of the Hotel des Archives. Decades of traffic have worn spots on the elegant upholstery on the Louis XIV chairs and the red faux-Persian rug. A musty smell hangs everywhere. A large red painting with a scruffy black frame glares opposite the dark stained wood-paneled wall behind the front desk.

"Good morning," she says to the clerk. "I made a reservation for a room yesterday. Stuart, Carolyn."

The clerk, a middle-aged man in a charcoal and green uniform with large round glasses and graying hair combed straight back, smiles with a serene air, holding the smile as he searches papers in a drawer. He seems surprised to find something, and still smiling, says in a factual voice, "Oui, Mademoiselle, we have reserved a room for you. For tonight?"

"Oh no, Monsieur, I will need a room for at least a week."

He nods in his serene way and smiles once more. "You are here as a tourist, I presume?"

"Not at all." Inner joy floods Carolyn as she continues. "I am going to live here in the 4th arrondissement. I'm staying at the hotel while I search for an apartment."

He peers over his glasses at her.

"Is something wrong, Monsieur?"

He sighs and hesitates, losing his serenity, before telling her. "I am sorry, but this is the 3rd arrondissement."

"But the map…"

He's in his element now, teaching an American, and shrugs. "I don't know about your map, Mademoiselle. If you observe, there, across the street...." He points out the door. "You will see city hall for the 3ʳᵈ arrondissement."

"But it's so close to the Beaubourg Museum."

He laughs a little laugh of derision which he tries to stifle. "Oh. That. You want to be close to that?"

Carolyn doesn't quite know how to take his condescension, how serious he is. "No, not right next to it."

"Ah," he says, relaxing, knowing now he may not lose a customer. "It's the same neighborhood, the same people. You're right next to it, the museum. In truth, the 4ᵗʰ ends 500 meters from where you are now." He frowns and thinks for a moment, his elbow on the desk, head in hand, then looks back at Carolyn. "Do you have a special need to live in the 4ᵗʰ?" He observes her straight on for the first time.

Carolyn doesn't know how to answer. It was Nathalie who suggested it. She shakes her head. "No, it's that, there are art galleries near the museum, and that's what interests me."

"Of course, we have galleries here, too. But let me tell you something." He leans on the counter to be closer to her. "Let's say that here you're in the 3 and a half arrondissement. There's no boundary line. It's all the same place. 3, 4, those distinctions are for the politicians and mapmakers."

She smiles with relief. "Oh, well, then it doesn't make any difference, Monsieur..."

"Oh," he says, impressed and warming up, "Hervé Villechaize, at your service, Mademoiselle. No, it doesn't. Not one bit. Except they have the ugly building." He chuckles to himself as he completes the paperwork. Then he lays his pen down and again becomes conspiratorial because he remembers something. "It's the Marais, think of it that way. 3, 4, who cares the exact district? You'll find your art galleries down every street."

"And an apartment?"

"Oh," he said, "those too. I recommend you find a real estate agent." He laughs again, he obviously feels more comfortable with her. "We have even more of those. And what they have is all in the window. You'll find it very easy, I assure you. Are you in need of an elegant apartment?"

Ah, there you go, she thought. Pegs me for an American. Funny, coming from someone in this careworn hotel. "Elegant? No," she replies, "enough to get by." Then she thinks to drop the issue. "Starving student, you know."

"Ah. Well, we don't have a garret," he says, once more with his little humorous sigh.

He gives her a room that overlooks the park on one corner and a small outdoor café on the other. Perfect. She puts her things away and goes for a walk. She waves to him as she walks out the door. "On the hunt!" But she reaches behind her to stop the door from closing and peeks back in. "And thank you Hervé." Her smile shows him she means it.

Carolyn walks down Rue des Archives for three blocks, then turns right three more, and repeats this trajectory until she is back in front of the hotel. Now she's developed a first sense of this neighborhood. Narrow streets with narrow sidewalks. No spectacular buildings or vistas, but apartments and street-level stores. Cafés, hair salons like Il Fait Beau, and the many real estate and insurance offices, one on every block, and small grocery stores. And the many small art galleries. She studies the apartments available in the window fronts and finds that there are all kinds that she could be happy with.

She does the same again going left out the door instead of straight, and catches the atmosphere of the other side of the street. This time she does not note the hair salons or cafés, but pays attention to the art galleries. While there are several with old paintings, with impressionists and old masters, most of them are full of contemporary works of art.

She winds her way back to the hotel, taking several trips down side streets. This wonderful neighborhood in Paris, this Marais, is the perfect home for her. She never imagined she could live in a quiet neighborhood and be surrounded by this vibrant, urban life. Even the cars, going by on every street, are quiet and slow compared to the zooming avenues of San Francisco or New York. People walking with small bags of groceries, with baked goods, the big baguettes sticking out, with flowers. But people walking in a measured pace. In New York they walk, but they're always in a hurry. Here, people are all taking their time getting home. That's it. They all seem to be going somewhere near, somewhere warm and inviting. No business. They live everyday Parisian lives.

Back inside the hotel, Hervé greets her with a thumbs up. "I can tell by your face, Mademoiselle, that you have had a successful journey around the Marais."

Carolyn smiles at him, because he had become her first real French friend, or maybe just acquaintance, but still, someone who seems to care about her. A neighbor. It isn't only his thumbs-up in greeting. It's on his face, too, in his eyes. She is sure that tomorrow she will find her apartment.

"Yes," she says, holding up two fingers in a victory gesture in his style. "I've seen enough already to think of this as my future home. There are a lot of apartments small enough for me."

He winks at her. "But what if you find a nice French boy?"

Carolyn narrows her eyes and squints at him, to let him know, even if she isn't too serious, she doesn't like it. "*O là là*, no Monsieur. Not for me. I'm not here for *l'amour*. I'm here for myself, for art. None of these smooth-talking French men for me."

His cheeks flush and he puts up his hands in defense. "Oh, I'm sorry, Mademoiselle." But then he narrows his eyes, too. "I will say no more." He moves his hand across his mouth as if he's zipping it shut. "So you will be leaving soon?"

"Yes, I'll find an apartment tomorrow. High windows to catch the light." She steps back from the counter.

"I haven't thought of that." Hervé cleans some imaginary dust off the top of the counter. "You must be tired. Thank you for your conversation." He bows to her, and gives her a meek smile.

She senses he doesn't often have long conversations with clients of the hotel. "Yes, you're right." Carolyn goes up to her room and takes a long hot bath, then opens a bottle of Chablis and calls Beatrice. It's still morning in New York.

"Hello?"

Carolyn hesitates at the sound of her aunt's voice. She shakes the question off. "Hi. It's me, Carolyn. In Paris."

Excitement permeates Beatrice's voice. "Carolyn, how wonderful. I was afraid I would never hear from you again."

"Oh, now that's an exaggeration."

"You were very angry when you left."

"But now I am in Paris. Who can be angry?"

"I'm happy to hear you say that. Have you talked to your mother?"

Carolyn puts the receiver down on her knee for a moment before she answers. "It's too soon for that."

Now she waits while Beatrice thinks. "Tell me, then, where are you?"

The warmth in Beatrice's voice begins to work on Carolyn. "In the Marais."

"Oh, the Marais. 3rd or 4th arrondissement?"

Carolyn smiles to the phone and brushes her hair back. "You do know Paris well. 3rd. Across the street from the mayor's office. In a small hotel on the Rue des Archives. I think I'm close to getting an apartment."

"You don't think you'll have trouble finding one?"

"No, not at all. I don't need much. It's for me. I did decide I need a bedroom so I can set up a kind of artist's studio."

"Okay, you sound like you have a plan."

"I think so. I'm not sure about the art yet."

"Don't worry about that. You're doing fine."

"Listen, Beatrice, I've got to go. I'm pretty bushed, walking around all day. I'll call you again."

"Wait, what about your phone number?"

"I'm at the hotel. I'll call you when I have my own phone."

"What should I tell your mother?"

Cold sweeps over Carolyn. "Tell her whatever you like."

Beatrice sighs. "Yes. All right, I understand and I love you, Carolyn."

"I love you too." She hangs up, her feelings mixed. She loves her aunt, but her aunt seems too close to Elizabeth, and Carolyn does not want to settle things with her mother. Yet.

THE NEXT MORNING, she speaks to three different real estate agents, until she finds an apartment that is right for her. On the Rue de Sévigné, and, as she requires, old enough to have large wide windows flooded with light. And, as she discovered for herself from walking around, it has to be high up above the street to avoid being in the shadows. With an elevator, none of that walking up so many stairs it becomes strength training. That tip she learns from the real estate agent. She's convinced that the agent, Marie-Claire, Parisian-thin and well-dressed, with elegant gold jewelry and a pearl necklace, is figuring her for a rich American. Why else is a girl a little past twenty renting her own apartment in the Marais?

Following on her new acquaintance, Hervé in the hotel, she now finds a second helpful French person. For the first time in her life, she feels lucky. Marie-Claire shows her an apartment on the seventh floor, with elevator of course, in an older building, she says. Which is a joke, saying it's older. There are no newer buildings in the neighborhood. Maybe the elevator makes the difference.

An elevator that holds one person and certainly no furniture except maybe one lamp pole. But it goes to the top and stays there until she gets out and that's what matters to Carolyn.

The beautiful thing is that this apartment is not on street level. Not even on the corner. It is in the middle of the block, it faces a park and there is nothing whatsoever to block the light coming in from the windows which look out from the seventh floor perch at the park on Rue de Sévigné. She wants to sing *La Bohème* out loud. The windows are ten feet high, Marie-Claire says, and the ceiling twelve feet high. And two very wide windows. Really tall and really wide.

"Thank you, Madame. This is perfect."

Now, she thinks, my life begins.

Hervé is sad to lose his best customer, but he consoles himself by helping her with getting a telephone, and giving her advice on where to find furniture. "Au revoir, mon amie," he says, shaking her hand and giving her a polite bow.

"I'll come by and see you once in a while," she replies. "You're around the corner from Café Sancerre."

"Ah, yes, of course," he said, but he sounded like he didn't believe her. He raised his eyes up to heaven. Then he waved her off. "Welcome to Paris."

Carolyn walks the few short blocks to her apartment, and christens it with a bottle of Dom Perignon Brut. The walls are still bare. She'll take her time on that. And she has been modest with her furniture.

The small corner has light wood cabinets and a cook top next to a white sink substitute for a kitchen. The floor is nice-looking varnished wood, polished to a sheen. She will have to pick up some area rugs. Maybe a large Persian rug dominated by red.

Her bed, for one person only—that's good enough. There are no plans for anything bigger than that. It's a day bed, useful as a second sofa. The dark blue quilted coverlet gives it an air of practicality. Three people can fit on her red sofa. The simple oak table stands in the center of the room, big enough for four people, that's more than she'll need. On top, she has already placed a crystal bowl with red apples, oranges and ripe peaches, topped by a cluster of dark purple grapes. She stands and studies the still life scene, maybe she'll make it her first painting in Paris.

Along one wall is a long dresser, painted ebony, a nice contrast to the sofa and daybed. Modern, but not too modern, not something for an *artiste*.

She's in no hurry. More furniture will come as time moves on and life develops and she understands who she is in Paris, France.

Carolyn drinks up her glass of champagne and pours another. She has no plans to go out today. The windows are open and a cool breeze blows into the room. Outside, dark clouds are moving and she watches the rain as it approaches across the rooftops of Paris. Beautiful Paris, even in the rain. Wary, she closes the windows as the first small drops hit her face.

Into her bedroom, she leisurely walks with a new glass of champagne. An empty room. Not a bedroom. The walls are Colombe Blanc, white dove. Like a hospital, but reflecting light. The high windows, the high ceilings, the huge white walls, perfect for a painting studio. She twirls around to catch the light of the whole room, drains her final glass of champagne and moves to the main room.

The tools of an artist are missing. She remembers what Nathalie told her, about sketching around Paris. All she needs for that is a sketch book and graphite pencils. Which, this being the Marais, she finds a mere two blocks away, an easy walk when the rain lets up, in the Rogier art supplies shop. On the way back, she can't resist and stops in to see her friend Hervé in the hotel. Her appearance in the lobby surprises him. His smile is wide and genuine.

"Oh, mademoiselle, I didn't expect to see you so soon. I hope you haven't been thrown out by your landlord." He laughs at his little joke, then stops, his frowning face betraying his worry that he is having fun at her expense.

"No, monsieur, I have not. As you see, I have purchased my first art supplies, and was passing by on my way home to say hello, and to thank you again for your help."

"Ah, thank you. Perhaps when you have a showing in a gallery you will invite your little friend?"

She smiles at that. "You are quite premature, monsieur, but I assure you that you will receive an engraved invitation. I must hurry now, before it rains again." Carolyn waves her sketch book at him and leaves the hotel. Before arriving back at her apartment, she stops at Les Délices de Marais and takes forever to decide on her dinner. After frustrating two clerks, she brings home a baguette, *de rigueur*, and then sliced filet mignon of pork, a little bit of *foie gras*, a beautiful little duck pâté. And a small rosé.

When she arrives home and has put her packages on the counter of her little kitchen corner, she surveys the room and notices she doesn't have a wine rack. And she has forgotten cheese. So she isn't Parisian the way she wants to be, a natural one. A true Parisian would go out and get the cheese. Now. So she does, to the laughter of the clerks she had frustrated a few minutes ago. She tastes a Roquefort and a Camembert before settling on a thin wedge of local Boursault. The wine rack will have to wait until she has established a good relationship with a local wine merchant. The Cave Saint Antoine comes recommended by Hervé, and she resolves to get to know them. After this wonderful dinner.

She dines on the sofa using the coffee table, with the windows open and the sun already gone down, orange lights appearing in the distance. As she pours the rosé into her glass, she makes a mental note to get excellent crystal wine glasses, too. And she congratulates herself. Here she is. Set. Ready to go. The last of the rosé into her mouth, her eyes become heavy, she lies back on the sofa and lets herself go. The world fades away.

Chapter 37

IN THE MORNING, she awakes on the sofa with a headache and bright light streaming in the windows. She sits up, looks around the room, and smiles to herself.

There is but one thing to do. The day is nice, a few clouds, warm enough. She now has to get her sketchbook and graphite and go out there and pick someplace.

Out the window, below, she sees children in the little park, a dog, parents, people walking by. A pretty little scene beneath the trees. Paris. But where to start?

The grand monuments? Notre Dame, Eiffel Tower, the canal? She can't decide, so she goes downstairs and out the door with no particular destination. She'll know when she's arrived at the right place.

But she doesn't arrive. Two hours of walking around the Marais, with beautiful shops, the Pletzl with Sascha Finkelstein's bakery, the medieval buildings, the courtyards.

Soon Carolyn is back home at her end of Rue de Sévigné, in front of her building staring at the park across the street. The afternoon rain threatens not far away. Instead, she goes upstairs to her refuge, where she can see the details of the storm clouds coming and keep the windows open to smell the air and yet keep dry.

She drops her sketchbook on the table and calls Nathalie.

"Hello?" comes Nathalie's familiar warm voice.

"Nathalie, it's Carolyn. Have I caught you at a bad time?"

"No, not at all. You caught me daydreaming, but there's no way to prove it, is there?"

Carolyn laughs. She runs her fingers through her hair and takes the phone over by the window. "Thank you. For the first time, it was a surprise for me, I was lonely in Paris. I didn't think that was possible."

"I understand the loneliness," Nathalie says. "Have you made any friends?"

"Friends?" The question catches Carolyn by surprise. She doesn't want any friends. "No. I'm not trying to find any. My friends are hotel clerks, shopkeepers, and real estate agents. Except for you, of course. I don't need to go looking for friends."

"I'm sorry, I didn't mean to pry."

"No, you're right. I'm the one who called you up to say I'm feeling lonely."

"But I do understand. The woman who takes care of my children, I've known her a long time, but she's not a friend."

"I surprised myself today. I bought a sketchbook, you know, and went out around the neighborhood."

"From your hotel?"

"Oh, no, I forgot to tell you. I have a lovely apartment on Rue de Sévigné. It's perfect. Now I know why I called you. I'm lonely because I haven't seen you. And I owe you dinner. When do you think you can come over?"

"Well, that's very nice of you. It doesn't have to be so soon, Carolyn. When you're more settled in."

Carolyn wonders if she made a French faux pas. "I'm settled in. There isn't much to settle in to. I'm happy with my small apartment. It has a beautiful view of a park, and huge windows. Lots of light. Perfect for my studio."

"Your studio?"

Carolyn laughs, embarrassed at how pretentious that sounded. "Well, it's my bedroom, but I don't sleep in there, it's perfect for painting."

"And you have been painting already?"

"No, that's not what I really meant. You see, I bought a sketchbook and decided it was time to go out and draw something."

"That sounds like the right thing to do," Nathalie says in a sympathetic voice.

"But I couldn't do it. I couldn't find anything."

"Nothing? Where did you go?"

"Nowhere. Around here."

"You mean you walked around the Marais and you couldn't find anything to sketch?"

"You know, Nathalie, I wouldn't put it that way. There were places to sketch everywhere. Modern, medieval, historic, everything, all the picturesque scenes, all the interesting people. But I couldn't find anything I wanted to draw. Can you understand that?"

There's silence on the other end of the phone. Then Nathalie speaks. "It means you're not ready yet." She is quiet for a second. "You know what I think?"

"What?"

"It's too pretty for you. You know, the Paris everyone loves, super beautiful Marais. I think it means you want to be different. I wouldn't even worry about it. Something will hit you, and you'll know."

"Well, you're right about that. It's what I was thinking today, that I'd come on some scene and know that was what I wanted. But it never happened."

Nathalie's voice took on a harder tone. "Carolyn, it's not so dramatic. It means you don't want to do pretty street scenes. What's so horrible about that?"

Carolyn sighed. "Nothing, the way you put it. Let's change the subject. What about you coming over for dinner? I don't have much of a kitchen, but they have nice shops around here. Is Bernard still here?"

"No, he's gone to his station. It's me and the kids, I'm afraid."

"Okay, then, why don't you come over here. There's a perfect park for them. Anne will love it, I'm on the seventh floor and she can use the small elevator. How about it?"

"Yes, then, it sounds nice. The weekend? Saturday?"

"Yeah, Saturday. Tell you what, I'll come over there first and we'll bring the kids back together. It will be fun. And you know what, I think I'll go to the shop called Thanksgiving, on Rue Saint Paul. They have American food. I'll get hot dogs and buns, baked beans and potato salad. Tell Anne, I think she'll like it. I hope."

"That's a brilliant idea. Don't worry, Anne eats anything. See you then, Carolyn."

"All right. And thank you, Nathalie." Carolyn takes the phone away from her ear but hears Nathalie's voice still speaking.

"Carolyn, what about you? Are you all right?"

"Yes, I'm fine. Why do you ask?"

"I guess, because, it doesn't matter. I thought maybe you had a craving for American food. You aren't weakening, are you?"

"Oh my god, why would you think that? Because of the hot dogs? Not me. No, I thought it would be fun for Anne, that's all. Don't read anything into it."

IN FACT, the first hot dogs are a bust without Kraft yellow mustard. But Anne warms up to them when Carolyn puts Dijon mustard on them. Even the baby likes a spoonful of the sauce from the baked beans. The kids love the park, and the two women reminisce on the history of the last two years.

After they clean everything up, and Nathalie is changing the baby, she says, "Carolyn, I want to invite you next weekend to my grandmother's house. Grandma lives outside town, so it's like a country estate. Small, but beautiful. Why don't we go down on Friday afternoon and stay the weekend?"

"That's wonderful," Carolyn replies, excited. "But if a lot of people are going to be there...."

"Oh, don't worry about that. I've already talked to Grandma. We're the only ones staying the weekend, so there'll be plenty of room."

Anne jumps up and down. "Say yes, Aunt Carolyn, please say yes. You can save me from my awful cousins."

Carolyn gives her a mock frown. "Ooh, they sound awful."

"Yes, boys can be mean."

"Well then," Carolyn says, "I'll be sure and watch out for you."

"Good, it's settled then. I'll take Friday off, why don't you come over for lunch, bring a little suitcase and your sketchbook, and we'll do it."

"That's fun," Anne says, smiling impishly.

"And we'll eat lunch there."

"The restaurant serves wild boar," Anne says, looking at Carolyn to see if she can scare her a little bit.

"Mm." Carolyn replies, her eyes widening, "Sounds horrible. But once in San Francisco I had ostrich. Have you ever had that?"

Anne shakes her head, and then moves her eyes sideways as if she were trying to think of something else exotic to eat.

"What about ostrich eggs, have you ever seen those?"

She shakes her head again.

"They are almost as big as a soccer ball."

Anne laughs and put her hand over her mouth.

"Come on, you guys," Natalie says, "we'll never get home if you keep this up."

THEY LEAVE and Carolyn sits down, reviewing the day in her mind. She never dreamed to find such a friend in Paris. She picks up the phone and dials Beatrice, but puts it down before it can be answered. No, she thinks, that would be weakening, like Nathalie said.

Instead, she tidies up the house, and takes a walk in the neighborhood. She stops at La Verrière, and enjoys white Dubonnet and crème brulé. People pass by, her neighbors, as she thinks of them.

Now she has a week to kill before the trip. Maybe she will try sketching again. Hervé might have some good ideas. But he's not there. She has no interest in talking to the skinny boy behind the desk in the lobby.

She returns home and opens a bottle of pastis and finds her favorite spot at the window, watching the somber shadows of evening overtake Paris. It is so nice to relax as the sky darkens and the city lightens.

And she senses, now that she has a week before the trip, she doesn't have to make decisions, or make progress, or live up to anything. Kill time until next weekend.

Which she does. She walks the streets of the Marais, down to the Seine, but away from the huge Pompidou modern art museum. Instead she walks toward the Saint Martin canal. Waiting to understand what she seeks for real in Paris.

On the Rue du Parc Royal, she observes a sign pointing to the Musée Picasso, but nothing pulls her in that direction. She stops before a large white building opening on to an inner courtyard with cobblestones. The clean white marble-looking walls are offset with red, white and pink geraniums in tubs. The entrance indicates Hotel de Retz, 1613, which intrigues her.

Inside the courtyard, gold renaissance lettering on the wall spell out Desson Galerie. Inside a second courtyard, she finds two black modern mobiles which don't interest her, but she continues on through the door to a white interior space with paintings on several walls. No one else is in sight.

The paintings shock Carolyn. Not as a person, but as an artist. Their point, in garish blues, greens, bloody red seem to be that there is some kind of beauty to be expected in the portrayal of violent death. Almost all the victims are women, and the scenes are of naked women, often watched in their death throes by groups of people who seem out of place. She walks out. As she closes the door, a face appears in one of the windows, but she dismisses the face with a wave of her hands.

She hurries out to the street and turns left, then turns right at the end of the block. Halfway down, another gallery. Now she is curious to see if the Desson was typical for the neighborhood. But it isn't. Here there is no representative painting wall, in fact no painting at all. There are two rooms with an assortment of red or black square boxes. Someone's idea of simplicity of space or something. In the second room there are two life-size statues made of wire thick as rope, seeming to be people, with wire eyes and mouths, each strand of wire a different primary color.

A young skinny girl with long black hair and outsized glasses watches her from behind a desk with brochures scattered across the top. The girl does not smile, she sits there and watches. Carolyn turns to go out and laughs out loud when she sees a skull, drawn with detailed care, with a droopy carrot sticking out as a nose. She keeps on walking, but not in a hurry, and she doesn't wave goodbye.

Two down. This is Paris, she thinks, it's not a big enough sample. I will keep going. But at least I now know what I'm going to do this week. Somewhere in Paris there must be art galleries that will appeal to me. Or an artist.

Several doors away she enters Galerie Jean Broullet. A young man with unkempt blond hair, a day's beard on his face, slides toward her from the back of the room. "Are you lost?" he says, his face betraying his dismissal of her.

"No, I'm out for a walk. Do I have to commit to buying something before I come in here?"

He puts his hand up to his mouth and studies her. "Not at all. I didn't mean to offend you. I'll be in the back."

"Thank you," she says, with a sincere smile.

The smile has an effect on him. His voice becomes warmer. "Perhaps I might give you a tour of my little gallery."

"Oh, you are Jean Broullet?"

"Yes, I am. Pleased to meet you. You are?"

"Carolyn Stuart."

They stand before a canvas of a man on a prairie, sitting before a fire, with an old train or bus behind him, then a fence, then more countryside. All in subtle shades of blue, gray, brown, green.

"This is Stefan Cruvet. He lives in Normandy, up north. It's our first exhibition of one of his paintings. His first time in Paris, I believe. Tell me, what do you think about it, Carolyn?"

"I think it's derivative. It's like Andrew Wyeth, but without the inherent drama."

Jean studies the painting for a moment, then says, "You may be right. Except that Wyeth doesn't have the color that you see with Stefan. A different temperament."

She nods and waits a moment before speaking. "More color perhaps, but less emotion."

She thanks him and leaves, but first says to him that she does like the Stefan Cruvet painting.

"Oh, I thought you said it was derivative."

"It is, I think, and so it is overpriced" she says as she opens the door to leave. "But I still like it. Perhaps he has other paintings that are more original. You have an interesting gallery. I will come back another time."

"As you wish, Mademoiselle. You have great confidence in your personal opinions. I wish you a good day." Jean stares at Carolyn as if he doesn't believe what she says.

She doesn't care. She walks out. But she thinks about what she has seen. True, it is right to call the painting derivative, but it does have a strong personal center to it. It has the young man in the center, and you wonder what he is doing there.

She understands now what she is doing today. She understands that she is capable of entering any gallery in Paris and holding her own, and it gives her confidence to continue.

What she has seen so far is such a meager sample of what Paris has to offer. Three galleries and from all that she saw, one painting she liked, and no sculptures. It makes her think that she will have to view a much wider range of Paris galleries before she discovers what she is really after.

She remembers back to Berkeley, to Marc Silver's comments. He said that she is still experimenting with her styles. And she has to admit that it's true. Even now, here in this great international city of art, she is experimenting with her styles. She is trying to figure out what appeals to her and she doesn't yet know what it is. So, she knows something, however vague and incomplete.

Well, in California that lack of concentration cost her the entrance to a school. Here it doesn't matter. She isn't hoping for entrance to anything.

The words on a window catch her eye. Galerie Parent. A large gold-lettering sign on a black background. A small storefront in an old building with a Parisian grayish-green façade. Inside are a couple dressed in habitual jeans and jackets, and a man in a gray business suit, with white wavy hair, dark blue fedora in hand. The couple are looking around as if they don't know where they are, but the man is studying a painting.

A painting, she thinks, that's a good start already. But when she studies the painting, it doesn't touch her. It seems representational enough, a human torso against a plain light gray background, with a playing card, a Jack of Hearts, sticking out of a woman's rear end. She wants to laugh. And now her respect for the serious businessman disappears. She turns away to see what else is on the wall.

A small sculpture in the middle of the room catches her attention. It is shiny black, a woman, naked, sitting on the floor, her legs turned under her and her arms resting on her knees. She is a young woman, with high breasts, and hair flowing straight out the back. Carolyn studies it. The woman is at rest. The sculptured surfaces are all smooth. There is no attempt to show any kind of struggle with the image coming out of the material. This is different. Is the artist interested in the person? Or maybe the material? She can't figure it out, but it intrigues her.

A large woman with several strands of pearls around her neck and three or four gold bracelets, catches Carolyn's attention. She is wearing a red dress and high-heeled shiny black shoes.

Carolyn becomes uncomfortable as the woman stares at her.

The woman smiles at her, then walks toward her, stopping on the other side of the sculpture. "I see you're interested in this."

Carolyn nods. "I don't know if I would go that far. If you mean am I going to buy it, then no. But I do like it as a work of art."

The woman speaks knowingly so that Carolyn understands that she, not Carolyn, is the expert. "Yes, many do. It's by Paola Piccolo. She has work in several places around Paris. I was very fortunate to get this piece."

"I can see that you are," Carolyn replies. "It's very, human, I would say. It draws me in, to wonder about it. And yet I can't help thinking that maybe the artist, Paola, is thinking beyond that, to the expressiveness of the form alone. I'm sorry, I don't know her, this Paola, but I feel like I do."

The woman opens her eyes wide and purses her lips, trying to think of what to say next, as if this were a game of artistic expression chess. "I've heard that about her work."

This puts Carolyn off. It's so easy to say, when someone makes a comment, that you've heard it before. "But then it's what makes it interesting, isn't it, this tension between different elements. Paola, what did you say?" But then Carolyn sees the label on the floor. "Piccolo. She has succeeded very well."

The woman holds out her hand. "Céline. How do you do?"

Carolyn shakes the woman's hand and smiles. "Nice to meet you."

Céline points to the sculpture. "She's almost your age."

There. Again. Carolyn's age. This woman has pegged her as a student. Carolyn's face turns cold and solid. "She has no age," she says, "she could be 19th century, but I presume she's contemporary. I don't think age has anything to do with it.

"I'm sorry," Celine says. She puts her hand on her breastbone, fingers her pearls, and looks around the room in embarrassment. "You're right, I didn't mean it that way. Or, at least, I didn't want to.

I do appreciate your comments, however. You have a well-developed artistic sensibility."

Carolyn puts her hand out again to Céline. "Thank you. My name is Carolyn. I live a few blocks from here. Today I'm out getting to know the Marais, the galleries. What I like and don't like about art in Paris today. Is this your gallery?"

"Mine? Yes and no. It belongs to my daughter. She bought it from me. But I opened it many years ago. I live upstairs and manage it for her when she's away." She steals a look at the man who has moved from the painting of the naked *derrière*. "We do have our differences. I adore this sculpture, and she likes things like the painting on the wall with the…" An impish smile takes over her face. "Jack of Hearts. We clash sometimes, but we do separate commissions, so it works out." She puts her hand down and smiles. "Would you like a cup of tea? Or coffee?"

Carolyn warms to this woman, who has revealed personal information to her. "Yes, either would be fine. That's very nice of you."

"I can't leave the gallery for long," Céline says, "but let me go start the water and I'll be right back."

"If you don't mind, I'll walk around some more."

"Make yourself at home."

And Carolyn makes herself a new friend in Marais. They have a long talk about the Paris art scene. Céline gives her advice on other galleries to visit. And some contemporary painters to watch out for.

"If you see anything you like in Paris, Carolyn, if you have any questions about it, please come and see me. I don't need to make a living off this stuff. It would give me an excuse to get out of this building for a while. I live upstairs, and I go out for shopping. Even when my daughter's here, she tries her hardest to keep me here watching the shop."

"Thank you. I appreciate your offer, Céline. I'm not out to buy art. Well, I'm not against it. It's more for myself. I'm not sure what I like for myself. So I'm not sure what I want to paint. Or draw."

"Oh, now you've said something new. You are an artist? You've been kidding me."

"Oh no, I haven't been. Please don't think that. It seemed like the next thing to say to you. That I'm not searching for art to hang on the walls, I'd like to see art that appeals to me. I'm doing it for myself, if you will."

"That's understandable, young lady."

CAROLYN VISITS MANY galleries during the week. She also takes her sketchbook, and plans to go beyond her neighborhood to try the famous and beautiful views in Paris. The Eiffel Tower, Sacré-Coeur, Notre Dame. In Notre Dame she starts sketching the outline of the cathedral from the plaza, but she draws only a few lines of the towers and loses interest. She walks up the stairs of the tower and stands close to one of the gargoyles. Her hand hovers over the sketchbook, but she can't move the pencil on the paper. At Sacré-Coeur, on the very top of Montmartre, she finds the vista of the city below her too vague and ambiguous for sketching. At Place du Tertre, she enjoys a glass of white wine, and sees the prettiness of the place, and sighs and can't relate to it. Too picturesque. She observes the stairs cascading down Mont-Cenis, then, even walks down them all the way to the bottom and watches the merry-go-round outside the 18th arrondissement mayor's office.

This, she thinks to herself, isn't what I want to do. She takes the metro home to her apartment, opens the window to see Paris. She begins to wonder if it has not all been a huge mistake.

Has she, all this time, been coming to Paris? Or has she been running away from New York?

If I can't draw, she thinks, how am I ever going to paint? Her white bedroom, empty and set up as a studio with the light from the big window, now seems a gigantic mistake. I am no closer to figuring out who I am.

She pursues her art no more for the next few days. Instead, she studies different restaurants for lunch and dinner, goes into clothing stores and jewelry stores.

Chapter 38

FRIDAY AFTERNOON, SHE packs a change of clothes for the weekend. Dressed in her brown corduroy slacks and a light gray blouse, she takes the subway to Nathalie's house. Nathalie and her two daughters are waiting for her.

"So, did you have a good week, Carolyn?" Nathalie is beautiful and glamorous in her black jeans and white cowl neck cashmere sweater. She has pulled her brown hair back in a tight bun, which accentuates her green pendant earrings and hazel eyes. She carries Marie and lets Anne go down with Carolyn to the car.

"The car?" Carolyn raises her eyebrows. "Not that it matters."

"Yeah," Nathalie says, "I didn't want to take the bus from the train station. And we'll have more freedom when we're there. To explore.

Anne adds her opinion. "And we might be stuck driving with Marc."

TWO HOURS LATER, they approach the outskirts of Senlis.

"I'm so happy we came this afternoon," Nathalie says. "Even though traffic has slowed us down, we'll have Grandmère to ourselves tonight."

"And no boys, either," Anne volunteers from the back, loud and clear.

"Now, ma Chérie, you know you'll have fun."

"Yes, with Sidonie and Yolande. But not Marc. Or François. They're mean."

"All right, young lady, we get the picture. You don't have to play with the boys if you don't want to."

"And I don't want to eat with them, either."

Carolyn turns to the back of the car and gives Anne a high-five. Anne hits her hand and says, "Oui!"

"Oh, now don't you go encouraging her," Nathalie says, switching her view between Carolyn and the road. "It's not so bad as she makes out."

Carolyn nods and laughs, then turns to the back again. "Will you introduce me to your friends?"

Anne nods. "My friends."

"Oh," Nathalie says, with relief in her voice. "We're almost there." She turns to Carolyn again. "We don't go into Senlis proper. We can do that some time while we're here. It's a beautiful town."

Nathalie turns off the road and approaches a large white wrought-iron gate. She gets out of the car and goes to the side of the gate, where she punches a button. She says something and nods. The gate opens and Nathalie returns to the car. They drive along a dirt road past a large lawn and toward a three-story mansion.

Carolyn looks over to Nathalie. "You didn't tell me your grandmother lived in a grand house like this."

"No, but it's not so grand inside."

"Your family must come from nobility or something."

"Not at all. My great-great-grandfather built this house. I'm not sure how he came to do it. It's always been there for me. My grandmother and my mother grew up here. I've been coming here all my life."

"Me, too," Anne says in the back.

Carolyn turns around and smiles at her.

"Yes," Nathalie says. "Over to the right, there beyond the trees, are the vineyards. That's all that's left of the estate. It's enough to support my grandmother and grandfather and keep the house in the family. But when they're gone, who knows. My aunts and uncles will all fight over it."

"Oh," Carolyn says, as if surprised.

"What?" Nathalie replies, sounding a bit worried.

"Well, I don't know their names, your grandparents."

"You're right, I never said. My grandmother is Marthe. And my grandfather, Luc. Luc and Marthe de Voisier."

"That sounds impressive. Aristocratic."

"Maybe, we don't know. There aren't any genealogists in our family."

"Marthe. And Luc. Thank you, that makes it easier to greet them. Even if you introduce us."

The gray stone house looms over them, three stories high, plus gabled windows on the roof. Four stories then, plus a basement, no doubt. The house is as aristocratic as the surname of the family. And two people are living there? Carolyn is already curious for answers when they pull to a stop in front.

The front door opens and an older woman comes out. She is tall and thin, but she seems strong. She has pushed her graying hair to the back, like Nathalie, but a large section in front hangs down in front of her face. Her large dark red sweater spreads out like a cape over her shoulders. She wears a dark blue dress with large white buttons and a black scarf around her neck. She steps to the top of the steps and waves, her smile showing her happiness.

The man who follows her out, full of a grand smile himself, has a white goatee and mustache and white hair that billows out on top. He is much bigger than the woman, with great shoulders and chest, but his hips are narrow.

Anne practically jumps from the car then runs up the steps. She hugs Marthe first, then runs to Luc and hugs him.

"Come on," Nathalie says. She goes around to the side of the car and takes the baby. She holds Marie up for the grandparents to see, although the little girl is somewhat frightened by the exuberance of it all.

"Ah, petite Marie," Marthe exclaims. She steps down to the ground, as if she were no older than Nathalie herself. "My little baby." She takes the child away from Nathalie and gives it wet kisses on both cheeks.

Marie seems to recognize her great grandmother. She smiles and claps her hands.

"And my Nathalie," Marthe says, with a happy wide smile, and she embraces her granddaughter as they exchange kisses on the cheeks. "And this must be your friend Carolyn," she says. She gives Marie back to her mother, takes Carolyn's hands in her own and kisses her on both cheeks. "Welcome. Welcome to La Chêne Cloîtré."

Carolyn looks into the woman's eyes. Light blue with flecks of black. They shine with a slight mist, not tears, but of joy. The woman's warmth comes over her.

"Thank you. It's so very nice of you to invite me here."

"I'm happy you came today. Tomorrow the others will be here and it will be crazy. I've made tea and we'll have some nice cake."

"Cake," Anne yells. "Grandma makes the best cake in the world."

"Yes, it's true," Marthe says, "I made your favorite, Anne. Do you know what it is?"

"Plum cake?"

"Yes, I'm glad we agree." Marthe smiles at her granddaughter.

As they go up the steps, Luc holds the door for them. "Nice to meet you," he says to Carolyn. He bends over and kisses her on both cheeks.

"Thank you," she says. "Thank you for having me." The soft warm glow of his light brown eyes welcomes her.

"Yes, but, you know, you are someone different for us. Nathalie says good things about you." He smiles and gestures for her to enter the house.

"Oh, that's nice of her. She's my best friend in Paris, so it's very warm of you to say so."

The hallway is classic French, with worn wood parquet floors. The ceiling is high, like a miniature cathedral, with a large crystal chandelier hanging over the middle. A room opens to the right, another to the left. In the back, a wide staircase leads to a landing facing up to a bright stained glass coat of arms, with the blue French lilies and red lions.

Carolyn points up to it. "Is that your family?"

He laughs. "Maybe. I've checked in Paris, and there is no registered coat of arms for de Voisier. So I suspect my grandfather, he was one who would do it, I think they found a local glazier and had them make it. It was important to him, I remember, all the family stuff."

A voice comes from the room to the right, and Luc leads Carolyn in there. This room has beautiful antique furniture, and several old landscape paintings grace the walls. Translucent lace curtains let in a gentle light from large windows, and red and gold drapes make an elegant frame around them, on two sides of the room.

Marthe smiles at their arrival. "Come, my dear, sit next to me." She pats the blue brocade Victorian sofa and smiles at Carolyn in expectation. Nathalie and Anne sit in elegant chairs. Nathalie holds Marie, asleep, in her lap.

Carolyn sits next to Marthe. "Such a beautiful home. Such beautiful furniture."

"It's not antique," Marthe says, dismissing the furniture with a wave. "It's nice, but it's beginning of the 20th century, not older than that."

Luc lets himself into a deep armchair. "We do have a few pieces, but they are in the attic. At least until Marc and François grow older and settle down.

At that, Anne laughs out loud. "See, see, I told you so," she says to Carolyn.

"Told you so what?" Luc says, leaning forward toward Anne.

Nathalie answers for her. "She already told Carolyn that Marc and François are, shall we say," she smirks down at Anne, "they're rambunctious and not good company for little girls."

Luc laughs and slaps his hand on his knee. "Oh, I understand that. I'm on Anne's side. They're good boys, don't misunderstand me. But, as I said, it's best not to let them near the good furniture."

"Oh, you're being too hard on them," Marthe says. "They're boys. You would hurt their feelings if they heard you talk like that."

"Yes, you're right. I'm getting it out of the way today so I can keep quiet tomorrow." He laughs to himself. He faces Carolyn and says, "Anyway, it's not that bad. Let's say that Anne and I have a more elegant view of things."

"The baby's sleeping well," Marthe says.

"Thank god," Nathalie replies.

"Did she do well on the trip down?"

"Oh, Anne was an angel and kept her occupied the whole way. I am grateful for that." Nathalie strokes Anne's hair and looks lovingly at her daughter.

Marthe stands. "Anne, will you help me serve the plum cake? Maybe we'll have a sample before we bring it in?"

"Oh, yes, Grandma, I'll help you."

The two of them disappear out into the hall.

"Grandpa," Nathalie says, "how are you? Has your arthritis been bothering you?"

He shakes his head. "It's been fine. We've had warm weather, so I've been out checking the vines. I don't trust them...you know, the workers."

"But they've been doing it for years."

"I know. And they do an excellent job. It's, I used to do a lot myself, you know, and it's hard to let it go. I need to see for myself. That's what I mean."

"What kind of grapes are they?" Carolyn asks.

"Ah," Luc says, nodding, "I see you appreciate wine. My grapes are Chenin Blanc."

"Oh, I know that variety. We have that wine in California, too. In Napa Valley, north of San Francisco."

"Yes," Luc says, "Napa wines. I have heard of them, too. But I have never tasted them."

"Is there a chance I might taste your wines? Are they the grapes that are outside the house?"

"Two questions. Let me see. Yes, tomorrow with dinner, we will serve our 1975, and maybe the 1977. We'll see. Tell you what, come with me down to the cellar, if you're interested."

"Not now," Marthe says, as she and Anne come into the room. Anne carries a tray with a beautiful round cake topped with plums.

"Oh, that looks delicious," Carolyn says.

"We'll go to the cellar another time. You're staying the weekend, right?"

Nathalie answers for her. "We are, Grandpa. I don't want to leave until Sunday afternoon. I was hoping to show Carolyn some of Senlis Sunday morning."

"But, I do want to see the cellar" Carolyn says. "I'm not a connoisseur of wines, but I want to learn more. Would you also take me out to where the grapes are planted?" She surprises herself with the way she invites herself. But everyone is so warm, she believes they'll welcome her.

"I would love to show you," Luc says.

"There, you've said the perfect thing." Marthe smiles at Carolyn as she makes the table ready. "He's afraid that none of the children are interested in keeping up the vineyard."

Luc addresses Carolyn. "You know what happened in the middle of the 19th Century?"

"Yes, I think so. I understand that a fungus killed the French grape plants. Is that it?"

"You are correct. And so they imported vines from California and grafted them on. I don't argue with that. It saved the French wine industry. French wine culture, I mean to say." Luc nods, his eyes dark and glaring. "I don't want to take anything away from the Americans. But it's the ground that matters, the dirt, the history."

"That's true, Monsieur. Every wine region is distinct because of the particular soil. I do know that."

"But, what you don't know is that these grapes escaped the fungus. There has been no grafting on these vines. There were many others also, I don't want to make too much of it. I'm not anti-American. Believe me, I know, the Americans liberated this house from the Germans. I'm saying, these grapes, this Chenin blanc on this land, they are special. And now no one cares but me." He is breathing harder, his voice getting louder.

Marthe goes over to him and touches him on the shoulder. "Mon chéri, will you please calm down. We're ready to have our cake."

Luc nods in exasperation and sighs. "Yes, of course, I'll stop this nonsense."

"It's not nonsense," Carolyn says. "I'm sorry no one wants to carry on. If I had a grandfather like you I would do it." Deep inside, the loneliness she has grown up with all her life swirls around her. "I still want to see the grapes. And the cellar."

Luc laughs at her and says, "Thank you." He cocks his head and raises his bushy white eyebrows in theatrical exaggeration. "Marthe is right. I think we should have our cake now before Anne gets too hungry."

Anne sighs in relief, unaware that anyone notices her reaction.

"This cake is delicious," Carolyn says, turning to Anne. "I've never had plum cake. And it has, what, brandy in it?"

Anne's eyes open wide, and she looks at her mother again, this time in alarm.

"Oh no," Marthe says, "Anne, there's no alcohol. It gets burned away. You remember the flambé I made last year?"

Anne nods, but remains serious.

"Well, it's the same thing. And anyway, you haven't had any ill effects from my plum cake, have you?" She watches Anne with a serious face.

"No."

"Fine, it's all right then," Nathalie says. "You're not eating any alcohol."

Luc becomes conspiratorial with Carolyn. "Anyway, it's not brandy, it's plum liqueur. One of the many ways that Marthe invents to make ordinary food extraordinary."

"Oh, Luc, stop that, will you? I like to cook, that's all."

"No, I won't. It's true. She thinks I'm bragging for your benefit, Carolyn, but in reality I'm doing it to keep the good stuff coming."

"That's right. He flatters me because he likes to eat like a gourmand. And you can see it on him."

"Go ahead, Marthe, make fun of me. It's all right. I don't mind. Tell me what we're having for dinner. Is it bread and water again?"

Nathalie and Anne laugh at the silly conversation.

"I guess you'll have to wait and see, won't you?" Marthe says, winking at her husband.

"No, I can't. You have to tell me so I can go to the cellar and choose the right wines." He says to Carolyn, "Yes, there, you can come with me and help me choose the wine."

"I'd love to," Carolyn says. "Not choose the wine but go to the cellar. My mother has a winery."

Marthe, Luc, Nathalie and Anne stare at her.

"A winery?" Luc says, his face showing his surprise.

"Oh, I don't mean she's like you. She doesn't make wine herself. She has an investment in a winery in Rutherford. That's the best grape terrain in California. Cabernet sauvignon. They make Bordeaux-style wines."

Luc's face lights up. "I see. Bordeaux. Cabernet. So your mother is serious, is she?"

"She likes her wine, if that's what you mean. She doesn't have a cellar at home, but she does have a climate controlled wine cabinet."

He leans over and speaks in a whisper, with an exaggerated frown. "You didn't happen to bring any with you, did you?"

She laughs and enjoys his camaraderie. "No, I'm afraid not. It's private, for a wine club she belongs to. But if it's possible, I'll try and get you some."

"Yes," he says, smiling at his wife. "Do they have a distributor in France? I find this most interesting."

"I'll find out," Carolyn says. "You know, I haven't paid much attention to it at home. It was something she always did and I wasn't part of it."

"You were too young, wasn't that it?" Nathalie says. She strokes her daughter's hair.

"We didn't drink much wine at home, and then I've been away at school these past years."

"And your semester with me," Nathalie says.

"I do like French wines," Carolyn says. "I admit to being partial to Côtes du Rhône. At home they call that grape *petite syrah*."

Luc looks up in companionable joy, his eyes open wide. "I think you know more than you let on, young lady."

Carolyn shakes her head and smiles with laughter as she turns to him. "No, I think you mistake my meager knowledge for more than it is."

"I think you're losing the rest of us," Marthe says. "I'll do the dishes, then let's walk. It's beautiful outside."

"Yes, yes, you're right," Luc says. "But people are interesting." He raises his teacup to Carolyn.

Carolyn returns the gesture, then raises hers to Nathalie and Anne. "Thank you so much. And thank you Anne, for asking for this cake. It's pretty marvelous."

"It's my favorite," Anne says.

"Let me help you," Carolyn says, picking things off the table.

"Why not?" Marthe says. "I'm not going to do the dishes, I'll wait for Querubina tomorrow." She turns to Carolyn as they walk to the kitchen. "She's my housekeeper."

"That's a beautiful name," Carolyn says.

"She's Portuguese, such a hard worker. She comes in three times a week. Anyway, thank you for the help. Nathalie has her hands full with little Marie."

333

"She's a beautiful baby. It must be hard with her, you know, with Bernard away so much."

Carolyn stops and stares in awe when they enter the kitchen. She turns around for a sweeping view of the room. It is cavernous. At the end is a huge fireplace, and above the center table a copper bar, with what looks like a dozen gleaming copper pots hanging down.

Marthe observes Carolyn with amusement. "That's Querubina for you. She's a fanatic about keeping things polished."

"She works hard."

"It seems so, yes. But there's only Luc and me here, so she takes her time."

"But it's so majestic. The whole room. I think of rooms like this as being a museum."

"Oh, come now. You're not a tourist any more, Carolyn." Marthe's face displays her satisfaction even though her voice bears a note of criticism.

Carolyn isn't sure how to respond. "But I worked in the Louvre, so I know what a nice place is. I've been to Versailles. It's that—this is your home. You baked your cake in this room, in a kitchen so beautiful."

"I'm glad you like it, then." Marthe nods to herself, accepting Carolyn's feelings.

Carolyn studies the rest of the rooms, the high beamed ceilings, the windows looking out over the park-like setting outdoors. The kitchen with the large rooster pottery and baskets on the mantelpiece high up, the gas stove with six burners, the huge ovens. Delft dishes in the breakfront. Wooden spatulas sticking out of a tarnished brass pot like a whittled bouquet.

Carolyn turns to Marthe who studies her with a frown and concern in her eyes.

"I guess, you're right," Carolyn says, "it's a French country home." She watches Marthe's eyes and winces inside. "It's your home. It's Luc's home. That's it. Nathalie's been such a friend to me, you are so kind. Yes, it's not the room. It's that I myself put some dishes on the counter."

"Are you all right?" Marthe says, puzzled.

Carolyn intertwines her fingers and holds them up. "Yes, I don't mean to sound difficult. I love it here in this house, this kitchen. Does that make any sense to you?"

Marthe shakes her head. "My dear, as they say, if you're happy, I'm happy. But you are a bit emotional, if you don't mind my saying so."

"I know what it is," Carolyn says. "It's because I never knew my grandparents."

"Oh, I'm sorry." Marthe holds out her arms to Carolyn, then embraces her. "I'm very sorry. But I do certainly understand what is troubling you, you see. We have lost so many people in France from two wars. It's not so strange to me to feel alone in this world."

Heat flushes Carolyn's cheeks and tears form behind her eyes.

"Sit down, my dear, and let me give you something." Marthe opens a cabinet and takes down an unmarked bottle with clear liquid in it. "Homemade liqueur. Luc's concoction. It works wonders for the soul." She pours it into a shot glass. Then she pours another. She lifts her glass and gives one to Carolyn. "To your health."

"To your health, Marthe," Carolyn responds. She downs the liqueur and other tears from the liqueur replace her tears of emotion. "Wow. Luc knows what he is doing."

"He wins prizes with his wine and liqueur. Are you feeling better now?"

"Yes. Now I feel like I have this kitchen inside me."

Marthe laughs and touches her lightly on the shoulder. "We'd better go back. They'll wonder what happened to us."

"But, I have a favor to ask of you."

"How can I help you?"

"Will you let me draw your portrait?"

"Me?"

"Yes, yes, if you please. I've been wandering around Paris trying to sketch things. Nothing. Now, today, in this kitchen, I'm ready. You've made me very happy. Oh, I don't want to take up your time." Carolyn doesn't see any trouble in Marthe's face, but she is demanding too much. Tomorrow, so many people will be here, so much to prepare. And tomorrow so many people to love. "Maybe some other time, you have your family coming."

Marthe moves her head from side to side in disbelief. "Yes, perhaps you're right. But I don't care. I would much rather sit for you than cook for them. Querubina can come over, and then instead of cooking we'll go into Senlis and, you know, they're all like you, everybody loves this kitchen. They'll enjoy it while they use it. They always say I do too much. Well, then, not this time."

Carolyn's heart is singing. "Thank you so much. I would love to draw you outside, in your garden."

"How about now? It's fine with me. There's still plenty of daylight. Come on, we'd better get back in there, if you're feeling all right now."

"Yes, I'm fine, I was overcome with emotion a moment ago. My sketchbook is in the car. Give me a minute to go get it."

IN NO TIME at all, they are all sitting outside surrounded by red, pink and white roses. Nathalie holds little Marie by the arms and helps her walk. Anne and Luc pretend to play chess together. Carolyn sits opposite Marthe, pencil poised over a blank page.

"You can't do that," Luc says, laughing. "She knocked over my king. That's not how you win."

Anne's voice pierces the air as she laughs in childlike glee.

Carolyn studies Marthe, her graying hair standing out from the dark green and pink of the rose bush behind her. Her eyes are now a shade of darker blue, the black flecks more prominent. And her mouth, upturned and smiling even though closed and trying to be serious. Her skin, soft and radiant within, with very few wrinkles.

Marthe sits straight in her chair, her hands on her knees. She cocks her head a little to the side and looks at Carolyn's face. She doesn't sit blankly for a portrait, instead she makes herself open to the artist, she exposes her heart to her. Her eyes above her high cheekbones observe Carolyn with love and sympathy.

Carolyn sketches the outlines of the broad shoulders, narrow waist, and thin arms. Then she puts in the outlines of the face, draws the hair, adds shadows on the face, hair and neck. She pencils warmth to the shadows between hair and face and underneath cheekbones, then merges the outside of the hair with the background.

"Carolyn," Marthe says, "do you know nothing of your grandparents."

Carolyn shakes her head and resists the temptation to think back to feelings of loneliness. Not now, not here. "Nothing on my father's side. He left my mother before I was born. On my mother's side, I didn't know them, either. My grandfather died when I was young. I

336

did see a portrait of him painted by my grandmother. But she died in 1943 in Versailles."

Marthe sits up in surprise. "Oh my. Versailles. Have you seen her grave?"

Carolyn puts her pencil down. She slumps in her chair and speaks without lifting her head. A pain grips the back of her throat. So close. "No. I haven't gone."

"Oh, I'm sorry." Marthe snatches a glance at Nathalie before continuing. "I didn't mean to bother you about it."

Carolyn sighs. "You haven't. Not at all. I haven't settled down yet."

"I won't go on about it. And I didn't mean to interrupt my sitting." Marthe smiles.

Carolyn is drawn by the sympathy that comes from deep within. She hears Nathalie's voice.

"How do you know about your grandmother? That she is buried at Versailles?"

"I don't think she's buried there. Her grave is in New York. It's a small cemetery downtown. The gravestone says she died in Versailles, September 4, 1943."

"That's not very far," Marthe says. "Oh, there I go again, telling you what to do."

"No, no, it's fine," Carolyn says. "Having met you, here, with your family, it makes me want to try and find out what happened."

"Doesn't your family have any record?"

"My mother says she knows nothing. My aunt in New York said my grandfather kept no records of it."

"Go to the town hall in Versailles," Marthe says. "Or the Red Cross in Paris. They have whole basements full of records, and they will be very willing to help you."

"I will do that. Thank you." Carolyn narrows her eyes, then smudges some here, deepens shadows there, and adds a few lines on the edges. "There. For what it's worth."

"Let me see, let me see." Anne comes running over and stands by Carolyn, who holds it up for her to see.

"Is it good?" Marthe asks.

"It's beautiful," Anne says.

Carolyn takes the drawing over to Marthe, who smiles in gratitude.

"Thank you, my dear. I will cherish it. Oh...I presume I may keep it." She appears sheepish. "Maybe you want it."

"No," Carolyn says. "I did it for you. I can't thank you enough. As I said, I haven't been able to draw at all in Paris. You have taught me something about myself. I am grateful to you all."

Marthe says she will take the drawing in to Senlis and have it framed, and then determine where to hang it.

The rest of the weekend flows by, with Carolyn helping Anne to avoid her cousins. On Sunday morning they say goodbye to Marthe and Luc.

Carolyn trembles as she hugs Marthe.

"God bless you, my child," Marthe says. "I think you have real talent. Don't forget what I said. I'm sure you will find something about your grandmother. What is her name?"

"Julia. Julia Stuart."

"Well, Luc knows some people, too. I'll make sure that he follows up with this. You never know. You have to believe that you will find something about her. If you make it to Versailles, and walk around the town, you will be where she walked. That is important in itself."

"I will. Thank you again." Carolyn waves, amazed at Marthe's last remark, and they get into the car and return to Paris.

She doesn't wait. The next day she boards the RER train and steps off at Versailles Rive Gauche. Within minutes she stands before the Monuments To the Dead, around the corner from city hall on Avenue General de Gaulle. She searches all the names, even though she doesn't expect to find anything on the wall about her mother. Still, her mother is American, and they didn't put her name up on the wall, but she could have died with some of these people.

Inside city hall, Carolyn talks to warmhearted and sympathetic people who take a long time searching their records, but they sadly find no mention of any Julia Stuart. But now she is on a mission. Even if it leads nowhere, Carolyn will find out what she can. Anything.

AT HOME, WITH the window open, she gazes out once more at the beautiful, warm, Parisian shining nighttime. She becomes aware that she is a different person, now interested in someone other than herself. She picks up the phone and calls Marthe in Senlis, and spends

338

an hour with her, going over her day in Versailles. Carolyn talks too much and too fast, guilt driving her.

After all, Marthe is not her grandmother, and she vows to make this one call and then not bother her new friend again. But when she says goodbye, Marthe insists that she keep her informed of the visit to the Red Cross.

"Carolyn, it's been thirty-five years since the end of the war. It's not very long. I have many graves that I visit every year. Thank God, Luc was spared during the war, I am grateful for that. But I pray. I pray for you, and now I pray for your grandmother. I sense that I am very close to you. Miracles do happen, we do find people we thought were lost forever. So promise me that you will let me know. All right?"

"Yes, I promise." The warmth and strength in Marthe's voice pierce straight through to Carolyn's heart.

"Thank you. Good night, darling."

The next morning, Carolyn walks out to a rainy morning and carefully heads to the bottom of the steps on Rue du Mont-Cenis. One left turn, one block and she stands at the corner of Rue du Mont-Cenis and Rue du Baigneur. A small store front window displays the lettering Croix Rouge de Paris. Her heart beats faster as she enters the office. Posters show Red Cross disaster relief in Martinique and Guadeloupe, an earthquake in Turkey. Behind the counter are two desks. At one of them a young man stands when she comes in the door. He is not much older than Carolyn. He is tall, and thin, and wearing jeans and a white shirt. His face bears a couple days' worth of black beard, matching his hair falling in ragged misdirection.

But he smiles at her. "Yes, mademoiselle. Welcome to the Red Cross of Montmartre. How may I be of service to you?"

Carolyn studies his dark brown eyes, the eyes that are going to help her find her future. "I have information that my grandmother died in Versailles in 1943. I know her name, Julia Stuart, but that is all. What I'm asking is, is there any hope at all of finding out what happened to her?"

The young man nods seriously but waits for her to say something more.

"I know it's not much to go on," she continues. "But it's all I have. I am prepared to accept that it's not enough information."

"Have a seat." He points to a chair opposite his desk, and raises a board at the end of the counter for her to come through.

"You know, of course, we don't have any information here. And you say you have made inquiries with the authorities at Versailles?"

"No, I didn't say. But, yes, I was there. They have no information. My grandmother is American, and they have no information on any Americans. A friend suggested I try the Red Cross. So I'm here."

"I think what I can do is help you get started."

"It would mean a great deal to me if you could." Carolyn doesn't really expect much help from him, but she knows it's her only choice at the moment.

He takes out a blank sheet of paper from a drawer and lays a pen on top of it. "Her name, Julia Stuart. Please spell that for me. This is a note for myself. And do you have any dates?"

"It says on her gravestone that she died on September 4, 1943, in Versailles."

He sits back in his chair and looks at her in disbelief, as if she were a curiosity. "Her gravestone? So you know where she is. You are not actually trying to find her grave. You want to know where she died? Is that correct?"

"When you say it like that, I must tell you, I'm not asking for you to spend any effort. It would of course mean a great deal to me to find out what I can about my grandmother."

"Yes, I understand," he says. His voice speaks of wasting his time.

Carolyn's heart sinks. She sees herself as a stupid fool on a fool's errand. She stands. "I'm sorry. This doesn't make any sense. In my head, it seemed like a logical idea. I realize it's a waste of your time. All I know is Versailles, and there's nothing there."

"Yes, I'm afraid I have to agree with you. We can't help you." He stands and puts his hand out. As they shakes hands he says, "Where is the gravestone? Is it here in Paris?"

"No, it's in New York."

"New York?" His eyes open wide and he smirks, almost choking on the words.

Carolyn blushes in humiliation. Without looking at him, she leaves the office and returns home. She calls Marthe, desperate to talk to someone sympathetic. And Marthe can help more than Natalie.

She dials Marthe's number, and when she hears Marthe's voice, the comforting voice, a soft current of warmth runs through her.

"Marthe, it's me, Carolyn."

"Oh, so soon. That's unexpected. Have you found something out already?"

Carolyn sighs. "No, I'm so stupid. It was embarrassing. I went to the Red Cross in Montmartre."

"Montmartre? That's strange. Why there?"

"I was near it at the time and I didn't think it made any difference."

"What was there, an ambulance?"

"Oh, you are making fun of me, too." Her cheeks burn and she is glad Marthe can't see her.

"No, my dear. You are going to have to develop a thicker skin, Carolyn, if you are to make any progress in this."

Marthe's advice is what she needs.

"What happened? Tell me in detail."

Carolyn relaxes. "It was …when I told him what I knew, that she died in Versailles, and, and then when I said she was buried in New York, he laughed me out of there."

"Now Carolyn, you cannot give up hope. You went to the wrong place. I have to admit, I thought they would be more helpful. He could at least have given you some addresses or phone numbers."

"But it seemed so useless. I have a date and a city so I thought there would be records." Carolyn wonders to herself what is motivating her to even pursue this. Why continue when it seems to start from nowhere and lead to nowhere. The image of her grandmother's grave in New York City Marble Cemetery flies up before her. The name, the dates, the places, they seemed so real back then, with Beatrice.

Now they are nothing. They don't lead anywhere. Now she doesn't trust her own feelings. She wants to put the phone down, but she spies the sketchbook, empty now after she has given her one Parisian drawing to Marthe. It is open but blank on the coffee table in front of her. She wants to put Julia's face on it. She thinks of Hugh's portrait in the attic in New York and forms the idea of putting it on paper, a sketch from memory.

"You listen to me." Marthe's voice is now serious and harsh and wakes Carolyn out of her reverie. "There's more in you than that.

What about your love for your grandmother? That's what's driving you. You cannot give up now. You haven't even begun."

Carolyn sighs in relief. It is as if now it doesn't matter whether she succeeds. It matters that she tries as hard as she can. "You're wonderful, Marthe. I wish you were my grandmother."

"That's a lovely thing to say, my child, but I'm not that person. We must continue to look for your real grandmother until there's nowhere else to go."

Marthe's statement hits Carolyn hard. She feels like she's blowing back and forth in the wind. "I hear what you're saying. I don't know where to go."

Marthe sighs in near disbelief. "The first thing is, young lady, you don't give up."

"But I don't know where to begin." A tightness grips Carolyn.

"So, you went one place, talked to an idiot, and now you're giving up?"

Carolyn hears the disappointment and frustration coming from Marthe. The tone in the voice on the other end of the phone makes her sick. "No. I'm not."

"Don't you have a phone?"

"What? Of course, I'm talking to…." Carolyn becomes confused.

"Then use it. Call the Red Cross in Paris, the International Red Cross. Call Geneva. Can't you do that?"

Carolyn starts shaking. She waits in silence for a moment, afraid of the sound of her own voice. She has always known what to do. "Yes. Of course. I think what I did was give up after the first try."

"That's better." Marthe's voice sounds softer, but it still carries that note of disappointment in Carolyn. "And you keep me informed. I'm in this with you. Do you understand?"

"Yes. I do. And I will." A great heavy fear leaves Carolyn.

"Good. Goodbye for now." Marthe hangs up.

Carolyn puts the phone down and steps to the window. She opens it wide and takes long breaths of cool fresh air.

Chapter 39

CAROLYN TELLS HER story to an operator on the phone in Paris, and wants to laugh and cry at the same time when the operator gives her the number of the International Red Cross in Geneva. But she is puzzled when the Red Cross there informs her that the place she must contact is Bad Arolsen in Germany.

Bad Arolsen? She has never heard of it. She learns that the German government, after the war, set up the International Tracing Service. The Germans did it because the Germans had caused the need for a tracing service and the Nazis had kept the best records. And everything over time became centralized there. The records were in an old SS barracks in a town that hadn't been bombed during the war. If there is any information on Julia Marie Stuart, that's where it is.

She calls the Tracing Service and is at first surprised by the extraordinary warmth and sympathy in the voice of the woman on the other end of the line. Then she comes to realize that this person has long experience talking to people who have lost mothers and fathers in concentration camps.

"My name is Frau Hanne Koehler. Who are looking for?"

"I'm trying to find out what happened to my grandmother, an American. I believe she died in France in 1943."

"So, I'm sorry that you must undertake this difficult task. I hope we may be able to help you."

"Thank you Frau Koehler."

"Sometimes it is easy, sometimes not so easy. Let me first inform you of how the process will take place. We cannot do this over the

343

phone. We have records, and we even have an alphabetical listing, a central name index. But after that, it's going through a very large warehouse of paper records and they're not always well organized. You do understand this?"

"Yes, I do." But Carolyn feels relief already.

"Then you can do this through the mail. I can send you a form...."

"But...."

"But what? I know what you are going to say. First, what is your name please?"

"Carolyn Stuart."

"I see. Miss or Mrs.?"

"Miss."

"Yes, then, Miss Stuart. We have people dedicating their lives to helping others connect to refugees, victims and people who have disappeared. The number is in the millions."

Carolyn shrinks inside herself. Here she is again, as she is with Marthe, unable to get beyond her own limited feelings. Wanting everything right now. But this is about her grandmother, her mother's mother. This comes from the deepest corner of her soul. She determines to change. Now.

"Frau Koehler, I am grateful for any help you can give me. I want to do things the proper way."

"All right, Miss Stuart, the proper way is the most efficient for you, I assure you. We need a form. You understand when you are looking up boxes and boxes of paperwork you need to have something appropriate to guide you."

"Thank you. How may I obtain a form?"

The voice resumes its earlier sympathetic tone. "I will be happy to mail you a form. You mail the form back to us and it often takes eight weeks for a reply. The reply will be a statement of what is in the Central Name Index. Of course, there is another choice."

Carolyn feels a strong desire to be still and let this woman's voice carry her into the future. "Please, what is the other choice?"

"You can come here yourself. We give priority to people who come here in person. We understand it is more important for some people. If you are willing to make the effort."

"Thank you for that information. Yes, it is worth it for me to come there in person. It makes me feel already closer to my grandmother."

"You are where, now?"

"In Paris."

"Paris. All right. You have our phone number in case you get lost. But you take the train. There's a German Railway train from Paris, the Gare de l'Est, it's about 8 hours altogether, but it's straightforward. You will arrive too late to talk to us. The next morning you can come here, talk to someone, me if you like…am I…are you following me?"

"Oh, yes, Frau Kohler, I have heard everything you said. And I do understand the chances are small. But it is important to me to come, even if I leave with nothing. If I don't find my grandmother, you have records of people who were there with her. So I will learn something, I'm sure of that. When can I come?"

"Well, Miss Stuart, you are serious. The real question then, is when will you be arriving?"

"I can leave tomorrow, and see you the next day. And it will take eight weeks after that?"

"Oh no, if you make the effort, so will we. If you come at eight o'clock in the morning, we will have someone available to start searching our index file, then we'll see after that."

The words 'start searching' intrigues Carolyn. "So, it depends…."

"Ah, I see. Okay, Miss Stuart, I think I know the direction of the thinking. I must tell you, some of the researchers are former concentration camp inmates. Or their children. And many are Germans who have a conscience about what happened during the war."

"Yes, I know what that means. Of course, I do."

"Then, well, can I be honest with you?"

A pang of worry jolts Carolyn. "Yes, please."

"Okay, so these people, an incentive, it helps them to improve their lives, and…"

Carolyn lets out a little laugh of relief. "Oh, you mean…"

"Miss Stuart, I do not want to be too direct. I think you understand me. But if you come prepared, then we will have someone, someone who is in need, and they will dedicate their time to your grandmother. You can see the city, visit our beautiful baroque Arolsen Castle, have lunch maybe a little wienerschnitzel and our local beer at the Hofbräuhaus, you know, then walk it off for a bit, and in the afternoon come back here to us and we'll know what our records are. It's after that when things can get complicated, depending on what we find."

"I'll see you the day after tomorrow. And I'll be prepared to help out one of your researchers. Thank you. Thank you."

"In two days' time, then. Auf Widersehen."

TWO DAYS LATER, Carolyn was in Germany, and two days after that, she returned to Paris. And called Marthe.

"Hello?"

"Marthe, it's me, Carolyn. I'm back from Germany."

"Oh, that's interesting. A week ago, you were distressed. Now you're back from Germany. That's very impressive. You must have found something out."

"I did. It's like good news and bad news."

"Oh, always give me the bad news first."

"My grandmother. They lost trace of her, and that's a bad sign. For someone who was interned in World War II by the Nazis."

"I understand that, dear girl. For us, the French, it is a common story. Now tell me the good news."

"It's not good news, I shouldn't have said that. But I learned what happened to her. She was put on a train in Paris in 1940, and sent to Vittel."

"Ah, I know Vittel. A spa town. Luc knows those camps better than me. He knows people. And then?"

"Then, that's the end. She went to Vittel and did not come out."

"You mean she died there?"

"No. Well, that may be what happened to her, but there's no record."

Marthe's voice becomes more sympathetic. "Carolyn, my dear, I'm very impressed with what you have done. You knew already that your grandmother was dead. So this is not a surprise. But in an important way, you have become closer to her. And you have proven to yourself that you loved her. You went through very much trouble to find out what happened to her."

"I must again thank you, Marthe. For teaching me how to be more serious about my life."

"So now you can go on with your life. Now you are living it a little more…thoughtfully…than before."

"Yes. It's not over. In two or three months, they will send me a document with the details of what they have, what they know from French sources, Germans, the Red Cross."

"Until then, why don't you come over to Senlis and have tea with me? I have framed your picture and I want you to see it."

"I would love that."

CAROLYN TAKES THE train to Senlis and relaxes with the warm sun on her face as she watches the beautiful green countryside pass by the train window. She looks up in the sky, trying to find figures in the clouds. She finds several, including a teddy bear, but realizes she is finding what she wants to see.

When she rings the bell in front of Marthe and Luc's mansion in Senlis, the door opens.

Marthe comes out laughing. "Sorry," she says, "we saw you coming up the driveway. We were upstairs. I made it to the door in time, I thought, but then the bell rang." She shakes her head and waves the thought away. "Never mind." She embraces Carolyn and kisses her on both cheeks. "Luc is inside with some special wine for you. We're both very interested in hearing all about your trip."

The warmth in Marthe's light blue eyes draws Carolyn in. "I can't thank you enough, Madame, for your advice."

"Oh, come now, it's not Madame for you and me. Not anymore. Luc's waiting for us, he wants to hear all about it. You have awakened his interest in his family and friends. He was interned, too, you know."

Carolyn feels guilty because she has not talked to Luc about his experiences during the war. Instead, she is fixated on her own interest. She resolves to make up for it.

Inside, Luc is standing next to a chess table, playing a game with himself. When he hears them come in, he looks up, smiling with his mouth, but more with his eyes. "Carolyn, how nice to see you. We are both waiting to hear what you have learned in Germany."

"Oh, thank you, Luc. Both of you have been so kind to me, and you're the ones who gave me the impetus to do all this. And I have never asked you about your experience. After all, you were here during the war. And I remember the first time I was here, you mentioned that the Germans took over this house. I want to hear about that."

Luc made an almost imperceptible nod. "Yes, in time. But tell us about Bad Arolsen. We want to hear from you first." He points at his wife. "Marthe tells me too little."

Marthe waves his statement away. "Yes, tell us everything."

Carolyn begins the story with her conversation with Frau Koehler. At the center in Germany they took her information, and when she came back in the afternoon, Frau Koehler was waiting with the results of her research.

"And, what did you learn?" Marthe says, closing her eyes and sighing with impatience. Then she smiles, but glances at Luc with a sense of guilt. "I haven't told him much about your story. I wanted for him to learn for himself. Because it's very exciting."

"Oh," Carolyn says, surprised. She turns to Luc. "Um, I went there in the morning, the lady, Frau Koehler, she was very nice, very sympathetic. She took my information. It seemed odd to me, that she would take down what I said and she could help me so soon. It's such a big place, several floors, crammed full of cabinets even in the hallways. Frau Koehler took me into a room, in the afternoon, after they'd done their research."

"They don't let you do it yourself?" Luc says, frowning.

"Well, they would," Carolyn replies, "if I was doing research, but coming in off the street to find something about a person, they don't. Frau Koehler showed me the microfilm they had. She told me, in the middle of explaining the images, that researchers sometimes had to leave because they hated seeing swastikas on everything, day in, day out, even on birth certificates."

"Ah, yes," Luc says, nodding in contempt, "the Germans, that would be natural for them. More efficient. More horror for those that have to see them constantly. It's as if they are screaming at us from hell."

"Luc, let her continue," Marthe says, with criticism in her words, but not in her voice.

"That's it. There is a record of her being put on a train for Vittel, and a record of her in a census in Vittel. But that's the end of it. Frau Koehler said there are records of people leaving Vittel at the end of the war, and some Americans leaving it during the war, but it seems my grandmother disappeared."

Luc is a little agitated. "Then maybe she escaped."

Marthe shakes her head. "Well, if she did, there's no record of that." She's sad. "I'm sorry, Carolyn, I shouldn't have said that. Luc's unwarranted optimism made me do the opposite. I am sorry."

"No, that's fine," Carolyn says. "It's over with now. I feel I made contact with my grandmother, that's what's important. I never thought I would find her."

Luc purses his lips. "Why not? Did you give up?"

"It seems to me, if my grandmother were alive, she would try and contact us, wouldn't she? Wouldn't she want to find us, too?"

"Yes, that's true," Luc says.

"But, I understand you," Marthe says, "and you have her grave back in New York. Didn't you say that."

"Yes. I've been there. I touched her gravestone. It's not very nice, a square piece of stone flat on the ground. My mother does that every time she's in New York, and she's the one that said I should do it."

Luke is puzzled. "Then tell me, why have you been searching for your grandmother?"

Marthe turns to him with darkened eyes. He returns her look with raised eyebrows.

"It feels like I'm in the trees without the forest. I wanted to find out how and where she died. Now I know at least that they put the wrong place on the gravestone. It wasn't Versailles, it was Vittel."

"But this is very curious," Luc says, standing. He puts a finger in the air. "It's odd that she died in France, though, and then they were able to get her body back to the United States. In the middle of the war."

Carolyn nods, but says, "Yes, I understand, but my grandfather was wealthy enough to do it. It's kind of odd. And I don't know if it was during the war. I think after the war. And he kept no records."

"What?" Marthe says, glancing quickly at Luc then at Carolyn.

"Well, still, it's a wonderful thing to do, don't you think? And a lot of expense. He must have had connections. And then…" But Carolyn doesn't want to continue. She doesn't want to drag these generous people deeper into her own history.

"What is it?" Marthe says, concern showing in her voice.

"It's that he disowned my mother."

"Disowned her? What for? Oh, never mind, Carolyn, it's your family business, not ours. We have no right to ask you about this. Now this is strange. You feel closer to your grandmother, and you're making us feel closer to her and you." Marthe touches Carolyn on the arm. "You don't have to go on like this."

A sense of guilt about dominating this conversation overwhelms Carolyn. "I'm sorry. Let's— I want to drop this. I know more than I ever thought I'd learn about my grandmother." She turns to Luc. "Marthe said you had some special wine. I would love to taste it. And I haven't forgotten your promise to show me your vineyards."

Luc smiles and stands, says he'll be right back and leaves the room.

Marthe turns to Carolyn. "Your grandfather disowned your mother and he brings his wife's body back from France. People are a mystery, my Dear, and the farther away in time they get, the more mysterious they become. I think now it's time for you to concentrate on your own life. Don't you agree?"

Carolyn nods and sighs. "You're right. I'm starved, and I can't wait to see what wine Luc has to show me. But before he gets back, there is one thing that interests me."

"What is that?"

"You, or Luc, said the Germans took over this house during the war? What did you do?"

Marthe nods, and becomes serious, her eyes darker. "Yes, we lived in one of the houses up the road. They were part of the property then. Now they've been sold as separate houses. We stayed there and they used this big house as some kind of headquarters. We never saw much activity, cars coming and going, generals, that sort of thing. Oh...." She sighs and shrinks into herself for a moment. "I'm sorry, now I'm going to get into family history. I'm thinking back what a scare it was. They gave us a week's notice. Which was lucky. We were able to avert a tragedy."

Carolyn now forgets herself, her own life. "A tragedy? What?"

"We have an attic. One day a man, a carpenter he said, well he was dressed like it, overalls, tools, paint on his boots, he said he worked for the Resistance and he was going to build us a secret room. He knew how to hide it. I was in shock. I didn't order someone to come to the

350

house. But of course, I knew it was Luc who had arranged it. It was what he would do. So the man came in, and when he was through, in the top floor, the attic, you would never know there was anything there. So we had whole families stay here. Never very long, it was too close to Paris, but they always came in the back door at night, and up the back staircase without lights, and up to the hidden room in the attic."

"Oh my god, you're brave."

"Yes, maybe brave like your grandmother. But one day an arrogant German officer came and said we had to vacate the house. We had a week's time, and the Resistance came and took these refugees away and the carpenter sealed up the hidden room so no one could ever find it. And we moved out."

"Here I am," Luc's jolly voice announces, "with our new wine."

"Oh, my, I didn't know you had new wine so fast," Carolyn says, now distracted and wishing she could hear more of the story from Marthe.

"It's not new," Marthe said. "It's, he has a new partner who's bringing in a new wine from Alsace."

And so Carolyn enjoys the wine, grows closer to Marthe and Luc, learns more about their experiences during the war, and before leaving, is thrilled to see her drawing of Marthe hung with an expensive gold frame in the hallway.

WHEN SHE ARRIVES home and peers out the window to the park on Rue de Sévigné, she still doesn't know what she is going to do with her art. Yes, she has some talent for portraits, but that's not enough. There is something puzzling about it.

She has a longing to know what art is like today, what are artists doing, what are they showing. And there is one way to do that.

She laughs as she remembers how insulted she was back in New York when she was offered the opportunity to pursue a certificate in art dealership at NYU. She isn't going to get a certificate out of this, but she is going to find herself. That's all she wants, that's all she needs and it's better: search the galleries.

Chapter 40

THE NEXT MORNING, she goes down to the park across the street for practice sketching. She finds plenty of scenes and produces a dozen sketches, and makes a couple of friends as well. She can take her time searching for out-of-the-way streets, or outside the city for now. Every day she goes down to a different park nearby to find material for her sketches. She'll split her day. Sketching in the morning, galleries in the afternoon.

TWO DAYS LATER, in the Park across from her apartment, she sits on a green bench by herself, surrounded by laughing children and watchful nannies. Her sketch pad lies open on her lap and she finds herself attracted to trees and flowers. She puts her pencil down as cool wind flows on her and sees a familiar face. Familiar but she doesn't know who it is, she doesn't remember where she's seen that face. A young man with a dazzling smile under hazel eyes, his neat black hair waving off his forehead in the wind.

"Carolyn," he says. A familiar voice, too, but not familiar enough. "How nice to see you." He's carrying something in a small case that he puts down on the bench between them, then he sits down. He looks at her patiently, waiting to see if she recognizes him.

She smiles, but with formal politeness. "I'm sorry, you're going to have to help me out. I apologize for not remembering."

He's handsome, with a striking cupid's bow and a strong jawline. He's wearing neat blue jeans and a black jacket over a gray sweater.

"I'm afraid I have an advantage over you. Your aunt Beatrice gave me your address."

"Beatrice?" She puts her hand on her mouth. "Oh, yes, New York, the hockey game, the bar." She nods. "Now I do remember. You didn't make a good impression."

He laughs. "Yes, you walked out on me, and I don't blame you. I was acting like a fool. But I think I'm over that stage."

She senses that he's somehow different now. His neat hair and jeans. The way he respects the distance between them. His manner of looking at her, at her face. "So, my aunt, she gave you my address, like that, and now you're here? Not like it's a coincidence or something." He's handsome and attractive, but not yet believable.

"No, it's no coincidence at all. I'm here for my film."

"Your film? Wasn't it about subways or something?"

"Yes it was. Well, remember, part of it takes place in a subway. I thought I could fake Paris by using the Montréal or New York subway. I shot some film, but my mentor said I had to do the real thing. So here I am." He picks up his case.

"What's that?" she says. She points at the case but she's more interested in studying his eyes.

"My camera. 8mm."

"8mm? For a film?"

He hefts it up and down in his hand and sort of smiles, sort of smirks. He seems more reserved now, not so confident and overbearing as he was in New York.

"Film is expensive. 8mm is affordable. I need to scout locations, as many as I can, to see what I want to use."

"How long have you been doing this here?"

"In Paris? Not long. A couple of days."

"Oh. It didn't take you long to find me."

"Well, I have a precise address, so I didn't need a lot of time. Anyway," he says, leaning a little toward her, running his hand through his hair to keep it down in the wind, which it doesn't need, "I am here, and your aunt knows I'm here, and I'd like to take you out to dinner. If I may."

His smile is sincere, but maybe mischievous, maybe playing. Whatever it is, it draws her in.

"Dinner. Do you know Paris well?"

"I know a couple of restaurants, if that's what you mean. I'll take you anywhere you like. But I did make a reservation at Restaurant Colbert. Do you know it?"

"I do, le Grand Colbert, from a long time ago. It's pricey. And touristy."

He shakes his head and frowns. "Touristy if you want, but it's beautiful turn-of-the-century, and Parisians love it, too. And we don't have to eat caviar."

"Aren't you presumptuous to make reservations?"

He nods and grins. "Not at all, I can unmake it. Nothing lost. I wanted to have someplace impressive to take you, to increase my chances."

Carolyn studies him. He seems at the moment to be out of place in Paris. A face from the past. A funny Quebec accent. But his hair has changed, that's in his favor. His manner is much more civilized. Not arrogant.

No. He is still arrogant. Now she remembers. In New York he ordered her drink for her without asking. And here in Paris here he shows up with reservations at an elegant restaurant. Again, without asking. Without having had a conversation with her. Still, he got his hair fixed. And he's shaved clean.

"Good," she says, trying to instill arrogance in her own voice, "you can unmake it."

He's taken aback by her words. "What? I'm sorry, but why?"

"Because you come barging into my neighborhood and think you're going to make decisions for me. It's a lot like ordering things for me in New York and I don't care for it."

Robert sits still for a moment, looking back and forth between her eyes. Then he seems to grasp her meaning. "Of course. I understand. That isn't at all what I wanted to do." He leans back on the bench and purses his lips, preparing what to say. "That's not how I meant it. I was being nice, but, I apologize, I do."

Carolyn doesn't know how to take Robert's words now. Is he being sincere, or is he still trying to sweet-talk her into drinks and dinner and whatever comes after? She turns to him to say what's on her mind, but he talks.

"Tell you what. Let's start over. I'm hungry. Do you know a little place around here where we could get something to eat?" His voice is low and apologetic. He holds his hands out to the side, palms up in supplication.

Carolyn smiles warmly, impressed with his willingness to make things right. "Sure. It is nice to see you, Robert."

She puts out her hand for a shake as a way of showing him that she isn't ready for any kind of relationship. And she resolves to not invite him up to her room any time soon. She's not ready for that invasion of privacy at all. Let alone intimacy. And is furious with herself for thinking about it and for finding herself a fraction off balance.

"Walk with me," she says. "We'll find someplace close."

"Thank you," he says, smiling and making sure he doesn't get close to her as they walk. "I am hungry."

"I like l'Osteria, down the street."

"That's fine with me," Robert says, showing relief in his voice. He picks up his film camera and follows her, still being careful to avoid bumping in to her.

That's nice, she thinks, he's not backing away. I'm glad. But that's all. It's nice.

At 10 Rue de Sévigné, she takes him inside the small restaurant, with no name on the street, windows with weather-beaten brown woodwork and three-quarters lace curtains giving the patrons some privacy. They face each other at a small table along the earthen-brick walls underneath black and white photos of scenes in Venice.

A waiter with a strong Italian accent takes their order and serves them glasses of dark red Amarone, recommending it as being the best vino of Veneto, the region surrounding Venice.

As they eat pizza, they laugh and share the humor of paring the good wine with good pizza.

Carolyn notes how they laugh together. How welcome it is that Robert, when he's relaxed, has a great sense of humor.

"So, tell me," she says, enjoying the last sip of delicious wine from her glass, savoring, for the first time she's in Paris, the complexity of the wine, some sort of earthy fruit. The thought jumps out in her head that she enjoys wine tasting with this man. "Tell me again why you are in Paris?"

He looks down, seems to study his fingers through the glass as he starts talking. "Well, I had a rough time in New York. I made a small film with these romantic scenes in the subway. A short film, 15 minutes." Then he hesitates and drinks the last of his wine without tasting it.

Carolyn thinks she could teach him to drink wine, then realizes that's the last thing she wants to do.

"So, why was it rough?"

He glances at her and then around the restaurant. "When I showed it to a group at a film club, they laughed. It was quite humiliating."

Carolyn frowns and a wave of sympathy comes over her. "Oh. I'm sorry. What do you think happened?"

"I realize it now. It's called production values. The romanticism of the film is lost in the shooting."

"But, I don't see why? Explain that to me?" Carolyn is quite happy to be having an impersonal, and yet also personal, conversation about a professional subject. She's interested in him on some level.

"The film was in French, the scenes were supposed to be in France, but the subways were in New York and Montréal. It was obvious to the film club people."

"That wasn't very nice of them to be laughing at your film. I would have thought they would be more appreciative. And I would like some more wine." She signals to the waiter.

"While we're waiting," she says. She's curious about his slight French Canadian accent, which she hears now and then.

"Yes. It doesn't matter. Other filmmakers are very competitive, you know. And arrogant. They were quite happy about my film's problems. Those people all made these social films, you see, that was part of it. Their films showed homeless people and cruel bureaucrats. My film was about romance. So outdated."

"But there are lots of good romantic films made," she says, bothered by the insult from the other filmmakers. As if they were insulting her.

Robert is also viewing Carolyn with sympathetic eyes. He nods and says, "Perhaps you're right, but that makes my point. Yes, there was another film, about two old people, and the man's jealous. They didn't laugh at that, but they sat bored all through it. Anyway, since you asked, that's why I'm here in Paris. So that the location doesn't take away from the film."

She's puzzled. "Why didn't you make the film in New York? Make it a New York film."

He laughs, but in a dismissive way. "Oh, I can't do that. I'm supported by the Quebec Film Council." He leans forward, elbows on the table, happy to share his story." It's a story about French Canadians. I don't have any money on my own. Well, not enough."

Carolyn took a long sip of her wine. The thought occurs to her that Beatrice might have told him about her trust fund. Then she drops the thought. Beatrice isn't like that. She looks directly at him to hide the idea she wasn't paying attention a moment ago. "I'm sorry, I don't mean to bother you with all these questions."

"No, no, not at all. I'm very happy to talk to you about it. It's, it's kind of refreshing. You know what they say. It's as hard to make a bad film as a good one."

She laughs. "Oh, I heard that too, about painting. And writing." She also wants to ask him how long he's going to be in Paris, but she's afraid he might then think she is being serious. "But you aren't letting them get to you, are you?"

Robert smiles and toys with his silverware. "No, I'm not. That's why I'm here. I learned from my mistake, so now I'm here where my story is set."

"Do you have actors, too?"

He shakes his head. "No, I'm scouting. I have my little camera and I will go around and film locations inside the metro until I find the three or four locations I need. They have to be clearly Paris, you know, Metro signs, direction signs, trains arriving with Paris Metro destinations on the front."

She furrows her brow. "Forgive me for acting like a producer, but what good are the Metro locations without actors?"

"When I'm ready, I'll get some French Canadian actors in Paris." He drains his glass of wine, a signal, "Carolyn, this was nice, meeting you. I'm glad your aunt helped me see you again. But I don't want to take up your time with talk about my movie."

He takes out his wallet and Carolyn puts what she thinks is half on the table. He smiles, and makes up the difference.

Carolyn feels guilty, not about taking up time with his film, but about maybe giving him the false impression she's interested in him. "I've enjoyed it, Robert. I'm glad, too. It's nice to see someone from New York."

He twists himself around to pick his jacket off the chair, then picks up his camera.

She gets up and they walk out to Rue de Sévigné together. Now she's winging it, and realizes she can do anything she wants and doesn't have to worry any more about whether she can control herself. Then she controls her mind back to just the street, the people, the shops.

He studies her, his jacket over his shoulder, film camera at his side, smiling. "Look, what about your art? We haven't even talked about it. Could we meet again, in a couple of days and we'd talk about your art?"

Nice. Very nice, she thinks. "Why not. I don't have any art to show you. But we could meet at a gallery and talk there. Is that okay?"

He smiles, happy with himself. "That's fine. Can I call you and set it up?"

"I'd like that. Let me give you my number." She writes it on a piece of paper, even though he probably has her number anyway from Beatrice.

"Thank you," he says. He takes out his wallet and folds the paper inside so she can see that he is taking this seriously. "Can I give you mine?"

Carolyn smiles and nods.

He holds his hand out to her with a small card, but she instead kisses him on the cheek and takes the card.

"See you in a couple of days," she says. She turns toward her apartment, saying "I'm going this way."

"I'm afraid I don't know which way I'm going." He seems genuinely lost.

"Where do you live? Oh, maybe you're not going there."

"No, I am going to my place. I live on Montmartre, on the backside. Rent's more to my liking there."

"Well, that's the opposite direction. The Saint Paul Metro is that way." She points to the end of the street to Rue Saint Antoine.

"Ah, yes," he says, finger in the air, "that's where I came from." He turns around, steps backward and says, "Au revoir," then walks to the subway.

"Au revoir," she calls after him. She stands still and watches him walk down the street. Then impulse takes over her again. "Wait," she calls out.

He stops, turns and smiles. "Yes?"

"Are there any art galleries near your apartment?" And she regrets saying that as a hot flush fills her face. "Oh, don't take that the wrong way."

He shakes his head. "No, of course not. And I didn't." He walks back to where she's standing, outside a fabric shop with a clear glass front. When he's next to her he says, "Art gallery? I haven't noticed. But this is Paris, there must be."

She nods and smiles without saying anything.

He hesitates, but when she doesn't talk, he says, "I know. I'll call you and let you know what there is. Would that work?"

She doesn't want to say anything. She's shocked to find herself attracted to him.

He lowers his head as if to study her. "Would that work? Or we could do something later, if you like. And it was nice to meet you."

"No," she says, in a quiet voice. "This is Paris. There will be galleries anywhere we want. Call me."

"I will," he says, as he leans over and kisses her on the cheek and then walks away, a few steps later turning back once to wave to her.

Carolyn wants to watch him to the end of the street, feeling still flushed and warm, but she forces herself to turn toward her apartment. When she arrives, she opens the window, her view of Paris, and lets the cool fog-like breeze rush past her into the room. She looks out over the rooftops, at the darkening sky, and puts her arms across her chest.

I arrived such a short time ago, she thinks, and already so much has happened. Nathalie, Marthe and Luc, Bad Arolsen. She feels so close to her grandmother Julia. She imagines Julia walking below, anyplace out there. What was she doing here during a war? Why had she come? Maybe the report that she'll be getting in a couple of months from Bad Arolsen will answer that question.

Why hadn't her mother Elizabeth tried to find out? Why did Elizabeth go every year to Julia's grave in New York and never go to France to find out what happened to her? What about Julia's painting? Did she do any of that here?

The air cools Carolyn down too much. She closes the window and goes into her bedroom-studio. I, at least, she thinks, will follow in Julia's footsteps. I will develop my talent as an artist. When I feel comfortable with myself, and maybe then feel close enough to Julia, I will get my mother to come to Paris and we will search for the spirit of Julia together.

Yes, she says to herself, that's what my mother is missing. She has given up on her own mother. I have not. Our time will come.

THE PHONE AWAKENS Carolyn the next morning. Beatrice. Carolyn asks her why she didn't tell her about Robert. But as soon as she has the thought, she knows she's happy about seeing him, with or without advance notice. Because it means she's over Damian and that she's in control.

Beatrice apologizes, saying she had meant to call. Carolyn said it's fine, he's quite nice, and she's going to see a couple art galleries with him. Beatrice then brings up Carolyn's mother, who has asked about her. Carolyn responds with scorn that she'll get around to it when she gets around to it.

When Beatrice continues on the subject, Carolyn reminds her that Elizabeth had called Beatrice in New York to find out what was going on, not her daughter in Paris. And she asks Beatrice to not bring it up again.

Carolyn begins tapping her fingers on the table, anxious to end the conversation. So she does, and not politely. But she feels guilty now, and reaches to call Beatrice back, but she also wants to call Nathalie, or Marthe, and then finds she wants so much to talk to Julia. And she knows that she won't be able to do that, but at the thought of Julia's name, she remembers back to San Francisco, to the picture her mother has of Elizabeth as a little girl in Central Park. She feels sick, wishing she had remembered that picture when she was in New York, or better yet, wishing she had made a copy, or even stolen it so she could figure out where it was in Central Park, and go to that spot and…but that isn't going to happen.

She can talk to Robert now. The new Robert. On the other side of Sacré-Coeur, down the far side of the hill.

Hell. She takes the card out of her purse and calls his number. He answers. She says hi, he says hi.

An hour later, she takes the funicular up to Sacré-Coeur and meets him in front of the basilica. Together, they walk to Place du Tertre and wander around looking at all the art, stop in the church of St. Pierre, where Robert says that Dante came to pray, and Carolyn kneels for a moment and thinks of Julia and then they go down the steps of Rue du Mont-Cenis, turning left for a long walk past the Moulin Rouge, before walking down into the lower heart of Montmartre.

The Montmartre with the farmers market, that tourists didn't even know existed. He takes her to houses where Picasso, Apollinaire, Modigliani all worked. That means something to her, not the famous people, but Robert's interest is what she cares about.

At the end of their walk, they climb half way back up Montmartre again and sit in the rickety chairs outside le Lapin Agile. She takes her sketchbook and makes Robert assume a pose while she works on the outline of him, the whole person in the chair, relaxed, quiet, smiling, unassuming, and whatever else she might believe is true about him. They sip an aperitif until dusk overtakes Rue des Saules and the rest of the back of Montmartre.

She goes home without him, without showing him her sketch, but with a plan they have made to meet again the next day and combine their efforts. He promises to follow her into as many galleries as she likes, and she offers to take a subway anywhere he likes and after he films they can search for galleries around the Metro exit.

They do this for the next three days. He shoots rolls of film at Pigalle, Louvre, the art nouveau Abbesses, Concorde, Varenne with its Rodin Thinker statue. And then Palais Royal with beautiful glass beads at the entrance, Arts et Métiers which is like the inside of a submarine, and the Bastille, with its murals of the French Revolution.

Carolyn is happy to learn of the beauty available among Metro stations, and becomes even more impressed with this young man.

He's true to his promise, and at each station they visit they leave the Metro and search out galleries. They go inside 59 Rivoli, the cool Galerie W, the hip Point Ephémère, the huge green plants that overtake the interior of the boxy, clear-glass Fondation Cartier.

Each day, they finish their work with dinner in a small, inexpensive restaurant near the last place they visited, and each day they part company as the French do with a kiss on both cheeks, and a promise to continue tomorrow. Neither of them says a word about when this might have to come to a stop.

The next afternoon their dynamic changes. Carolyn says she wants to watch the film they're shooting. Robert smiles with pleasure. Together they go to Montmartre Pathé Studios near his apartment on Rue Caulaincourt.

Robert's French-Canadian contacts allow them to use a small 8mm editor. Little movies float across the 4-inch screen as they sit close in the dark room. Funny people get in and out of subway cars.

Scenes with Carolyn in them surprise her, causing her to smirk and sock him on the shoulder. But she grows to enjoy them.

And Carolyn learns something else. The talent she has for drawing would help him flesh out the ideas for his film. With his script in hand, she'll draw storyboards. On a chair outside a restaurant they sit and sip wine as she draws four boxes on a piece of sketch paper. Inside each she put a minimal picture of someone from the subway.

"You're worth your weight in charcoal," he says, smiling and focusing on her eyes.

Carolyn nods in mock solemnity. But the idea bores deeper inside her. That she might use her talent in the film industry. Not painting, but working on expressing a story on paper. Something for the future.

Chapter 41

AT THE END of this exciting day, they stand on the corner. Chilly clouds in a sunless sky settle over Montmartre. Neither knows what to say or how to move into the twilight. Carolyn turns to walk a few hundred feet to the Lamarck-Caulaincourt subway station. The glint from a store catches her eye. Galerie Petit Moulin in gold letters on the window surface. Several pastoral landscapes hang on a wall behind it.

Carolyn takes Robert by the arm. "Come on, one final visit. Then can we get dinner someplace?" After her generous offer of doing storyboards he'd have to say yes.

"Of course," he says, not waiting. "As long as it's romantic."

Carolyn leans toward him and gazes into his eyes before she replies. "Yes."

Black paint surrounds the door and window of the small, narrow gallery. Inside, the room is old European, with dark wood paneling, muted cream walls, and a ceiling with dozens of ornate plaster panels.

Carolyn leans in to Robert. "You know what, I find this attractive."

The walls of the gallery hold figurative paintings. Nothing abstract or absurd. After a day of crazy postmodernist shapes and colors, Carolyn bathes in the warmth of the room.

A thin young man sits motionless, absorbed in a book at the back of the room. Just sitting, he's tall, and wears black jeans and a dark blue turtleneck.

Carolyn glances at books on a table, *The Art of Religion, Picasso And Writers, Ansel Adams*. Landscapes fill the wall in front of her, castles, rivers, moonlight, coastlines, a racing horseman on a dusk-darkened golden field. The horseman strains his neck searching for danger behind him. Carolyn imagines someone is following him with sword drawn.

"This is amazing." Robert's voice behind her, sounding surprised.

"What?" She turns toward the sound.

Robert scrutinizes portraits on the opposite wall.

Interesting, Carolyn thinks, a wall of landscapes on her side of the room, portraits on the other.

He doesn't reply to her question, but waves her to him. "This is you," he says, when she doesn't move.

"What's me?" she's now curious. A portrait on the wall, a life size head. In a way he's right. It is her. The substance of Carolyn, and her thick blond hair, bright hazel eyes, the oval face, the confidence. Across the room her painted double returns her gaze from within a frame. "Well, yes, it does resemble me." The painting keeps her attention. "You think?" Something pulses inside her. Alright, it's uncanny, but coincidences do happen, and this is one of them. A closer view shows a canvas without an artist's name. "That's odd," she says. She raises her eyebrows at Robert. "No name."

A deep but quiet voice comes from the other side of the room. "That's because it's the owner's. It's not for sale." The thin tall man stands in front of a table. A small blemish on his left cheek shows under a high forehead beneath thick brown hair. "And I must admit, it does resemble you. But I don't think it can be." He grins as if he knows something.

"Well," Carolyn says, her interest piqued, "it's not me, I know that, too, but how can you be so sure."

"Because the painter made it forty years ago." He puts his fingers up to his lips as he studies Carolyn. "Would you excuse me a moment?"

"Of course," Robert says, a slight mocking tone in his voice. "It's your gallery."

"Not mine, but you won't go anywhere will you?"

"We're not here to buy and it's late," Carolyn says, irritated. She turns to Robert, so the young man sees that they had other plans.

"But you did stop in. I won't be long. Wait here." He takes a step, turns around to put up his palm to get them to stay where they are, and disappears.

"Yeah, he'll try and sell us something, probably a print," Robert says.

"I don't know. We'll give him two minutes, and we'll leave. I'm hungry," Carolyn replies. But she returns to the intrigue of, she thinks, "my portrait," and a flush creeps across her cheeks. What makes that jump out of her subconscious?

The tall man comes back into the room with a woman in her fifties or sixties, maybe a little older, you can't tell, petite, with a slim waist.

Pearl earrings and necklace stand out against a dark red sweater and tan slacks. She favors her right leg, but walks with elegance, her posture straight. Pure self-confidence. Wavy hair streaked with silver streaks enclose her oval face.

The woman's hair mimics Carolyn's blonde hair, but it's straight. An expensive cut. An air of Parisian glamour surrounds her. Subtle makeup, the delicate curve of her nose. Hazel and green eyes study Carolyn and Robert as she approaches.

"Yes, Vincent, I see a resemblance. Remarkable, as a matter of fact." As she smiles at Carolyn, her eyes beam empathy for her. "I'm sorry, he is thoughtful to bring me out, and you do share features with the woman in the portrait. But, if I may judge from your own faces, I agree with you." Amusement or condescension curls her mouth up. "I don't quite get the point because you look like someone in a painting."

Carolyn stares at the woman. At that moment, she understands how she'll appear at fifty or sixty years old. The face is graceful, there are few lines behind the eyes, the skin is perfect, lustrous. "The resemblance is remarkable, as you say. There's nothing more."

"Fine," the woman says, nodding in an irritated way, "Vincent said you weren't interested in any of the art. I thank you for your visit. Good day to you both." The woman makes a quick dismissive wave of the hand, turns to leave, and stops. "But, as long as you're here, why not take one of my cards?"

The young man hurries to the desk and brings a card back to Carolyn.

Carolyn sees the card and her heart skips a beat. Breathless, she swallows, dizzy. Sound escapes her lips with awe as she says, "You're Julia Stuart."

The woman's face shows great concern, her voice soothing. "What's the matter, are you okay?" she says, as she puts her hand on

Carolyn's shoulder. "You look sick. Here, come, sit. Vincent, go, go get a glass of water."

Carolyn freezes. "No, I'm fine." The painting draws her attention, and then the woman. "I don't have a card, Madame, but if I did, I..." Hot air parches her throat. When she continues, she speaks with deliberation in a low voice, confident. "My name is Carolyn Stuart. Spelled the same way as your name."

The woman puts her hand on her chest. "You are good-looking, young woman, and you resemble me when I was your age, the painting attests to that. It's a wonderful coincidence. But it's nothing more than that."

Carolyn blinks several times and wipes her eyes. Robert holds her hand.

"You're my grandmother. I've searched for you all over Paris. Germany, too."

Julia takes Carolyn's other hand. Carolyn inhales and holds her breath for a moment when the warmth of the woman's skin touches her hand.

"I know the names may be the same, young woman...Carolyn...," Julia looks at Robert and Vincent for corroboration, "but I don't have any children, and so," and now Julia's eyes well up, "you can't be my granddaughter, as good as that would be."

Carolyn's voice shakes with pleading. "But it can't be a coincidence. It's not possible."

Julia's face hardens, her eyes narrow, and she nods as if she grasps something new. "Yes, I understand what's happening. You've walked by, saw the painting, decided to do research, and here you are in the shop. I don't know what your game is, young lady, but it won't work."

Carolyn falls into a bottomless pit. She loses everything she had found.

Julia holds Carolyn's shoulder and stares. "My dear, my daughter Elizabeth..."

Carolyn lets out a scream. She trembles. "That's my mother's name."

Robert puts his arms around her to keep her from falling.

Julia's face reddens, her eyes widen as she studies Carolyn in anger. "As I was saying," she speaks with a hard voice, a voice of finality and resignation, "my daughter is dead. She died when she was two years old."

Carolyn bites her lip and moves her head back and forth as she deliberates. She pleads with her voice. "No. She isn't dead. She's my mother, she lives in San Francisco, and she's your daughter."

Julia looks at Carolyn with a mixture of irritation and pity. "Please, don't continue. My daughter, my Elizabeth, may have the same name as your mother, but she's buried in the ground. I saw her death certificate. I saw her gravestone in the New York Marble Cemetery on Second Avenue. So, young lady," Julia glances at Vincent and Robert and back, "I can't be your grandmother."

Carolyn's eyes open wide. She looks at Robert. She holds out her hands in supplication. Her voice strong and unwavering, her eyes focus on Julia, "I saw your gravestone, Julia Marie Stuart, in the New York *City* Marble Cemetery just around the corner on Second Street."

The intrigue on the face of Julia tells Carolyn to continue with confidence. She speaks with a serious voice even as joy fills her spirit. "You were born May 23, 1920 in Lewiston, Maine. My mother has a picture of you in Central Park with your husband and your daughter Elizabeth, my mother."

Julia folds her arms across her body, stunned, doubling over and leaning as if to fall. Carolyn and Robert reach out and keep her standing. Speech is impossible for her. Vincent brings her a tissue and she controls herself and wipes her cheeks. Now she looks up in supplication at Carolyn. Her voice comes out in little whispers. "And… and…" but she halts. She takes several long breaths. "My little Lizzie?" Her mouth twisted, trembles with disbelief as her red eyes fill with tears. "My little Lizzie?"

Carolyn sees that it's too much for her grandmother. How is this possible? How can there be gravestones for both Julia and Elizabeth, both so close and so far apart?

Julia reaches out to Carolyn and draws her closer. They hug each other with silent tears and quiet breathing.

But Julia pulls back, her voice calm. "Tell me, Carolyn…," her voice changes to something hard in disbelief. She becomes overwhelmed, still, at the thought that it's a hoax. "Where is your mother Elizabeth?" Her eyebrows rise above unblinking eyes.

Carolyn sees the strange new look in Julia's eyes and understands that it's difficult. "My mother is in San Francisco, as I said. She doesn't know you're here in Paris. But she goes every year to visit your grave in New York. She made me promise to do it, too. I went there with my Aunt Beatrice a month ago."

"Beatrice?" Julia's face lights up with joy, and yet, in the next moment, it disintegrates into confusion and doubt. After a moment of self-absorption, she continues as if testing Carolyn. Her whole being wants to believe, but life doesn't give gifts as great as this. "Beatrice who?" Her face shows that her wish to believe is stronger than her fear.

"Beatrice, my aunt, in New York. She lives on Park Avenue, in the house left to her by Hugh Stuart. She moved there from Montreal when her own husband Pierre died."

At the mention of that name, Hugh, Julia's eyes darken and her lips form a grim line. She nods as she speaks. "Now I understand." Her chest rises and falls in great breaths.

"Do you have a telephone?" Carolyn says.

"Of course. In the back."

"I'm going to call my mother so you can talk to her. You thought she was dead. She thought you were dead."

Julia holds tight to Carolyn and leads her to a small room in the back of the gallery. Carolyn picks up the phone and starts to dial her mother's number in San Francisco. She turns to Julia. "I'll let it ring till her secretary answers." Her eyes open wide when she sees the photograph on the table. Pointing to it, she puts the phone back on the hook. "That picture, that's you and Elizabeth and Hugh in Central Park. That picture is in my mother's house in San Francisco."

Julia picks up the picture and holds it tight to her chest. She waits in silence for Carolyn to dial, watches her face, her frown, showing how hard this is for her to accept.

Carolyn waits an eternity as the phone rings. She's ready to give up and try again when someone answers. "Hello?"

"This is Carolyn Stuart. I'd like to speak to my mother."

"I'm sorry," the voice comes in a flat tone on the line, "she's in a meeting and can't be disturbed."

Carolyn's voice rises. "I'm calling from Paris. This is urgent. Get her to the phone now."

Silence. She waits with nervous energy for one minute, and then Elizabeth's voice comes on, not happy.

"Carolyn, what is this? I am in the middle of important negotiations."

"Mama! Mama!"

Elizabeth's voice is harsh and irritated. "Carolyn? What's wrong? Are you okay? Has something happened?"

"Oh, Mama!"

"Carolyn, what is this Mama talk? Have you been drinking?"

"Mama, I'll make you so happy you'll think you're in heaven. In fact, I'm giving you a gift that people who go to heaven get. I'm giving you your mother."

"What? You're not making any sense." The voice is even more irritated.

"Mama, your mother, Julia Marie Stuart, is here with me. I found her." Carolyn squeezes her eyes shut and contracts her whole body before she goes on. She raises herself up on her toes, and talks in an excited pitch. "I found her. You know what? She has the same picture on the table here that you have. Of you and Hugh and Julia in Central Park. The same picture, Mama." Her voice reaches a fever pitch. "The same one!"

Dead silence on the other end of the phone, but Elizabeth's breath is fast and deep.

Carolyn doesn't wait for her mother to speak. "Mama, I'm passing the phone to your mother."

Tears fill Carolyn's eyes, blurring Julia's face. She gives Julia the phone and helps her sit at the table.

"Hello? Hello?" comes the voice from the phone.

Julia hesitates before she speaks. "Lizzie?" Julia takes in a long, deep breath. "Is that my little Lizzie? Is it you?"

The answer that came out of the earpiece is a series of sobs and sniffling, and then, "Mama? Mama?"

Julia shakes her head, looks at the phone in disbelief, then puts it back to her ear. "Forty years he stole from us, your father." Her voice breaks. The next words come out with the greatest depth of bitterness. "He put you in one cemetery and me in the one around the corner and stole you from me."

Julia lays the phone on her lap, and looks in fear at Carolyn. She's not sure any more. Too many ideas have been thrown at her too fast. She puts the phone back up to her head and holds it there for a moment before speaking. It's as if there's an endless stream of doubts. "Lizzie, tell me, do you remember the last time you saw me?"

Elizabeth's voice cries in the phone. "Yes, Mama, I do. You were on the boat, at the railing, looking out at the dock for me. But they put me in the car and took me away."

Julia's voice gives out. She's breathing too hard and crying.

Carolyn takes the phone from her grandmother and speaks to Elizabeth. "Mama?"

Elizabeth, almost frantic, says, "My mother, where's my mother?"

"She's overcome, Mama. Now you have to come. You have to come."

"I will, darling, I'll be on the next plane that gets me to Paris," Elizabeth says. "I'll see my mother tomorrow morning. Let me say goodbye to her, then I have to call the airport. Give me your phone number. I'll call you back there." The phone is silent for a moment. "Where are you?"

"We're in an art gallery in Montmartre, Mama, Julia's art gallery. Can you believe that?" She puts her hand on Julia's shoulder.

"I must call Beatrice, too and have her fly over from New York with me."

Carolyn hands the phone to Julia and reluctantly leaves the room to wait with Robert in the gallery.

Half a minute later, Julia comes out. She wipes her eyes with a handkerchief and rolls it up into a ball in her hand and puts both hands out to Carolyn. "I'm the one who has heard a ghost. I didn't want to hang up. But Lizzie said she had to hurry to the airport to take a private jet. She must be well off, my daughter Elizabeth Stuart. Oh, that's not her name"

Carolyn laughs. "Yes it is, she never married and she's very rich I can tell you." She puts her arms around her grandmother. "Lizzie. That seems a strange name to me."

Julia pulls away, but keep hold of Carolyn's hands. "I'll never let you go, my granddaughter. Tonight you must stay with me. We can walk home from here. I do every night. Oh." She looks at Robert and confusion sweep her face, a slight fear she's taking too much for granted. "I'm sorry, but I have not been introduced to you, young man."

Robert smiles, with warmth on his face, amazed at what had transpired in the past few minutes. "I'm a friend of Carolyn's from New York. We've seen Paris together. Needless to say, I'm happy to meet you. But it's time for me to leave you alone." He kisses Carolyn on the cheek. "May I call you sometime?"

"I want you to call me. Give us a day or so. My mother and aunt arrive tomorrow." She returns the kiss on the cheek. "You know, I don't have your phone number."

"You do have it, but here's another," Robert says. Taking Julia's card from Carolyn, he writes it on the back. "And yours, sorry, another copy?" He laughs in a shy way.

Vincent, following the conversation, brings Carolyn another card.

"Here," she says. "I want you to meet my whole family soon. You are part of this now. You helped me find my grandmother, and I will never forget you for it."

Robert leaves and waves to them through the window from the sidewalk.

"And now, Vincent," Julia begins, "you should go home, too. I'll close the gallery today. You can open up tomorrow."

"Yes, Madame," he replies. Turning to Carolyn, he smiles. "It was nice to meet you, Mademoiselle."

"Oh, and Vincent, take petty cash and buy champagne. Anyone who comes in, offer them a glass."

He laughs. "Of course."

When he's gone, Julia takes Carolyn by the hand and sits with her. She breathes without making a sound, her gaze controlled by the portrait on the wall. "I can't keep that hidden any longer on a wall of other paintings. I have to take it from here and put it up at home. Oh," Julia smiles warmly at Carolyn for a long moment, "I think you should have it."

"Or my mom, your daughter, it would be a wonderful gift for her tomorrow."

"Yes, but now, no, first I want her to find it on the wall where you first saw it."

"Oh yes, she will be thrilled. Thank you," Carolyn says, her heart beating faster, you're my… Grandmother, my *grandmother!*"

Julia nods, but she concentrates on her own thoughts for a moment. "We will have to go through that whole scene for Lizzie. The portrait on the wall, you, Robert. Several times." She falls silent and pensive again.

"What is it?" Carolyn leans in to her grandmother and forces her attention.

Julia touches Carolyn's cheek. "It's my fault. If I hadn't left, if I'd stayed in New York forty years ago…oh…if you'd have stayed in New York…"

"Oh, please, don't," Carolyn pleads, wincing. "It doesn't matter anymore. All that matters, is that we'll all be together tomorrow."

"Yes, you're right, of course."

"And you're not alone in this," Carolyn says.

Julia sits up straight and looks at her granddaughter with curiosity. "What do you mean by that?"

Carolyn smiles. "I mean, I shouldn't have left my mother in a hurry, or New York. But I did. And now I have you. And I have my mother."

Julia shakes her head briefly, bewildered. "But you have always had your mother."

Carolyn sighs. "No, I haven't. We haven't been close for years. This changes everything. You, me, Mama, Beatrice, we're a family now. I never had a real whole family. Not my mama either. And you, the same."

Julia frowns and puts her hand on Carolyn's knee. "And your father? Where is he? On the phone Lizzie said she didn't have a husband. Ever."

"I never knew my father."

"Oh, my dear, I'm so sorry." Julia sinks into herself again, remains quiet, then turns to Carolyn. "We three women seem to be the same."

Carolyn moves her head downward, eyes pointed at the floor. Her voice floats in from nowhere. "He left my mother before my birth." Then she pulls herself together and shakes her head as she leans in to Julia. "Oh, I have so much to tell, Grandmother."

"Carolyn, call me Grandma."

Carolyn laughs. "Grandma? That sounds old. You're not old, you're young, you're glamorous. You're a Parisian woman with an art gallery, not a grandma."

"I know, but, Carolyn, old fashioned is what I need right now. We have so much to learn, so much to tell. It's overwhelming. Do you understand? I want something familiar."

Carolyn puts her arm around Julia. "I do, believe me, Grandma, I do."

Julia takes Carolyn's hand. "I don't want to go over the past anymore today. I'll have to do it again with Elizabeth. My heart is so full of joy, I'm so glad you are here with me. Tomorrow, I will find joy and heartbreak again. I can't imagine how hard that will be." She pats Carolyn's knee. "Come. We can't sit here the rest of the night." She runs her fingers through her hair. "Even if I'm awake till morning. Let's take the Montmartre bus up to the top and have dinner. After that we'll walk the steps back down to my home."

"But we don't know when Mama's plane gets in."

"There's a fax machine at home." Julia touches Carolyn's arm. "I'm not so old fashioned." A smile lights up her face and her hazel-green eyes grow vivid. "You have my eyes, that's wonderful. Do you have a picture of your mother? I haven't even thought about it until now."

Carolyn grins. "No, I don't. When I left San Francisco, I was so angry, it didn't even occur to me to bring a picture of her"

"Well, I guess I'll have to wait until tomorrow. I don't know how I'm going to last that long, but with you by my side, we can do it together. Come on," she pulls Carolyn to the door, "we'll go home and go up to Place du Tertre for dinner. Pick up your things and…" Julia points to Carolyn's valise. "What's that? Too big for a purse."

Carolyn blushes. "My sketch book."

Julia's face takes on an air of magical epiphany. "Sketch book? As in drawing?"

Carolyn nods in silence.

"Bring it with you, I'll want to see everything in it while we have some wine up on the top of Montmartre."

A FEW MINUTES later, when they've settled down at Chez Eugene, in the shadow of Sacré-Coeur, the white picket fence cornering them opposite Mère Catherine, a bottle of Le Clos Montmartre between them, Julia insists on seeing Carolyn's sketchbook.

Carolyn takes a sip of the wine and nods, cocking her head. "I can taste why this is hard to find." She laughs a little.

"Oh, yes, it's no good, I know. But it is, contrary to rumor, very drinkable. And it's not a great vineyard, but it's like you, my granddaughter. It's very rare. It's not available in stores or restaurants. Except here, and Eugene finds things like this for me."

"I've seen two of your paintings, Grand...ma...." Carolyn muses that it will take time to get used to saying that.

"Two? Oh. My. I know about the portrait of me that resembles you. And another one?"

"Yes. Beatrice showed it to me. In the attic in the house in New York. A painting, half finished, of my...of Hugh."

Julia's face turns sour. "I don't believe it. I can't imagine there's anything in that house from me. When I'm supposed to be dead."

"Somebody kept it." Carolyn puts her hand on Julia's. "That's not all. Your letters, your telegram from the ship. Those are the things that gave me hope, don't you see. Even when I gave up hope."

Julia brings her hands up to both cheeks in astonishment, then squeezes Carolyn's hand. "I'm puzzled. Did you come here to find me?"

"Yes, but I didn't think I would find you alive." Carolyn takes another drink of the wine and puckers her lips.

Julia laughs and called Eugène over. "Monsieur, please, thank you for keeping this for me. But now it's time for a good Chablis."

The waiter bows and leaves to fetch a better wine.

"I came here to flee my mother. When I found out she had kept my trust fund from me, I...I...I had to leave the country, so I came here because I knew someone at the Louvre. I went to find something about you where your grave said you died, at Versailles. But there was no record there. So, I did give up hope. And then I found out about Bad Arolsen, the Germans had all these records, and I found out that you went to Vittel, but you didn't come out. So I gave up hope again."

"But my darling, you did find me. How did you manage that?"

"I tell you I didn't find you because I was searching for you, it was because I was in so many art galleries in Paris, with Robert."

"So you found me because you wanted art."

"And isn't that perfect." Carolyn picks up her glass of Chablis and offers it to Julia to toast.

"It is. So, back to where we started. Can you draw me a picture of your mother?"

"Yes, of course. I'd love to. Something like her, anyway." Carolyn puts her sketchbook on the table, and lays pastel sticks next to it. The first stick she chooses is a light gray charcoal and she draws the outline of a diamond shaped face with a delicate chin. Next she adds a small, elegant nose and the outline of the eyes, the almond shape, nothing inside. For a moment she searches, then selects a dark red stick and sketches hair pulled back."

"Oh my," Julia exclaims, raising her eyebrows.

"I'm not done yet, Grandma, I need to put some brown in to get to her auburn hair."

Julia puts her hands up to her face and can't contain her joy and anticipation. "Ah, yes, her auburn hair. That's my little Lizzie."

"But she always wears it pulled back with a pony tail or a bun. That's my mom." Carolyn raised her head up from the paper to catch Julia's attention. "It works quite well for Goldman Sachs."

"Excuse me?" Julia's bewildered.

"Mom is caught up with making money."

"Good for her!" Julia raises her glass of Chablis in a toast.

Carolyn's face registers surprise. "To be totally caught up in it?"

Julia shakes her head back and forth. "Young lady, you concentrate on getting me a picture of my daughter." Then she sits back in her chair and folds her hands on her knees. "I doubt my Lizzie neglected you. I'm old enough to know that there's plenty of guilt to throw around." She sits up again, serious. "Listen to me…look at me." Julia waits for Carolyn to put her pastel stick down and raise her head. "I've waited forty years for this day and you are not going to ruin it for me. You have no complaints, do you hear me? None."

The hardness in Julia's voice penetrates deep inside Carolyn. Her eyes narrow in anticipation.

"You think you've had a tough time, do you? Have you ever gone hungry?"

"No." Carolyn sits in a sulky twitchy silence.

"Have you ever seen people commit suicide because Nazis are coming for them?"

Carolyn's eyes grow large, but she says nothing. Her heart beats faster.

"Have you?" Julia stares at Carolyn.

Carolyn responds in a quiet voice. "No, I haven't." Her bright eyes grow dark. She fidgets with her hands.

Julia leans forward and puts the tenseness of her whole body into her words. "Have you ever seen someone die right in front of you," she stabs the table with her finger, "when a bomb was dropped on them?"

Julia's piercing eyes dumbfound Carolyn.

"No." Carolyn bites her lip.

"Do you want me to keep going?"

"No, Grandma." Carolyn's cheeks are burning.

Julia relaxes a little bit, but not much. "You have no idea how lucky you are to have your mother, Carolyn. Your mother made everything possible for you. This is the last I will hear from you on this subject."

"Yes."

"Do you understand?"

"Yes." This woman, a war hero, chastens Carolyn.

"Good. I'm sure your mother will understand that tomorrow. Now finish the picture. Do those striking pale blue eyes. And have some more wine."

Chapter 42

CAROLYN AND JULIA, arm in arm, stand before the enormous glass wall of the Concorde terminal at Charles de Gaulle Airport. Far behind the rows of empty seats are several men in limousine livery ready with signs for arriving passengers. But the two women remain alone at the window. This is the Concorde, and business people and celebrities arrive. Outside, a light drizzle dilutes all the colors to the same unending gray. Little tractors pull empty cars of luggage into place. On the runway in the distance a huge Air France 747 with its blue and red tail lumber in slow progression on its path across the ocean. Then the vast concrete field before them once more becomes a lonely empty space.

Carolyn sees at the desk two women in dark blue suits with bright red scarves who are typing away at terminals, ignoring the world around them. Don't they know what's happening? A small jolt of excitement goes through her as she feels Julia's warm hand.

Julia speaks, her voice quiet with awe, her finger pointing. "There, now."

On their right, the white Concorde with its nose unhooked and pointing down, appears, growing longer and longer, as if it will never end. Carolyn's heart jumps. When the plane turns toward the window, its wings spread like a giant bird, she feels Julia's hand tighten. A heart pounds, but she doesn't know if it's hers or her grandmother's. Carolyn stares intently at Julia, who trembles and seems to have stopped breathing.

Again, Julia speaks in the barest whisper. "It can't be happening? Can it?"

Without warning, Julia folds and becomes a heavy weight. Carolyn steadies her grandmother.

"After 40 years?" Julia's eyes beg Carolyn for this to be reality. She lets out a sharp little cry. "What if she doesn't come through that door? What if she's not on the plane?"

"Grandmother, are you all right?" Fear grips Carolyn that the end of forty years will be a heart attack, or a stroke. Her mouth is dry.

Julia puts her hand over her mouth, shaking all over.

Carolyn leads her grandmother to a chair and helps her to sit down, but Julia steps backwards to the chair, not taking her eyes off the approaching airplane. Then she watches the great Concorde, which is not seeming to move at all, just becoming larger in the window.

"What if I don't recognize her?" Julia's gripped as much by fear as anticipation.

Carolyn laughs and puts her arm around Julia. "Of course you will. Just as she will recognize you."

Julia strains to see passengers coming off the plane, but the jet bridge keeps them out of view. And then, without warning, without consideration for the hearts waiting, Elizabeth appears inside the terminal. Elizabeth, her face transcendent with joy, sees her mother, and Julia lets out a little stifled scream when she sees her daughter. Julia stands, takes a step, Elizabeth takes a step, as if they just want to be in this moment of seeing each other, then they run to each other and wrap their arms around each other and stand, locked, immobile, crying, shaking.

Beatrice walks around them, tears falling down her cheeks, and Carolyn runs to her and they embrace. Carolyn holds tight to Beatrice, but then wipes her face and studies her mother and grandmother, still holding each other tight but not shaking any more.

Elizabeth opens her eyes, won't let go of her mother, but looked at her as if there's nothing else in the wide world but this woman in front of her. "My mama."

"My Lizzie."

Elizabeth, a new Elizabeth who has never before existed on this earth, holds her hand out to Carolyn, who walks to her and takes the hand, and feels Elizabeth's strong grip pulling her in, and then she senses Beatrice with them, and the four of them are still, and it seems forever. Finally, they break, and Julia holds her daughter in one hand and her granddaughter in the other, and lets go of them and opens her arms to her sister-in-law.

A LONG BLACK Citroën limousine brings them to Julia's apartment at 32 Rue du Mont-Cenis, in the shadow of Sacré-Coeur. Inside, they open a bottle of champagne.

And they're ready to hear Julia tell them what happened forty years ago. Lizzie holds her mother's hand, and says she remembered the ship and being taken away and put in the back seat of the limousine with Grace. As Julia tells them how she came to stay in France, they're all in silent tears with the death of Christine and the disappearance of Isabelle.

They hear that Julia has never been to Versailles, that she was in Vittel until the end of the war. When the Germans fled, she had not waited for refugee processing, she just came back to Paris, found that the neighbors had kept the apartment in the hope that Isabelle might come back, and when Julia appeared, they were happy to let her stay there.

"But, Mama, why didn't you come back for me?" Elizabeth says. For this moment, Elizabeth is little Lizzie.

Julia nods in sorrow. "I did, darling. I did." She talks with a broken heart, desperate for her daughter to understand. "I came back to New York as soon as it was possible after the war, to look for you, sure you would go back to Paris with me." She drinks champagne, rests her hands on her lap and sighs. "I came to the house, and Mrs. Willow answered the door and almost fell over with shock when she saw me. She said that Lizzie wasn't there, and I would have to talk to Hugh. She said come back later. Later? Later when, I said, this is my house. No, you will have to talk to Mr. Stuart. In an hour, he will be back.

So, I came back in that one hour and he was there. He wouldn't even let me in the house. 'Julia,' he said, 'Julia, Lizzie has died.' His voice pretended to be sorrowful, but he didn't have any tears in those eyes. He showed me the death certificate, signed by Dr. Rivlin."

She focuses on Lizzie's eyes. "He showed me that. Then he got the car and he took me down to Second Street and he showed me your grave, Lizzie, in the New York Marble Cemetery."

Julia breaks down and puts her hand to her forehead, and sighs from deep inside. "So what was there for me? I had seen the certificate and I had seen your grave. In Paris, I had a life there, and friends. I could do something with art. Not paint."

She softly touches Carolyn. "The one painting, the one painting that has been waiting for forty years for you to come and see it." She turns back to Lizzie. "Oh, you must come tomorrow. Oh, of course you will, come to my little gallery, it's just a short walk from here. To see the painting that has made a miracle."

Elizabeth nods in solemn acceptance of this new reality. "Now I see. My father. Hugh Stuart. A monster. When I was five or six, or maybe older," she brushes her red hair away from her face, beads of sweat appearing on her forehead, "he took me in his office, and he seemed so sad. He said that you had died of fever in France, that he had brought you home. And I went to that cemetery on Second Avenue, the New York City Marble Cemetery. I never even knew there was another one. It was so beautiful, along the sidewalk, with a wrought iron fence, and I could see your grave even from the street. I've gone there on your birthday every year of my life. I even flew in from Stanford, I wouldn't tell anybody."

When she finishes, the silence that fills the room keeps the heaviness of all those years around them.

"To think," Beatrice says to Carolyn, "we went there." She smiles at Lizzie and Julia. "We went into that cemetery on Second Street, we would have found your false grave, Lizzie, but it didn't look right, the cemetery was not like your description, so we left."

"How close we were," Carolyn says.

"And now," Beatrice continues, "you must come to New York and reclaim your house. It belongs to you."

Julia is stricken. "Thank you, Beatrice. You're wonderful, you are. But I don't want to live in that house. He gave it to you and it's yours."

Elizabeth interrupts before Beatrice can continue. "Mama, you're coming home to live with me in San Francisco. I'm never letting you out of my sight. We'll all have this home in Paris, and a home in New York, and a home in San Francisco.

MARTIN F. SORENSEN

THE NEXT MORNING, they all meet at Julia's gallery and stare in silence at the portrait that brought them together, and then Carolyn shows them her apartment, where they are introduced to Robert, and late in the afternoon, they drive out to Senlis for an introduction to Marthe and Luc. Carolyn explains that it was Marthe who had shown her how to contact the International Red Cross.

The next day, they find themselves at Notre Dame cathedral and light candles before a statue of the Virgin.

Julia picks up a match and lights two more candles. "For Christine and Isabelle," she whispers. She puts her arms around Lizzie and Carolyn and looks up at the Virgin for a long time. Lizzie sniffs. Then Carolyn. Beatrice pulls tissues out of her purse and passes them around.

And then the four of them walk out together into the bright Paris sunshine.

Acknowledgments

I want to thank, first of all, my wife Charleyne, for her encouragement and editorial advice; Tory Hartmann, a publisher par excellence; Roy Jackson for his editing.

www.ingramcontent.com/pod-product-compliance
Lightning Source LLC
Chambersburg PA
CBHW030629020726
47493CB00006B/1639